YOU
DON'T HAVE
to TELL
EVERYTHING
YOU KNOW

a novel

YOU DON'T HAVE to TELL EVERYTHING YOU KNOW

a novel

LIZ NEWALL

DUDLEY COURT PRESS
SONOITA, AZ

Author's Note: This is a work of fiction. Names, characters, places and incidents are either the product of the author's imagination or are used fictitiously, and any resemblance to actual persons living or dead, business establishments, events, or locales is entirely coincidental.

For information about permission to reproduce selections from this book:
Email: publisher@dudleycourtpress.com
Please put Permissions in the subject line.

Author photo: Patrick Wright

Published in the USA by
Dudley Court Press
Sonoita, Arizona
www.DudleyCourtPress.com

Publisher's Cataloging-in-Publication Data
Names: Newall, Liz, 1948- author.
Title: You don't have to tell everything you know / Liz Newall.
Description: Sonoita, AZ : Dudley Court Press, [2021]
Identifiers: ISBN: 978-1-940013-98-5 (Paper) | 978-1-940013-99-2 (EBook) |
LCCN: 2021918630
Subjects: LCSH: McGee, Isamar Woods Jones--Diaries. | Women authors--South Carolina--19th century--Fiction. | Reconstruction (U.S. history, 1865-1877)--South Carolina--Fiction. | South Carolina--History--1865- --Fiction. | South Carolina--Social life and customs--19th century--Fiction. | Families--South Carolina--19th century--Fiction. | LCGFT: Historical fiction. | BISAC: Fiction / Historical / Civil War | FICTION / Cultural Heritage | FICTION / Small Town & Rural
Classification: LCC: PS3564.E8558 Y68 2021 | DDC: 813/.54--dc23

Dudley Court Press is committed to publishing works of quality and integrity. We are proud to offer this book to our readers. The story, the experiences, opinions and words are the author's alone.
www.DudleyCourtPress.com

This book is dedicated to
Ellie, Will, and Trey

*We tell other people's stories
to understand our own.*

Early this morning, right before dawn, when the stars lose their luster, it happens again.

Alexander comes to see me. He rides the same gleaming black stallion beneath my window. The window that always sticks. But he opens it soundlessly and slips into my room.

Even without the light, I can tell he hasn't aged. The same curtain of blond hair across his forehead. The same sky-blue eyes. He kneels beside the bed, takes my hand, and whispers, "Wake up, Isamar. Wake up. I've come back for you."

I try to pull my hand away. Suddenly Willis bursts into the room. He's wielding a cane and angrier than I've ever seen him. He leaps across me and lights into Alexander.

I gather all my strength, rise from the bed, push between them.

I wrap my arms around Willis, press my head against his heart, and find my voice. "Stop!" I scream over and over until the bloodied Alexander disappears.

Then Willis disappears. Even the horse, such a magnificent phantom, stomps its hooves, breathes out smoke, and is no more.

Only I am left to be awakened by Anah shouting, "Ooooh Lawdy! Mizz Icie done had another fit!"

PART I

Lay down my brother

Family affair ⌐ ɾ ⌐

Mama said I was conceived in grief and brought joy to sorrow. As it turns out, it had more to do with a waning war and a leg wound. Either way, you'd think my parents would've named me "Joy" or something equally pleasant.

Instead they named me Isamar Woods Jones. Jones is obviously from my father. Woods is from mother's side. "Isamar," pronounced "EYE-sah-mar," is from the Bible. I'm not sure that's the correct pronunciation, but that's the way my family says it. So I do, too. At least they shortened it to "Icie." I should be grateful. Granted, it sounds cold, but I'd take it over "EYE-sah-mar" any day.

I was born May 25, 1865—one month after General Lee surrendered the South at Appomattox. Mama said that the wives weren't sorry. Most had been trying to keep their farms going until the men got home. So the ones who still had husbands with most of their limbs rejoiced.

My sister Bessie was born in 1861, three and a half years before me and about the same time the Confederates fired on Fort Sumter. Papa said we were like little bookends to the war. We're Papa's second family.

He had five children by his first wife, who died several years before the war.

My Papa, William Jones, served in the Confederacy, the same as his father, his oldest son, Dock, from the first family, and all his brothers except the one who'd died as a child. All of Papa's brother-in-laws served, too. Aunt Eliza would say "brothers-in-law." But I don't say it that way in front of the first family because I'll be accused of acting uppity.

So the war was a family affair.

When Grandpa Jones joined the army, he was well into his fifties. Instead of combat, his job had been to take home the dead for burial. Before the war, he'd been a merchant, farmer, coffin maker, and sometimes undertaker. In other words, he'd done whatever he could to provide for a wife and twelve children. He'd been accustomed to dealing with both the living and the dead.

When Bessie and I were still quite young, my oldest half-sister Mattie used to tell us, "Grandpa Jones was Death's delivery man. We knew when he was bringing home a body—even before he got here. We'd see a high circle of hungry buzzards, getting closer and darker as the day wore on."

Bessie and I would always cringe at the mention of "hungry buzzards."

Grandpa Jones caught a disease from dealing with dead soldiers and died himself early in the war. All that was before I was born.

As for Papa, he'd enlisted with the Hampton Legion of South Carolina, which served mostly in Virginia. Shortly thereafter, my half-brother Dock left Mama with the farm and joined the Confederate Army, too. He was fourteen at the time.

For all the Joneses who served, only one died from gunshot. Uncle James. And he wasn't even armed. The story of how Uncle James survived, then died, and was buried twice pretty much shaped my view of the war. And just maybe my understanding of family.

Frayser's Farm ❧

Papa didn't talk about the war all that often. But when he was into his brandy, he would sometimes recount how he'd brought his brother James's body home from Virginia to be buried in the family plot in upcountry South Carolina.

Uncle James had been serving in Richmond, when, as Papa put it, "Brother James took a minie ball to the leg." It was at the Battle of Frayser's Farm during the summer of 1862.

It'd been fairly early in the war and the Confederacy appeared to be winning. Papa said, "Back then, hope was high as God's blue sky." Although Papa had been in his middle-thirties at the time, his brother James had been only seventeen. My uncle's job had been to carry his unit's flag into battle.

When Papa reached the flag-bearer part, he would always say, "Them boys was the bravest of the brave." He would usually pause, take another sip of brandy, swallow, and add, "The fella carryin' the colors, he had a bull's eye on his chest, and just a rag and a stick to defend hisself!"

My half-brother Dock had been in the very same battle. If he was present at the telling, he would add, "We had God at our back and the Yanks at our front!"

The gist was that General Lee had driven the Union's main army into full retreat at Frayser's Farm in Richmond, and he'd intended to cut it in two. But after heavy losses on both sides, the Union had managed to escape to fight another day.

Both Dock and Uncle James had survived the terrible battle, but James had been wounded. Dock would always say, "Soldiers around Uncle James said he never let go of the colors, not even when the Yanks shot him down."

Sometime later, the newspaper printed an account of the battle wherein James had dropped the flag and a childhood friend had retrieved it and carried both the flag and James off the battlefield. Over the years, I learned that the war has many versions.

If Dock was helping tell the story, he would end with, "I tell you what, if the General had just succeeded in splitting the Yanks' retreat, the whole damn war woulda been over and done!" He would pause and finish with, "Then and there!"

But General Lee hadn't succeeded.

And neither had Uncle James. By the time he'd received medical attention, the leg had turned black and the doctor had to amputate it. He'd died a week later. And because it'd been July hot, he'd been buried in a Richmond cemetery.

Therein lay the problem. Not that James had died carrying the flag for the Confederacy, but that he'd been buried far away from home. If Grandpa Jones had still been alive, he'd have gone after James himself. But Grandpa had died the year before from hauling the bodies of other men's sons.

At that point in the story, Papa would usually hand his glass to Mama for a refill and say, "Fetchin' brother James's body home for a second buryin' fell heavy upon me."

In March 1863, eight months after James had been buried in Richmond, Papa finally received a funeral furlough. He'd been camped with his unit in Petersburg at the time so he walked from his camp to the Petersburg train station and rode on to Richmond.

There he'd met the undertaker, who was somehow able to find Uncle James's grave. They'd taken turns digging. The grave had been shallow, as Papa said "dug in haste," and the casket had been fairly easy for the two men to hoist up with ropes.

As though "dug in haste" was her cue, Mama would hand him a refilled glass of brandy so he could continue. When he reached the point in the story where they pried the lid off the coffin, he would take another slow drink, then say, "That coffin was fulla water and that face didn't bear no semblance to brother James!"

Bessie and I would always shiver at the mention of Uncle James's dead face. And Mama would usually frown and intervene with, "William, don't scare the girls!"

He'd finish with, "I'm just sayin' I wouldn'ta recognized my own kin if the undertaker hadn't knowed who be in that shoddy box."

Evidently, Uncle James had been tall like Papa. And because the body in the waterlogged coffin had been long and missing a leg, Papa had surmised it to be James. He and the undertaker had repacked the body and taken it to the depot. Papa said he'd tried to get Uncle James shipped home for free or at least half fare, considering his service and sacrifice. He had no luck.

He and Uncle James had ridden the train out of Virginia, through North Carolina, stopping at Raleigh and then Charlotte and some smaller places, and on to upcountry South Carolina and the courthouse in Anderson. He said, "Brother James mighta enjoyed the ride on a diff'rent occasion. Least he didn't feel the cold."

From there Papa had borrowed a wagon and driven Uncle James home to Varennes about eight miles south of Anderson.

He could recount the exact dimensions of the coffin because, like Grandpa Jones, he was a skilled coffin maker. "Seven feet, three inches long and two feet, three inches at its widest," he would say. Then he would add, "The grave was gonna take consider'ble diggin.' I just hoped it'd be dug 'fore we got home."

Uncle James's second burial had been at Cross Roads Baptist Church Cemetery in Varennes, where Grandpa Jones's grave still appeared as newly turned dirt.

Papa used to say, "The number of folks comin' to a funeral depends more on the weather than the good works of the departed." Either way, Uncle James's reinterring, Aunt Eliza's word, had been well attended. If, in fact, it really was Uncle James.

During the rest of his furlough, Papa had visited with family on all three sides. Since we were his second family, he had two sets of in-laws, along with blood kin. He'd gotten to see my sister Bessie, who was only a year-and-a-half old, and his children from his first marriage, all except Dock who was still in Virginia. I hadn't been born yet.

Mama would usually say, "We visited my kin and William's kin and tried to get the farm in shape for however long that war was to last."

Papa would sometimes add, "I went squirrel huntin' twice and shot five." Then he would smile as though it were an appropriate ending.

And so concluded the account of Uncle James's homecoming. A sad occasion had become a joyful occasion, at least for Papa and Mama. Mama sometimes said, "There's a reason for everything." I guess she was right, although on this particular occasion I doubt that Uncle James would've been a willing participant. Nor the squirrels.

At the end of the furlough, Papa had to go back north to Petersburg. He didn't come home again until the summer of 1864. This time, he was the one who'd been shot in the leg.

Mama said it was an awful time because she couldn't help but think of Uncle James and all the other soldiers who'd been wounded, lost a limb, and died anyway. But the doctor had dug the ball out of Papa's leg in time and sent him home to heal. That's when I was conceived. Mama never said so, but it didn't take a genius to count backward.

So that was the backdrop of my conception, a lost cause and a war wound. I was born the month after the war had officially ended. My family had sent three generations of soldiers into a bloody struggle that changed them all.

I suppose every family has war stories, men lost or maimed, women left to go on, babies conceived in grief or joy. Still something in Papa's account of bringing home Uncle James to be buried with his kinfolk seems to resurface again and again in my adult life. And each time I find something different to consider.

It's like looking at a blue jay feather. On the bird, most of the feathers look to be blue, with a few others either black or white. But when you find a single blue jay feather and study it, you see that it's a perfect balance of the three colors—the beautiful blue layered between stripes of black and then dipped in pristine white. The whole of the bird is in each feather.

At this moment, how I wish I could sit beside Papa one more time with Bessie and Mama and my half-brothers and sisters close by. To listen again to the telling of Uncle James's story. To hang on every thrilling, dreadful detail. To once again be united by the ironies of war and the bonds of kinship. Or maybe it's the other way around—the bonds of war and the ironies of kinship.

Baked apples ⌐ ⌐ ⌐

Sadly, the war hadn't really ended with Appomattox. But I was too young to understand much about the early years after the war, who made the laws and who enforced them. I did learn that there were hard years at first, followed by decades of ill will. And that the dirtiest word in the English language, at least in South Carolina, was "Reconstruction."

When I was around eight, I asked Mama what the word meant. We were shelling butter beans at the time. Papa had gone to check a field, and Bessie had quickly decided she needed to go with him. Bessie didn't like shelling butter beans. She said it took too much sitting.

I didn't mind as much. The bean shells were velvety curves. And inside were three or four small white beans. Together they made me think of babies in a canoe.

Mama was quite an accomplished sheller. She'd set a basket of unshelled beans to her left and another basket to her right for the empty shells. Next, she'd balance a large bowl on her lap. She'd scoop a generous handful of unshelled beans and drop them into her bowl. Then in rapid fire fashion, she'd lift an unshelled bean with her right hand, drag her right thumb across the seam to pop it open, scoot the shiny oblong beans out with her left thumb, and throw the empty shell into the basket on her right.

I would pull my little chair up close facing hers with my own small bowl on my lap and try to do the same. Scoop up the unshelled, dig out the beans, discard the empty shell, start over.

But I was slow. I had to press the seam with both thumbs, pry it open with my thumbnails, and then scrape out the contents with both hands. More often than not, I'd leave little crescent cuts in the tender beans. Then my fingers would get slippery from bean juice. You wouldn't think a tiny bean would have liquid in it, but once it was mangled, the juice seeped out. Mama could shell a dozen beans to my one.

Such was the case on that particular summer day of butterbean shelling when I decided to ask about Reconstruction. Although Mama and Papa hadn't talked about it in front of Bessie and me, sometimes the walls whispered the word.

And so I asked. And immediately wished I hadn't.

Mama's face soured. She looked as though she might throw up in the bean bowl. "Federal occupation," she said.

If words had a taste, I knew those were bitter.

Still I couldn't stop myself from asking, "What's that?"

"Revenge for the war, Icie, pure evil." She grabbed up another unshelled bean.

"Wasn't losing bad enough?" I asked, hoping I hadn't upset her too much.

"Evidently not. Do-gooders and scoundrels poured into our state before the ink was dry at Appomattox." She popped open the hapless bean so hard that it broke in the middle and flew out of her hand.

"Who? The North?" I asked as I chased down her bean. I studied it closely. I was afraid to look directly at Mama.

"Outsiders," she said. "They even divided the churches as much as they could."

"Our church?" I asked, trying to remember if I'd seen an unfamiliar face in the Cross Roads congregation.

"No, honey," she said, a bit calmer. "But even in our church, folks have been more in the mind of the Old Testament than the New."

That was my first inkling of Reconstruction. It was a difficult concept for a child. But I knew it was bad. And the walls continued to whisper the word.

About two years later, a large number of men in South Carolina, mostly from the upcountry and the Edgefield area, came together to put an end to Reconstruction. The men organized into horseback groups that would soon unite and become known as Hampton's Red Shirt Legion.

The legion's purpose was to take back our state's representation in the government by electing Wade Hampton. I read later that it was "to terrorize colored voters and unwelcome Northerners." So the purpose differed dramatically depending on who you asked. Or as my Aunt Eliza would say "whom you asked." She was a schoolteacher.

Wade Hampton had been a senator before the war started. By the end of the war, he'd risen to the status of living saint throughout the state because of his battle skills, leadership, and undying love of South Carolina. Once federal occupation began to turn ugly, he started campaigning against it. But he was shut out of the State House.

Because all of this started about ten years after the war, it appealed to many of the young men who hadn't been old enough to serve in the 1860s. So was the case with my second half-brother Sammy, who'd come of age during Reconstruction.

Mama said that joining the Red Shirts was a way for young men to fight a war that had passed them by. The movement had a large force of veterans, too.

The men called themselves "the Reformers," and their symbol became "the bloody shirt." Women began sewing shirts out of yellow homespun and then splotching them with red paint, pokeberries, or whatever they had that looked like blood. I remember seeing a few of the shirts as a child. They were truly terrifying. I asked Mama if she was making any of those frightening shirts for the men in our family.

"No," she said. "Your papa doesn't need one, and the others have wives able enough."

Mama didn't appear to be caught up in the fervor. She not only kept Bessie and me close, she seemed especially watchful for Anah and Lee "Red" Jones, two colored children who lived on our place. She refused to send them to town, and she forbade them to leave the farm after dark.

One night at supper, Bessie asked Papa about the bloody shirts, probably not the best time to bring up the subject as we could tell by Mama's reaction. She put down her fork.

We were having cornbread, green beans, and thick bacon. Papa called it "streak-a-lean-streak-a-fat," which was a lot more exciting than "thick bacon." Either way, Mama fried the fat right out of it until it was streak-a-leather.

But I thought I smelled syrupy baked apples in the kitchen. That's what I hoped, so I kept eating.

Mama looked as though she'd lost her appetite. "Blood will have blood," she said. "I'd just as soon Manse Jolly come back and start killing again."

Papa held a forkful of green beans in midair. "He's a veteran, Em'ly. He deserves respect. You know he lost five brothers to the Yanks." Then he cleaned his fork and chewed.

Bessie slumped down a little and nibbled on a wedge of cornbread. I did too.

"I know," Mama answered, "but that didn't give him the right to ambush those boys at Brown's Ferry."

"Yankee soldiers," Papa said. He took a swig of tea.

"Boys, no more than sixteen, if that old," she countered.

Papa set down his tea glass harder than need be. "No younger than Brother James when the Yanks shot him down." He lifted a stiff piece of bacon.

"The war was already over when Manse Jolly killed those boys," she said.

Papa didn't respond. So Bessie ventured in again. "What boys?"

"Yankee soldiers," he said, laying down his bacon. "Young soldiers," he added, glancing toward Mama. "And it wadn't all that long after Lee surrendered. Not ever'body got the word."

Mama gave a slight nod.

Papa went on, "Manse Jolly, a fella from these parts, kept fightin'. One night, him and his band of four or five men took back some horses from Yankee soldiers that come here durin' Reconstruction."

"'Took back some horses'!" Mama interrupted. "He stole them!"

"They was likely Confederate horses to begin with," Papa said, looking at his plate. I think he wanted to get back to eating.

"They may have been," she said. "But he surely wasn't returning them to their rightful owners."

"What happened at Brown's Ferry?" Bessie asked, trying to get the story back on track.

"Manse Jolly and his men had some horses they wanted to take across the river to Georgia." He picked up his bacon again. "And they needed the ferry."

He looked at Mama, probably expecting her to interrupt. When she didn't, he continued, "He come upon what he thought was a bunch of Yankee soldiers, so him and his men shot 'em."

Papa stopped the story there and said, "Em'ly, supper's gettin' cold. You tell the rest." He bit into his bacon and twisted it a full circle until a piece broke off.

"Turns out," she said, "it was just three boy soldiers sent there to guard some bales of cotton." She shook her head slowly. "Their commander probably thought he was keeping them out of harm's way. He wasn't expecting a bunch of war-crazed idiots to shoot them and throw them into the river."

Bessie and I shivered at the same time. We'd just been on Brown's Ferry with Mama and Papa to visit our half-brother Johnny in Elberton, Georgia.

"Are there dead bodies in the river?" I asked.

Papa swallowed hard. "Now who's scarin' the girls?" he said looking at Mama.

"What happened to Mr. Jolly?" Bessie asked.

"He drowned," Mama said, flatly.

"In the Savannah?" I asked. I sensed some sort of irony although I didn't yet know the word.

"Texas," Papa said.

Bessie shot me a funny look. I pinched my lips together to keep from giggling. Mama must have taken it for fear.

She softened. "Didn't mean to scare you. Now clean your plates. I baked some apples for dessert."

With that we got back to the business of supper and let the Union boys and Manse Jolly rest in peace.

The baked apples were a welcome ending. The sugary crust on the tender peels gave way to the warm, wonderful center of the fruit. As I loaded a spoon of the soft goodness, I said a silent prayer for the Union boys.

⸘

The Red Shirt movement grew with or without Mama's blessing. As more and more small groups of mounted men united throughout the state, they began wearing red flannel shirts, rather than the bloody ones, to give themselves a uniform look.

Dock, my oldest half-brother, was a leading force in the Anderson area. According to him, the red shirts signified blood, but they also set the Reformers apart from the Ku Klux Klan, a loosely formed gang of men who disguised themselves with bed sheets and struck at night, burning and killing anyone they surmised to be the enemy.

The Red Shirt movement reached its height in 1876. Groups from across the state rode all the way to Columbia and stormed the State House to reclaim a voice in government. The result was the election of Wade Hampton as our governor and pretty much the end of Reconstruction in South Carolina.

Papa seemed proud of Dock and Sammy, but even though people still called him "Capt. Jones," he didn't take part. And Johnny had been too busy clearing land and building a barn to do much else. Papa was more concerned with getting back to farming, making an occasional coffin, and trying to earn a profit. Land was cheap, so Papa bartered and bought as much as he could. More than he could farm by himself.

He soon turned to sharecropping, letting a few families live on the land and do their own farming in exchange for part of their crops. By the time Reconstruction was over, Papa had more fields and sharecroppers than he could keep up with, so he hired a farm manager named Preston Allen.

Things settled down somewhat all around, and two years after the Red Shirts had made their famous ride, Gov. Hampton was scheduled to come to Anderson to thank the people for supporting him. It also happened to be his sixtieth birthday, which was in March during the final blow of winter.

Everybody in Varennes appeared excited, except Mama. In fact, she and Papa had a heated discussion about Wade Hampton shortly before his visit. Not in front of Bessie and me, but we heard them through the bedroom wall.

Mama said, "Why should I go listen to a man who helped bring that war upon us?"

"The war wadn't his doin'," Papa said.

"He was the biggest slave owner in South Carolina!" Mama said, her voice rising, "probably in Mississippi, too!"

"Em'ly Jones, you best not be judgin'!" Papa's voice rose too. "Have you forgot your kin in Edgefield?"

"It wasn't my doing," she replied a little less emphatically.

"Not mine neither," he said. "Anyway, you'll be goin' to honor me."

They talked on, but I couldn't make out the rest. Still I had no doubt that Mama would give in to Papa's wishes.

When the day arrived, folks bundled up in their Sunday best and came from all the surrounding towns to see Wade Hampton. They'd also taken up a collection throughout the county to buy the governor a fine horse. It came from Rivoli Plantation in Pendleton and cost a whopping $300.

For the occasion, Papa planned to take Mama, Bessie, and me in the buggy while our new farm manager, Preston Allen, followed behind in the wagon. I was almost thirteen and Bessie was sixteen. Mama said if we had to go into Anderson anyway we might as well take the wagon, too, and get some supplies that we couldn't find in Varennes.

Bessie decided she needed to ride in the wagon with Preston

to help keep up with the list and get the supplies. She asked Papa, and he said "yep" before Mama could say "certainly not."

As we were about to leave, Mama said to Preston, "Drive careful with Bessie there. And stay in sight."

"I will, Mrs. Emily," he said, glancing at Bessie. She blushed. He looked back at Mama. "I'm happy to see you're going to this momentous occasion, too. The governor's address should be impressive."

She sniffed and said, "I'm not going to see the governor. I'm going to see the $300 horse."

Papa smiled and off we went.

By the time we arrived, the Anderson Courthouse was surrounded with wagons and carriages along with single mounts. Someone decided the crowd needed to shift over a few blocks to a large vacant lot for more space. Several men lifted a platform with three steps and carried it to the center of the lot. Men on foot quickly surrounded the platform. Behind them, onlookers like us in carriages and men on horseback filled in the rest of the lot.

The air was cold and the crowd was noisy. Someone shouted several times for silence to greet the governor. Then the men on foot began to part like the Red Sea as a single gentleman strode through the crowd. He reached the platform, climbed the steps and soon stood above the crowd.

The governor wore a white shirt with a silky red tie tucked into a black vest. His black coat and trousers looked to be tailored of thick wool. His boots gleamed from polish, and his gloves ran halfway to his elbows. He wore no hat. His thick hair was mottled with gray, and he had enough whiskers for two men.

I was already shivering, but I got a fresh case of cold chills looking at the most revered living person in the state, maybe in the whole South.

The crowd grew silent except for the whinny of a horse behind us and the muffled cries of a baby nearby.

Gov. Hampton stepped forward and began to speak.

"My fellow citizens of the great state of South Carolina!" He paused and surveyed the crowd. Someone yelled. He continued, "I thank you for your Service! Your Sacrifice! Your Support! Your Steadfastness!" He paused after each S-word as more shouts went up.

Papa yelled too. Mama shot him a look, but he seemed not to notice.

I remember that part of Wade Hampton's speech because of all the Ss. I don't remember much more of what he said, but I do recall the way he delivered it. Like a preacher, only smoother, building up speed and volume, then catching his breath while men yelled and women attempted to clap in thick gloves. The cadence repeated over and over until his delivery was done. And the cheering was exhausted.

Just as he was about to descend the platform, the crowd began to part again. This time it was for a man leading the most beautiful horse I'd ever seen. It was at least sixteen hands high with a long graceful neck and powerful haunches. As it pranced and blew out frozen breath, its black coat glowed like polished coal. Its bridle was the color of walnut, and on its back sat a brand new English saddle.

That's when I realized the man leading the horse was my half-brother Dock!

Papa straightened his back and smiled. He looked at Mama. "See?" he said. She nodded.

The governor seemed truly surprised. He pulled off his gloves and quickly descended the platform. Dock said something to him, handed him the reins, motioned to the crowd, and stepped back into the circle. Gov. Hampton nodded to Dock and to the crowd several times in what I took to mean, "Thank you."

Then he turned to face the horse. He looked down the right side of the horse and ran his hand along its neck. He did the same on its left side. He led the horse in a small circle to the right and then back to the left.

Next he moved to the horse's left side. He tugged gently on the stirrup. He took a step back and stretched his left arm straight out to where his hand barely touched the saddle. With his right hand, he pulled the stirrup toward his chest and measured the length of the strap by the length of his left arm. I'd seen Papa do the same before mounting a horse, so I knew he was checking to see if the stirrups were right for a man his size. After that he ran two fingers underneath the girth.

Murmurs among the onlookers increased with each new motion the governor made toward the horse. The horse began to bob its head and dance around, but the governor held on firmly, stroking its neck.

"What kind of horse is that?" I asked Papa.

"Thur-uh-bred," he said. "Thur-uh-bred," he repeated louder, perhaps thinking Mama hadn't heard him. "Finest in the state."

"Male or female?" she asked. "I can't tell from here."

"Male," he answered. "And he ain't been cut."

The governor slid his hands down the reins and quickly looped them over the horse's neck. With his left hand holding the reins and a thick portion of mane, and his right hand on the pommel of the saddle, the governor left the ground. In one flow-ing motion, he slipped his left boot into the left stirrup, arced his right leg over the horse, and landed lightly in the saddle.

He quickly secured the right stirrup just as the crowded erupted. The stallion sprang forward, white breath shooting out like smoke, the rider every bit as regal as the legend.

Right there in the center of Anderson, the sixty-year-old governor transformed back into a fearless warrior leading his troops into a cause that, at the moment, did not seem entirely lost after all.

The crowd noise reached a new high. And this time the women cheered as loudly as the men.

Papa shouted over the noise, "Now, Em'ly, ain't you glad you came!"

"Yes!" Mama shouted back, "The horse is magnificent!"

Second family ☙

Mama was little but she was used to being in charge. The old-est of six children, she'd helped raise her brothers and sisters. The youngest, Euphronius, was more than twenty years younger than Mama. As children, Bessie and I called him "Uncle Eufee" because we couldn't pronounce "Eu-phro-ni-us" without losing at least one syllable.

All that responsibility may have soured Mama on marriage. That is until she met Papa when she was already thirty-five years old. Thirty-five! That used to seem old. Not so much now.

Mama, whose maiden name was Emily Woods Adams, caught Papa's eye just over a year after his first wife, Elizabeth, had died. Mama said she hadn't planned to marry unless she found the proper gentleman. But there stood Papa, a widower with a houseful of young'uns and in need of a wife.

She said he was a charmer and the handsomest man she'd ever seen. Papa was four years younger than Mama, but I guess he was proper enough. They married soon after meeting, just a few years before the war.

Bessie and I loved to hear how they met. Papa would tell us more than Mama, but she'd chime in with details. The time I remember most was when I was almost seven and Bessie ten. It was a winter morning. Mama had cooked a big breakfast—scrambled eggs, bubbling grits, big puffy biscuits, blackstrap molasses, and thick slices of sweet ham.

We ate until we couldn't eat any more. It was a Saturday, and Papa didn't seem in a hurry to start the day. So Mama got up to put on another pot of coffee.

Bessie started it. "Papa, tell us how you met Mama."

"You girls done heard it many a time," he said. But I'm sure he knew what was coming.

"P-l-e-a-s-e," Bessie said, drawing it out into the next county.

"P-l-e-a-s-e, Papa!" I chimed in.

He looked toward Mama at the stove. Then he began, "When my first wife, Liz-buth, died, I didn't know what I was gonna do. We had five young'uns." He counted them on his fingers as he named them—"Dock, Mattie, Sammy, Sallie, and little Johnny. Johnny was just a babe in arms."

Papa hesitated and looked toward the window.

Bessie said, "And then you saw Mama."

By then Mama was on her way back to the table with a fresh pot. She poured Papa a cup. He blew on it, then set it down. "Your mama's brother Frank, he was sweet on my sister Jane.

They were gonna marry. Your mama's whole family, the Adams, they lived in Edgefield so's I'd not met your mama."

"But we have relatives in Abbeville, which is a lot closer than Edgefield," she said as she poured herself a cup. "That's where Frank and Jane met."

Papa continued, "It'd been just over a year since Liz-buth died. I mourned her proper. Then put away the band I'd wore on my sleeve since her death."

He looked at Mama. She nodded in agreement. "So there we set at Cross Roads Baptist Church all cleaned up for Frank and Jane's weddin'."

"The day before the wedding," Mama corrected. "On the day before the wedding, the families got together to size each other up."

"The day before the weddin'," he said. "And there stood Mizz Em'ly Adams. She was a tiny slip of a woman, but she had a spark about her. And purty blue eyes. And shiny brown hair with just a little bit of red stirred in."

"Auburn," she interrupted.

"The color of cherry wood," he said, "and all piled up in pins. You could tell her hair wanted to bust loose and come down swingin'."

"It did not," she said, patting her hair knotted in a bun. But she was smiling. Bessie and I loved the part about her hair.

He went on, "I asked Jane about Mizz Em'ly. She said she heard Mizz Em'ly had chances enough in Edgefield but wasn't lookin' to wed."

Mama nodded again.

"I decided to give it a shot anyhow. I talked her into stayin' with her kin in Abbeville so's I didn't have to ride clear down to Edgefield."

"I agreed," she said, "but I wasn't planning on moving. I'd meant to live out my days in Edgefield."

Papa laughed and said, "I won her heart anyhow."

They looked at each other, weaving a stream of light like a slice of sunshine slipping through a gap in the curtains. Even as a child, I knew it was a moment. One that seemed outside the realm of my own young experience. "Jesus-God moments," as Papa called them, ordinary but extraordinary at the same time—ones that you store away for harder times.

Neither one of them mentioned that Mama was thirty-six when they married. But that might have had something to do with the fact that she didn't think she'd have babies. And with Papa's five, she said she hadn't felt the need.

But lo and behold, she had Bessie when she was almost forty. And she had me when she was forty-three. Lordy, forty-three! I was lucky to be born at all. Mama had a baby before Bessie and me, a little girl they named Frances. But she didn't live very long. Mama never talked about her. Papa mentioned her a few times but never in front of Mama.

One evening when Mama was at her sister's and Papa was enjoying some brandy, Bessie decided to ask him again about Frances.

He was reared back in his chair in the front room with his feet on a stool he used only when Mama wasn't home. The stool came from Mama's grandmother, but Papa made the chair himself. The frame was pine, and the arms and legs were cherry wood all stained to match. Mama had covered the seat with layers of combed cotton and muslin.

Sometimes I'd try to sit in it when no one else was around. My feet wouldn't touch the floor. Not even when I was grown.

Papa had made small chairs for Bessie and me, too. He called them his angel chairs. Bessie pulled her little chair closer to him and said, "Tell us about Frances, our sister." She had a good sense of timing with Mama gone and brandy in Papa's glass.

He took a sip, looked around, closed his eyes for a few seconds, then said, "Your mama was so proud of little Frances. It bein' her own babe after helpin' raise her sisters and brothers. I was too."

He took another sip and swallowed. Then he drew in a deep, slow breath and exhaled until his lungs were surely flat. "The baby took sick and died less than a year old." He said it fast, as though it still hurt.

"I'm sorry, Papa," Bessie said, as soothing as she could. She patted his arm.

"It was summer," he continued. "After we buried Frances, your mama took to the bed. She didn't get up for two days. We all worried but I let her be. She laid there in her weepin' weeds, hot as it was, her hair all down and tangled.

"But on the third day," he said, "sorta like in the Bible, she got herself off the bed, cleaned up, and started over like nothin' much happened."

He took a long pull of brandy, swished it around, and swallowed. "She did pretty good after that, and you might not know she was grievin' cept for her weeds. She wore 'em six months to the day, then packed 'em up for later heartaches. But she didn't really come back to life 'til Bessie was born."

He looked at Bessie and smiled. "I wanted to name you 'Blessin',' but your mama, she wanted to name you after her sister Bethia. So we did. I started callin' you 'Bessie,' and it stuck."

That was the end of the discussion about little Frances. Bessie and I both knew never to ask Mama about her.

And yet, I thought of Frances from time to time. I wondered

if she'd be tall and good with animals like Bessie. Or small and musical, more like I was turning out to be. If she'd have hazel or blue eyes. Or even emerald green. And if I died during my sleep, if I'd recognize her in Heaven. But mainly, I just wanted to give her life, if only in my mind.

Devil's garden ⌒ ⟋ ⟀

There were other things Mama didn't talk about. She had a sack-load of sayings, one being "You don't have to tell everything you know." She'd say it to Bessie and me at the dinner table if we had a story that went on too long. Or after church, if someone stood up and confessed his sins.

I learned it early on when I asked about Anah and Lee "Red" Jones, the two colored children Mama helped raise.

Their mother, Alice Jones, started working for us when I was barely old enough to remember. Her mother had been with Mama's family in Edgefield, probably as a slave, but Mama never said so. Alice's children, Anah and Lee, were born during Reconstruction. She died soon after Lee was born. I never knew why or what of. I was around six or seven. Their nearest relatives were in Edgefield, but Bessie and I didn't want them to leave. Neither did Mama.

She decided she could best take care of them right here in Varennes with the help of another colored family living on our farm. Lee had brown hair with a hint of auburn so folks called him "Red." Actually, his hair was no redder than mine, but it wasn't black like Anah's. Papa called him Red so we did too.

When Anah was old enough, she got married and went to

work for the McGees a few miles south of our home where her husband was already working. Red stayed and worked for Mama and Papa until much later.

One time when I was about eight, I asked Mama if Anah and Red were kin to us. Mama was perched on a tall stool at the sink, silking corn with a soft brush. She looked from the ear of corn to me, then back to the corn. "Why do you ask?"

"Because their last name is Jones like ours."

"Oh, silly child," she said, "there are lots of Joneses."

"Colored?" I asked.

Mama put down the brush. "After the war, freedmen could take the name of the family that'd owned them if they wanted to."

"Papa owned them?" I asked.

"No," she said. "They could take any name they liked." And back to the corn-silking she went.

"Then who's their father?" I asked.

Without looking up from the corn, Mama said, "Idle curiosity is the Devil's garden."

I should have embroidered that on an apron for myself.

Mama knew a lot of things she didn't tell. Or didn't care to remember. But she did occasionally talk about her grandmother Isabella. Mama's mother came from a large family of landowners in Abbeville County who'd been wealthy before the war. Mama's grandfather had died shortly after she was born, so she never knew him. But she was especially fond of her grandmother. Mama said Isabella had been quite the lady and that she'd managed the entire plantation on her own. That is until the war.

Evidently, her grandmother never came to terms with the war or its aftermath. Soon after Reconstruction turned ugly, her beloved grandmother had, as Mama put it, "come down with a bad case of the nerves." She'd lived a long time afterward but was never the same.

Mama also told us about her favorite aunt, Arabella, who'd found herself in an even worse situation. She and her husband had eleven children. During the last months of the war, her husband had been assigned to move Union prisoners from a stockade in South Carolina to one in North Carolina and then to join the front line to prevent Sherman from taking Richmond.

Sherman was in the midst of his ungodly march from Savannah, Georgia, through South Carolina on his way to North Carolina and ultimately Virginia. Union forces were near Columbia when Arabella's husband had started his last letter to her, still hopeful of a Confederate victory. It was mid-February 1865, three months before I was born.

By the time he'd been able to finish his letter, Columbia had fallen.

Mama had read the letter herself and said that it began with joyful expectation of a husband soon to be reunited with his family. But it ended in quiet desperation as he realized it wasn't to be.

Arabella had received his letter in March, the month before Lee's surrender at Appomattox.

Each day thereafter, Arabella had waited for her husband to come home. But he did not. In the following weeks, word came trickling in of his death, possibly from disease among the Union prisoners. Other returning soldiers said they thought he'd died in the final battle in North Carolina.

Mama said that the family never found out for certain how he'd died or, worse yet, where he'd been buried.

"I can't imagine not having a gravestone," she said, "a place

for his widow and children to mourn, evidence that he walked
on this earth and was loved. I can't imagine." The telling of such
sad events left Mama near tears. So when it came to stories about
her relatives, I learned not to ask. At least not to ask Mama. Not
even when Uncle Euffee eloped to Georgia with a thirteen-year-
old bride.

'Forty acres and a mule' ⸱ ⸱ ⸱

The elopement happened during early Reconstruction, so Mama
had other matters to keep her mind occupied. One was helping
Papa find freedmen to work the fields. She wasn't above working in the fields herself as she'd done while Papa was serving the
Confederacy. But Papa had managed to accumulate more land
since then.

Like other planters, he'd had little money to pay for help,
but he could provide simple shelter for families willing to farm.
They'd give him a portion of the harvest in return. In a few years,
Papa had earned enough profits to build more small houses and
bring in more families.

So while some of the Joneses had joined the Red Shirts and
were trying to take over the government, Papa had been as he
put it "seein' to the land." That's when he'd hired Preston Allen
to help manage the fields and the sharecroppers.

With the fieldwork taken care of, Mama became the record
keeper. By the time Wade Hampton had become governor of the
state, things were going pretty well on our farm.

About a week after Hampton's famous birthday visit to
Anderson in 1878, everyone in our household was back to doing
what they normally did. Since it was nearly time to plant corn,

Papa and Preston were touring the fields to decide which ones should be sown in corn. Bessie, as usual, joined them.

That left me at the piano where I was supposed to be practicing and Mama at her desk where she was tallying up the sharecropper records. Her desk was underneath a large window in the front hall. My piano was at an angle across the room.

Mama kept all of our household records right there at her desk. It was quite dainty and a little shaky. It'd been her grandmother's writing desk imported from England. She'd given it to Mama's mother, whose middle name was Woods. Then it had come to Mama, whose middle name was also Woods. Because my given name—Isamar Woods Jones—carried on the tradition, I hoped the desk would come to me eventually.

It was made of fruitwood and had thin, curvy legs. The front pulled down for a writing surface. Little compartments held an ink well, two fountain pens, a cloth for dabbing ink, a sachet that smelled like gardenias, and several ledgers. It also had two drawers on the front. One drawer had a false back that opened to a secret compartment.

I sometimes wondered about the stories it could tell of my relatives, particularly female, on my Mama's side.

Papa didn't seem to think much of the desk. He told Mama more than once that he'd make her a new sturdy desk of oak. She said she didn't see the need.

But back to the subject at hand, which on that particular morning was Wade Hampton's recent visit to Anderson. As Mama sat at her desk, I decided to ask why she hadn't been as impressed with him as the rest of us were.

I kept glancing at her from my piano stool, hoping to catch her attention between sweeps of her pen.

"What do you want, Icie?" Mama asked, without looking up.

"I was just wondering," I said, "why you weren't excited to see Gov. Hampton in Anderson last week." I was half-expecting to get "the Devil's garden" comment.

Instead she marked her place and laid down the pen.

She turned to face me. "He's a great man," she said, "and he sacrificed as much as anybody, more than some. But we lost the war."

"What about getting rid of Reconstruction and the Northern outsiders?" I asked, "the ones that came in and stirred up trouble?" I was careful to use her own words.

"We're better off with them gone," she admitted. "And although we lost what money we had, we still have our land."

She turned back toward the desk. "But so many men died, some better than others. With all that suffering, nothing really changed for the good of the colored people."

"Didn't they want to get freed?" I asked.

"I would think so," she said as she looked out the window above the desk. "And I'm sure they wanted '40 acres and a mule' like that bastard Sherman promised them!"

I sucked in a breath without meaning to. I'd never heard Mama say such a word before. She wouldn't even say "hell." She called it "the bad place." I expected her to take it back, but she didn't.

She turned to me and explained, "After the war, most colored folks became house servants or field hands, doing the same things they did before, except they were called 'freedmen' and they got paid a little and had to buy things themselves. Even though they were free to leave, not that many left. At least not many from around here."

I thought that maybe just knowing they could leave was change enough. But I didn't say so.

Mama held up the ledger she'd been working on and said, "Many of them ended up in here, share-cropping for folks like us."

"Is that a bad thing?" I asked.

She turned back to her desk and said, "It's better than nothing."

"What do you mean by 'nothing'?" I asked. "Being dead?"

"No. It's being without hope. As long as you have a little land and some seed to plant, you have hope of a harvest. Whether or not you get one is another matter."

She picked up her fountain pen, tested the nib, and started writing again. Over her shoulder she said, "Now play something pretty."

"Jesus Loves Me" seemed like a safe choice.

'Death don't wait'

Papa was the oldest in a family of a dozen children. He had four brothers and seven sisters. All of the males—except for the brother who died as a child—joined the Confederacy. Most survived the war. Some suffered long after. Others didn't.

Of my aunts on Papa's side of the family, I had two favorites. Aunt Louisa, whose daughters were my best friends, and Aunt Eliza, a schoolteacher who taught me to knit, expanded my vocabulary, and told me many a story.

Papa's mother, Elizabeth Austin Jones, came from Greenville, two counties to the north, from a long line of Austins that went all the way back to London, England. King George III had made an estate grant of 15,000 acres in the upper part of South Carolina to Papa's great-great-grandfather Nathaniel Austin.

When Papa talked about that bit of family history, he would always laugh, and end with, "That king didn't know Nathaniel Austin was gonna be 'bout his worst enemy." Obviously, Papa was proud of his kinfolk who fought for American independence. The lineage of Papa's father, James Vandiver Jones, was less traceable. He too came from Greenville where his mother had given birth to him in the early 1800s. Those who'd known her said she was as smart as she was pretty and that she'd made a good life for herself and her son.

I knew all that because Aunt Eliza told me so. As for Grandpa Jones's father, the matter was, as she'd said, "debatable." Regardless of his parentage, Grandpa Jones must have been charming and ambitious. He'd convinced Elizabeth Austin to marry him in spite of her family's lineage. Whether or not her family had approved was another matter.

Together they'd made a good home in Greenville where Papa and his brothers and sisters were born. When Grandpa Jones inherited a bit of money, or more likely when his wife did, he'd bought land here in Varennes.

He and another man had opened a store, but the Jones family had remained in Greenville. That is until some years later when Grandpa and Grandma Jones were kicked out of their church. The Jones family moved to Varennes shortly thereafter.

Not even Aunt Eliza seemed to know why they'd been given the boot. If she did, she never told me. That may be the reason Papa didn't get too angry with me for upsetting our own church.

Papa and Grandpa Jones helped build the church here in the 1850s. Cross Roads Baptist. There was already a building at the time, but members decided they needed a bigger, stronger brick structure. They made the bricks near the little stream just south of the church.

The church used the same little stream to baptize folks. That's where Rev. Wright dipped Bessie and me. In hindsight, I'm sure he'd have taken back my baptizing if he could've.

Papa was a religious man, but he was a practical man too. He seldom passed up the opportunity to increase what he had. He said he was using his talents like the good and faithful servant in the Bible rather than "diggin' a hole like a fool." Along with farming, he lent money to folks, including fellow soldiers during the war, and he charged interest. Not everyone approved.

And like Grandpa Jones, he made coffins. Evidently the coffins were much finer than the graves he dug. Papa said he loved working with wood, but he hated digging. Sometimes the grave digging was figured in with the cost of the coffin. So Papa usually paid someone else to dig the grave a little less than he was charging the grieving family. That way, he made a good profit on the coffin and a small profit on the digging, all the while avoiding the shovel.

Because of the coffin business, Papa was considered something of an expert on dying. He had as many sayings about dying as Mama did about living. Things like "Death's a remedy for all ills." "Death shows up like a wormy dog lookin' for a bone." "All's forgiven in death if you didn't do nothin' too hateful in life."

He was self-educated, meaning that he didn't get to go to school like his younger brothers and sisters. He was too busy helping his father make a living. As a result, deciphering his writing was like solving a puzzle. And his speech was a wonderful mix of grammatical errors, abbreviated words, and biblical expressions.

Bessie and I loved the way he talked. But when we'd try to

sound like him, Mama would correct our grammar. She didn't correct us in front of Papa, though.

His woodshop was near the barn. It faced north and had large widows on the east and west sides to catch the light. He had various saws and planes as well as clamps and all kinds of nails. He used different woods depending on what he was making and what was available.

He sometimes used hardwoods for finer furniture even though he said it was tricky to work with. He preferred pine because of its softer nature and ease of nailing. I preferred it because of its wonderful smell. For coffins, he almost always used pine.

When Bessie and Mama were busy somewhere else, I liked to follow Papa around in his woodshop. I could find plenty to do while he worked. I would line up tools by size, sort nails, and practice writing my name in sawdust until he'd pay me attention or send me to the house.

One such afternoon, Papa was busy making a coffin. He kept measuring and checking the numbers he'd written on a scrap of wood. He seemed to be working faster than usual. I noticed an unfinished coffin across the shop on the other workbench.

I didn't want to annoy him, but my curiosity got the best of me. I cleared my throat to get his attention. "Papa," I said, "why are you starting another coffin before finishing the other one?"

"Cause death don't wait for no coffin maker," he replied. I looked around, wondering if Death was somehow watching. I wiped away my name written in sawdust, just in case.

Papa laughed. "This coffin's for a young fella from Dean Station. He died with nary a sign. He was alive one minute and dead the next."

I shivered. "What about the other coffin, the one that's half-finished? Who's it for?"

He answered without looking up, "That's for a fella up in Rock Springs. He's been bedbound for better'n a year."

"So he's not dead?" I asked. I walked over to his coffin and looked in.

"Just a matter of time," Papa said. "I couldn't use his coffin cause the young fella's lots bigger. People can get them fact'ry-made caskets now, but most folks 'round here want 'em made special."

I walked back to the coffin at hand. "Why do some people die fast but others take a while?"

Papa put down his tools. I thought he might run me out, but he didn't.

"I've pondered the question many a time," he said. "Each coffin I build, I think about the new departed and the why of his life and death."

He took out a handkerchief and wiped his face. I waited.

"I think if'n a person dies in a hurry, he's ready to meet the Maker. That's if he's good to begin. In the case of a bad person, I think he goes straight to hell."

I blinked without meaning to. "What about the person who's bedbound for a long time?" I asked. "Is he not ready to go to Heaven?"

Papa put his handkerchief back in his pocket. "That ain't what I meant, Icie. I think the person what lingers has something unfinished, maybe just in his head. That's if he ain't done nuthin' too hateful. I think he gets extra time to look over his life, tidy up, maybe let go of things. Then he's ready to meet the Maker."

He picked up his tools and went back to work on the coffin.

And I returned to the house feeling a bit more grownup. I wondered if Papa had ever had a similar conversation with Mama. I guessed not, since Mama was much more about the travails of life than the specifics of death.

'Rules for Mourning' ⌐ ⌐

Papa's expertise on death included the prevailing convention for demonstrating grief. Those who hired him to build a coffin often asked him how to show proper respect to the recently departed.

Varennes was probably like most towns in the South in that people observed a mix of ways to demonstrate grief. But there was nothing in writing.

Although Papa had little education, he took his knowledge of mourning seriously. In fact, it's the only "ing" word that Papa pronounced all the way to the end and then some. It sounded like "MOUR-NIN-guh." Not a complete extra syllable but like the tail on the g wrapped around and came back above the line. G with a flair.

Late one evening he decided that Mama should set his expertise to pen and paper. We were sitting in the front room shortly before bed. Mama didn't seem keen on getting up from her cushioned chair and going to her desk.

She said, "William, surely everyone knows the weights and measures of mourning. Especially with all the death from the war."

"That's the point," he said. "People couldn't mourn on the outside durin' the war. They were too busy tryin' to keep theirselves alive. They mourned in their hearts and got back to fightin' Yanks."

"Or farming. Or feeding hungry mouths," she added, not making a move from her chair.

"Yep," he said. "But now the war's done. Folks need to get back to mour-nin-guh, proper."

Mama stood up. "And you don't think they remember how?" she said more than asked as she made her way to the desk.

He replied, "My dear wife, you'd be surprised."

He waited for her to light a candle, open her desk, and get her fountain pen flowing.

When she was ready, she asked, "What do you want to call this?"

"Rules for Mour-nin-guh."

"Go ahead then," she said.

He began dictating. "How long a person shall mourn for a dead relative," he paused, giving Mama time to catch up, "it depends on age, closeness of kin, and if said mourner be the man or woman."

"Alright," she said.

"Departed babes and young'uns under ten take six months of mour-nin-guh."

"Alright," she said again.

"Same for grandparents," he said.

"Is that a new sentence?" she asked.

"Nope."

Mama sniffed. Bessie and I looked at each other, but Papa acted like he didn't notice.

"A parent be mourned six months to a year."

"I always heard it was a year," Mama said.

"Six months to a year," he repeated, then waited.

"Go on," she said without looking up.

"For a spouse, if the mourner be the widder, she'll mourn

two years or more." He let Mama catch up and then continued, "The first year, the widder wears black weeds and stays home." He quickly added, "'Cept for church. She goeth to church."

Mama looked up at Papa. "Goeth?"

He nodded. She made the sniff sound again.

"The second year, she wears sober colors and goeth out sparin'."

"What's 'goeth out sparin'?" Bessie asked.

Mama answered before Papa could, "Going anywhere necessary for running the farm but nowhere she really wants to go."

I chimed in, "What color is 'sober'?"

"Somber!" she said. "And it means nothing pretty."

Papa breathed in and out a time or two and resumed, "If the spouse in mourn-in-guh be the man, he wears a black armband for a year."

"Papa, why does the wife mourn two years and the man just one?" Bessie asked.

Mama laid down her fountain pen and looked at Papa.

He seemed to think about. Then he answered, "I don't make the rules. I just know 'em."

Mama put away the pen, blew on "The Rules for Mourning," and closed her desk for the night.

Bessie and I'd thought mourning was just for older people until our niece died. She was our half-sister Sallie's second baby. Sallie was eleven years older than me. By the time she'd turned nineteen, she'd married J. E. Seigler and was on her second baby.

Her first child, Lillie, had been born fit and fine and had remained that way. Sallie hadn't let me hold Lillie, although she'd let Bessie, because Bessie was older. But when her second child, Ola, came along two years later, Sallie decided I was old enough to be trusted with a baby. Sometimes she even let Bessie and me play with Lillie and Ola as though they were our own little sisters.

One day, just after Ola reached her first birthday, she ran a fever. The very next day she died. I couldn't comprehend how the little girl I'd held in my arms could possibly be dead.

Her death hit our entire family hard because Ola was the first of the grandbabies to die so unexpectedly and, no doubt, it reminded Mama and Papa of their baby Frances. For the first time in my young life, I ached with grief.

Sallie and her husband mourned properly, attributed Ola's sudden death to God's will, and within two years, Sallie had her third baby. They named him William after Papa, which was quite an honor considering it was their first son. Papa was understandably proud.

I'd been only ten when little William was born, but I thought he looked too pale and delicate. He wasn't as pink and pudgy as the first two babies. We soon learned he had something wrong with his small heart. He lived less than a year.

William's funeral was the first I remember attending. Mama saw to it that Bessie and I were properly dressed. Bessie, who was fourteen by then, was as tall as Mama, so she wore one of Mama's mourning dresses without alterations. I was smaller, of course, so Mama cut down one of her other mourning dresses to fit me. As strange as it sounds, at the time I liked wearing that dress because I felt grown up in it.

But I hadn't felt nearly so grown up at the graveside as I watched William's little coffin being lowered into the ground. Neither had Bessie. We both began crying. When Sallie saw us, she walked to where we stood and put her arms around both of us. Even though she wore a veil, I could see the pain in her face.

"Stop your crying, girls," she said. "William is in Heaven with his sister Ola."

That made us cry even more.

"God has a special place in Heaven for babies of all kinds. Don't ever forget that." Then she breathed deep, returned to J. E.'s side, and left Bessie and me to ponder the possibility.

I imagined William and Ola and our own sister Frances in Heaven playing with lambs and fawns, kittens, maybe even a friendly bear cub. It was comforting at first. Then I started to wonder if they would grow up like we would on earth.

After the service, Mama went to the Seigler home with other ladies to put out funeral food while Sallie and J. E. greeted mourners. Bessie and I rode home with Papa. He went into the front room and poured himself some brandy.

We shucked off our new old mourning clothes. As Bessie pulled her own dress over her head, I asked her, "Do you think babies in Heaven grow up?"

She smoothed her bodice and straightened her skirt. "Seems like they'd grow up a little bit," she said, "but not so much that their family wouldn't recognize them when they got to Heaven too."

She seemed to consider her answer, then added, "Let's ask Papa."

He was in his chair so we sat in our little chairs near him. Then Bessie did the asking. He didn't respond right away. He looked from Bessie to me. "I'm glad you girls got outta them widders' weeds. I don't like you wearin' black."

"Yes sir," Bessie said. We waited.

He took a sip and swallowed. "I think when babes die, they go to Heaven first. But, I think they might get another chance at life, considerin' the first one didn't work out."

I looked at Bessie. She nodded. I nodded too. It did make sense.

He finished with, "Babes are too young to sin, so their little spirits get new bodies and come on back down."

That satisfied Bessie, and it satisfied me until I thought about it a bit more. Then I began to wonder if Bessie was really Frances, our sister who died, come back down for a second chance. It was a hard concept for a child.

Mainly, I wanted Frances to be Frances and Bessie to be Bessie.

But I better understood Papa's reasoning when Sallie's next baby, another boy, was born less than two years later. They named him Jackson after Stonewall Jackson, and he was healthy looking like the girls had been—pudgy and rosy and full of life.

Papa immediately loved Jackson. In a way, he was little William, only healthy. And when Jackson made it through his second birthday, we all thanked the Father, the Son, and the Holy Spirit.

As Aunt Eliza used to say, "Ignorance is bliss."

PART II

All God's children tell stories

First family

As for Papa's first family, by the time I was born, his oldest son, Dock, had already moved out. Dock's given name was a mouthful—James Thomas Crayton Jones. Little wonder everybody called him "Dock." Even Mama.

The other first-family children—Mattie, Sammy, Sallie, and Johnny—were still living with Mama and Papa when I was born.

Then Mattie married Franklin McGee, a Confederate veteran, and started her own family near the Savannah River. That made her name Mattie McGee. The sound of it always made me smile.

What I remember most about Sammy was how he'd chase me with snakes he'd found at the river. Needless to say, I feared him and the snake-infested riverbank. Of my three half-brothers, he seemed to be the most unsettled. Like Dock, he'd been old enough to remember his mother, but unlike his older brother, he'd been too young to join the Confederacy or to strike out on his own. He grew up during Reconstruction, certainly not the best of times for forming lifelong beliefs.

By the time I was old enough to remember much more about Sammy, he'd found some land in the Rock Mills area and moved out. Sallie and Johnny were the only two of Papa's first family who lived with us any length of time. Sallie was eleven years older than me and Johnny was nine.

When I was a baby, Sallie wanted to mother me. Mama did too. Papa said they got in each other's way until Mama put her foot down. But Sallie kept a close watch and let them both know she didn't approve of the way they were raising me. According to Mama, she'd make a face or quote the Old Testament just beneath her breath.

The odd thing is she reminded me of Mama. She was feisty like Mama and had her own little sayings. But she was more outspoken. Much more.

When I was six, Sallie married J. E. Seigler. And pretty soon she started having babies, eleven in all, though some died early.

She became one of the best-known mothers in Varennes. In addition to having her own slew of babies, she was midwife for folks throughout the county, colored or white, kin or strangers, well off or just getting by.

Sallie and J. E. were what people called "staunch members" of Cross Roads Baptist Church. Papa called them "starched members." J. E. had more than one of his brethren reprimanded for immoral behavior. As we grew up, Bessie and I respected Sallie, but we were careful not to brush skirts with her.

Johnny, my youngest half-brother, was easier to get along with. He'd been born with an afflicted foot, the only one of Papa's children to have something wrong. At least on the outside.

The story was that when he was just a little fella, a blacksmith noticed his foot and told Papa that he thought he could fix it. The smithy had then set about making a contraption of blocks and metal that attached with leather straps to Johnny's foot. He made new ones along as Johnny grew. Seems to me it would have hurt like the devil, but Johnny never complained according to Mama. And sure enough, his foot had slowly straightened out until he walked with just a slight limp.

Mama called it a miracle. Papa said it was "the grace of God and some mighty fine smithin'." Whatever it was, Johnny gained some powers of his own throughout the ordeal. For one thing, he could talk warts off man, woman, or child.

We discovered, first hand, he could talk them off cows, too. It happened shortly after he'd gotten married and was living nearby.

One morning at breakfast Bessie noticed that the milk tasted funny. I took a sip and agreed. Papa said we were imagining things. Mama took a taste and said that Molly, our milk cow, must've gotten into some wild onions. Bessie and I went outside and into the paddock to see what Molly might have grazed on. We didn't find any onions. But a closer look at Molly revealed little warts around her left eye and on the side of her face.

We ran back inside. "It's warts!" Bessie shouted. "We're tasting warts!"

"She's got warts on her utter?" Papa asked.

"No, on her face!" I chimed in.

Mama and Papa looked at each other and laughed. Then he said, "That don't have nothin' to do with her milk."

"We can taste it," Bessie insisted.

That's when Mama thought about Johnny and his special powers. She said, "We'll get Johnny to talk those warts off."

"Yes!" Bessie and I shouted in unison.

Then Papa threw cold water on the idea. "That's for people, not cows."

But Mama was undeterred. She sent for Johnny, who came right away. When she explained the situation, he said he could cure Molly. He went out the back door and down the steps with Bessie and me behind him. Papa just shook his head.

Mama called us back in. "Where are you girls going? Not to bother Johnny, I hope."

"No m'am," Bessie said. "We're gonna gather eggs."

"Eggs, is it?" she said. "Then you'd best take the egg basket.

And stay out of Johnny's way. The cure won't work if he's interrupted."

Bessie grabbed the basket, and out the kitchen door we flew.

The chicken coop was on the far side of the barn. Bessie hung the basket on the coop door and headed for the barn hall with me right behind her. She twisted around her skirt and pulled herself up the ladder that led into the loft, no simple matter because the ladder rungs were spaced for a grown man. It was even harder for me. Bessie had to reach down from the loft and pull me up the last rung by my elbows.

Johnny had gone into the paddock and was bringing Molly into the milking stall. We crept to a spot high above and lay down to listen. We could see a little bit through a crack in the loft floorboards.

Johnny rubbed Molly's face, warts and all, then started talking in a language I'd never heard. It was frightening. He spoke in a singsong tone something like a preacher.

"How does Molly know what he's saying?" I whispered.

"He's not talking to Molly," Bessie whispered back. "He's talking to the warts."

"How do the warts know?" I asked.

Bessie cut me off with a "Shush!" and an elbow to my side.

He kept at it for what seemed like forever, and the whole time we were afraid to move. When he stopped and led Molly back into the paddock, we scrambled for the ladder. Bessie descended first and came back up a little ways to help me. Then I struggled down while she pressed my body against the rungs and eased me to the ground.

We ran straight for the chicken coop and gathered eggs as fast as we could. Bessie kept telling me not to break any.

When we got back into the kitchen, we were still brushing

off straw from the loft. Johnny was inside talking to Mama. "The warts should come off in a week," he said. "Don't drink her milk 'til then."

One week to the day, Molly's face was clear of warts, and her milk tasted sweeter than ever. My very own half-brother was a miracle worker.

Johnny stayed in Varennes with his wife, Etta, for a few more years. Then they moved across the Savannah River into Elberton. As close as Varennes was to the river, I seldom went there, much less crossed it, until he moved.

The only way we could get to his farm was to take a ferry across the river. Boarding the ferry for the first time was frightening. I held tight to Bessie's hand and tried to stay in the center. The water was calm where we crossed, but it seemed dark and mysterious farther down. The banks looked like they might crumble with a wash from a rainy spell. I imagined copperheads coiled in the thickets along the banks. And said so aloud.

"Don't be afraid," Papa said. "This old river been flowin' since the Lord madeth the earth. Just treat it with respect. Mostly, it giveth life."

"But it can taketh it, too," Mama said.

How that was supposed to reassure me I never knew, other than the fact that I was holding onto Bessie's hand.

Johnny came to see me not long ago. He talked about Etta, his children, and an orphaned colored baby they'd taken in. That's Johnny, heart and soul and a bit of magic. I wish I could talk to him now, ask him to speak in tongues over me. To work a miracle.

Bessie ❧

*Last night's dream comes back to me. I'm a child again,
maybe four or five. It's late fall. Papa and Johnny are in the
woodshop making a coffin. Mama's in the kitchen cooking
dinner. Sallie's keeping Bessie and me out of the way by
playing a game of Going to Heaven on the back steps.*

*Bessie and I sit on the lowest step. Bessie wears a
Sallie-hand-me-down, and I wear a Bessie-hand-me-down.
Sallie has on something Mama probably altered from her
own wardrobe. I can still see each dress, all in various shades
of faded blue.*

*Sallie stands over us, her arms crossed at her wrists, her
hands gripped in soft fists. One hand holds a small smooth
stone. The other holds nothing. To advance a step closer to
Heaven, Bessie and I have to guess which hand holds the
stone.*

*Bessie chooses the hand with the stone and moves up a
step. I choose wrong and stay on the bottom step. And so it
progresses with Bessie choosing right more often than not and
me doing the opposite. When Bessie reaches the top step, the
game is over.*

"Why does Bessie get to Heaven and I don't?" I whine.

"Bessie is better," Sallie says.

I start to cry.

Bessie comes down the steps and hugs me. "It doesn't mean
I'm a better person," she says. "I'm just better at guessing."

As we grew up, it became apparent that I looked more like
Mama's side of the family—small, blue-eyed, and round-faced.
Bessie took after Papa's side. She was tall with high cheekbones
and hazel eyes just like Papa's. She had dark brown hair like
the rest of Papa's children. Except for me. My hair was a lighter
brown with a hint of auburn like Mama's.

Papa used to say I looked like a little china doll, which was
embarrassing, except I knew he meant it as a compliment. He
would sometimes say, "Icie, you look just like Em'ly, but without
what time and worry does to a body." He didn't say that in front
of Mama.

Bessie may have looked like the Joneses, but she had a double
dose of Mama in her blood when it came to taking charge and
mothering.

As children, I was Bessie's shadow. I followed behind her
pretty much during the waking hours. I don't know how she
stood it, but she didn't seem to mind most of the time. She kept
me out of the barn paddock if the bull was nearby. When we
picked blackberries, she'd beat the bushes ahead of us to scare
off snakes. She even taught me the alphabet and numbers before
I was old enough to start school.

She was always faster, wiser, abler than me. But she was kind
too and sometimes said, "Don't worry, Icie. You have your own
talents."

When she wasn't mothering me, she was taking care of other

babies on the farm. And we had quite an assortment. Chicks, calves, kids, and any wildlife baby that came our way.

She even raised a fawn.

Not long after Papa had hired Preston Allen, Bessie and I walked up on them in the yard just as Papa said something about a fawn left alone in the woods. It was early fall, and summer hadn't quite let go.

"What happened?" Bessie asked. Both men looked surprised. I don't think they realized we were within earshot.

Papa said, "I was down by the creek huntin' when I spied a fawn all by itself!"

"What do you think happened to its mama?" Bessie asked.

"I spect a hunter shot the doe," Papa said.

Preston agreed. "He probably never saw the fawn. Too bad, though. So late in the season."

"It don't have a chance," Papa added. "We best leave it be."

Bessie, however, wasn't about to let a motherless fawn starve in the woods. Down to the creek we went, Bessie and myself, Papa and Preston. The men kept trying to convince Bessie that the fawn wouldn't live in captivity even if we found it. But find it we did. Bessie insisted we take it to the barn.

Preston carefully picked it up and carried it with Bessie close by making baby talk. Papa led the way to the barn while I brought up the rear.

When we reached the barn, Papa opened the door to a stall, and Preston set the fawn down. It had a surge of energy and bolted into the corner. Bessie eased toward it and kept up the baby talk. Papa held the door shut while Preston spread clean straw around the stall. I stood next to Papa out of the way.

As Bessie tried to sooth the fawn, Preston said, "It needs milk, but cow's milk is too strong. Goat milk isn't much better."

Papa spoke up, "It might drink on its own. But I wouldn't be countin' on it."

The fawn appeared to calm down or simply give in to exhaustion. Bessie stroked its head.

Preston came closer. "It might be old enough to eat a little," he said. "Maybe something soft."

"Deers like acorns. And apples," Papa said, his tone a little less hopeless.

Bessie looked from Papa to Preston. Then to me. "Icie, come over here," she instructed. "Squat down next to me."

I did so.

"Take my place and keep stroking its head, just like I'm doing." She demonstrated. "See?"

I touched the small head between its ears and pulled my hand slowly along the nape of its neck. It was silky and warm. I could feel it tremble. Bessie watched me make several practice strokes until she was satisfied I could manage. Then off she went to the kitchen.

I kept petting it, trying to apply the right pressure and maintain the right timing as though the fawn's life depended on it.

Just as my arm was starting to ache, Bessie was back. "Mama put on a pot of apples," she said, reclaiming her spot.

Papa and Preston left the stall, shaking their heads. I stayed with Bessie in case I was needed again. But the fawn soon fell asleep, and we both slipped out.

Once the apples were mushy, Mama fished one out to cool. As soon as Bessie could stick her finger into it without getting burned, she plopped it on a dishtowel and took it to the stall. I followed.

She knelt beside the dozing fawn and offered up some mushy fruit on two fingers. The fawn opened its eyes and sniffed. Then it slowly licked the sweet succor from Bessie's hand. She repeated the strange finger feeding until the fawn had eaten the entire apple.

Preston returned. He leaned against the stall door watching Bessie feed the fawn. The late afternoon light shown in sheets between planks in the barn wall. No one spoke. No one needed to. Another Jesus-God moment.

And so the fawn survived on cooked apples, boiled acorns, and watered-down goat's milk. Preston said it lived because of Bessie's special touch. Papa said it lived just to prove him wrong. But he was as happy as the rest of us.

The fawn grew into a beautiful doe. I see her now, the long delicate neck, the silky white bib of fur across her chest, as content in the pasture as the milk cows with fences she could have topped at will.

She could've returned to the dark woods where she would've been pursued by bucks and borne fawns of her own. I wonder if she knew how easy her escape could have been. Or if it would have been an escape at all.

Preston Allen

Even though Papa spent time in the fields, my half-brother Johnny oversaw much of the work when he still lived with us. But after Johnny got married and started his own farm, Papa and Mama had to go back to managing the fields themselves. They farmed what they could and rented out the rest to smaller farmers, white and colored, for a share.

Pretty soon, Papa decided they needed a farm manager. He asked around and found out that a certain Preston Allen was looking for just such a job. He lived one county over, in Lowndesville, where he'd grown up.

The first time Bessie and I heard Preston Allen's name was at dinner shortly before he started working for us. I'd set the table while Mama and Bessie put out supper. Papa came in from the field, washed up, and joined us. We were having ham and grits and red-eye gravy, Papa's favorite. He was in a good mood.

He asked a blessing and started the platter of ham and bowl of grits around the table. But Mama examined the gravy.

"I believe the red-eye's gone tepid," she said. She scooped up the gravy boat, and back to the stove she went.

While Papa waited for the gravy, he said, "I think I found a fella to keep up with the share-croppers."

"Who might that be?" Mama asked, stirring the thick liquid in a frying pan until it bubbled.

"Preston Allen from over in your folks' direction."

"Abbeville?" she asked.

"Closer," he said, "Lowndesville."

Mama put a spoon in the gravy boat. Then she wrapped a dishtowel around the pan's hot handle and poured the gravy slowly into the spoon in the boat so as not to break the dish.

"Allen," she said. "That's a good name." She returned to the table and handed Papa the hot gravy.

"Full name's even better," Papa said as he poured a pool of the steaming liquid into the center of his plate. "It's Preston Brooks Allen. Named after Preston Brooks, the senator. His parents thought it honor'ble."

He handed the gravy back to Mama. She took a splash and passed it to Bessie.

"Honorable?" Mama said, her voice a few notes higher than usual. "Preston Brooks caned a man senseless right in the middle of the Senate floor!"

"The man was senseless to begin with," Papa declared. "That's why Brooks caned him."

"Who's Preston Brooks?" Bessie asked.

"He was in Congress before the war," Papa said as he looked at his plate. "He stood up for us. He was from Edgefield, your mama's hometown."

"No kin," Mama said.

"What's 'caned'?" Bessie asked. She took a spoonful of gravy and pushed the boat my way.

"It's beating someone with a walking cane," Mama answered before Papa could.

"Did the other man have a cane?" I asked.

"No," Papa said. "He didn't need one."

"Why did Mr. Brooks need one?" Bessie asked.

" 'Cause he got shot in the hip," Papa said.

"In the war?" I asked. "Did he serve with you, Papa?"

"Nope. It was a war with Mexico."

"Was he at the Alamo?" I asked.

Papa smiled and said, "No, Icie, it was a diff'rent war."

"But that's not how he got wounded," Mama quickly added. "He was dumb enough to get shot in the hip during a duel!"

"With the man without the cane?" Bessie asked.

"No," she said, "with some other fool."

Papa looked at her. "Em'ly, don't confuse the girls."

Mama didn't flinch.

Then he looked at us. "Preston Brooks was a great man. A sorry son-of-a-gun insulted his kinfolk and our state. So Brooks caned him good."

"What's a 'son-of-a-gun'?" I asked.

"Is it a pistol like someone sticks in his boot?" Bessie asked.

"No," Mama answered again for Papa. "It's a crude expression." She shot him a look.

He cleared his throat. "As I was sayin', I'm gonna hire a young man named Preston Allen."

He clearly meant the discussion to be over, but Mama came back with, "I just hope he doesn't take after that crazy Brooks man."

Bessie said, "I just hope he doesn't have a cane." She glanced at me. I stifled a giggle.

By the time I poured my own gravy, it was tepid again. I let it be because I knew Mama wasn't about to heat it a second time.

Papa hired Preston Brooks Allen the very next week. I was twelve and a half at the time. Bessie was sixteen. I think Preston was twenty-one. He was the oldest in a family of seven. His family, like most small farmers, had little to nothing after the war other than their good name.

Preston apparently wanted more. What he lacked in education, he taught himself. He usually had a book of some sort nearby.

He added a kind of energy to our family that we hadn't felt since Johnny left. A certain eagerness to make his way in the world.

It was contagious. Papa seemed to have more giddy-up in his step. Preston quickly won us over, including Mama although she was less generous with her enthusiasm. At first, she watched him like a hawk around Bessie. But she gradually became more trusting. Or accepted the inevitable.

Preston wasn't as tall as Papa, nor as lanky. His face was sort of square, and he wore his hair combed back from his forehead in the style of young men. His eyes were grass-green, unlike any of my kin.

His job was to take care of planting, harvesting, leasing, and sharecropping. A full slate he not only managed well, but turned enough profit that Papa started talking about fixing up our house.

Papa said more than once, "Bringin' on Preston Allen is the best dang decision I ever made." If Mama was in earshot, he'd say "the second best decision."

Preston lived in Lowndesville when he began working for us, which was about fourteen miles away. His work often carried into the evening, so he shared many a late meal with us and occasionally slept on a cot in the front hall. Mama made sure it was as far away from our bedroom as possible.

He treated Mama with great respect, same as with Papa, and he teased me like I was his little sister. Not mean teasing, just enough to make me laugh.

But Bessie was another matter altogether. They acted quiet around each other at first, but then Bessie resumed her tagging along to the fields with Papa. And Preston.

As time passed, Papa went less and less, and Bessie went more and more. If Preston was driving a buggy or a wagon or even a pony cart, there'd be Bessie alongside. If he climbed on a mule, she climbed on behind him. By the time Bessie was seventeen, she knew nearly as much about managing as Preston did.

One evening at supper, when Preston had gone out of town on a farming matter, Papa looked at his vacant chair next to Bessie's. He helped himself to some rice and sent it past the empty space next to Bessie. Then he ladled on some gravy and passed it her way.

Just as he was serving himself a chicken breast, he said, "Bessie, you know the crops and tenants and mules and plows good as Preston."

"Thank you, Papa," she said, taking the chicken platter. She went for the wishbone, the piece she always took if I didn't get it first.

She passed the platter to Mama. But Mama didn't take it right away. She was looking at Papa. I didn't know where to look. The rice and gravy had made their way around the table to me. So I concentrated on forming a little well in the top of my rice for a mud puddle of gravy.

"You know what?" Papa said. Then he took a bite of chicken and chewed it more that it needed. We all waited.

He swallowed and appeared to be going for a forkful of rice. Then he commented, "I could save a lot of money if I just fired him and let you run the farm."

Bessie went pale as the rice. "No! Papa! No!" she shouted. "I couldn't do half the managing that Preston does!" She sucked in another breath.

I thought she was going to cry, and maybe I was too, until I looked at Mama, who was smiling.

"William, you shouldn't tease the girls like that," she said.

He started laughing. Bessie exhaled.

He said, "Bessie, I 'spect Preston'll end up with double the land we got. And he'll be askin' for your hand 'fore long."

"But not before you're eighteen," Mama said.

Bessie blushed.

Papa was right on both accounts. Mama wasn't. A month before Bessie turned eighteen, she became Mrs. Preston Brooks Allen.

Sometime later, I learned that Bessie was Preston's second wife. His first had died in childbirth along with the baby. I came to realize that our odd little second family of Joneses was as important to him as he became to us.

Ironic how joy follows sorrow. How sorrow follows joy. And on and on. It's almost too much to comprehend close up. But at a distance it seems like the normal course of things. The way life ebbs and flows.

Aunt Eliza

Aunt Eliza, Papa's next-to-youngest sister, lived with us off and on when I was young. She'd leave for a while and return, sometimes with a different last name, sometimes with the same. I never knew what to call her other than Aunt Eliza.

She had more education than the rest of the Joneses and made her living as a schoolteacher when she needed to. From time to time she would teach in Anderson or Greenville or even Nashville, Tennessee, depending on what relative or husband she was living with.

She once lived in Louisiana. When she came back to live with us for a while, she brought a ruby red thumbprint pitcher for Mama. It said "New Orleans" in fancy silver script. She gave Bessie a rainbow-beaded purse and told her to keep her first gold piece in it. And she gave me a silver-backed hairbrush and mirror.

Needless to say, Bessie and I always welcomed Aunt Eliza.

Mama did some of the time although she said Aunt Eliza put on airs. At the time I didn't know what "put on airs" meant, so I assumed it meant dabbing on perfume.

Aunt Eliza came to live with us again right after Bessie had married Preston and moved to Lowndesville.

She'd been in Greenville teaching school when her husband took ill and died. I was sorry for her loss but glad to have her back in our house. I missed Bessie so much I was nearly sick with separation. Having Aunt Eliza to spend time with was almost as good as having my sister back. She was playful and artistic, and her cheeks were always pink. Mama said she used "tinted powder" pronouncing it as though it were questionable. Aunt Eliza wasn't as gaunt as Papa's other sisters, and she usually looked happy even when she was in mourning.

I loved the way she talked, almost like singing. She didn't sound at all like Papa. She pronounced her "ing" words to the end and often reminded me to do likewise.

"You know there's a 'g' at the end of 'knitting,' don't you?" she once asked.

"Yes, m'am," I said. "I see it in my head, but it doesn't come out of my mouth that way. It's like the 'g' forgets to be heard."

"Then you must remind it," she said. And on to the next new stitch she went.

She taught me how to embroider, crochet, and knit. Mama was equally talented with the needle but much more practical. Mama made dresses for us when she had time and mended Papa's clothes more than anything else.

But Aunt Eliza made dainty pillows covered in embroidered pansies, towels with big cross-stitched Js on the corner, and a tablecloth of white crocheted lace for special occasions.

She taught me to knit with a little rhyme:

Needle to needle and stitch to stitch,
Pull the old woman out of the ditch.
If you aren't out by the time I'm in,
I'll rap your knuckles with the knitting pin.

"Pulling the old woman out of the ditch" was wrapping the yarn over the loop and pulling it through to create a knit stitch. The "by the time I'm in" was the process of creating a purl stitch with the second needle.

She taught me another silly rhyme to keep track of the rows:

Jenny and I, Jenny and I,
For a good pudding pie,
A loaf of wheat and another of rye,
Jenny and I for a good pudding pie.

The name would change with each new row. I didn't understand the rhyme, but I sang along with Aunt Eliza. She told me it was an old English verse for knitting, but Mama said it sounded more like a drinking song for shiftless men. To escape Mama's ire, we'd hum the tune softly except for the new name in each row. More often than not, we'd break out laughing as soon as Mama was out of sight.

Aunt Eliza also taught me about literature. I suppose she couldn't go without teaching school, even during mourning, so I became her one and only pupil. She explained things like dramatic irony, tragic hero, and star-crossed lovers. Aunt Eliza illustrated each with a sad story. And at the end, she would say, "Now there's a lesson to be learned."

But I didn't want lessons about people I didn't know. I wanted stories about my family, ones I didn't think Mama or Papa would tell me.

"So it's family stories you want," she said late one afternoon when Mama was at her sister's home and Papa was in the field.

I was setting the table for an early supper at the time. Aunt Eliza had just made a custard pie and was putting it into the oven.

"Yes'm," I said. "You're the best storyteller I know."

"I'm not sure how to take that," she said, then laughed. "Your papa used to say I'd climb a tree to tell a story rather than stay on the ground and tell the truth."

"Did he mean lying?" I asked. I finished setting out the forks and started on the spoons.

"I don't think so. All God's children tell stories. Some just liven them up a little to make them more interesting." She removed the lid from a pot of beef and vegetables on the stove. It smelled wonderful.

She looked at me. "But sometimes the truth is too painful to tell, either for the one doing the telling or the one doing the listening." She put the lid back on the pot. "So the story gets changed a little, but the meaning is still true."

"The meaning?" I asked. It'd never occurred to me that a story might have meaning.

"Yes. The best stories make you contemplate more than just the characters or what happens. They make you think."

"About what?" I asked, laying out the knives.

"Life," she said.

I didn't respond.

"Like with Jesus telling parables," she explained. "Nobody ever said Jesus was lying."

The very idea seemed sacrilegious. I looked around as though Mama might hear us all the way from Abbeville.

"His stories had meaning," she added.

Just as I was starting to understand, she said, "Of course, with family stories, sometimes we're just trying to make sense of our own little lives."

I finished setting the table and let the complexity of story-telling rest for the time being.

But a few days later, when Aunt Eliza was talking about her childhood, I decided to revisit the subject of family stories. I began by asking her what had happened to her youngest brother, Ben.

I was embroidering Bessie's new initials "B. A." on an apron that Mama had made for her. Aunt Eliza was knitting a shawl for herself.

Her expression turned serious, "Oh, Icie, that was such a sad time for us. You know there were twelve of us children."

I nodded.

"William, your papa, was the oldest and already grown when little Ben was born. But I was only five. His full name was Benjamin Franklin Perry Jones. Why our parents named him after Ben Franklin Perry, I'll never know! But that's another story."

She caught her breath. "The last four children in my family were James Jr., myself, Louisa, and Ben. We were all born in the 1840s. I don't know how our mother managed to bear twelve children over three decades! I'll never do it. That's for certain."

"So I know Uncle James died in the war," I said, trying to get her back to the question at hand, "but what happened to Ben?"

She resumed, "I was fourteen years old at the time. The same age as you."

"I'm almost fifteen."

"So you are," she said. "Ben was only nine when he died."

"From what?" I asked. I expected her to say a fever or a hole in his heart or something else to do with his health.

She put down her knitting and leaned toward me. "A mule! He was kicked in the head by a mule and died in a few hours."

I was too surprised to say anything. I wondered why Papa'd never told me. But he did often warn Bessie and me not to walk behind a horse, mule, cow, or any critter bigger than we were.

Aunt Eliza went on, "I don't know what it is about boys, but they think they're impervious to the slings and arrows and rifles and bullets of misfortune."

"What's 'impervious'?" I asked.

"Indestructible," she said. "Boys seem to think that nothing bad can happen to them. I don't know if they're born that way or raised to believe it."

Aunt Eliza picked up her knitting. "All those men, young and old, who marched off to join the Confederacy thought they'd come home unscathed."

For once, she sounded like Mama. But just as quickly, she was back to Ben. "Ben never got the chance," she said, resuming her stitch. "At least he didn't linger."

"What happened to the mule?" I asked, assuming it was dangerous enough to be shot.

"Nothing," she replied. "It was our best mule, and Ben knew better than walking behind it. We all did."

I can't say I enjoyed the story. I decided to let Papa's family rest in peace.

What's sauce for the gander

Aunt Eliza knew history on Mama's side of the family, too. So one day when Mama and Papa had gone into town, I decided to ask her about one of Mama's uncles. The uncle had two families, not like Papa who had one family with his first wife who died and then a second one with a second wife. The uncle in question had two women bearing his babies at the same time.

I'd heard bits and pieces from my cousins, but I knew I'd get the "Devil's garden" if I asked Mama.

We were crocheting granny squares from leftover yarn at the time. I was new to crocheting so Aunt Eliza had started me with granny squares. They were fairly simple to make once you got into a rhythm. She could turn them out like biscuits, but I had to concentrate.

"You know your mama came from money," she said. "At least her mother did."

I nodded, having realized that much on my own.

"Before the war, Emily's grandmother owned half the county where they lived. The uncle you asked about was quite wealthy." She eyed my attempt at a granny square. "You missed a stitch. It's chain three, two double chains in the space, and chain two to form the corner. See?"

I pulled out several stitches and tried again. "What about Mama's uncle?"

"He married a fine young lady from another wealthy family in the area, and soon they began their own family." She looked at me. "You do know that most of the large landowners back then had slaves to do their hardest work?"

I nodded again. She looked at my needlework. "Now three

double chains in the same space, chain two. Then repeat in the next space and the next to form another corner." She finished her first square as I rounded my second corner.

"But after his second or third child was born," she continued, "he caught sight of a pretty slave girl, not much older than you, at his grandfather's farm."

She started a new square and asked, "Know what he did?"

"I can guess," I said, feeling the wisdom of an almost fifteen-year-old.

"He took her away from her own folks, brought her to his plantation, and soon began a second family with her."

I didn't know what to say, so I kept quiet.

"Times were different."

She shook her head. "The poor girl had no choice in the matter. Things are somewhat better now—except for godawful Jim Crow."

"Jim Crow?" I asked. "Is he kin to Mama?"

"Oh Lord no!" she said. "But that's a different lesson for another day."

"What about the wife?" I asked, looking at my scrawny crocheted square and trying to get back to the story.

"Add another round, just like you started the first round." She watched my fingers. "The wife didn't have all that many choices either since she was legally bound to him—although she could have chosen poison."

"Like Juliet?" I asked.

"No, not for herself. For Romeo. She could have solved the problem for both families! Anyway, the story goes that when the wife found out, she kicked him out of her bed."

"Good!" I said.

She shook her head again. "Evidently it didn't bother him

because he kept fathering children with the slave girl. And his wife must have accepted it because she had more children, too. He was quite the virile fella," she said as she finished another square.

"What's 'virile'?" I asked.

"It means your mother's uncle ended up with fourteen children in all, nine with his wife and five with the girl."

I tried to picture a family gathering. "So he had nine white children and five mixed?" I said.

"Not exactly," she said, looking at my square. She examined it and helped me start another one.

"Several of the children he had with his wife turned out to be as olive-skinned as his children with the young colored lady."

"What's 'olive-skinned'?" I asked.

"Having a tawny complexion, neither brown nor pink—like Varina Davis."

"Who's that?" I asked.

"Jefferson Davis's wife," she said. "I think you need a better education, both in vocabulary and history!"

"I know who he is," I said, feeling ignorant. "The Confederate president. I just didn't know his wife's name."

"Have you ever seen her?"

"No, m'am."

"She's a lovely lady with an olive complexion, large brown eyes, high cheekbones, and thick black hair. It's glossy like fudge just before it sets. Her parents contend she got her looks from her Welsh heritage."

I wasn't sure who the Welsh were, but I wasn't about to ask.

Aunt Eliza seemed to read my mind. "Icie, our ancestors are Welsh."

"I thought we were English," I said, "like the pilgrims."

"Not everyone came here from England. Some came from Ireland, Scotland, Wales. Some from Italy, Spain, and other countries."

"So we're Welsh?" I had visions of English pilgrims and Indians sharing food for the first Thanksgiving. Somehow I had to make room for these other people.

"The Joneses are Welsh—although by now we have quite a bit of English blood, among others, mixed in."

I was getting more education and fewer answers than I wanted.

"So some of Mama's uncle and his wife's children were darker than their parents because of their Welsh ancestors?" I asked.

"Maybe," she said. "But some folks thought they looked to be part Indian."

"Indian?" I looked at my needlework. My new square had five corners. I pulled it apart and rewound the yarn.

"Yes," she said, "Cherokee or Creek. That would've been before our government stole their land and drove them west."

My head was spinning. I gave up on granny squares altogether. I tried to remember if I'd ever seen a real Indian. A few folks around Varennes were thought to be part Indian, but they didn't look much different.

"So how could they be Indian?" I asked.

"One possibility is that both parents had Indian blood from way back, and it came out together in some of their children."

"Like Welsh," I said, thinking I was starting to understand.

Although no one else was within earshot, Aunt Eliza leaned close and whispered, "Of course, only the wife knows for sure."

Before I could ask what she meant, she added, "A woman's heart is a sea of secrets."

Aunt Eliza's story had more questions than answers. More

history than I knew what to do with. And a bit of wisdom I didn't yet understand. But it did make me think. Maybe that was meaning enough.

By the time she completed her year of mourning with us, I had two granny-square coverlets, several embroidered cushions, a heightened sense of drama, and a much broader vocabulary to show for her stay.

Papa told her that according to the rules, one year was too short for "a widder to be done mourning-uh."

But she replied, "What's sauce for the gander is sauce for the goose." She went back to Greenville to take up teaching again, and according to Mama, to catch a new man.

After she left, I wrote long letters to her. I tried to use proper grammar, my most adult-sounding words, and my best penmanship. She would usually respond with a letter in kind complimenting my effort and encouraging me to practice my stitches and pronounce my g's.

Sometimes I still write to Aunt Eliza in my mind. But after Mouchet Hill, all real letters stopped.

Bushwhackers and a strange affliction

No sooner had Aunt Eliza left than one of her sisters, my other favorite aunt, was struck with a strange affliction. Louisa Jones Mouchet—"Aunt Lou" to me—was nearly twenty years younger than Papa.

She was a handsome lady. By handsome I mean she looked

like a younger version of Papa without whiskers. She was tall and thin and kept her dark hair pulled back in a bun.

After the war, she married Tyler Mouchet who'd served with Papa in the Hampton Legion of South Carolina. His claim to fame was that he'd survived capture by Yankee bushwhackers, a tale retold many times at family gatherings. I knew it by heart before I could read.

The bushwhackers in the story were a band of renegade soldiers who took orders from the hated Yankee Colonel Kirk. The colonel, a native of Tennessee, had found particular pleasure in terrorizing his former neighbors who'd tried to remain neutral.

Uncle Tyler's ordeal had come near the end of the war when he'd received a furlough to come home to Varennes for a few weeks. He'd traveled with another Rebel soldier, also from Anderson County.

At the time they'd been stationed in the Tennessee mountains in the dead of winter. Getting home would have been difficult even without Yankee bushwhackers. But that was not to be. Colonel Kirk and his gnarly bunch of followers had been camped near the area where the furloughed soldiers needed to pass.

As bad luck would have it, the bushwhackers came upon Uncle Tyler and his fellow traveler sleeping in a farmhouse. They were taken captive and soon learned they were to be hanged the very next day in retribution for the deaths of several of Col. Kirk's men. Realizing their fate, Uncle Tyler and the other man made a desperate escape when their captors fell asleep. They became separated, and Uncle Tyler ran so hard his worn boots fell apart. But he kept running all night and into the next morning, nearly ten miles in the snow, until he found a camp of Rebel soldiers.

His fellow escapee followed Uncle Tyler's trail and reached the same camp some hours later. His account was that Tyler had run like a scalded cat and left bloody footprints in the snow.

As children, Bessie and I always shuddered at the end when the tale reached the parts about the "scalded cat" and "bloody footprints."

Luckily, for Aunt Lou and their children to come, Uncle Tyler recovered and managed to get on with life after the war. He married Aunt Lou, and they set out to make a living from the land.

They had a houseful of children including two girls, Carie, who was my age, and Lenore, who was a year younger. They lived fairly close by, and I spent time with them in the summers and they with me, especially after Bessie married Preston and moved away.

As to Aunt Lou's strange affliction, late one morning the girls came running to our house to tell us something bad had happened to their mama.

"We found her in the kitchen holding her throat," Carie cried. "And when we asked her what was wrong, she tried to answer, but . . ."

Lenora interrupted, "Nothing came out but air and spit!"

And so back and forth, the sisters told their frightening account. The gist of the story was that after they'd found their mother in distress, they'd run to get their father, who was in the field. Uncle Tyler returned to the house and found Aunt Lou in a sad state.

He then sent for Dr. Dean, who was eating breakfast at the time. Dr. Dean come shortly thereafter. He said it might be a stroke. He examined Aunt Lou for other signs but found none.

He pressed around her neck and peered down her throat making her gag but still found no physical cause for her distress.

Carie summed up the diagnosis. "Dr. Dean said she must have 'ah-FAZE-yah.'"

"What the heck?" Papa said.

"It's aphasia," Mama said. "It means you've lost your ability to talk. My Grandmother Isabella had it in her later years."

Lenore added, "The doctor said there's 'no known cure'!"

At that point, Mama, Papa, and I hurried to the Mouchets with Carie and Lenore. When we got there we could see that Aunt Lou was agitated. Mama tried to comfort her while Papa stood and watched. Uncle Tyler looked helpless.

Mama led Aunt Lou back to the bedroom, away from the family, and onto her bed. When she returned, she said, "Louisa is probably worried sick over how she'll take care of the children, one of them still a baby, and manage the household without her voice."

No one said anything for a few minutes. Then Uncle Tyler spoke up. "Lou can carry around a pencil and a tablet to write down what she wants to say until her voice comes back."

Papa agreed. Mama sniffed. We stayed long enough for everyone to calm down and for Aunt Lou to fall asleep.

A few days later, the Mouchets were back to doing what they usually did except without Aunt Lou's voice. She tried the tablet and pencil for a while. It worked somewhat at first, but it soon became obvious that she couldn't manage the household, balance the baby on her hip, and carry around writing supplies, too.

Uncle Tyler came up with yet another solution. He tied a string around the pencil. Then he punched a hole in the corner of the tablet and attached the pencil. Next he added a longer string so Aunt Lou could wear the tablet and pencil around her neck.

After that, whenever we saw Aunt Lou, be it at church, in her kitchen, or in the field, she'd have that tablet around her neck like a big odd collar.

One day on the ride home from church, Mama said, "Did you see Louisa sitting there with the baby on her lap? I know she was trying to listen to the sermon, but the little fella just kept pulling on her tablet. I thought she might choke."

I agreed. "Carie and Lenore told me it was nice at first not having their mama telling them how to do everything. But soon they started missing her advice. Now they feel so bad for her they're trying to help out more."

Papa shifted the reins. "Lou's just talked herself out."

Mama straightened her back, made her little snorting sound, and adjusted her seat in the buggy. "Louisa didn't talk that much to begin with. Maybe something bad happened that she can't put into words."

Papa gave a snort of his own.

"Or maybe," she suggested, "Louisa just got tired of no one listening."

Papa didn't wade back in. And neither did I.

After that, Mama and I visited the Mouchets at least once a week. Mama helped Aunt Lou do chores or held the baby while Aunt Lou combed her hair or took a bath or just sat quiet for a spell. In the meantime, Lenore and Carie and I took care of the other children and did outside chores.

I didn't know what to say to Aunt Lou. I didn't want to ask something that she'd have to write a reply, so mostly I just smiled and nodded my head. Looking back, I can see it was a foolish thing to do, but neither I nor any other member of her family had dealt with such an affliction as aphasia. At least not yet.

Whatever the cause, Aunt Lou remained speechless for more than a year. Then one morning after the men had gone to the fields, she spoke.

She told Carie and Lenore, "Go get your father. Tell him I can speak again. We must give thanks!"

Uncle Tyler finished the row he was on and returned to the house to find a cured wife. He and Aunt Lou decided to have a large dinner the following Sunday for friends and relatives to celebrate the happy occasion. Mama, Papa, and I were invited along with some other Jones kinfolk, several Mouchet in-laws, the minister, and Dr. Dean.

It was a fine dinner with ham and chicken, rice, two kinds of gravy, tomatoes, squash, and beans. Aunt Lou smiled, poured tea, and chatted with the ladies, while the men talked about the weather and crops.

Then Aunt Lou brought out two pound cakes. They were golden with a shiny glaze. She waved a large knife in the air for a moment until everyone was quiet. Then she said, "I want to thank each one of you for your help in my time of great need."

I was sitting at the kitchen table with my cousins, but I had a clear view into the dining room.

To Mama she said, "Emily, you've been a dear friend and a constant source of encouragement. You've helped me more than you know." She carefully sliced a piece, slid it onto a small china plate, and passed it Mama's way.

She called Carie and Lenore in from the table in the kitchen. "Dear daughters, even though I saw you making faces from time to time, you two have become my most trusted helpmates.

You've grown from carefree children to caring young ladies during this ordeal."

The girls beamed as their mama sliced a generous piece of cake for each of them.

"And here's one for you, Icie," she added. "You've been like a daughter, too."

I'd never been served before the adults, much less the men. I quickly took my plate and returned to the kitchen.

She resumed doling out pieces of cake with heart-felt gratitude to several more people until the first loaf was gone.

Then she took a deep breath as though she were gathering up new energy, waved the knife around again, and started on the second loaf.

First she turned to her sister-in-law. "Dear Caroline, I don't guess I've seen you in nearly a year," she said sweetly. "Did you think I didn't hear you say, 'It might be catching'?"

Caroline sucked in.

Aunt Lou went on, "I see you didn't have a problem eating the dinner I cooked. Do have some cake. I'm not contagious." Down went the knife on a chunk of the new cake. Caroline's mouth was still open when Aunt Lou slid the plate in front of her.

She turned to Rev. Wright. "Pastor, your visits meant so much. Too bad they were so few and far between." She smiled and asked, "Cake?"

When he didn't answer, she whacked him off a piece and shoved it at him.

To Dr. Dean, she said, "Your understanding and treatment went a long way in *not* helping me recover. Thanks for all the research you *didn't* do." She slammed down the knife again at the hapless cake and flung the plate his way.

By now, Uncle Tyler's face was pale as cotton, and his eyes

were so big I could see the white all around them. Even Papa was speechless.

Aunt Lou finished in a controlled fury, waving the knife while she eyed other people at the table. "Did you think I couldn't see? Hear? Think? Feel? Did you take me for some simpleton who could somehow keep on doing everything I've done without a voice?"

She gave the knife a final flourish. "So to the rest of you, cut your own damn cake!" She flung the knife down the center of the table and sent dinner guests scrambling.

It was a Jesus-God moment.

Mama didn't speak all the way home. Neither did I.

After a while Papa said, "Did you see Tyler? I bet he ain't been that scared since he was a'runnin' from them bushwhackers."

Aunt Lou was here just a few days ago. She visits every week or so. She tells me what's going on in town and how Carie and Lenore and their families are. Each time before she leaves, she holds my hand and says, "Icie, I know you're in there. When you're ready to come back out, we'll be waiting."

PART III

Stings and honey

Revelation ⌒

After Preston married Bessie, he turned his attention to his small house and farm in Lowndesville. As much as he wanted to keep working for Papa, Preston said he didn't think he could manage two farms fourteen miles apart and be a husband, too.

Papa said he understood and set about to find another manager. Over the next year he gave several men a try, but none could measure up.

At the same time, Mama and I missed Bessie more and more. So did Papa. To ease the separation pangs, we'd take the buggy to Lowndesville to visit once or twice a month. Bessie would be happy to see us and show us the latest improvements she'd done to the little house to make it more a home. Mama would take baskets of pecans or whatever produce was in season, and I'd tuck in needlework pieces for her. Preston would guide Papa through his field and show him how well whatever he'd planted was growing.

Our ride home would be bittersweet with Mama worrying that Bessie was working too hard and not eating enough and with Papa wondering out loud why his own crops weren't as healthy as Preston's and why he couldn't find a good farm manager.

And that's the way things stood until Papa's war-wounded leg began to give him problems again. The area where the minie ball had been dug out fifteen years earlier bothered him from time to time.

Sometimes it would develop into what Dr. Dean called a carbuncle. He said the old wound had healed on the outside before it healed completely on the inside. Which meant that occasionally it would create something like a boil deep inside Papa's leg. When this happened, all Papa could do was to wait until the carbuncle came to the surface of the skin. Then Dr. Dean could lance it, clean it out, and hope it would heal from the inside out.

Once the leg started hurting, it would be a week or two before it could be lanced. Those are the only times I remember Papa getting heavy into whiskey. The day of the lancing, Papa would get squinty-eyed drunk to no one's objection. A few days after the lancing, Papa would start to feel better. Within another week, he would be up and on the leg again.

Such was the case more than a year after Bessie and Preston had gotten married and moved to Lowndesville. First, Papa began to limp. Then he stayed in his chair most of the day. In a few more days, he took to the bed. Once he was bedbound, Mama brought him whiskey and sent for Dr. Dean.

The doctor did his work with his scalpel while Papa shouted words I'd never heard of. And so it went as usual, except following this particular episode, Papa woke up in a sort of visionary state. At the crack of dawn, two days after the lancing, Papa began to yell for Mama and me.

Mama had been sleeping with me during Papa's carbuncle episode so as not to disturb his aching leg. She was already awake but not fixed for the morning, and I was still drifting in and out of sleep. She shook me awake, and we rushed into their bedroom.

Papa had propped himself up in bed, clearly feeling better although he still looked haggard. I blinked back sleep.

"I've had me a revelation!" he said excitedly. He sounded like a preacher.

"Like Moses and the burning bush?" I asked.

Papa seemed to consider it for a moment, then shook his head.

Mama pushed her hair back and began winding it into a knot as though she might need to take action. "Like Paul and the talking donkey?" she said.

"Not no talkin' ass. Not none of the Bible stuff," he said. "The revelation is this—I should offer Preston Allen fifty or so acres on the east side of the farm for next to nuthin'." He paused and let the first part of his revelation sink in.

"Go on," Mama said.

"Next to nuthin'," he repeated. "Him and Bessie can come on back to Varennes and manage for us in exchange for land."

"Indeed," Mama replied. I was awake by now but not yet talking. Papa looked at me. I nodded in agreement.

Papa went on, "He can build Bessie a house close by. And they can put all their energy in the land right here."

Mama took over, "And we'll have Bessie back within a short walk. But Preston will be a fellow farmer rather than a hired hand."

Papa carefully bent his knee and eased up his sore leg. He barely grimaced. "I 'spect they'll agree." He rocked his sore leg slowly from side to side.

"William, it's a fine revelation, and one we should act upon lest some unforeseen circumstance taketh it away," Mama said in her scripture-quoting voice. She sounded oddly like Papa. She left the bedroom and went into the kitchen to put on a pot of coffee. I followed. We were still in our bedclothes.

As she stirred the embers and added a piece of wood, I asked, "Do you think it was the pain or the whiskey that made Papa come up with such a fine revelation?"

She shoved another piece of wood into the stove. "Probably the combination," she said. "Everything happens for a reason." At least she didn't say "happeneth."

As soon as Papa was up again and able to manage the buggy, he drove straightway to Lowndesville and made his offer. It was a proposition that the Allens quickly accepted. Mama and I were over the moon. And Bessie seemed as happy as we were.

Once Preston was managing for us again, Papa turned his attention to something he and other farmers had talked about for years. The need for a railroad.

Folks in Varennes and other small communities in the county wanted a railroad to run through town to help lower the cost of getting crops to market. Cotton in particular. Without a train they'd have to continue hauling the bales by wagon to Anderson where the current railroad line stopped or move them by barge down the Savannah River and on to Augusta.

In response, several businessmen formed the Savannah Valley Railroad Company. The plan was to extend the current tracks that stopped at the Anderson Courthouse to the southern part of the county.

That meant the tracks would pass through Dean Station, Varennes, Lowndesville, Abbeville and on to McCormick. The ultimate goal was to go all the way to Augusta where tracks already ran from Augusta to Savannah and then to Charleston.

For preparation work, the company officials wanted to use contractors and laborers from communities along the proposed railroad. They announced a call for bids to clear and grade land in twenty-mile increments for the new tracks.

Papa thought he could manage a crew to do the work in our area since Preston was overseeing most of our farm again.

After a week of figuring, which involved Mama's pen and Papa's dictation, he put in a bid for the stretch that would go from the center of Anderson, south through Dean Station, and on through Varennes. From there, another contractor would clear the way for tracks to run through McCormick. The contracts were to be announced in early 1881.

The morning they were to be awarded was a typically cold, damp January day. Papa decided to take the buggy to the Anderson Courthouse rather than go by horseback because he didn't want to irritate his leg.

He asked Mama if she'd like to come along. She said she was already feeling the cold in her bones and a buggy ride all the way into Anderson wouldn't help. So Papa went alone. He didn't ask me. I guess he thought if it was too cold for Mama, it was too cold for me.

Mama regretted her decision almost as soon as he was out of sight. She fretted throughout the morning and into the afternoon.

Finally, I said, "We should surprise Papa with an apple pie."

She looked at me as though she didn't know me. Then her face softened. "Yes!" she replied, louder than I expected. "Let's do!" She checked the stove's embers and added wood.

And so we set about soaking dried apples and making dough. I put several cups of dried slices into a pot, covered them with cider and put them on the stove to heat.

Mama began making the piecrust at her bread table. The table was small with thick legs and a marble slab on top. It stood to just below her waist. Papa'd built it for her to roll out biscuits. She scooped flour into a dough bowl, sprinkled it with salt, and threw in a chunk of lard.

"I should've gone with your papa," she said, cutting in the lard until the mixture looked like a bowl of white peas. Next she sprinkled water into the dough mixture and began to ball it up.

"It's a mite sticky," she said as she added a bit more flour, and like a magician, turned the dough into a smooth white ball. She sprinkled flour across the slab of marble, then placed the ball of dough in the center.

"You know William's a proud man," she said, more to herself than me.

In criss-cross motions, she rolled the dough flat until it looked like thick paper. Then she placed a pie pan, bottom side up, in the center of the dough. She traced around it with the tip of a knife adding about an inch all around.

She gathered the scraps into another ball, put it aside, and flipped the pie pan right side up. She rubbed the rolling pin with flour and gently laid it on the dough circle. She lifted one side of the dough sheet onto the rolling pin and rotated it until it balanced. Then she held it above the waiting pie pan and unrolled the dough, perfectly centered, into the pan.

"You make that look easy!" I said, stirring the filling. I added sugar to the apples.

"I've done it enough," she said as she fit the dough across the bottom and sides of the pie pan. She dipped a fork in flour and pressed it into the sides of the dough, making a snug fit. Next, she pricked a line of little holes across the bottom of the pan with the fork. As I child, I'd thought they looked like bird tracks.

I stirred in a bit of flour to thicken the apple mixture. "Seems those little holes would let the filling leak through."

"Keeps the bottom crust from bubbling up and throwing out the filling," she explained as she began to roll out the second ball of dough. Then she stopped and looked at me. "He'll be heartbroken if he doesn't get the bid. I should have gone."

The boiling apples had thickened nicely. I removed them from the heat.

"It wouldn't change the outcome," I offered. "Besides, he'll be happy you stayed home and made him this fine apple pie."

She seemed to relax. She even smiled. I realized I had done and said exactly what Bessie would have. It was a heady feeling.

When the filling had cooled enough, I poured it into the waiting crust. Mama added several chunks of butter and covered it with the second sheet of dough. She rotated the pan, cutting off the extra dough, and crimped the edges of the top and bottom crusts with the pointy end of a teaspoon, making a rounded zigzag pattern on the outside edge. She carefully cut several small slits across the top, sprinkled it lightly with sugar, and slid it into the oven.

I'd no sooner taken the golden bubbling pie out of the oven and set it on the bread table than Papa walked in.

"I got it!" he shouted before he'd even taken off his coat. "I got the contract!"

Mama launched herself at Papa. Luckily, he caught her and swung her around. They were a sight.

"I knew you would," she said as he set her down. "That's why we baked you a pie." She looked from Papa to me and smiled.

For the first time in my young life, I didn't feel like a child.

Varennes

Papa started gathering a work crew for the railroad project right away. He planned to begin clearing and grading in mid-February and complete his twenty-mile stretch of roadway before the first frost.

The week before the work was to begin, the Savannah Valley Railroad Company held a ground-breaking ceremony near the Anderson Courthouse. It was supposed to be a small event, but it turned into the biggest to-do since Wade Hampton's visit.

The day was seasonably cold for early February, but Mama didn't hesitate to make the trip. Preston and Bessie came too. So did the first family.

Papa sat on the platform with the railroad company president, the Anderson mayor, and some other dignitaries. The mayor talked about how the new stretch of tracks would benefit not only the county but the entire state.

Next the company president took the podium and outlined plans for running the tracks through the southern part of Anderson County. He explained where other railroads would tie into the new one, making our part of the state as accessible as larger towns and cities.

Then he turned his attention to the first leg of the plan, the twenty miles south of the courthouse that would go through Varennes. At that point he asked Papa to stand.

Papa was the tallest man on the platform. He seemed even taller than in life as though he had transcended into a character straight out of history. (I learned "transcended" from Aunt Eliza.) Mama had made sure that he was dressed in his finest. She'd also trimmed his hair and beard and polished his boots.

"From everything I hear," the company president boomed, "Capt. Jones here is the man for the job!"

Someone shouted "Hip, Hip, Hooray!" The crowd quickly picked up the cheer and repeated it for several more rounds.

Mama beamed. So did the rest of us. It was a glorious day for the Joneses.

Then came the actual work, which was less glorious. Papa's clearing and grading proceeded in fits and starts, depending on the manpower of his crew. He hired colored and white alike, any able man who needed a job. But the size of the crew fluctuated with the planting season, as with the chopping and picking seasons. At times, Papa had as few as twelve workers and, at other times, as many as two hundred.

There was talk of using convict labor during the busy cotton season, but Papa stuck with locals. The convict labor would come later, much to Mama's consternation, when the company laid the tracks.

Everyone watched the progress, and the talk of the town was how the railroad would change Varennes.

Before the railroad, the town had one general store that Grandpa Jones and another man had opened when Papa was a boy. My half-brother Dock later owned it. He added onto it several times and built a warehouse. The store was second in popularity only to the cotton gin, the first stop for most farmers on their way into town.

Varennes also had a livery stable with a blacksmith, a small grain mill, and a public well beside the gin. Near the middle of town was a Masonic Hall built some time before the war. It was a social center for everything from dances to rifle clubs.

The community had three churches—Cross Roads Baptist that Papa had helped build, Good Hope Presbyterian that was a little south of town, and Bethesda Methodist, a small log building west of town.

The colored folks had two churches, one fairly close to our house and another almost dead center in the McGees' property.

As children, Bessie and I loved to listen to the colored church near us in the summer when windows were open and the congregation held daylong Sunday services. We could usually make out words to familiar hymns, but the voices transformed them into something altogether different. We would sit on the porch and clap to the rhythm of the singing.

I don't recall hearing an organ or even a piano. The congregation probably couldn't afford one. But they didn't really need accompaniment. Their voices were their musical instruments, and what a joyful noise they made. I can still hear them singing, "Walking in Jay-ru-zah-lem just like John."

Varennes also had a school that Bessie and I attended along with most of our cousins and other neighbors. But it didn't have a post office before the train came.

As for doctors, Dr. Dean was the one most of my kinfolk sent for when possible. He was brother to Papa's first wife so he was uncle to the first family. When my half-sister Sallie Seigler was old enough, she became the town's midwife. She probably delivered more babies in Varennes than Dr. Dean did.

How Varennes got its name was a bit of a mystery.

I once asked Papa, who said, "There's a church up north of here with the same name. Must be from the Bible. Go ask your mama."

So I did. Mama said, "If it's in the Bible, I've never seen it. More likely, it's named for some fur trapper who came through a long time ago. Maybe French."

Aunt Eliza was staying with us at the time, so I asked her if our town was named for something in the Bible or for a French fur trapper.

She and I were sitting close, embroidering pillow covers.

"Your mama's right about the French," she said. "But it's the name of a town, not a man. And it should be pronounced 'VAAH-ren.'" She said it again, pushing air through her mouth and nose at the same time.

I was trying to make a French knot while I listened. I stuck my finger on the underside. Somehow it seemed ironic. I put my needlework aside.

I thought it was, "Vah-REN-ez," I said. "That's how everybody here says it."

"The accent's all wrong."

"What about the 's'?" I asked, looking at my wounded finger.

"The French don't often pronounce 's' at the end of words," she said. Then she repeated "VAAH-ren" several times perfecting her delivery.

I attempted saying the French version myself, which came out, "VAAH-RENZ."

Aunt Eliza laughed. "No one here pronounces it like the French. It's been anglicized." She looked up from her embroidered bachelor buttons. "That means converted to English and changed in the process."

"Is 'anglicized' a bad thing?" I asked. I squeezed the tip of my finger and watched a tiny spot of red appear.

"It's just what we tend to do. We make things fit our own experience. As for meaning," she explained, "I've seen Varennes translated as 'wasteland' and as 'cemetery of the gods.' You can choose the one you prefer."

I didn't particularly like either meaning, but I chose "cemetery of the gods" considering how many of my kinfolks were buried behind Cross Roads Baptist Church.

Then she launched into an account of French King Louis

XVI and his wife Marie Antoinette and their escape from Paris to VAAH-ren in France. How they were spotted, sent back to Paris, and sentenced to the guillotine, which she pronounced "GEE-yo-teen."

Whatever the origin of our own Varennes, it was an exciting time to live there. People began to talk less about the past, specifically the war and Reconstruction, and more about the future.

The coming railroad gave Papa new purpose. He cleared and graded his section of the Savannah Valley Railroad on schedule as did the man contracted to clear the next twenty miles.

In the meantime, Preston farmed his and Bessie's land near ours, managed Papa's fields, and completed their new house. Mama set about helping Bessie furnish and settle into the Allen's new home.

That left me pretty much on my own, certainly more than I'd ever been before. The only time during the railroad work that Mama became especially protective was when the company contracted convict labor to lay the tracks. She imagined angry, lusting convicts at every twist and turn. But they completed their work in Varennes without incident.

When a problem did arise, it was later in Abbeville. And it wasn't an uprising of convicts inflicting pain on their contractors. It was just the opposite. A guard whipped several convicts so badly that one died and the other was crippled. Another convict in the same railroad camp died from illness left untreated. And there were other reports of mistreatment.

As for Mama's concerns, once the convict danger had gone down the track, she was back to helping Bessie.

As much as I'd tried to be Bessie's little shadow when we were growing up, I'd also lived in her shadow. Her marriage to Preston Allen forced me into the light, to depend more on myself and make my own decisions. That is, when Mama or Papa didn't intervene, which they did less and less.

I didn't feel nearly as lonely as when Bessie first left. Over the next few years, I made new friends, female and male. And I began to attract attention from the latter. If I'd wanted a boyfriend, I had several to choose from. But I hadn't found a young man yet that I looked at the way Bessie looked at Preston, the way Mama looked at Papa.

I was in no hurry because I had other things to do with my time. I'd become the organist for Cross Roads Baptist, and I played piano for several of my kinfolks' weddings.

Besides, Varennes had plenty of young folks. We went to parties and dances and holiday gatherings. And if there weren't any social events on a particular weekend, we would find something else to do. It was a magical time. I was blissfully ignorant of just how quickly life can turn.

Mouchet Hill

During the spring, we'd sometimes go to Mouchet Hill right at dusk. The hill was part of the land Uncle Tyler had inherited. Bare spots between the hardwoods offered the perfect place at night to view the enormous starlit sky.

The hill seemed enchanted. Uncle Tyler and Aunt Lou had spent time there when they were courting. As parents, they'd taken their children to watch the constellations light up the sky. Sometimes I'd tagged along.

As we got older, we'd go to Mouchet Hill on our own. We'd usually begin after March's last blow of winter. Finding and naming constellations became our game.

We'd search the wide-open sky for the North Star, the Big Dipper, the Little Dipper, and other familiar constellations. And if we didn't know a name, we'd make up one. Like Big Mule, Little Bucket, Sallie's Apron. I felt smart and worldly and part of a place far beyond my own little Varennes.

Mouchet Hill was about a mile and a half from our house. Even though I considered myself grown, Mama and Papa never would've let me go if I hadn't promised to get one of my cousins to walk me home.

Such was the case one clear night in April, a month before I was to finish school. Summer was nearly two months away, and the air still turned chilly in the evening. But Carie, Lenore, and I were itching to leave winter behind and sit out under the night sky.

Easter was early that year, which meant an early spring. So the Saturday following Easter Sunday, we headed up to Mouchet Hill. We weren't alone for long. Soon, some of our cousins and friends and their friends showed up.

Because the ground was cool and damp, I brought a small quilt, one that Aunt Eliza and I had stitched several years earlier. It made for a drier seat and would keep me warm if I needed it on the walk home. Carie and Lenore sat fairly close by, but others settled in around them and between us.

Around dusk a young man eased down onto the bare ground beside me. He sat silent for a few minutes looking off into the distance. I didn't recognize him and wondered if he thought I was someone else.

Then he turned where I could see his face. His hair was blond and straight, cut short against his neck but longer on top. It flopped across his forehead nearly covering one eye. He looked a little older than me.

He pushed his hair back and said, "Icie Jones, you look beautiful in the waning light." I laughed, flattered and embarrassed at once. Even in the falling dark I could see his eyes were sky-blue.

"How do you know my name?" I asked, my mind trying to sort faces from school, church, special occasions.

"I know your cousin," he said.

"Which one?" I asked, laughing again from nervousness, trying hard to make the connection.

He ignored my question. "Icie's an unusual name."

"It's short for Isamar." I pronounced it again slowly, "EYE-sah-mar. It's from the Bible."

"Or IY-Zaa-Mar," he said, making my name sound foreign. "I believe that means 'island of palm trees.' If you were in Charleston, it would be palmetto trees."

"I'm not an island or a tree!" I protested.

He laughed. "In Biblical times, palm trees were considered a blessing. They were beautiful. Always green and fruitful. They provided all sorts of things that people needed."

He had a handsome voice, if sound can be handsome. I liked hearing him talk. Perhaps, he did too.

"It's symbolic of riches," he explained. " 'The righteous shall flourish like the palm tree.' That's from Psalms, I think."

"Probably," I said, wondering who this person was and how he knew so much.

"I'm Alexander," he said, as though he read my mind. "I'm the product of too much education."

I looked at him closely. He seemed older than I'd first thought. "Where are you from, Alexander?"

"The lowcountry," he answered.

"Well, Alexander from the Lowcountry," I said, regaining my wits, "what are you doing in upcountry Varennes?"

"Give me some of that quilt you're sitting on, Miss Isamar, and I'll tell you." He patted the ground between us.

I moved over a little and he slipped in close beside me. "I'm here for a wedding," he said, settling on the dry quilt.

"A wedding here?" I asked. I was puzzled again. I was almost certain I'd have known if anyone in Varennes was getting married, at least in a public way. But the railroad had brought in a mix of folks from everywhere it seemed. And the truth is I saw strangers every time I went into town. It was both exciting and a little frightening.

"In Anderson," he answered easily. "I have friends in VAAH-ren, so I'm getting in a visit while I'm in the area."

I should tell Aunt Eliza about him in my next letter, I thought. "Who are your friends here?" I asked.

He didn't answer. Instead he leaned in toward me and asked, "What's your favorite constellation?" This time he looked up at the night sky instead of me where the stars were beginning to sparkle.

I felt more at ease.

"Orion," I answered quickly. "He's my favorite."

"Why?" he asked, still looking up.

"He's a warrior and a hunter. And he's easy to spot tonight!"

Alexander laughed. "What does he hunt?"

"Rabbits and squirrels," I said, realizing at once how silly that sounded.

"Or even larger game," he added. He was quiet for a moment. Then he said, "Orion is quite vain, you know."

"So he is, but he's beautifully adorned in stars. You'd be vain, too."

He laughed again. "Did you know that Orion gets chased out of view about this time of year?"

"No!" I said disappointed. I'd never thought about it. My stargazing had been mostly in the spring before mosquitoes came out.

"The Scorpio constellation runs him right out of the night sky."

"A good thing we don't have scorpions around here," I said quickly.

"Scorpio also means 'hissing serpent,'" he added.

"Snakes we have," I replied, "but I've never heard one hiss."

"And I hope you never do," he said.

I thought a bit. "But Orion comes back in the winter. Right? And then he chases Scorpio out of the sky!" I felt I'd rescued Orion's reputation.

Alexander replied, "A matter of perspective, pretty Icie, just a matter of perspective."

He laid his hand on top of mine. "Have you ever been to Charleston?"

Unsure whether or not to move my hand, I didn't answer.

"Or Savannah?" he added.

I decided a hand on hand was acceptable. "No, neither Charleston nor Savannah."

"Would you like to?" he asked.

"Certainly," I said, realizing I'd never been farther south than to visit Mama's folks in Edgefield. The idea of travel became enticing.

"With the new tracks, you could catch the train from here and ride it all the way to Augusta. Then you could catch another train and make a long winding trip to Charleston."

"I could," I agreed, thinking of all the places I might see.

"If you did," he said, squeezing my hand lightly, "I'd be honored to show you around the grand old city. We could stroll along the Battery. Have you ever seen the ocean?"

I shook my head.

"Then at dusk, we could watch the fireball sun drop into the Ashley River. Would you like that?" He looked into my eyes.

I tried not to blink. "I'd be delighted."

"The houses are painted the colors of the rainbow. And the gardens are all lush green."

"What do they grow in their gardens?" I asked. "Tomatoes and such?"

"I meant the grand gardens surrounding the grand homes," he replied.

I felt myself blush. I hoped he wouldn't notice in the moonlight. "Then they grow 'grand,' I suppose," I said, trying to regain my wit.

He laughed. "They grow magical oak trees."

"We have oak trees here," I said, "and they aren't magical."

He slid his fingers between mine. "You have red oaks and white oaks."

My hand tingled from his touch.

"But the lowcountry has live oaks. Their limbs reach out far beyond a regular oak tree's span, like long muscular arms." He held his arms out and tightened his muscles in exaggeration.

We both laughed.

"The limbs are draped in Spanish moss like loose woolen yarn."

"We have moss, too."

"That you do. But Spanish moss isn't really moss. Nor is it Spanish."

"Then why's it called Spanish moss?"

"Because," he said, slipping his arm around my back, "in early times, a Spanish soldier chased a beautiful Indian maiden up an ancient live oak that was growing along the river."

"Why?" I asked.

He paused, then answered, "To make her his own."

"Oh!" I began to visualize the chase.

He leaned in closer until his lips nearly touched my ear. His warm breath covered my cheek. "She climbed all the way to the tip-top," he whispered, "then leaped into the rushing river to escape."

He paused again.

"Go on," I whispered back.

"The Spaniard reached out to grab her as she flew by, but he lost his grip and began to fall himself." He caught his breath, then continued, "As he fell, a tree branch snagged his coarse, thick beard. And there he hung. The birds pecked away his flesh, and the squirrels carried away his bones, but the beard remained."

I pulled away at the horrible ending.

He pulled me back. "The story goes that from that day on, Spanish moss, which is Indian for hair, has grown throughout all live oaks to serve as a reminder."

"Reminder of what?" I asked, drawn back in.

"To remind young men not to chase beautiful maidens up trees."

I laughed. "Serves him right! But what about the maiden? Did she drown?"

"No one knows for sure. She was never seen again. But everywhere she'd touched the tree, there grew green resurrection ferns."

"Resurrection?" I asked. "Like in the Bible?"

"Sort of," he whispered, warming my cheek. "They're called resurrection ferns because nothing can kill them, not even drought. They seem to die and disappear, but soon come back greener than before."

And on throughout the evening, Alexander captivated me with stories about the lowcountry. I listened spellbound, unaware of time. But when I saw others leaving, I knew I should too. I looked around for one of my cousins to walk me home.

As though he read my mind, he said, "I'd be honored to walk you home, Miss Isamar." I looked around again and didn't see any Joneses or Mouchets left.

I can't say I was sorry. At least not yet.

And so down Mouchet Hill and toward my house we went as he carried my quilt with one hand and guided me with the other. We'd gone about a mile when he put his arm around my shoulders. I didn't object. After a few more steps, he stopped, spun me around, and kissed me.

I'd been kissed before, little kisses, but not like this, deep and long and blurry. A kiss that sent all the constellations spinning. And before I knew what'd happened, I was on my back and he was still kissing me.

I should have stopped him. Part of me wanted to jump up and pretend nothing had happened and finish the charmed walk home. But the other part of me wanted to stay as I was, with my back on the cold ground and my front weighed down like I was covered in a dozen warm blankets.

Then it was too late. My skirt flew up and over me and he did more than kiss me. Much more. I was surprised and confused and in the moment all at the same time. A whirling dervish of heat and sound, skin on skin, fire on kindling. I thought I heard a voice in the distance calling my name, again and again.

And then it was over. We lay still except for beating hearts and rushing breath. The mysterious visitor from the lowcountry was a stranger to me no more.

Without a word, he helped me up, brushed off my back, took me by the arm, and started again in the direction of my home. We walked the rest of the way in silence other than the rustling of my disrupted petticoats and the footfall of his boots crushing the spring grass.

When we reached my house, he tried to turn me toward him. But this time, I wouldn't give in. I bolted up the steps and through the door. He called to me, but I wouldn't look back.

Mama and Papa had gone to bed. I went straight to bed myself but slept little. I was in the grips of a fever turning from hot to cold, shame to anger. All the while I was too stubborn to let myself cry.

The next morning, I slipped away as soon as I could to retrace the path to Mouchet Hill and look for my little quilt.

About a half mile from home I found it on the side of the trail crumpled into a pile. I picked it up and tried to brush off the grass and dirt. It was damp from the morning dew. I carefully folded it and pressed it to my face. The sobs I'd held in the night before came rushing out in heaves, turning my stomach.

I didn't return to Mouchet Hill for a long time. Luckily I didn't have to make excuses right away because we had a wet spell that kept everyone at home. By the time I did go back, it was midsummer. Sure enough Orion had left the sky. Many bright and beautiful stars had taken his place, but I refused to acknowledge any in the Scorpio constellation.

I tried to make peace with the whole incident, laying as much blame on myself as on the mysterious Alexander, if that was, in fact, his real name. I finished school and felt mature enough to put it behind me and carry on normally with my life.

And if he did come back, apologize profusely, and behave like a true gentleman, I would consider seeing him, though not alone.

But by the end of summer, all that changed. There was no normal. My newfound confidence, maturity, boundless joy in young adulthood—like dandelion puffs in the wind—were blown away.

Suffice it to say, I was with child.

Reason for everything ⌒ ꝰ ꙩ

Mama realized I was pregnant almost as soon as I did. She knew the signs. And if she knew, Papa wouldn't be far behind.

They began watching me like a pair of hawks, a tall one and a small one. I quit going anywhere except to church on Sunday. I didn't visit friends anymore nor ask any to visit me.

I couldn't find the courage to talk about it to anyone, not even Bessie, so I played my piano and did my chores and tried to stay in my bedroom as much as I could.

The loneliness I thought I'd outgrown came back double-fold. It was nearly paralyzing.

Then one morning in late fall when it became obvious that I had a baby growing inside me, Mama could contain herself no longer. We were in the kitchen and I was about to go outside when she positioned herself between me and the screen door.

"Who's the father, Icie?" she asked, her voice shaking.

My face flushed hot and my throat tightened like I was choking. I didn't answer.

Mama began to cry. Papa heard the dam break and in he came.

I felt faint. "I'm so sorry," I said to both of them, fighting back my own tears.

Mama composed herself. "Is he married?" she asked quickly. "No," I answered, not really sure. She looked slightly relieved. "Then who the hell is he?" Papa shouted.

I lowered my head.

Mama asked slowly, "Is he kin?"

I raised my head. "No!" I said emphatically. They both looked relieved.

"I'm gonna ask you one more thing," Papa said. "Did he force hisself on you?"

I was unsure how to answer. But my hesitancy fueled Papa's suspicions.

"Got-dammit! Icie!" he shouted again. "Did the son-uva-bitch rape you?"

I looked at Mama. She didn't flinch.

"No, sir," I answered quickly. Papa stared at me. He looked doubtful. "No," I repeated. Whether they were relieved or not I couldn't tell. But I knew I wouldn't be testing the believability of my strange story on Mama and Papa or anyone else.

Mama asked one more question, "Does he know?"

"No," I said.

Papa spoke up. "You sure?"

"I'm sure," I said with certainty.

They both exhaled.

Mama hugged me and Papa hugged us both. They still loved me. Relief and guilt blended into something I'd never felt before, like opposite emotions pumping through my veins at once.

When Bessie found out about my sorry state, she blamed herself.

The day after I'd told Mama and Papa, Mama went early morning to the Allens' house and told Bessie. Then Bessie ran straight to our house. I was changing my bed when she flew into the room. I nearly jumped out of my skin.

"Oh Icie, I didn't mean to scare you!" she said, looking scared herself.

I caught my breath and returned to stripping the bed. "I'm a bit jumpy these days."

She stood across the bed from me, still breathing hard from running. "I should've paid more attention to you," she said. Before I could object, she continued, "I've been so busy trying to be a good wife, building our house, helping Preston keep the books. I haven't made time for you."

I didn't know what to say so I shook my head and waved my hand to dismiss her concerns.

"And Mama! I distracted Mama from paying attention to you."

I shook my head again.

"How do you feel?" she asked.

"Awful," I said. "I've shamed Mama and Papa. And you. And the whole first family, too." I didn't look up.

"No," she said, "I mean your health."

"Not so bad as I did in the beginning," I said, staring at nothing in particular.

She began removing a pillowcase. "Good. And don't worry about shaming the Joneses." She slipped off the second pillow-case. "This won't be the first child in the family to be born out of the confines of matrimony."

I looked up. Bessie balled the cases together, handed them across the bed to me, and smiled. "We have a history."

"A history of what?" I asked, pulling off the rest of the bedding and piling it on the left side of the bed where I was standing. Bessie took clean linen from the chest at the foot of the bed. One Papa had made for me when I'd turned sixteen. He'd lined it with cedar. The fresh smell filled the air and permeated the cloth. She shook out a sheet and billowed it over the center of the mattress. I caught the edges. "A history of unknown fathers," she answered.

"Who else?" I asked as I smoothed my side of the bottom sheet.

"Grandpa Jones, for one. His mother wasn't married when she had him."

I slowly pushed the edges of the sheet under the mattress. "Aunt Eliza hinted as much to me in a past visit, but she stopped short of telling me Grandpa Jones was illegitimate." The word hung in the air. I realized I'd better get used to hearing it. And worse. Much worse. I shuddered.

"Papa doesn't even know who Grandpa's father was," she said, tucking in her side of the sheet. "I don't think anyone knows. I guess our great grandmother took it to her grave."

"Evidently," I commented more to myself than to Bessie.

She was wound up. "But just think if she hadn't given birth to Grandpa. There'd be no Papa. No first family. No you. No me."

I let the new bit of family history settle in as I tucked the top corner. Bessie did the same. Then we moved to the bottom corners.

"As for Aunt Eliza, remember when she went back to Greenville after mourning for her husband?"

I nodded.

"A year later, she gave birth to a baby girl."

"What! Aunt Eliza?" I exclaimed. I stopped making the bed. "How do you know?"

"Mama told me."

"Damn! Just damn!" I cried with as much energy as I'd had since Mouchet Hill. "Why didn't she tell me!"

"Probably because she knows how much you admire Aunt Eliza," Bessie said. "She didn't want to upset you."

I didn't reply at first, letting something close to anger pass. "Now there's some dramatic irony," I noted. "Double irony since Aunt Eliza taught me the term herself!"

Bessie looked at me like I was talking in tongues. Then she said, "Aunt Eliza named the child Willie. A girl named 'Willie'! They've since moved to Nashville where she's teaching school."

I suddenly recalled Aunt Eliza's words—"A woman's heart is a sea of secrets." I began to understand.

We tucked in the lower part of the top sheet, the same as we'd done so many times growing up, me on the left, Bessie on the right, always faster but pacing her time to match mine.

"I'll bet that's one story Aunt Eliza won't be telling," I said. Bessie laughed, and so did I, the first time in months.

"And then there's Mama's family," she said. "Lordy, they were a busy bunch."

We continued to make the bed, one Papa had built for us when I was old enough to be out of a crib, an adult bed but not as high. The head and foot were made of oak. The sides and slats were poplar. I always slept on the left, Bessie on the right.

"How do you like having our bed all to yourself?" she asked.

"I didn't at first. But I've gotten used to the extra space."

"Must be nice!" She laughed, then added, "I'm still sharing a bed."

She dug into the cedar chest again and came out with a quilt. Not my little quilt but a larger, older one. It was the color of unbleached muslin, probably white at one time, with a large medallion of appliquéd flowers in the center and a smaller bouquet in each corner. The flowers had faded from their original vivid colors into soft pastels.

Bessie shook it out and whipped it across the bed toward me. "The gunboat quilt!" she said. "I'd almost forgotten about it. Remember when Mama gave it to us for our bed? And I asked her where the gunboat was?"

"She told us, 'At the bottom of Charleston harbor most likely!'" I answered. "She never did say where she got the quilt."

"Grandma Isabella probably sewed it with her group of ladies for the Confederate naval cause," Bessie speculated. "She must have gotten her 'case of the nerves' before she could sell it."

By the time my bed was freshly made and my family's graveyard was newly disturbed, I felt a little better.

"Don't guess you want to tell me who the father is," Bessie said.

My face flushed. "No one you know, and knowing wouldn't change anything."

She didn't persist.

By then Mama had made the walk back from the Allen house at a sensible pace. We soon sat down to a breakfast of biscuits and coffee. For the first time in months, I could taste.

And so I was at peace with the second family, but the first family and the entire community of Varennes was another matter.

Most of Papa's first family went to Cross Roads Baptist Church where I played the organ every Sunday. I'd taught myself when my legs were long enough to reach the pedals. "The Old Rugged Cross," "Amazing Grace," "I Go to the Garden." Whatever the preacher and the congregation wanted to hear, I learned to play. I'll admit—I'd felt important.

My relatives held posts throughout the church. Two of my half-brothers were deacons, Sallie's husband, J. E., was treasurer, and several of my cousins were ushers. Papa had helped build the church. And now I was the main musician.

The point is, what I found the greatest pride in, playing the organ in church, started causing me the most pain. The stares increased as my body bloomed. I began wearing a shawl in early autumn before it even turned chilly. It was a soft gray wrap that I'd crocheted in record time. Mama said my fingers flew like a bevy of mourning doves as I made it. I wore it every Sunday.

In the latter months I had to ease the organ bench back, an inch or two at first, then nearly a foot, until I could barely reach the pedals. Still, no one asked me not to play. Not even Rev. Wright.

But some members left the church.

Papa said I swelled the ranks of Good Hope Presbyterian and spurred the growth of Bethesda Methodist. Cross Roads Baptist had expelled folks for less so I'm sure they wanted to do something about me. Especially Sallie and J. E.

But nothing happened. Perhaps, Sallie's loyalty to Papa outweighed her outrage. Or she was counting on delivering the baby. As for the other members, I think Papa had too much influence, and none of them wanted to be the one to complain. He still made the best coffins in the county. Maybe they thought he'd leave some wormholes in theirs if they made him mad.

I kept right on playing until the end of December. By then, I couldn't reach the pedals at all, and, truth be told, I didn't feel much like making music anymore.

Bessie tried to keep my spirits up. She said if my waist hadn't been so small to begin with, no one would have noticed. A few other kinfolks were kind too. Aunt Lou went out of her way to be pleasant to me, and my half-sister Mattie seemed strangely understanding.

But most everyone else was cold. I think it was my not telling who the father was that church folks hated in me more than the sin itself.

Mama and Papa acted as though the outrage didn't bother them. Occasionally, Mama would mutter, "Idle curiosity is the Devil's garden." Papa would simply say, "It ain't nobody's got-damn biz-ness!"

As for myself, I'd already made up my mind—come hell or high water—I was taking it to my grave. It would become, like Grandpa Jones's birth and Aunt Eliza's Willie, one more secret in the Joneses' family history.

Feaster Ithamar cometh

I wondered from time to time what'd become of Alexander from the Lowcountry mostly with anger but also with the slightest little hope he'd return.

Varennes didn't have any Charleston connections that I knew. Anderson probably had a few. But several families from Charleston did have homes in Pendleton, a half-day's ride north of Anderson. Wade Hampton's magnificent black stallion had come from one of those farms.

At first, I scoured the Anderson newspaper each week for any reference to Charleston or Pendleton weddings or visitors. But to no avail. I suppose it was simply a distraction, something to do with my mind, since I had little control over my body.

Bessie spent more and more time with us that fall and early winter while I was swelling like a wet sponge. She claimed she was just helping Mama since I wasn't able to do as much as usual.

I was glad she did, especially in January, when the baby decided it was time to come out.

Luckily the air was cold or I think I would have caught on fire. Bessie stayed in the bedroom with me. So did Mama. They waited for Sallie.

Papa'd insisted on Sallie for the delivery. The minute I'd started to show signs of labor, he'd sent for her although Mama had tried to talk him out of it. She wanted Dr. Dean.

"Sallie's with child herself, well into her time," she protested.

"Won't slow her down a bit," Papa said. "She's seasoned at birthin'."

And so it was settled. Sallie would be lording over me and I didn't care. I just wanted to quit hurting. My whole body started to cramp and squeeze like I was turning inside out. I thought I would surely die. I cried and cried, louder than I wanted to.

Mama hovered on one side and Bessie on the other. Papa stayed outside.

"Hush up, Icie Jones! You'll wake the dead!" Sallie shouted, sweeping into the room with a basketful of cloth and tools. She shooed Mama and Bessie away like they were pesky chickens.

I was lying on layers of old cotton sheets with a wool blanket on top. I could smell wet wool. I wondered why the blanket on top of me was wet. I asked between cramps.

"Cause you're squirming around so much," she answered, already sounding impatient. "Quit wiggling and concentrate on pushing this baby out."

Mama spoke up, "For God's sake, Sallie, show some compassion. The girl's in pain."

"The girl's a full-grown woman," Sallie said, pulling the blanket off and having a good look at the blood and liquid squirting out of my body. "She might not be in such a fix if you hadn't spoiled her so much! Both of them!"

Mama bristled. "Judge not, Sallie Jones Seigler!"

"I work as hard as you do. And Icie has her own talents," Bessie snapped. I couldn't focus on her face, but her voice was low and sharp.

"I can see that," Sallie said, leaning against the mattress with her thick middle.

I wanted to slap her face. Then another wave hit. And another. And another until it was one long agonizing train blasting through a crossing. The last one sat me up. I gripped the mattress and did the hardest thing I'd ever done in my life. I gave birth.

Something pink and red and shiny appeared on the bed with me—its little arms and legs kicking out. It made a sound I'd never heard before, more like a cat than a baby. Little wisps of sound that soon connected into a high-pitched wail.

"It's a stem-winder!" Sallie shouted, her voice joyous. "A baby boy, with a fine set of lungs."

Bessie and Mama and Sallie began laughing together like that hadn't hated each other just minutes earlier. I wanted to be among them, to share in the sisterhood, the wondrous gratitude of having created life. But all I felt was relief from pain.

Sallie wiped the baby dry and slipped a clean sheet underneath him. She tied off the cord and cut it and wrapped the baby in a little cotton blanket.

By then my heart had quit racing and I could focus more clearly. Sallie handed the baby boy to Mama. Bessie crowded in.

Then Sallie started pushing on my belly. I thought she was hoping I'd scream out the father's name. "Dear Jesus!" I shouted. "Quit pushing on me!" It wasn't the name she expected. She pushed harder.

Mama smoothed back the hair on my forehead and said, "Hush, Icie. She's getting rid of the afterbirth so you don't get the fever."

And I didn't. Sallie had done her job.

I woke later with a sense of gratitude that I was still alive, not fully aware of the lives I had just changed. Mama was holding the baby to my breast. It was the first time I could see him close up. He had blue eyes like Mama and me, but deeper, and a little smudge of light brown hair. And evidently large lungs. I tried my best to feed him, but he'd suck a little and then scream a lot.

This went on all night and into the next morning.

Once it became obvious that I just didn't have enough milk, Mama mixed up what she called pabulum—a little bread dipped in goat's milk that he could suck on. Over the next few days, the baby survived on the concoction. Bessie stayed close to Mama watching everything she did. Bessie and Preston Allen had been married long enough by then to have a child of their own. But nothing had taken.

She quickly became comfortable handling the baby. A week after the birth, she was as easy with him as Mama was. I was not. A pattern had formed. Bessie or Mama would feed and burp him and then hand him to me. He would begin to cry. I would try to soothe him. He would cry louder.

A deep sense of failure and loneliness rolled over me like a cold gray fog. By the second week, I began crying as loud as he did. I was in a shameful, sorry state of despair.

Mama looked from me to Bessie and back to me. I knew what she was thinking. I heard the words, screaming inside my head. My heart convulsed—love and sorrow, all knotted together. I swallowed hard and said, "Bessie, you're a better mother to him than I am."

I handed the baby to her and she took him without a word. She jostled him a bit until he lay silent against her shoulder.

How she convinced Preston to raise the baby as their own, I never knew. Probably he was just eager to get Bessie home and thought the boy would be a good starting point for their family.

They named him Feaster after someone in Preston's family, I suppose. And Ithamar, the male version of Isamar, for his middle name! I imagine it was to honor me, but I doubted Feaster Ithamar would appreciate it.

As for church, I didn't go back for another month. Not until Mama said it was time, and Papa agreed. Bessie had settled into a routine with little Feaster in her own home, and I could fit back into my clothes, so I didn't have an excuse.

I hadn't thought about church, the congregation, or who might be playing the organ. It didn't even occur to me to ask about the music until we were in the buggy on the way to church.

"Has there been any music at church?" I asked.

Papa didn't answer.

Mama said, "Rev. Wright found another lady to play." She didn't look at me.

I was dumbfounded. My eyes watered. I don't know why I was emotional, but I was.

Papa didn't look at me either. He said, "She ain't very good."

Mama said, "The preacher's sister-in-law, a widow, moved in with him and his wife. Miracle of miracles, he discovered she could play the organ."

"Or claimed she could," Papa added.

Mama glanced at Papa. "Her name is Myrtle Murphy."

Any other time, her name alone would have made me giggle. But the laughter had gone out of me.

Walking into church felt like being thrown into the fiery furnace. Mama and Papa ushered me in quickly and settled into our pew. I could hear people whispering or thought I could. I tried not to look around, but I saw several familiar faces lean forward and look at my middle. My face flushed hot. I wanted to run out of the sanctuary, but Mama and Papa hemmed me in. Mama laid her hand over mine.

It was almost a relief when Rev. Wright took the pulpit. He began the service and announced the first song, "The Church in the Wildwood." It was popular with our congregation, especially the men who sang bass. They loved to sing the "Oh come, come, come" part of the chorus while the ladies sang the rest.

The widow started playing the song well enough. The congregation began, "There's a church in the valley by the w-i-l-d—wood."

I joined in on the second line, "No love-li-er place in the dale." Mama nodded at me as we sang, "No spot is so dear to my chi-i-i-ld—hood . . ."

But something happened to the widow's fingers between "child" and "hood." She stopped. Then instead of picking back up where she'd stopped, she started over at the very first line. The preacher quickly started over with her. Some of the ladies did too while others quit singing altogether.

But as for the men, the horses were out of the barn. They sang on, reaching the bass part of the chorus "Oh-oh come, come, come, come, COME to the church . . ." just as the start-over singers were back on "No love-li-er place in the dale." Papa was among the loudest, and I knew Mama would have elbowed him if I hadn't been between them.

I wished Bessie were there. I could imagine her lifting her eyebrows and pushing her lips together to keep from giggling. I glanced around and saw Sallie grimace at J. E. I quickly looked down and bit back my own smile. Music mayhem, Aunt Eliza's word, had come upon Cross Roads Baptist Church. Right or wrong, I felt a morsel of joy.

The preacher called a halt and plowed into his sermon. It was on sinners' need to repent and on non-sinners' need to tithe.

By the end of the service and a horrible rendition of "Bringing in the Sheaves," I felt almost benevolent. Another of Aunt Eliza's words.

On the ride home, Mama and Papa talked a little about the music, but mostly about the sermon. "That preacher best quit askin' for money," Papa said.

Mama nodded. "The congregation would be better served with a sermon about minding their own business."

"Amen," Papa declared.

. . ❧ . .

I didn't see the baby every day. It didn't bother me most of the time when I did see him because Bessie and Preston were crazy happy to be parents. But I had to be cautious, as I learned a few months after the birth. It was an early spring day, so I'd walked to their new house on the far side of Papa's property. Preston was standing on the front porch while Bessie was inside getting the baby ready for a stroll. We chatted, Preston about the weather, me about how nice the yard looked.

Then Bessie rolled little Feaster out the front door in a brand new baby buggy made of white wicker. He was dressed in a sky-blue crocheted bunting, the color of his eyes. When I looked at him, my heart went into my throat. It was all I could do to keep from reaching in and snatching him. And running away. Just running until I couldn't run anymore.

I stole a glance at Bessie and Preston. They were looking at him with such love that I knew he was theirs forever. I tried never to feel that way about him again. When the feeling blew over me in a gust of love and loss, I turned my back to it and folded in on myself like a collapsing shed.

I am a collapsing shed now. I would laugh at the irony if I could. But my heart still beats, and it still wants what it wants.

I think how different life might have been if I hadn't made the mistake of my young life. Not only for me, but for Bessie, Preston, and family to come. Perhaps, one's life is a matter of fate intervening with stings and honey. And maybe the challenge is telling the two apart. Or accepting both on faith.

PART IV

Joyful noise

Bad times don't last ⌐ ſ ⌐

A month or so later, Mama told me I had to take the bull by the horns and get back into the business of life. She said it was paining Papa and her to watch the life drain out of me.

I hadn't really thought about their feelings. I felt guilty. It was another moment of self-realization that I didn't welcome. I promised her I'd try to be a better daughter.

Mama did her part. She made sure I got to play the organ every other Sunday by alternating with the preacher's sister-in-law. Rev. Wright didn't argue. And neither did the congregation. So I had a sliver of purpose again if only every other Sunday.

Still I couldn't shut out the way I felt in just day-to-day living. I tried harder to act normal for Mama and Papa, but normal had changed.

In the meantime, Bessie and Preston put the final touches on their new home. It was wood-framed with a tin roof like ours. But it was larger. And, being new, it was fresher and crisper, if a house can be crisp. It was painted a bean-blossom white. Ours may have once been white, but it had weathered to the color of wheat.

Papa began to see the shortcomings of our own house. First he replaced the uneven, squeaky boards in the kitchen floor. Then he decided Mama needed a new stove, the coal-burning style, and a new icebox. Next he turned his attention to a new porch.

He'd talked about making improvements for years, but I think Preston's energy spurred him on. Papa had a touch of competitiveness when it came to his son-in-law. If he could get a crop in faster than Preston Allen or a bigger bull or a better deal on a wagon, he counted himself successful.

At the time of our house renovation, I'd thought he was trying to keep up with Preston. I later wondered if it was his way of giving us a fresh start, projects Mama and I could get lost in, whether deciding on colors and fabrics or making pretties for each room. Papa was wise more often than not.

Mama and I quickly caught the decorating fever. We added new curtains and rugs to all the rooms. We polished every brass fixture and every piece of silver. And on it went. Pretty soon a year had gone by. The inside of the house shone like it was suitable for royalty. Or as royal as you could get in Varennes.

A reporter for the Anderson newspaper came out for a tour and wrote a short piece about it. The line I remember was "Capt. Wm. Jones continues to enlarge and beautify his already handsome residence by the addition of porticos and verandas." It sounded so grand.

No sooner had we completed work on the house than Mama decided we needed new plants and flowers in the yard.

Papa added six pecan trees, two magnolia saplings, and several pear trees out front. He bought gardenia, camellia, and daphne bushes to go around the trees, and he planted three thorny but lovely rose bushes near the well house. Of course, he hired help for the heavier digging.

In the late fall and early spring, Mama and I dug little holes with lady-size trowels and dropped in bulbs. Once the danger of frost had passed, we scratched out flowerbeds and scattered seeds. I hadn't been that dirty since Bessie and I'd made mud pies on the creek's edge behind the church.

Our efforts soon sprang to life in the colors of a painter's palette—burgundy and gold from irises, white and red from gladiolus, a glorious array of greens from stems and leaves. For the first time in my life, I began to understand why Papa and Mama so loved the land and treated it like holy ground. I became blissfully lost in the seasons of planting and growing, harvesting and planting again.

Two springs later, our yard was well established. Delicate white hyacinths, buttercup daffodils, and lavender crocuses burst out overnight. Strawberry plants were already spreading, and the daphne bushes smelled like honeysuckle and lemons.

One morning, Bessie and I strolled through the yard admiring our wealth of blooms. As I pointed out various flowerbeds, Feaster lurched ahead making his own discoveries with the abandon of a toddler. He wore light blue coveralls, and his blond hair flew out into a silky halo. Bessie always dressed him in light blue or white until he'd grown old enough to put a stop to it. And he was far from that age yet, still a mother's dream.

A yellow butterfly fluttered by us, low and lazy. Bessie pointed at it. "Thank the Lord," she said. "No late frost this year. Preston and Papa'll be happy."

I'd almost forgotten about yellow butterflies as good omens. When we were little, Papa would give us the task of spotting the first yellow butterfly each spring. Bessie would see one first, but she'd show it to me and then we'd run to the barn or wherever Papa was, shouting "yella butta-fy!" What joy to remember. That sunny moment took me back to childhood when my senses were just awakening and everything was new and sweet and good. I'd absolutely believed the yellow butterfly sign.

"Do you still believe in yellow butterflies?" I asked Bessie as she watched the boy.

"As much as any other omen, good or bad."

"You're starting to sound like Mama," I said. We both laughed.

"You look like her, and I sound like her. We could do worse."

We scanned the landscape as though Mama might have heard us. When we were young, she seemed everywhere at once. She still did. We laughed again. Like the early blossoms around us, I felt fresh and planted in a family I loved.

Then Bessie broke the mood. "Since the yard looks beautiful, you should have a garden party!"

I froze. I'd been so occupied with the house and yard that I hadn't thought about social outings. The only time I'd left home was to go to church, the Allens' farm, or town with Mama to get supplies. The thought of hosting an event left me cold. I took a step back, folded my arms, and shivered.

Bessie frowned. "Icie, you've gone barn-crazy just like Papa's old mules!"

She waited for me to respond. But I didn't. My heart had started to throb in my temples, and my cheeks flushed. The beauty of the morning began to fall away.

Her face softened. She touched my shoulder and said more kindly, "I'm sorry. Maybe the time isn't right yet." She let it drop and didn't broach the subject of a social event again until nearly a year later.

Early the following year, she had another idea that was more appealing. She and some other ladies came up with a plan to raise money for several churches in the community. They called themselves the Faith Alliance. They decided to put on a grand dinner followed by a concert at the Masonic Hall, an event unlike anything Varennes had seen since before the war. Those who could sing and play instruments or perform recitations would provide the entertainment. Others would prepare their tastiest dishes for the dinner.

Bessie and Preston had started going to Bethesda Methodist Church a few miles west of home. It was made of logs and not nearly as nice as the one Papa had helped build, but the congregation seemed devoted and happy to have new members.

I'd thought at the time that Bessie didn't appreciate the way some of the Cross Roads Baptist congregation looked at Baby Feaster, as though they were trying to make out his features and who his father might be.

Bessie and the Faith Alliance's grand event was to raise building funds for the Bethesda Church as well as to help purchase new musical instruments for Cross Roads Baptist and Good Hope Presbyterian.

The ladies scheduled the dinner and concert for early December so the men wouldn't be concerned with planting or harvesting or going to market. The entertainment was to be a mix of hymns and non-church tunes, dialogues, and recitations. The thought was a full belly and a little laughter would loosen the purse strings.

Bessie assured me that the members who'd left the Baptist church on my account weren't involved in the enterprise. She went on to say that the alliance wanted me, along with Rev. Wright's sister-in-law, Myrtle Murphy, to play the music. Bessie and I called her "the good widow" because that's how the reverend described her. Papa called her "the good widder."

I couldn't refuse such a worthy cause. But the thought of being in front of folks from all over the county made my stomach churn. I said so to Bessie. She acted like she didn't hear me. She handed me a new Cokesbury hymnal and a book of sheet music and asked me to pick out some lively songs that would be nice for a varied group of singers.

I spent afternoons at the piano in the front hall picking out new tunes. Every time I told Mama I'd come help with something, she'd tell me she'd rather hear me play. I found a dozen hymns and other songs I especially liked, some simple enough for the good widow to play. Then Bessie, Myrtle Murphy, and I sat down and chose eight for the concert.

As for our choral group, we knew plenty of ladies and a few men in the community who could sing fairly well. We just didn't have many solo voices. The talent was probably there, but most folks were more concerned with cultivating crops and children than their musical abilities.

I'd had time to develop a solo voice, but I told Bessie right from the start I didn't want to be in front of the chorus at any time during the concert. I'd be happy to work hard behind the scenes and to play my heart out, but not to stand centerstage. She reluctantly agreed and that was that.

But Myrtle Murphy didn't have any qualms about being up front. In fact, she set about choosing her solo parts. The problem was that she sang like she played, adequate at best.

For the concert we did have some prospects for the solo parts. Preston's niece Allie had a beautiful voice. She wasn't a member of any of the churches in Varennes, but she visited often and was accepted as part of the Allen family. Several of Sallie's children also had pretty voices.

So as Myrtle Murphy picked out songs she might sing solo, Bessie gently maneuvered around her saying, "Yes, but that would be perfect for Allie. Preston would be so proud that he might give an extra donation."

Or, "Sallie Seigler works so hard and delivers so many babies for the community. Wouldn't it be fitting for her daughter Lillie to sing the solo part of that gracious song?"

And so it went until we got to the last selection, the Goodnight Song.

For the final performance, we chose "I Bid Thee Goodnight" from the new Cokesbury hymnal. The lyrics were simple but lovely.

Sleep on beloved, sleep and take your rest;
Lay down your head upon the Savior's breast.
I love you well, but Jesus loves you best,
Goodnight, goodnight, goodnight. Lord,
I bid you goodnight, goodnight, goodnight.

The song wasn't difficult to play, so we thought the good widow could handle it. I would sing with the chorus. But when she played it for us, it sounded more like a funeral dirge than a happy farewell to end the concert. Bessie kept asking her to speed it up a bit until it sounded like a call to arms, or as Bessie put it, "an effort to rally the troops."

This went on and on. But hearing it over and over in all sorts of tortured versions made me realize that it didn't have any difficult high notes.

At last I said, "Mrs. Myrtle, why don't I play the Goodnight Song so you can sing one of the verses solo?" I wouldn't look at Bessie, but I could feel her stare burning my forehead.

The good widow considered it for at least a few seconds and said, "Well, yes, I'll do my part." She seemed refreshed as she set about deciding which verse would be hers alone.

After she left, Bessie said, "Well, Icie, we just traded a winding path to the Bad Place for the flaming pits of Hell!"

I didn't respond. I settled onto the piano stool and started playing my own version. After hearing it so many times, I couldn't say that my version sounded right either. But I kept at it until I realized that it needed strings. My nephew Dolph, a self-taught picker, was rehearsing with the quartet on the front porch. He was only a few years younger than me so he seemed more like a cousin than a nephew.

When the quartet finished practice, I asked Dolph to get his parlor guitar and to strum the melody. The change was immediate. And after a few tries with both the guitar and piano, "I Bid Thee Goodnight" became magical, transformed from a cold choppy hymn to a warm embracing folk song.

Years later, I would hear Red and his choir sing their version of the Goodnight Song—under much different circumstances— their voices both weary and hopeful in a soulful contradiction.

The best cure ❀

"I Bid Thee Goodnight" turned out to be the best song in the concert. But it didn't go as planned. Not at all. In fact, the good widow exacted a measure of revenge on the rest of us.

As the early rehearsals began in February, Mama decided I must have a new dress for the grand event. She was a wonderful seamstress, much better than I was, although I was adequate at needlepoint, crochet, and knitting. I could hem well enough, too. In fact, I'd hemmed all the new curtains in our house. But my dressmaking attempts were the stuff of nightmares.

Mama announced to Papa more than to me, "Icie must have a new dress for the concert." They were in the kitchen, and I was in the dining room setting the table for dinner.

"Who's gonna make it? Icie shore as hell cain't," he said as though I couldn't hear him.

"I will," she said.

"Em'ly, your eyesight ain't what it used to be." I'm sure she gave him a cold look. "More important," he hurried on, "I need your help with the sharecroppers and whatnot."

Still nothing from Mama.

Papa cleared his throat. "Take her to that dressmaker woman at Brown & Osborne."

"What dressmaker?" she asked. Since I was still out of the conversation, I didn't offer anything.

"They got one from Pendleton," he said. "It was in the paper."

She didn't argue the point probably because she couldn't read the paper as closely as she once did. I thought it was ironic that Papa, who could barely read, was more informed than Mama. But I didn't share my observation.

"I suppose we could," she said, giving in. "We'll pick out the cloth though."

I rattled two plates together to make my presence known.

Mama called me into the kitchen. "We want you to have a new dress for the concert," she said, as though I'd been stone deaf and now miraculously healed. "What about black velvet for the skirt?"

"Black!" Papa shouted. "She ain't no widder."

Mama ignored him. "Fine distressed velvet."

"Distressed! What in the . . . ?" He stopped himself.

She looked at me. I wanted to smile but I didn't. She looked back at Papa. "Oh William! Distressed cloth means it has a design. It looks like lace over velvet."

Papa knew what lace was. He nodded slightly.

"And a satin bodice," she said.

"What color?" he asked.

"A deep cornflower blue." That's all she had to say because we both knew it was Papa's favorite color.

Going to Brown & Osborne for fittings was awkward at first. And having the seamstress measure me in my petticoat was downright embarrassing. But fairly soon she seemed more like an aunt. She and Mama got along well. She was kind and flattering, and she listened to me as much as she did to Mama.

She used deep blue satin for the bodice and black distressed velvet for the skirt. She added a black lace collar to the bodice and ran two rows of tiny pearl buttons from the bottom of the bodice to the top. She fashioned long, loose sleeves with soft cuffs at the wrists so I could maneuver the keyboard.

The skirt was flowing and dramatic, but we decided on a small bustle that wouldn't hang far over the back of the piano stool.

It turned out to be the most beautiful dress I would ever wear.

Papa wanted Mama to buy something new for herself, too. But she didn't take the time. I think she was too intent on getting me "gussied up"—Papa's term—as much for themselves as for me.

It gave me an idea. I decided I would buy the best yarn I could find and knit her a shawl as a surprise. The concert was in December so I wanted the wrap to be both warm and beautiful. I thought about some yarn I'd seen advertised, shipped all the way from England. Or maybe from Ireland. It was called cashmere, and it came from a special goat.

I knew that ordering the yarn might take several months and a pretty penny too because I wanted it dyed blue like my dress. I would need to do all the knitting during rehearsals for the concert so Mama wouldn't see.

I talked to Bessie and she agreed. But I quickly realized I couldn't order anything expensive without Mama or Papa knowing. I had no money. It was a moment of self-realization like a needle to the thumb.

When I was growing up and wanted or needed something, I could ask for it or put it on Papa's tab at one of the stores. I had my own coins from time to time, but I usually spent them on birthdays and Christmas presents.

Mama had money at her disposal because she managed our household. Bessie had her own purse for the same reason. Obviously, I did not.

Bessie had a solution. She said that paying for the yarn would be her part in the surprise especially since I would be doing the knitting. That's Bessie. She has a knack for working things out and making others feel better. We ordered the yarn, and I stored the painful realization of dependency in the back of my mind.

Rehearsing in the Masonic Lodge soon began. I accompanied the solos and joined in the choruses. I helped several ladies learn their lines for the recitations—"Aunt Betsy's Beaux," "The Best Cure," and "My Country Aunt Goes to Town."

My nephew Dolph practiced with the quartet and helped with the men in the chorus. Susanna McGee, a whip-smart five-year-old, quickly learned a recitation called "A Household Fairy." She also sang solo in "We Are Little Travelers."

Rehearsals continued through summer and into fall, and I knitted between piano pieces as often as I could.

At the same time, other ladies planned the dinner—ham, turkey, chicken, beef, even oysters from Charleston, along with breads, vegetables, pickles, pies, and cakes. Dock, who had several general stores by then, volunteered his brand new warehouse along with tables and chairs for the dinner.

Concert practice rolled on right up to the week of Thanksgiving, which came late that year. It provided a good break for us all. Myrtle Murphy took time to visit relatives in Charlotte. She hadn't returned the following week as we were completing our last rehearsals. Even so, it was nice to have her out of the way for a bit while I concentrated on the music and Bessie made final plans for the dinner.

But when the good widow hadn't come back by the day before the concert, we began to worry. Rev. Wright was so worried that he rode the train all the way to Charlotte to escort her back. Bessie called it "divine intervention," and we were both relieved.

The afternoon of the concert, Bessie stopped by on her way to organize the food. Mama and Papa had left earlier to check on a family of sharecroppers. And I was doing my best to get into my new dress. It was not, however, a one-woman job. I'd managed the petticoats, the bustle and the full skirt, but the bodice was proving difficult. I'd started it over my head with my arms straight up, but had gotten stuck.

Bessie found me in my awkward state. She grabbed the bodice, unfastened a few more pearl buttons, and pushed it the rest of the way over my head and past my arms.

"Good heavens!" she said, "you could have suffocated!"

"I just about had it on," I said, smoothing the waist and trying to rebutton all those little pearls.

Bessie was dressed much more sensibly—no bustle, less of a skirt, and no tiny buttons. She read my mind. "I'll be dealing with fried chicken and gravy, not music. And you look pretty enough for the whole family."

Just then, we heard frantic knocking at the front door. Bessie hurried to open it. There stood a stricken Rev. Wright.

"The good widow would not return with me," he said, stepping inside. "She refuses . . ." His voice faltered. He tried again. "She refuses to come back to Varennes."

Bessie and I sucked in at the same time. Guilt washed over us. I caught my breath. "I'm so sorry!" I told Rev. Wright. "If I offended her, I never intended to."

Bessie chimed in. "We should have complimented her skills more than we did, showed more gratitude."

The reverend looked at us as though we'd lost our minds. "She met some fella at Thanksgiving dinner. I guess she fancies marrying him." He sounded inconsolable.

Bessie turned to me. "What will we do without her?"

"I don't know!" he sputtered before I could answer.

Normally Bessie and I would have been curious about the reverend's outpouring of emotion for his sister-in-law. But we didn't have the time.

"Thank you so much, Rev. Wright, for going all the way to Charlotte," Bessie said.

"And back," he added.

"All the way to Charlotte and back," she said, grabbing him by the arm and leading him out the door. "And for delivering the news, even if it's upsetting."

He nodded, clearly unable to speak at the moment.

She kept him moving across the porch and to the steps. "I'm sure you and your dear wife will be just fine. And Mrs. Myrtle Murphy will be ever so happy."

He started to regain his voice, but Bessie didn't wait to see what he might say.

"Thanks again and good day," she said, quickly retreating into the house and closing the door with a thud. She turned to me, her face pale.

"I can play all her pieces," I said with lukewarm confidence. Then I repeated it, realizing that I really could.

"What about the Goodnight Song? The third verse that the widow was to sing solo?"

"Allie can sing it," I said quickly.

"Allie hasn't practiced it or memorized the lyrics," she said. "You'll have to sing it. You know all the verses. You could sing it in your sleep."

I didn't say anything for the moment, but my heart began to pound. I felt faint.

Dolph had come into the front hall by then and caught part of the conversation.

"I have to play it on the piano," I protested. "I can't sing a solo part upfront and play at the same time. The stage isn't set up for it and neither am I."

Bessie seemed desperate. She looked from me to Dolph and back to me. "It's the most important part of the concert because it's the final song. It has to be special. You have to sing the solo."

I shook my head. "I can't just get up from the piano and sing a verse with no accompaniment, even if I wanted to."

"I'll accompany you," Dolph offered.

Bessie looked hopeful.

"We'll do the first and second verses as intended, with both of us playing," he suggested. "Then you can get up from the piano and join me out front. I'll play the third verse while you sing solo." He caught his breath. And before I could object, he added, "Then I'll lay down my guitar and we'll all sing the last verse a cappella."

Bessie was nodding. "It'll be a good way to let the audience know you've put away your instruments and it's time to go home."

By then, we had no more time to make plans. Dolph and I headed to the Masonic Hall to set up for the concert. Bessie left for the warehouse to organize the dinner. We were in such a hurry that I almost forgot about Mama's new shawl. It had turned out just as I hoped. I'd knitted it in a simple pattern to let the wonderful yarn outshine the stitch. I left a note that said, "A mother as beautiful as a butterfly deserves a new cocoon. Love and adoration from your daughters." I placed the note and shawl on her and Papa's bed. The night would be chilly so I knew she'd need it.

Suddenly, I realized I didn't have a wrap to go with my new dress. And I certainly wasn't going to wear the gray shawl of shame. I spotted one of Papa's shirts thrown across a chair. I grabbed it up, hoping it wasn't meant for the wash, and wrapped myself in it. I rolled up the sleeves as I ran for Dolph's buggy. He pulled me in, and off we went.

Centerstage ↭

The Masonic Hall was a large building with a raised stage in the back. A piano had been placed onstage for the concert months

earlier. Because there was no curtain, the music itself would sig-
nal an imaginary curtain for each part of entertainment.

By the time Dolph and I arrived, several of the men had
already packed the hall with chairs almost up to the stage. I
checked to make sure the music sheets were in order, and Dolph
did likewise for the quartet's songs. As soon as we were satisfied
we could do no more, we rode to the warehouse and joined the
diners.

I've never before nor since seen so much food. Tables and
tables of it. Wonderful meaty smells of ham and fried chicken
with less wonderful smells of smoked oysters and chitlins. The
sweet aromas of yeast rolls and cornbread and every type of
dessert imaginable from fruit pies and ambrosia to blackstrap-
molasses cookies and Aunt Lou's legendary pound cakes.

The warehouse was filled with overlapping voices—so many
people inside and others outside waiting to go in. Bessie managed in her best boss-lady manner—kindly giving orders and
hurrying people along. I stood back and watched as though the
dinner were the show itself. I couldn't eat, but I enjoyed the
sights and sounds of joyful diners, cordial conversations, and
bursts of laughter.

Dolph had no trouble eating dinner. When it was time for us
to return to the Masonic Hall, he climbed into the buggy with
a handful of cookies.

Soon diners began surging into the hall and quickly filling
all but a few reserved seats. The chorus and other performers
gathered on the right side of the stage. Bessie hurried in from
the dinner still wearing an apron. When it was time to begin,
the chorus moved out front between the audience and the piano.
I took my seat and straightened the music. Just as I lifted my

hands to begin, I realized I was still wearing Papa's shirt. I jumped up from the bench, hoping my bustle wouldn't hang, and rushed off stage.

Bessie looked horrified. I pulled off the shirt, pushed it in her arms and whispered, "Don't worry! I won't let you down." And back out I went.

I began playing "Gathered Once More," the imaginary curtain went up, and we let our rehearsing take over. I felt strangely calm, even when I played songs the good widow was supposed to have played.

The event went beautifully. The songs, the dialogues, everything. Allie hit all her notes, little Susanna melted hearts with her recitation, the men especially liked the quartet, and all the pieces sounded better than in rehearsal.

I began to feel like I belonged to something larger than myself. It was an exhilarating state that lasted almost throughout the concert. Until the final song. The Goodnight Song. Where my fingers had been calm, they suddenly trembled. My heart rose into my throat. But I managed to play the first and second verses well enough for the singers and Dolph to carry on.

Then it came time for me to sing the third verse myself. Solo. In front of the entire audience. The town. The first family.

Dolph looked at me and nodded. I felt paralyzed. He nodded again, this time more urgently. My body pushed back from the piano and stood as though it was controlled by someone else. My throat was so tight I didn't think I could get out a single note. I focused on Dolph who was holding out his hand. When I reached him, I looked out over the field of blurry faces. I wanted to run for cover, but Dolph gripped my wrist.

Then, as though a gift from above, I spotted a tall man with a bundle of cornflower blue next to him—Mama and Papa. I knew I was singing for them and Bessie, for the second family, for whatever purpose we had in this town and on this earth.

I opened my mouth and let the song flow out. I almost didn't recognize my voice. It sounded distant, independent of vocal cords, better than my own voice could possibly be. By the time Dolph put down his guitar and the whole chorus sang the last verse a cappella, I could see that Papa had jumped to his feet, applauding. The rest of the audience followed.

It was the best night of my life.

Folks in the audience made their way to the stage and waited their turn to tell each of us how much they enjoyed the concert. Even half-sister Sallie, who was pregnant again, gave me a thick hug and said, "Well done, Icie. Now I see where your talents lie." I took it as a compliment.

The Faith Alliance dinner and concert was a financial success, too. We earned enough for a new organ for Cross Roads Baptist, a new piano for Good Hope Presbyterian, and a good chunk of building funds for the Bethesda Methodist.

The concert marked a change in my life—in the way I felt about my place in the family, both the Jones family and God's much larger one. I realized that I'd been in mourning since I'd given birth to Feaster. As happy as I was for Bessie and Preston, something in my own life had died—the person I'd been. Right then and there, I put away my mourning dress, even if it had been only in my mind, and started living again.

Mama used to say, "Good times don't last, but neither do the bad." Or maybe it was the other way around. Either way, my life improved for the better. I had my beloved place back playing hymns for church. Only this time, I did so on a new organ and with a wage.

It was Bessie's idea. She said, "Icie, you need to have your own money. The church should pay you."

"What!" I shrieked.

"The organist at the church we went to in Lowndesville got paid by the month," she continued as though I didn't look shocked. "Come to think of it, that lady earned the same amount whether there were four or five Sundays in the month. You'll need to get paid by the Sunday."

"I don't think I could ask for money," I said, feeling flushed at the thought. "I wouldn't even know who or how to ask."

"Rev. Wright," she said emphatically. "But don't ask him— tell him—kindly of course. Let him know that other churches would welcome your skills at the keyboard."

When I didn't respond, she went on, "You're in demand now. It's high time that the fine Cross Road folks came to realize your musical skills are valuable. Bethesda or Good Hope would love to have you." This time she waited for me to answer.

"I don't think he'd be willing, much less the congregation."

Bessie caught her breath. "He saw to it that Myrtle Murphy got paid."

I was too surprised to say anything at first. After a moment, I sputtered, "What? Are you sure?"

She nodded.

"How do you know?"

"While you were out, he told the church that the good widow was supporting herself and needed a wage. The majority of the congregation agreed." Bessie smiled and added, "I doubt Papa did."

"Why didn't anyone tell me?" I felt foolish and annoyed at the same time.

"You had enough on you already. Anyway, she got half a

dollar a Sunday." She let that sink in and added, "You'll need at least seventy-five cents. Maybe a dollar."

A weekly wage started to appeal to me.

"Make it a dollar a Sunday," she declared, "with additional fees for special services and programs. And you should collect your dollar before the service begins. You'll want to tithe."

I began to consider it. Then I thought about my folks. "What about Papa? I don't want to embarrass him any more than I already have. Or the first family."

Bessie laughed. "Oh, Icie, I don't know about the first family, but Papa will be proud!"

And so I made my case to the reverend, and he complied. If the congregation objected, they never said so, not even Sallie and J. E.

Bessie was right about Papa, too. The first Sunday that I had the organ bench all to myself and a dollar in my purse, Mama said Papa walked into the church "grinning like a mule eating briars."

PART V

Things seen and unseen

Peaches ✿

It's morning and Anah has brought me a bowl of soft, sweet peaches, the first of the season no doubt. I haven't thought about summer until just now. My second season of peaches in this sorry state. Peaches first. Then baked apples. Then boiled custard. Now peaches again. Outside my window, the black walnut tree is flush with green. It's summer—both under the clear blue sky and in the spoon Anah holds to my lips.

The new decade started well for my family. By 1891, Feaster had turned five and grown into a little whirlwind of energy with hair the color of sand. Mama described his hair as "tow-head blond." He was a mother's dream. Or an aunt's dream, depending on how you looked at it.

He clearly thought of Bessie and Preston as his parents. And no one corrected him. He was as strong-willed as the rest of the Joneses, which got him into trouble from time to time. In fact, Red, who worked for Bessie and Preston, rescued Feaster from an angry bull.

Bessie had been supervising dinner preparations when Red led Feaster by the hand onto the back porch and called her to the door. "Mizz Bessie," he announced, "Mr. Feaster done been chasin' Mr. Preston's bull."

She pulled them both into the kitchen. "Why on earth were

you chasing the bull?" she shouted. When Preston heard Bessie, he scraped his chair back from his desk in the hall and hurried into the kitchen.

"He hurt the cows!" Feaster cried in high-pitched protest. "He jumped on their backs!"

Bessie looked at Red, who looked down and said, "Mr. Feaster tried to chase him off. But the bull, he turn on Mr. Feaster."

"Thank God you saw him," she said. And to Preston, "You'd best have that talk about where calves come from."

She told me later that as she watched Preston and Feaster walk down the steps and toward the barn, she knew it was one of those Jesus-God moments, but she didn't know whether to laugh or cry.

After the bull incident, Preston called Feaster "the Little Rooster," and Bessie said he wasn't afraid of the devil himself. I thought they should rein him in a little, but it wasn't up to me.

Feaster didn't chase the bull again. But he did decide to ride Big Boy, Preston's high-stepping bay gelding, with neither permission nor assistance. One day not too long after the bull incident, while Preston and Red were in the barn repairing stalls, Feaster made his move.

We all knew how Big Boy loved peaches. He'd wrap his lips around the fruit, bite it into pieces, and roll out the pit with his long, thick tongue.

That day, while the men were distracted, Feaster gathered a few peaches, stuffed them into a small peanut sack, and climbed onto the paddock fence. Then he lured Big Boy alongside the fence where he was perched. While the horse munched on peaches, Feaster slipped onto his back, grabbed two little fistfuls of mane, and urged him to the far end of the paddock.

Red saw him first. "Look-a there, Mr. Preston. Mr. Feaster's a ridin' Big Boy."

The next week Preston bought Feaster a sure-footed mountain pony. A small fine-boned pinto as spirited as the boy. Preston set about teaching Feaster to ride properly with English cavalry tack and with his hands holding nothing but the reins. He was a natural in the saddle.

⟶ ⟵

The Allens' farm had grown into what people still called a plantation. Papa had sold Preston more Jones property, and the Allens had been quick to buy adjoining land whenever it came up for sale. They'd amassed nearly 2,000 acres. Preston had built eight more tenant houses, a new carriage house, and several other outbuildings. And his current crop looked to be a record setter.

In fact, the Anderson newspaper ran a feature on Preston Allen's farming practices, calling him "a self-made man," and "perhaps, the most successful grower in the upcountry due to his progressive ways."

The article didn't say so, but Preston conducted his affairs by what Bessie called his Masonic principles. To my best understanding that meant applying science to farming, generosity to his workers, and charity throughout the community.

The only criticism of Preston I'd ever heard was that he was too generous to his help. As a result, his sharecropper families often saved enough to buy their own small plot of land elsewhere and become independent farmers. But plenty of other families were eager to take their place on Allen land. He was able to get the best day workers, too, and avoid using convict labor.

The thorny issue of convict labor persisted beyond clearing land and laying railroad tracks. Since the war, growers who couldn't find enough day workers to take care of crops at peak times leased convicts from the county. The person doing the leasing was responsible for food and shelter during the work period. Some of the larger farmers set up camps on their property near the work site where they could lock up the prisoners at night.

Their investments were large, and so were their expectations. To make matters worse, sometimes freedmen worked alongside the convicts and stayed in the camps where they were locked up at night, too.

Papa said those freedmen agreed to be there. But Mama said they didn't know what they were agreeing to, since most couldn't read, and it was only one step away from slavery.

Thanks to Mama, Papa never used convict labor even though he said he'd needed at times when he was clearing land for the railroad tracks. Preston didn't use convict labor either because he had plenty of men willing to work hard for the best wages around.

So life was going well for the Allens. That is, until catastrophe struck. And it wasn't caused by convicts. At least, not directly.

It had been a typically hot July. Our peaches were smaller but sweeter than usual from the lack of rain. Mama had spread out several dozen on the kitchen table where their heavenly scent filled the house.

That particular night, I remember seeing the vague outline of a new moon in an otherwise coal-black sky. A small breeze had picked up at bedtime making sleep come quicker for our household. Then around 3 a.m., a great commotion arose in the direction of the Allens. We rushed outside to see flames leaping on the far side of the main house.

Still in our bedclothes, we ran straight there. We found Preston's new carriage house engulfed in fire with flames shooting out toward the house.

Papa joined the large group of men already slinging water. Mama and I found Bessie and Feaster at a safe distance outside. Bessie was shouting, "No, Feaster, you can't go to the barn! I need you here!"

She seemed relieved to see us. She said that Red had seen the flames about the same time she and Preston had awakened to a houseful of smoke. Once everyone was out, Red had run to get help from men living on the place.

The two-story building held a carriage, several buggies, and the bulk of Preston's tools. It also stored more than a dozen barrels of flour along with a year's worth of hams, bacon, and other provisions. And worst of all, it was next to the main house.

The Allens had several wells near the carriage house, so the men quickly manned each and did their best with buckets and pumps and wet croker sacks. When it became apparent that the carriage house was doomed, they turned their attention to soaking the ground next to the house. It took several hours and near depletion of the wells, but the Allens' house was saved by sheer manpower. "And the grace of God," Mama was quick to add.

Dawn was breaking by the time the fire was out. Preston went to each volunteer firefighter, said something, and shook his hand. Then he, Papa, and Red joined us in the front yard where the air was easier to breathe. The men were drenched in sweat and streaked in soot.

Bessie hugged Preston long and hard. Then she asked what was on all our minds, "How'd it start?" Before Preston could answer, Red let go a string of swear words I couldn't quite make out.

Bessie covered Feaster's ears and looked at Preston. But Preston was as angry as I'd ever seen him. His square jaw seemed thicker and sharper. "I'd love to get my hands on that sorry bastard!" he said through clenched teeth. "I'd beat the life right out of him!"

Bessie held Feaster tighter. "We can build another carriage house."

"Jesus Christ! It's not the damn carriage house! It's the fact that we could've burned up." His face was so contorted I thought he would spit or throw up. "Of all the outbuildings on this place, it was the one closest to where we lay sleeping!"

"How do you know it was set?" Mama asked. She tightened her hands around the neck of her robe and leaned against Papa.

"Kerosene," Papa said. "You can smell it all along the far wall."

"Why on earth would anyone set such a fire?" I asked, too naive at the moment to realize someone might be spiteful toward the Allens.

Preston spoke up, somewhat calmer. "It had to do with wages, I'm pretty sure. Goddamn wages!"

Red nodded in agreement. Papa seemed less convinced. "Least ways it wadn't the barn."

Whatever the reason for the fire, the main house had been saved.

The carriage house fire happened not too long before cotton-picking time. That season, Preston increased pay to his day workers, got his crop harvested in record time, and set up a night watch on his outbuildings until his crop had gone to market. Once again he had the first bale to hit the scales in Anderson, and it brought a record price.

Odd how a little peach can hold a world of memories. One taste and an entire summer rushes back.

Schoolyard ⌁

The next few years rolled by without incident. Papa and Mama stayed well, and Preston had no more fires to put out. None that I knew of.

Feaster started school and took to his studies like a duck on a pond, as Mama said. He could explain the life stage of a tadpole in one breath and recite the Ten Commandments in the next. And he easily made friends along the way.

Bessie stayed busy with the books, the household, and Feaster, yet she still found time to volunteer at church and in the community. Preston did likewise, including his due diligence as a county leader and his service through the Masons. Little wonder they were among the most popular couples in the county and in constant demand for social events.

I regained some confidence in socializing myself. Several of the young men in Varennes must have thought it was safe to come around again. And so they did. I'll admit I enjoyed their company although I saw no reason for anything beyond a daylight stroll, a dance, maybe a picnic. Nothing more. Most came and went.

But one in particular, Willis McGee, kept coming back. His family had been in Varennes before my Grandpa Jones had come here from Greenville to open a store. The McGees had served alongside the Joneses during the war, and Willis's father, Col. Jesse, had been one of the main forces in getting Wade Hampton elected governor. The McGees had large farms in the area with some acreage near ours and some along the Savannah River.

Bessie and I'd gone to school and grown up with many a McGee. In fact, my half-sister Mattie had married Franklin McGee, one of Willis's kinfolk. And my half-brother Dock had married Franklin's sister Sarah McGee.

Willis McGee was my age. He was handsome, smart, and quick-witted. He had a thick, tawny mustache and the prettiest eyes I'd ever seen. They were green with traces of blue and little flecks that caught the light. I hadn't seen the ocean, but Willis's eyes were the color I imagined it to be. Mama said the color came from his Irish ancestors. She lumped the Scotch and the Irish into one.

He could've had most any lady's heart in the county. Why he kept coming back was a mystery to me and probably to the rest of Varennes. But I didn't mind. So my little life was going well along with the rest of the second family.

Soon, however, one of Mama's sayings came true—the one about "Bad times don't last, but neither do the good." When it did, it had nothing to do with Willis McGee. And everything to do with Feaster. As much prestige and power as the Allens had in Varennes, they couldn't keep Feaster sheltered from life beyond the farm. And so it happened in grade school when he was around seven.

It was a late Friday afternoon, more than two years after the fire. Papa had gone to town, and Mama was in the kitchen baking a pie. I sat on the front porch with some knitting on my lap when I spotted Bessie rushing along the cart path that ran between our houses. She held her skirt up with one hand and thrashed the air with the other.

I jumped to my feet and called Mama outside. By the time Bessie reached the porch, she was nearly out of breath. She looked stricken.

"What on earth's the matter?" Mama asked, rubbing doughy hands on her apron.

Bessie caught her breath and dropped her skirt back into place. "It's Feaster!"

"What happened?" Mama shrieked. "Is he hurt?"

"No," Bessie replied, "not physically."

Mama let out a sigh. "Then what?"

"Feaster came home from school about an hour ago all upset." She paused. Mama and I waited. Then her words tumbled out like rocks. "Someone at school said Preston and I aren't his real parents."

I felt the blood drain out of my face.

"What did you tell him?" Mama asked.

Bessie looked like she might cry. "The truth—that Preston and I love him like a son."

I couldn't speak, but Mama asked for both of us, "Did you tell him who his mother is?"

"I didn't have to. Whoever told him that I'm not his 'real' mother also told him that Icie is."

"What did he say?" I asked. My voice sounded like it was coming from outside my body.

Bessie looked from me to Mama then down at the planks in the porch. "He asked, 'Who's my father?'" No one spoke for what seemed an eternity. The blood rushed back into my face and set my cheeks on fire.

Then she said, "I told him I didn't know."

I began collapsing from inside. I fell back into my chair.

The guilt I'd felt when I'd shamed my family came back tenfold. And for the very first time I began to realize what pain I'd laid upon a child.

"I know what you're thinking, Icie," she quickly added. "Now, stop it!"

Mama chimed in. "People make mistakes, but the good Lord doesn't." She grabbed my hand. "God gave us that child, and you've allowed him to have the best life possible."

Bessie grabbed my other hand. "We'll get through this."

"We should've prepared for this long ago," she added, looking at Mama. "Yes, you warned me often enough!" Evidently I hadn't been included in such discussions. I wondered if Preston had.

"The horse is out of the barn now," Mama said.

I couldn't look at either one of them. "Where's Feaster?" I asked through tears.

"I sent him out to take care of his animals until Preston got home." She took a deep breath and smoothed her skirt. "After he disappeared in the barn, Preston rode up. I told him what happened."

"What did Preston say?" Mama asked.

"He said for me to come here and stay while he and Feaster have a man-to-man talk."

I knew whatever Preston told him would be wise and loving, but I didn't know if it would be enough. I wondered what other child could be so mean-spirited as to tell him. Maybe the offspring of whoever set fire to the carriage house. Or maybe a cousin.

Regardless, I had to do what I hadn't done for years—think about Alexander from the Lowcountry all over again. I'd long given up on seeing him again, much less his coming back to claim his son.

In fact, by the time I'd realized for certain that I was pregnant, there'd come a terrible storm to Charleston and the surrounding area. Our newspaper had called it a cyclone. Its wind and water had nearly demolished the Charleston Battery that he'd talked about. The newspaper reported that the damage exceeded one and a half million dollars. I couldn't imagine that much money much less the destruction it represented. At the time, I'd worried that Alexander might have suffered great loss or even death. What a fool!

Then, the following year, about eight months after Feaster's birth, a fierce earthquake had shaken Charleston loose from its foundation. The great quake and several smaller ones over the next few days had brought more destruction to the grand old city than the war had. According to the newspaper, it'd struck indiscriminately both the rich and the poor. It had toppled mansions and shanties, churches and brothels, and anything else within its reach.

By the end of Charleston's second great catastrophe, I'd changed my mind about Alexander from the Lowcountry's survival. In fact, I hoped he *had* suffered great loss. Even death. And that's where I'd willed him to remain, buried in the rubble of his beloved city, and dead to Feaster and me. I'd vowed never to let him back into my heart. Or my mind.

But how does one explain that to a seven-year-old? Or a seventeen-year-old for that matter, let alone the fact that I didn't even know his father's last name. I'd briefly considered creating a story, perhaps a dramatic tragedy like those Aunt Eliza had told me. If the war had still been raging, I could've said how he'd served the South, perhaps a flag-bearer like Uncle James, and that he'd fallen trying to save a fellow soldier. Or I could have imagined him to be like Great Aunt Arabella's husband, to have succumbed to disease in the final months of the war and buried somewhere in an unmarked grave.

But the war had ended before I was born, and there wasn't any other war to bury him in. No, not even the truth would do after all this time. I was stuck with silence. I saw no other way.

Feaster soon quit saying he was "Feaster Allen." He quit calling Bessie and Preston "Mama" and "Papa" and started calling them "Aunt Bessie" and "Uncle Preston." It must have hurt them something fierce, but they didn't complain.

As for me, he called me nothing. He refused to acknowledge my presence, and he began avoiding me like the plague. I truly believed that God had forgiven me. I knew my family had, at least the second family. But I wondered if Feaster Ithamar Jones ever would. I opened a gash in the boy's heart that never seemed to heal completely. Like Papa's war wound, it closed up on the outside but festered from time to time on the inside. At least toward me.

Sometimes now when Bessie visits me, I think Feaster comes with her. If he does, I'm sure it's because she insists. I don't actually see him, but I sense his uneasy presence as he leans against the wall near the door. Or maybe I only imagine him here, his pain lingering in the shadows.

Tomcat ❧

Feaster's anger at Bessie and Preston didn't last long. But I was another matter. As he got older, he was civil to me on account of Bessie, but that was all. I never let myself expect more.

Luckily, Mama and Papa were still his grandparents and his feelings toward them didn't change. Nor their love for him. He was Mama's only grandchild, and she showed it.

Papa had lots of grandchildren by the time Feaster was born, but he too seemed to favor the boy. It was much the same way he'd favored Sallie and J. E.'s son Jackson. He'd taught Jackson to shoot a rifle and took him hunting whenever J. E. would let him. It was like Mama and Papa had their own little boy. At least until he reached that age where he'd rather spend what little leisure time he had with his friends.

When that day came, Feaster was old enough to take his place. In fact, Papa taught him to shoot a rifle when he was six. By the time he was eight, his aim was dead-on. Pistol shooting, however, was Preston's domain. He and Feaster culled potatoes and turnips from the root cellar and used them as targets. They lined up the hapless vegetables on the ground at first. And as Feaster got better, Preston threw yams and turnips in the air as moving targets. Sometimes Papa got in on the action with his rifle.

Eventually, Bessie had enough of the gunfire and put a stop to it. She told the men, "You've got Feaster shooting so much the hens are afraid to lay and I can't hear myself think."

Papa soon came up with something else for Feaster—and a way to get back into Bessie's good graces—a beautiful little kitten. It was brindle, yellow, and white. He said he'd found it all alone in the pasture.

When he brought it in to show Mama and me, she said, "The boy doesn't need another critter. A stray critter at that."

Papa said, "It ain't a stray, it's the pick of the litter."

"Pick of the litter? All alone in the pasture?"

Papa quickly corrected himself. "I meant it was probably the pick of the litter 'fore it got left all alone." He smiled at Mama. "You wouldn't want me to leave it to be trampled on, or get eat up by a fox." He held the kitten out to her.

She took it and cradled it in the crook of her arm like a baby. "The boy won't have time to study for taking care of his menagerie," she said, her voice softening.

"Barn cats take care of theirselves," he said. "They's mice enough and they drink outta the cow trough."

Mama handed the kitten back to Papa. He stroked its head with two fingers. "Besides, Red Jones is Feaster's shadow. He makes sure the boy's critters get fed."

Mama and I went with Papa to deliver the kitten. At first Feaster held it like it might break. But he soon flopped down on his belly so the kitten could pad around on the ground. Then he rolled onto his back and put the kitty on his chest. He was clearly smitten. He didn't even seem to mind that I was watching.

"Is it a boy or a girl, Grandpa?" he asked.

"A girl kitty most likely 'cause she's got three colors," Papa said. "God made her extra fancy."

He was right on both accounts. The kitten was female, and Feaster named her Fancy. But he was wrong about her being a barn cat. She may have slept in the barn, but she enjoyed a fine diet of bread and milk and meat scraps straight from a china bowl on the back porch.

She quickly grew into a beautiful cat. And as grown female cats do, she attracted an assortment of tomcats. Soon, to no one's surprise except maybe Feaster's, she became bloated with kittens. Since there was no putting it off, Preston used Fancy's bellyful of kittens as an opportunity to let the boy witness birth close up.

Red gathered some scrap wood and nailed together a low-sided box for Fancy's bed. Feaster filled it with clean straw and added a towel from the linen closet. They placed the box on the back porch next to her bowl and settled Fancy into it. Feaster checked on her obsessively. And the night she delivered the kittens, he and Preston stayed up until early morning watching Fancy push out and lick clean four wet squirming kitties.

Preston said experiencing birth through the eyes of a child reminded him just how miraculous and blessed life is. Papa's gift became even more special.

But as beautiful as nature is, it can turn ugly in the space of a breath. Not long after Fancy had her kittens, Mama, Papa, and I went to the Allens' house for a visit. Papa and Preston were walking the field closest to the house, Red was in the barn taking care of Papa's buggy horse, and Bessie, Mama, and I were in the kitchen talking about something that didn't matter. Feaster made an excuse and hurried outside, perhaps, because I was there.

All of a sudden we heard the terrifying squalling of a cat-fight. Feaster ran back inside and shouted that something had killed two of the kittens. He bolted toward Bessie and Preston's bedroom. We hurried onto the porch and saw Fancy trying to fight off a big gray tomcat. Two of her kittens lay dead, one half-eaten. It was a horrifying sight. Red ran out of the barn and toward the tomcat, which picked up a dead kitten and started down the cart trail. By then Feaster had run back outside holding Preston's pistol in both hands.

The tomcat trotted down the path until it was about thirty feet away. Feaster yelled at it. Instead of running faster, it made the mistake of stopping and looking directly at him. Before we knew what happened, Feaster raised the pistol, took aim, and dropped the tomcat where it stood.

When Preston and Papa heard the shot, they ran up from

the field. "What happened?" Preston yelled in Bessie's direction, but she was clearly speechless. Mama and I were, too.

"Mr. Feaster done shot him a bad tom," Red said, looking down at the dead cat. "Right 'tween the eyes."

Feaster was shaking. His blue eyes were rimmed in tears. The men asked him to repeat the story several times. They examined each dead kitten and the dead tom before Red took them off to bury. They told Feaster he'd done the right thing.

In the aftermath, they congratulated each other on fine marksmanship tutelage and adjourned to the front room. Feaster retreated to the porch to soothe Fancy and the surviving kittens. Bessie, Mama, and I returned to the kitchen.

"The men were clearly pleased," Bessie said.

"They were puffed up like peacocks," I added. I looked at Mama, thinking it was her turn to say something. I wished I hadn't.

She sniffed and said, "Pride goeth before destruction, and a haughty spirit before a fall." I didn't know if she was talking about Papa, Preston, or Feaster. And truth was I didn't want to know.

PART VI

Time and tide

Storm

This morning, I woke up to rain. I believe it will fall most of the day. I don't mind. I'll watch the raindrops roll down the pane. I've learned that each drop is unique, both in size and movement. Some pool together and hold onto the pane until their weight pulls them down in a wide, wet path. But others cling by themselves. Hold on longer. Then roll down leaving a small slender trail, taking their time as though they can stop at will.

Despite Mama's dire prediction after the tomcat incident, life continued without much drama. At least for a while. And when bad things started to happen, they had nothing to do with pride. The early 1890s were good years for most of the Joneses, both the first and second families. It was the quiet before the storm, "literally and figuratively" as Aunt Eliza would say.

Sallie had another baby, her eleventh. It would be her last. She'd borne seven by the time she delivered Feaster. And four more after him. Mama said she was trying to repopulate the South with Seiglers. But knowing Sallie and J. E., I'm sure it was part of their religion to go and bear fruit. They lived fairly close to us but seldom visited although we did see them most every Sunday in church.

My half-sister Mattie had a harder time than the rest of the first family. Even though she had healthy children, a respected husband in Franklin McGee, and a nice home near the Savannah River, Franklin had been ill for years with what Mama called "war nerves."

He'd served the Confederacy—Mattie would always say "with honor"—but he'd never gotten over the war. Two of his brothers had died on separate battle fields. A third had come down with the fever and died shortly after the war ended. Franklin was the only one to survive physically, but Mattie said he suffered from battlefield nightmares, waking up wall-eyed and soaked in sweat.

As a result, he spent long stretches at the mental hospital in Columbia. Mattie said it was a harsh place to visit and worse place to stay, but Franklin showed signs of hope from time to time. Their daughter had gotten married and started her own family. That left Mattie with her two older sons, Jones and Rube, to run the farm. Sallie's son Jackson was especially fond of his McGee cousins and would help them out when he could.

Then, in the spring of 1893, we heard reports of strange weather in Arkansas and Alabama. The men seemed more concerned than the women. And, at least to me, Arkansas and Alabama seemed a world away. By late May, farmers were talking about Georgia's odd string of rainstorms with hail. Still I don't think anyone on our side of the Savannah was prepared for what was about to come.

It started on a Sunday evening just at sunset. The sky turned green, and the air felt warm except for small pockets of cool air. Then the rain came. Mama and Papa seemed relieved. Papa said the clouds were emptying out and would lose their strength.

We went to bed. But sometime during the night, the wind picked up. I don't think any of us slept soundly. I heard something grinding in the distance. As I listened, it came closer. It sounded like the train I often heard in the night, only much louder, and barreling in the wrong direction.

At that moment Papa yelled, "Tornado!" I rushed into their bedroom. Mama was gathering quilts as fast as she could. I hurried back to my room and pulled the gunboat quilt off my bed. Papa pushed Mama and me into the inside corner of their room. He dragged the mattress off the bed and leaned it against the corner in front of us like a fort. He squeezed in with us and stuffed quilts around the openings.

The roar became deafening. It sounded like the Savannah Valley train had come off its tracks and was running full force across the upper part of our farm. Our walls shook. The floor creaked. Papa swore at the wind while Mama repeated the Lord's Prayer. Then as quickly as it had come, it was gone. We waited a while longer in case there was another one. By the time we pushed the mattress back and scrambled to our feet, dawn was just breaking.

Outside, all sorts of objects—clothes I didn't recognize, buckets, feeding troughs, pieces of fence posts—lay across the field and hanging in trees. Broken branches layered the yard. An old oak rested on its side, opening a jagged pit of dark earth where its roots had been. But a quick look around showed no major damage. The barn and outbuildings were intact. So were our tenant houses. The families living in them were terrified but unhurt.

The Allens hadn't been as lucky. We hurried to their property. The house was standing and so were Bessie, Preston, and

Feaster, to our immense relief. But the wind had ripped the roof off the barn, and more than 1,000 bundles of fodder were blown to bits.

That was only the beginning. As Papa and Preston surveyed the damage, they found that twenty of the older tenant houses were destroyed. Twenty! And tragically, in one of those, a collapsing wall had fallen on a child and his mother. Dr. Dean came quickly but couldn't save the child. He and Bessie did what they could for the mother, but she soon passed away too.

Later in the day, we learned the path and destruction of the tornado. It had blown through the upper part of Georgia heading east, some said three miles wide, where it killed several people. At Hartwell, it jumped the Savannah just below the Rock Mills area. Luckily its path was south of half-brother Sammy's home and north of Mattie's. Word was that it'd narrowed to a mile wide by the time it entered lower Anderson County.

It nearly destroyed Dock's home, badly damaged his barn, and leveled his outbuildings. The force had been so great that it'd driven a wagon spoke through a six-inch oak post. But mercy of all mercies, somehow his family had escaped.

And on it had gone, traveling east, blasting gins, barns, shops, and anything else in its path. It'd passed above our home. Then it'd hit Bessie and Preston's land full force. Everyone agreed it was a miracle that no one else died.

To this day I shiver when I hear a night train, remembering the mother and child crushed in darkness. I pray she never realized her loss. A bit of grace among the ruins.

Trouble in threes ⟋

Later that year, just as my folks were starting to get order back into their lives, word came that Mattie's husband, Franklin, had passed away in Columbia. The cause was never given, but I suppose a body eventually gives in to a sick mind. Franklin was brought home and buried in Cross Roads Cemetery. Sadness was weighed against unspoken joy that he'd been released from his hellish mental state. Mama said it was the loss of another good man to the war.

Little did we know then that we'd be back in the same cemetery in less than a year for a very different burial. It was in mid-June 1894, late in the day on a Saturday. Bessie, Preston, and Feaster had taken the train to Charlotte for the weekend.

Sallie and J. E. came by to invite us to Jackson's birthday party the next week. They seldom marked birthdays, but since he was turning seventeen and would be considered a man, Sallie wanted to do something special. It was a rare visit and pleasant surprise.

After they left, Mama and I sat on the front porch admiring the results of our flower planting. Papa had just taken to his chair to look at the newspaper. Then, out of the blue, we spotted Red running toward our house shouting, "Cap'um! Cap'um!" Papa put down the paper and hurried down the steps to meet him. We couldn't make out what they were saying, but Red's arms flew about like the wings of a trapped bird.

Papa turned and ran back up the steps. His face was ashen. "Jackson's missin'!" he shouted. "Him and Mattie's boys went seinin' down at the Savannah and now he's missin'! Red and me gonna look for him!" He ran to the barn and hitched up the mules. Red threw rope and grappling hooks into the back of the wagon, and they headed toward the river.

Mama and I got ourselves together and hurried to Mattie's house, which was about two miles away. When we got there, Mrs. Annie McGee, Mattie's mother-in-law, stood on the porch with Mattie, who looked to be in shock.

"What on earth happened?" Mama shouted before we reached the steps.

Mattie looked at her but didn't answer. Mrs. Annie said, "The boys, Rube and Jones, and Sallie's boy Jackson, they went to the river shoals about midday to seine. Then they decided to cool off and swim down the boat sluice."

Mattie shuddered. Mrs. Annie went on. "They musta jumped in together. Rube and Jones said they felt how bad the current was and climbed up on some rocks. But Jackson didn't."

No one spoke for a moment. Then Mama asked, "What happened to him?"

Mrs. Annie looked at Mattie and back at Mama. "Mattie's boys said he didn't come up. The men have gone to look."

"Where's Sallie?" I asked.

"Inside. J. E. brought her here so he could go searching. But she no sooner got here than she fainted dead away. She's in the front bedroom. I keep going back and forth between Mattie and her!"

Mama took over Mattie, and I rushed inside to Sallie. The room was hot and dark. I stood in the doorway until my eyes adjusted. Sallie was curled up on the bed facing the door, gripping a Bible. When she saw me, she sat straight up. "Anything?" she asked, her voice cracking.

She seemed to have aged by at least ten years. Her eyes looked battered. Her cheeks, splotchy. Her hair stuck out from her bun in tangled clumps. She searched my face.

I shook my head. I sat on the bed beside her and wrapped my arms around her. It was awkward. I expected her to pull away. She didn't. I was at a loss for my own words, so I recited the Lord's Prayer, then the 23rd Psalm, then every Bible verse I could pull from the thick summer air.

The search lasted until late that night. Georgia neighbors across the river joined in. The next morning just as dawn broke, they were back, raking the river and searching the banks. Then late Sunday morning, the Savannah gave up Jackson. The men carefully pulled his body to shore and brought him to the McGee house, still dripping from the river's dark water. Sallie dried his face, and the women wrapped him in quilts. When they were done, the men gently lifted him onto the bed of the Seiglers' wagon. They helped J. E. and Sallie climb into the front.

J. E. took the reins. Sallie leaned against him. Slowly they proceeded to bear Jackson home. Mama and I joined Papa and Red in our wagon and eased into the procession behind them.

My half-brother Johnny made the coffin. He knew it would be too hard for Papa. He said he'd started measuring and cutting as soon as he'd gotten word, and he'd stayed up all night finishing it. The next day Papa and I waited for him and the coffin at Brown's Ferry.

We stood in silence, except for the wash of water on the banks. I thought about the young Union soldiers ambushed by Mance Jolly's men more than twenty-five years earlier. I wondered if their spirits lingered.

I wondered the same for Jackson. I stared at the river, hoping for a sign—a dove, a cross, a butterfly—some offering from the river for taking such a fine young man. But the dark water flowed on as though nothing had changed.

'To be or not' ⌒

I dream that Willis and I are young again. We're dancing under an early summer moon outside the Masonic Hall. The party's inside, but Willis leads me outside and underneath two grand oaks strung with little lanterns. He's handsome. I'm pretty. We're in love.

He squeezes my hand and says, "Icie Jones, you know I'm crazy about you."

"Just how crazy?" I tease him in the moonlight.

He stops dancing, lets go of me, and takes a step back. "Enough to ask Capt. Jones for your hand," he says, looking down into my face.

It's a moment I've both hoped for and dreaded. I have no answer. But in the dream, no answer is needed. I step forward into his arms, and we dance throughout the night with the moon, the grand old oaks, and the flickering lanterns watching over us.

Jackson's death sucked the joy out of the rest of the summer. Fall's early cooling was a welcome change even if it meant winter's chill was coming soon.

I saw Willis McGee twice that fall. He came to call once to show me his new horse and buggy. It was a beautiful early October day. The leaves had started turning, and the maples already flamed out in yellow and orange. I was on the front porch when I saw him driving up. I didn't recognize him at first because of the new buggy. But once I could see the precise way he sat and held the reins, I knew it was Willis.

I walked down the steps to meet him. "What brings you here on this lovely autumn afternoon?" I asked.

He smiled and tipped his hat. "I've got me a new getup here. I thought you might take a ride and let me know if I paid too much." He smiled again. His eyes sparkled like water in the sunlight.

I admired the buggy. The body was a rich mahogany brown with a shiny black coating on the metal parts and the rims around the wheels. Thick brass filagree ran along the top edge of the dash. It gleamed in the afternoon sun.

"It's from the Rock Hill Buggy Company," he said, clearly proud of his new purchase. "I took the train there myself to see just how they put such a thing together. They've got their own blacksmiths, carpenters, painters and what not, right there on site." He caught his breath. "I came home with this one. I judged it to be the best."

He fixed the reins and stepped down to meet me.

By then I was admiring the new horse. He was dappled white with dark hooves and mane. A handsome horse, larger than the usual wagon horse but smaller than a draft. His new harness was thick and black with just a touch of brass trim.

"Did you get this big boy in Rock Hill, too?" I asked.

He rubbed the horse's forehead. "Nope. This fine fella came from Tennessee. He's a cross between a saddle horse and a draft."

I reached up to rub his neck. "What's his name?"

"Sugar 'cause he's sweet as sugar, just like me."

We both laughed as he led me to the step-up and lifted me gently into the buggy. He quickly joined me. And off we rode toward the center of Varennes. We passed the general store, the cotton gin, and several small shops. We turned at the Masonic Hall and rode past Cross Roads Baptist Church and the cemetery. We circled around and rode slowly back through town, laughing and enjoying the view from the new buggy.

Then, instead of turning toward my house on the return trip, Willis decided we should go to Dean Station a few miles north of Varennes. So we rode past Aunt Lou and Uncle Tyler's farm, past Mouchet Hill, and on to Dean Station. We stopped at the depot, gave Sugar some water, and let him rest a bit.

By the time we started back, the late afternoon sun had faded and the air had chilled. Willis pulled out a lap blanket from behind the seat, spread it across my knees, and drove us back to my house. I thought I could make out a star or two dimly shining in the waning light.

When we arrived, Willis jumped to the ground, tied Sugar, and came around to my side. As he helped me down, he leaned against me and gave me a kiss. His lips were soft and warm and welcome. It wasn't the first kiss he'd given me, nor would it be the last, but it was memorable just the same. Then he let me go, stepped back, and looked into my eyes. His eyes seemed as deep as the sea. My head took a minute or two to clear. I looked around and saw no one else. Still I imagined Mama at the window.

"Thank you for a delightful ride," I said, trying to sound normal.

He smiled. "So you think I spent my money wisely?" he asked, walking with me to the porch.

"Wisely and handsomely," I replied.

"Then you'd be willing to ride with me again soon?"

"I would. I truly would," I repeated as I reached the door.

He made a mock bow and jogged down the steps two at a time. He untied Sugar, hopped into his gleaming new buggy, and turned down the road toward the river. I watched him disappear, my heart aching with affection and apprehension.

I didn't see Willis again for almost a month. The next time was an early November morning, clearly cooler. This time Willis was driving a farm wagon pulled by two mules instead of the pretty buggy with the dappled Sugar. I walked out to meet him.

"Morning, Icie," he said.

"What are you up to, Mr. McGee, on this chilly morn?" I asked.

"I'm headed into Anderson for business and supplies. Don't worry, I'm not gonna ask you to ride all the way in this old wagon with me." He flashed a smile.

"Good," I said although I halfway hoped he would.

"But," he added, "what if I stopped by on the way home?"

"I'd be happy to make you a cup of tea," I answered, pleased at the thought of seeing him again.

"I just may have a surprise for you when I return," he said mysteriously. And before I could ask him what, he flipped the reins on the mules' backs and off he went.

The rest of the morning was a confused mix of excitement, curiosity, and a bit of something else, not dread exactly, just something. I steeped a pot of tea mid-afternoon in anticipation of his return. By late afternoon it was too strong to serve. I poured it out and put on a fresh pot. By dusk, the second pot was too strong. Still, I watched the road until darkness swallowed it completely.

Ultimately, I convinced myself that his business had kept him in town or he'd simply changed his mind about stopping by. I was disappointed, but in a small way I was relieved. That is, until a week later, when I found out what'd happened. I heard it from Bessie who got it from Preston.

Seems that Willis completed his business, had his mules shod, and loaded his wagon with supplies, just as he'd planned, by noontime. He'd stopped at the hotel for lunch with several other men before heading home. He'd then said his goodbyes and proceeded to climb onto the wagon bench. It wasn't clear if he'd touched the back of the mule to steady himself or if his hand slipped from the wagon dash as he was climbing up. But whatever the cause, the newly shod mule kicked him full-force in the left side of his head.

He fell sideways to the ground, his left eye bleeding profusely. Several men carried him back into the hotel and sent for the doctor. Fortunately, the doctor was in his office and came immediately. He said Willis's skull didn't appear to be caved in although he couldn't be sure. But he was certain that the left eyeball was ruptured and needed to come out. Willis refused. He said he'd stay the night at the hotel to rest and regain his senses and would drive home the following day.

But he couldn't drive the next day. Or the next. After several days of maddening pain, he gave in and let the doctor take out his left eye. The doctor said the pain should subside fairly quickly but that Willis would need time to heal before driving again. The day after that, his brothers came to get him and to take the other wagon home.

Bessie knew how I felt about Willis and told me as nicely as she could, but there was no avoiding the horror. She was quick to remind me that he could've been killed like Papa's youngest brother.

And so began a period of limbo, "a purgatory of indecision" as Aunt Eliza would call it, in my relationship with Willis McGee. I wanted to see him, but I didn't want to see him. I wanted to comfort him, but I didn't know how. I was back and forth, feeling guilty for what I didn't know, until the matter was put to rest. His family announced that Willis wanted no visitors until he had time to heal. In other words, until he could come to grips with the loss of his eye and regain his confidence.

I'll admit I was relieved. Acting or not acting was no longer up to me. But I couldn't help but mourn that magical blue-green eye gone in the flash of a hoof.

Grass widow ⌈ ⌐

Willis's run-in with the mule happened a few weeks before Thanksgiving. It was one more in a string of tragedies leaving the folks in Varennes grieving and unsettled. None of us felt much like celebrating the harvest that November. But Bessie insisted that Mama, Papa, and I join them for a mid-afternoon Thanksgiving dinner. It turned out to be a godsend.

The Allen house was filled with wonderful smells thanks to Janey, Red's wife, who was Bessie's cook. Bessie had her prepare double dishes so Red's family would have their own feast later in the evening with no extra work for Janey.

Bessie set the table with fine china from England, an anniversary gift from Preston. The silverware gleamed, and the stemware sparkled. We all dressed up for the occasion. Feaster wore a tie in a loose, uneven bow with his church clothes. Bessie quickly straightened it before we sat down. I wanted to say, "Leave his tie alone. It's perfectly imperfect." But I'd given up that right long ago.

Preston began by saying, "We've had painful losses this year. But we've also had many blessings. I propose, for this day, we concentrate only on the good."

Everyone nodded in agreement.

Preston delivered one of his eloquent masonic blessings ending with "So mote it be," which I later learned meant "So be it." The rest of the table followed with "amen." A fine meal commenced. We talked about the weather, the coming winter, the price of beef, the churches—all in a noncritical way. And we managed to stay pleasant from the first slice of turkey through the last slice of pound cake.

As the meal ended, Feaster asked to be excused so he could feed his menagerie. Bessie reminded him to change clothes, and out he went. The men moved to the front parlor. Janey brought in a fresh pot of coffee. She poured a cup for each of the ladies, and we joined the men.

Preston stoked the fire and pulled up several more chairs. Then he went to a nearby cabinet and returned with two stemmed, sphere-shaped glasses in one hand and a bottle of deep golden liquid in the other.

"Brandy?" Papa asked.

Preston nodded. "But it's a special brandy I've been saving for a special occasion. It's called 'cognac.'" He pronounced it "con-yak." He held up the bottle so Papa could see the label.

Papa squinted and said, "Looks foreign."

"It is," Preston said. "It's from a place in France where they age it at least ten years before they can import it."

He handed Papa a glass and poured him a generous portion. Bessie looked at Preston and held out her cup of coffee. He poured her a small amount. Bessie looked at me and smiled. "It's good in coffee with cream, sort of like eggnog only better."

I held out my cup to Preston without looking at Mama or Papa. He smiled and poured the same amount for me. I took a sip and felt the warmth go down my throat, into my chest, and out through my arms.

Mama held out her cup. "Just a drop or two to see if this foreign stuff tastes different from regular brandy."

Papa said, "Dear wife, you just told on yuh-self!"

Everyone laughed, even Mama. Then Bessie suggested we take turns telling something we were thankful for.

Preston began, "I'm thankful for my marriage."

Bessie smiled at him and said, "I'm thankful for that too, and I'm thankful that Feaster is having a good year in school."

Papa was thankful for Mama. Mama for Papa.

I was thankful for family. And so it went around several more times until it got kind of competitive between the men. Preston was giving thanks for having the first cotton bale in the county to go to market again and Papa was giving thanks for his outstanding cabbage crop that earned mention in the Anderson newspaper as the best in the county.

Preston refreshed his and Papa's glasses and our cups several times.

We let the men go back and forth until Papa declared, "I'm thankful for no dang carbuncles this year."

To which Mama chimed in, "I, too, am thankful for no carbuncles this year!"

That led to body parts. I was thankful that I had hands to play the piano and knit. Bessie was thankful for feet without bunions so she could keep up with Feaster. Mama was thankful that her ears still worked. Preston was thankful that he had two strong legs. And Papa was thankful that he had two good eyes.

Papa's pronouncement of "two good eyes" sent the grace fest in a different direction.

"Unlike Mr. Willis McGee," Mama said.

My throat tightened and my heart sped up.

"Lucky to be alive," Papa added.

"So's the mule," Mama said. "With his Irish temper, I'm surprised Willis didn't shoot it where it stood."

"He's Scotch Irish," Preston said. Mama didn't respond. "His brothers sold the mule," he continued, "before Willis could gather his wits about him and regain his aim." He refilled the brandy glasses and our cups until the bottle was empty. If I had any coffee left, I couldn't taste it.

"When I first heard about Willis losing an eye," Preston went on, "I thought maybe one of the grass widows knocked it out." The men laughed. The ladies did not.

I'd heard the term "grass widow" before, and I knew it wasn't a compliment, but I wasn't sure what it meant.

"What exactly is a 'grass widow'?" I asked.

Mama took a sip and swallowed. "It's a wife whose husband deserted her. Put her out to pasture so to speak."

"Or the other way around," Papa chimed in. The men laughed again.

"So she's not really a widow?" I asked.

"Not in the legal sense," Bessie said.

"I'll tell you the difference between a widder and a grass widder," Papa said as he swirled his glass of cognac. "A widder loses her husband. A grass widder just misplaces hers!"

We all laughed, including Mama, though I didn't find it very funny.

Preston added, "And the men who dance with her get hay fever!"

More laughter. But the idea of Willis with a grass widow started to sink in. I looked at Preston. "So, you're saying that Willis spends time with grass widows?"

Bessie frowned at Preston. He glanced from her to me. "Oh, no. I don't know that. It's just the way of some young men who don't have a fine wife."

I didn't respond. I didn't like the idea of Willis with another woman one bit, but I wasn't about to admit it out loud.

Papa spoke up, "Icie, ever'body in Varennes knows Willis is sweet on you. He'd marry you yesterd'y if you be willin'."

"Then everyone in Varennes should know I have no interest in getting married," I said, louder than I meant to. I drained my cup.

And so ended a memorable Thanksgiving.

Laundry ❧

The coat rack across the room has caught my eye. A ray of morning sun must have landed on one of the brass hooks. In the center hangs my Savannah Market hat with its wide black brim and band of blue grosgrain ribbon. I remember wearing the silly thing all over the Charleston Exposition. I haven't worn it since. Still, it hangs there, almost within reach, waiting.

Thanksgiving was the last time I saw Papa in high spirits. Not even Christmas the following month brought out his playful side again.

We spent Christmas morning with the Allens, the same as we'd done since Feaster had been born. Bessie and Preston glowed with pride as Feaster held their family Bible and read from Luke 2: 1–20. The familiar Christmas story seemed even more moving in his young, clear voice.

Then we exchanged gifts. Because I'd earned money of my own as church organist, I'd decided to buy presents instead of making them. For Papa and Preston, I'd bought thick leather driving gloves the color of black walnuts. Each man tried on his pair and seemed pleased. I'd also bought a smaller pair for Feaster. He seemed less pleased until Preston made a fuss over them and told Feaster to try his on, too. He obliged. He thanked me without looking up and took off the gloves as soon as he was no longer the center of attention.

For Bessie and Mama, I'd ordered hand muffs. The catalogue called the muffs "a warm and luxurious blonde French coney accessory for the fashionable lady."

Bessie slipped her hands into the round of golden fur. "Why, Icie, it's beautiful and so warm. But I won't be able to drive with this on my paws." Everyone laughed.

"Bessie, I do believe your mule driving days are over," I replied. "It's more fitting that you just sit close to your handsome husband and look fashionable." Preston and Bessie exchanged smiles.

"And Mama," I said, as I handed her the one I'd bought for her, "I haven't seen you drive a wagon in years!"

"I can if I need to!" she shot back. The rest of us agreed she certainly could.

"What kind of fur is it?" Feaster asked. "I mean what kind of animals did it come from?"

"French coney," I answered, realizing I had no idea what critters lost their lives to fashion.

"Bunnies?" he asked, his voice rising.

"Fancy rabbits," Preston said quickly, "bred for their fur like cattle for roast beef." He cut Feaster a glance that I took to mean, "Don't take this any further."

I had a second gift for Feaster, a mechanical pencil—"of the very latest engineering" according to the advertisement. Instead of a spring, it had a twist mechanism to advance the graphite. I handed him the slender box. No doubt, he knew that Bessie and Preston were watching, so he took the box and opened it. He studied the metal pencil, rolling it slowly between his thumbs and forefingers. He examined both ends. Next he carefully twisted it in the middle to see the inner workings.

Then, miracle of miracles, he thanked me without being told. He quickly fetched some paper and showed us how well his new pencil wrote. I don't recall what gifts I received, but none was as welcome as Feaster's genuine approval.

Papa, however, didn't seem to enjoy Christmas as much as he usually did. And by the new year, he ventured out less and less.

When March came around, he didn't even plant his cabbage patch. And by late spring, he was in bed more often than not. He wouldn't say what bothered him in particular other than he just didn't feel much like moving. Dr. Dean came and went several times, but offered no real hope.

Mama used to say, "Time and tide wait for no man." I doubt she'd ever seen the ocean ebbing and flowing any more than I had, but she understood the gist of it. I did too. So in 1895, while life for most folks rolled forward, Papa's was winding down.

Mama saw to Papa, and I saw to the rest of the household needs.

Bessie and Preston not only managed their own expanding operation along with Papa's, but they also began building a new church. The congregation at Bethesda had outgrown the structure. So the Allens donated land for a new sanctuary within easy walking distance from their home. They also added a good bit of the building fund begun by the Faith Alliance.

It was an English-style structure of dark brick with white wooden gables. It had windows on three sides and the tallest bell tower I'd ever seen at the time.

As the church went up, I reported to Papa on its progress. I kept hoping he'd feel well enough to visit the site and offer his opinion. But he never did. He seemed satisfied with my daily account and usually fell asleep before I finished.

Papa's children from his first family came to see him that year. Johnny and Sallie came the most often. I wish I could say we were one big happy family, but we weren't. Johnny was still close to Mama, and Mattie was kind, but the others were cool to us.

One July afternoon after Dock and his wife had visited Papa, Mama and I bid them goodbye from the front steps without much ado. The day had been warm, but dusk promised a bit of cool. I sat on the front porch while the sun slowly dropped. Mama checked on Papa, then joined me on the porch.

"We need to do laundry tomorrow," she said. "William's bedding must be kept clean."

"I'll do it in the morning," I said. But at the moment, I didn't want to think about chores. I was curious about the Joneses. "Mama, why do you think the first family doesn't seem to care as much for us as we do for them?"

She didn't answer so I continued, "I know my having Feaster

out of holy wedlock didn't endear me to any of them, but that shouldn't affect you and Bessie."

Mama shook her head. "Oh, Icie, it's not because of that. The first family has had it harder than we have."

"I think they're mostly happy," I offered.

"I hope so. But you have to remember, I took the place of their mother. They all must have felt a terrible loss."

"But you were a good mother to them."

"I tried to be." She looked into the distance at nothing in particular. "Dock was already gone. Sammy wanted to be. And sweet Mattie was giddy in love." She smiled and added, "Sallie was so very headstrong." We both laughed as we recalled how Sallie had always insisted on doing things her way, from cooking to sewing to praying.

"She'd have been a handful even if she'd been my own flesh and blood," Mama said. "But being strong-willed has served Sallie well. She's taken life head-on with more grief than a mother should have to bear. And her faith has endured."

I agreed, wondering if I'd ever be that strong. "At least Johnny loves us," I said.

"Yes, but even his name was on the lawsuit that they . . ." She stopped abruptly.

"What lawsuit?"

She hesitated, then said, "It's been settled."

"What lawsuit?" I repeated. When she didn't respond, I put my face right in front of hers. "I'm a grown woman! Tell me!"

Mama looked at me. "I suppose so." Then she stared into the distance again and began the Jones vs. Jones lawsuit story. "Some years after William's first wife, Elizabeth, passed away, her father, Thomas Dean, died."

"The first family's grandfather," I said.

"Yes. His estate was divided among his children. Since Elizabeth was no longer living, William took control of her portion."

"Was it a lot?"

"No. A bit of capital, some land, a few possessions. William added it to his own holdings and used it to grow our farm."

She stopped, took a slow breath, and let it out. "Once Dock and Sammy were grown, they began to think in terms of their own prospects. That led them to question their inheritance from the Deans."

"Or the lack of," I said. She nodded.

"They got a lawyer and brought a lawsuit against William. Sallie and Johnny joined them. Mattie may have too," Mama said. "I'm not sure. I tried to stay out of it."

"What happened?" I asked.

"It dragged on for over a year. And in the end, the first family lost their suit. But I think William may have given them what few possessions Elizabeth had and made some promises about the rest."

I sat silent for a moment trying to process what I'd just heard. "Did Bessie know about the lawsuit?"

"Yes."

"Then why in Holy Heavens didn't one of you tell me?" I asked as loud as I dared without waking Papa.

This time, Mama looked me in the face and said, "Because, Icie, you were occupied with a far more important matter."

I had no response. Of course I was occupied. I was throwing-up pregnant by a man whose last name I didn't even know. I was so wrapped up in myself that I hadn't noticed the turmoil the rest of the Joneses were in. It was a hard realization. But as I sat there trying to make sense of what Mama had just told me, I also realized it wasn't completely my fault, after all, that they were cool to us. I took a bit of solace in that.

She concluded, "We've been more prosperous than the first family was. Times have been better for us than for William and Elizabeth."

We sat silent for a while. The setting sun seemed to speed its descent, exploding into flames along the horizon. I pointed to the mass of yellow and red through distant pines. "Looks like the tree line is on fire."

She nodded. "Some days the sun burns brightest right before it disappears, like it's trying to hang on to the day a little longer."

No sooner had the sun dropped beyond the horizon than thousands of lightning bugs appeared above the yard and across the field. The sight immediately took me back to my childhood.

"I used to think they were light-in-bugs and they came out when the sun went down so Bessie and I could chase them."

Mama smiled. "They're just looking for mates."

We sat on the dark porch a little longer with nothing to distract us from our thoughts but an occasional creak from the house as it exhaled the day's heat. And the winking of lightning bugs claiming their place on earth.

In the final months, Papa started calling me "Em'ly." Mama didn't seem to mind. Once when Sallie was visiting, he called her "Liz-buth." I think she took comfort in it.

Then Papa barely spoke at all.

So it was a surprise when he seemed clear one day in late October. He woke up, looked from Mama to Bessie to me and said, "Icie, sing for me." We glanced at each other, heartened at the same time that he might actually be getting better.

"What do you want to hear, Papa?" I asked eagerly. I was hoping for something lively like "Little Church in the Wildwood."

But he said, "That Goodnight Song."

And I no longer felt so heartened. I couldn't look at Mama or Bessie for fear I'd start crying.

Mama spoke up, her voice unsteady, "Sing for him, Icie."

And so I did. I tried to sing it like we had at the concert when my life came back to me. But there was no denying the words now—"Sleep on beloved, sleep and take your rest. Lay down your head upon the Savior's breast. I love you well, but Jesus loves you best . . ."

Papa fell back asleep, and I kept singing. But it was for Mama and Bessie that I sang the rest.

He died a week later. If he'd needed time to make peace with death or to let go of something in life, he'd had nearly a year to do so. Either way, I convinced myself, he was ready to meet his Maker.

Lay down my father

Papa would have loved his funeral. It was a rare sunny day in early November. Most of the leaves had fallen, but the oaks glowed orange and golden. Two preachers presided—a sign of importance Papa would have noted. People came from all over the county. They spoke of Capt. Jones's bravery during the war and his place in the community afterward.

Papa's brothers and sisters and their spouses, and his first family and theirs were all present. I'd never seen so many Joneses on one plot of ground—even the ones who'd squabbled with him in the past were there, paying their respects and recalling the good times in place of the bad.

The entire town closed down for the service. Papa's kins-men wore black armbands, and the women wore their best black dresses, all in accordance with "The Rules for Mourning." Papa would have been pleased.

Johnny made Papa's coffin. It was as fine as any I'd ever seen—polished pine, lined in cedar. No worm holes for Papa. Mama said Johnny had been working on it over the past year as Papa unwound. I remembered seeing a fold-up measuring stick in his back pocket when he came to visit, but I hadn't made the connection. Mama knew the signs better than I did.

Papa's grave was in the family plot beside Cross Roads Baptist Church where his mother and father, his brother James, whose body he'd brought home from Virginia, and his brother Benjamin were all buried. His first wife, Elizabeth, was buried there, too.

Mama held up well through the service although she seemed smaller than ever. In the cemetery, she stood at the foot of Papa's grave. Mattie and Sallie stood to her left at the foot of their own mother's grave, while Bessie and I stood to her right where Mama would one day be buried.

We waited for the coffin to arrive. Bessie and I held hands. I whispered to her, "Think Mama minds him being buried next to Elizabeth?"

I knew it was inappropriate, but I had cried myself out. Evidently Bessie had too because she squeezed my hand and whispered back, "Mama's probably ready for someone else to take care of him for a while." We kept our heads down and stifled giggles. I felt like a little girl again if only for a moment.

Soon the men carried Papa's coffin from the church to his waiting grave. Dock, Sammy, and Johnny were on one side while

J. E., Preston, and Dolph were on the other. All the men looked somber except Johnny who had the slightest of smiles. I wondered if he was admiring his work. It was a silly thought.

But as they slowly lowered Papa into the open ground, the finality of the grave fell on me like a collapsing roof. My tears rushed back tenfold. I gritted my teeth and looked away to hold back sobs.

Then in my head, just as clear as day, I heard Papa's voice. "Don't cry, Icie. I had my time—more good than not."

· · ℰ · ·

For the next few months, Bessie, Mama, and I sorted through Papa's papers to make sure he didn't owe anybody and that nobody owed him. Bessie and I were surprised that Papa hadn't left a will, especially since he'd been so precise about loans and acreage and boundaries. But Mama told us there wasn't one, at least not one that she'd written down for him, and she thought he'd settled up with each of his children from his first family in that final year.

I guess she was right because none of them sued us.

Papa had already sold a good bit of the land that bordered the Allens' property to Preston, so Bessie was well taken care of. As for me, Mama said I'd inherit the home place after she died. I was in no hurry.

Mama and I managed throughout the winter. I'd become fairly handy around the kitchen and yard, and Preston made sure we had all the help we needed with the farm. Six months passed quickly and before we knew it, spring was breaking through. I decided it was time to put away my mourning clothes. I hoped I wouldn't need them again for a very long time.

A few days later, I opened the windows to let in the spring

air. I thought I smelled flowers so I went out on the porch to see what might be blooming. But instead of flowers, I saw a buggy approaching. It was still some distance but I recognized the horse and the driver. I went down the steps and waited.

"A good morning to you, Mr. Willis McGee," I said. "I don't think that buggy has aged much since the first time I saw it."

"Haven't had much occasion to take it outta the barn," he answered. Then he jumped down, looked straight into my eyes, and said, "What do you think?"

I was confused so I looked at Sugar. "He's as handsome as ever." I stroked the horse's broad, silvery head.

"And me?" Willis asked. He drew an imaginary circle around his face.

I looked from eye to eye. I was shocked. Both eyes were the same as ever—bluish green, the color of the ocean, with little flecks that caught the light. I began to wonder if the whole mule story was made up. Maybe he'd spent the past year or so with a grass widow, maybe several.

"Yes," I said, trying to regain my composure. "You look as handsome as ever, too."

He exhaled, took a long, slow breath and smiled again. "Then I've spent my money wisely."

"On what?" I asked, my mind racing.

He looked at me in disbelief.

At that moment, I realized he was talking about his eye. My face burned with embarrassment. I'd seen fake eyes that looked all right at a distance, but none so convincing close up.

"Oh Icie, I didn't mean to make you blush. I just wanted you to see my new eye. Evidently it passed the muster."

"It certainly did," I stammered, still not completely convinced. "How'd you find one to match so well?"

"Had it made," he said, his voice rising with excitement. "Went all the way to Philadelphia to find a fella who could do it. A 'German artisan.' He said the color was hard to get right, and it took him a number of tries."

I looked closer. "What about those little flecks?"

"Some kind of ground-up metal that he mixed in with the glass," he replied, obviously happy with my reaction. "I can't control it as much as I can my good eye, but I do have some movement in it. See?"

He looked up and down, then side to side. Both eyes moved, though not exactly in unison.

"I bought several in case I lose any."

He seemed to be waiting for me to say something, so I did. "It's been nearly two years."

"More like a year and a half," he responded, turning serious. "It took time to get myself in order. And I knew you were grieving for Capt. Jones."

I had to blink back tears.

"But that's in the past, he added sounding playful again. "I brought something for you!"

"What's the occasion?" I asked. I was starting to feel self-conscious. I wished I'd taken more time making myself presentable.

"Your birthday!" He pulled a small box from his pocket.

"That's two weeks away," I said. "I'm trying to put it off a little longer."

He handed me the box. "Then open it now and you won't be a year older."

A light blue ribbon tied in a bow held the box closed. I slowly pulled one end of the ribbon, careful not to tangle it. It fell to the ground. I picked it up and wound it around my wrist.

"For God's sake, Icie!" he shouted. "Open the box!"

I pulled off the lid and found a beautiful gold watch. I carefully removed it from the box, pressed the stem, and opened the front. The hours were in fancy Roman numerals.

"It's lovely," I sputtered.

"Look at the back. It opens."

I turned it over and pressed the stem again. The back popped open to reveal "ICIE" engraved in large graceful script. I squealed in surprise.

"I've never seen a watch quite this fine," I said, turning it back and forth.

"There's a chain that goes with it. Look under the cloth in the box."

I pulled back velvet to discover a long gold loop with a hook and a slide, studded with an opal. It was as beautiful as the watch.

"Put it on. Here, let me help." He took the watch, hooked it to the end of the chain, and slipped it over my head.

"It's perfect," he said. "Just as I imagined. I wish I had a mirror to show you."

"You're mirror enough," I said. And I hugged him in pure joy.

"That was the surprise I promised you," he whispered, "right before I tangled with that dang mule!"

I can still feel his warm arms around me, mine around him, my face against his beating chest. It's the Jesus-God moment I wrap myself in, like the old gunboat quilt, when I feel a storm blowing in.

PART VII

Best laid plans

Mama's move

Mama and I managed rather well for the next year or so while Preston helped with the farm. Willis would have, if I'd let him.

But nearly two years after Papa died, Mama got sick and took to her bed. I sent for Dr. Dean. Mama's illness was easier to diagnosis than Papa's had been. "Pneumonia," Dr. Dean said. He shook his head. The word sent chills through me. So did Mama's godawful coughs. I was afraid they'd rip her fragile body apart.

Bessie hovered over her as much as I did. We gave her chicken broth with rice and hot tea with honey as often as she'd take it. Every night we'd fill a pan with steaming water. One of us would hold it under Mama's face, and the other would hold a towel over her head like a tent so she could breathe in the warm, moist air. We did the steam treatment until the water turned tepid and she ran us out.

This went on for nearly two weeks until she declared we were killing her with kindness. We took it as a sign that she was better. She was soon back on her feet trying to do her usual tasks. But after the pneumonia scare, the Allens agreed that she should live with them where she wouldn't try to do so much.

Bessie broached the subject shortly after Mama had recovered. "Mama," she said, "Preston and I've been talking."

Mama didn't take the bait, so Bessie went on, "We'd like for you to live with us."

"Why? I'm not decrepit!"

Bessie smiled and touched her hand. "I know you're not. But if you fall sick again, it'll be easier to take care of you at our house." Mama didn't reply. Bessie went on, "We have more help, and it'll be easier on Icie, too."

Mama shook her head. "I don't intend to get sick again."

"You didn't intend to get sick the last time, did you?" Bessie asked sweetly. Mama didn't answer. Bessie added, "I could use your advice from time to time on household matters."

Mama's face softened. "I suppose I could be of help. But I don't see as well as I used to."

"Then we'll get you a pair of spectacles. We'll get you two pairs!" And with that she began making plans.

But just as I was considering Mama's move, Bessie added, "Preston can find a good family to rent the house so it won't sit empty."

I pulled her aside. "I'm happy for Mama to be in your care. But I plan to stay here."

She looked at me like my hair was on fire.

"I can run the house," I said. "I've done it since Papa took to his bed."

She kept staring.

"I still have the tenant family here if I have an emergency," I added.

She waved her hand in front of my face. "You can't live by yourself. It's too dangerous for one thing," she said, as though I were still her baby sister. "You can't protect yourself. You never did learn to shoot a gun, did you?"

She had a point. "I could learn," I said.

"I doubt you will. And even if you did, it wouldn't look right."

"Other women live alone," I argued, "like Mattie."

"That's not the same and you know it. Mattie's a widow. And she has those boys close by to protect her." Bessie was building up steam. "Folks might think you're a grass widow. Or worse."

Her words stung. Tears welled up. "I'm not a grass widow," I said, wiping my eyes, "and I'm not worse!"

She looked contrite. She tried to hug me but I stiffened. "I'm sorry, Icie. I didn't mean to hurt you. I just want you to be safe with us."

I felt my resistance falling away. I slumped and hugged her back. "What about Feaster?" I asked.

"It'll do him good," she said. "It'll do you both good."

Brand new century ↩

A cardinal has begun banging against my bedroom window. He must have spotted his reflection. Flaming crest, black mask, orange beak—a glorious, angry vision in red. He throws himself harder into each new attack only to be deflected by his own force.

I suppose he'll continue until he breaks his fragile neck or the sun's angle shifts and frees him from his own reflection.

If I were trying to sleep, his futile banging would be maddening. But these days I try to stay awake. From where I watch, I won't know his fate. Yet in the story forming in my mind, he tires of fighting his ghost, stretches his crimson wings, and flies away.

Sunday morning at the Allens became an interesting routine. Preston, Bessie, and Feaster went to Bethesda Methodist Church. Mama and I still went to Cross Roads Baptist. Preston had bought what he called a church carriage to transport us on Sundays and a matched pair of sorrel fillies named Blaze and Star to pull it.

On our rides to church, Preston, Bessie, and Feaster would sit on the front bench, and Mama and I would sit on the back. Preston would take Mama and me to our church first and then loop back to Bethesda. After the services, they would return to get us. Sometimes Feaster would take the reins.

A few years earlier, Rev. Wright had left Cross Roads Baptist to become a missionary in Africa. Rev. Charles Ligon took over the pulpit. Fair or not, Rev. Ligon was everything that the former minister was not. Most of his sermons were about making one's family part of God's larger family or tilling one's own farm in respect for God's creation. He didn't dwell on sinners. Nor on tithing. Papa would've approved. Little wonder, Rev. Ligon was warmly received. The only criticism I ever heard toward him was when he had guest speakers who enumerated the evils of alcohol.

Alcohol prohibition had become a hot topic throughout the state. Our governor had responded by setting up dispensaries in each county to control the sale and reap the benefits. Through dispensaries, citizens could still get liquor, and the profit went to the state.

Most of our family, both the first and the second, didn't object to the dispensary idea, especially since Dock was dispensary keeper for Anderson County. And like the Joneses before them, they didn't take kindly to being told what they could and couldn't do, especially by outsiders. Even Sallie and J. E., who were strict teetotalers, didn't see the need for any more laws regulating how we lived.

Rev. Ligon didn't rail against alcohol himself, but from time to time he was required by the Southern Baptist Convention to host a "visiting brother." Such was the case one early spring Sunday in 1900. On that particular morning I was especially eager to get to church in hopes Willis would be there. I hadn't seen him since we'd danced in the New Year together.

We still had a relationship of sorts. The previous year I'd accepted a few invitations from Preston's friends, and Willis had appeared from time to time with a few other Varennes ladies. Still, for the holidays and big events, we seemed to end up together much to the bewilderment of my family and probably his.

On that Sunday morning, as Preston helped Mama and me down from his church carriage, I spotted Willis's buggy. Then I saw him, his back to me, standing among a circle of men. My heart raced. I hurried into the sanctuary and settled behind the organ. As I arranged my sheet music, Rev. Ligon and another man entered and ascended the steps to the pulpit.

The organ sat at an angle where I could see both the pulpit and the congregation. I began playing the call to worship, and the group of men from outside joined the rest of those already seated.

The McGee men were members of Good Hope, the Presbyterian church in town. So most Sundays they went to Good Hope if they went at all. But their mother, Mrs. Mary, came from a family of lifelong Baptists. So occasionally the men came to Cross Roads and sat with their mother.

Rev. Ligon rose and announced the first hymn, "When the Roll Is Called Up Yonder." I'd chosen the song because, like "The Little Church in the Wild Wood," the men seemed to enjoy the chorus, especially the bass refrain of "I'll be-e th-e-r-e."

And they did. The men sang louder than the ladies. I could pick out Willis's voice in the refrain. The song seemed to put folks in a good mood. And when the collection plates went around, they appeared to hold more coins and bills than usual.

We proceeded through the order of worship rather joyfully until it came time for the sermon. Rev. Ligon introduced the man with him, a guest speaker from Pennsylvania. The speaker stepped to the podium and thanked the reverend for inviting him. It looked as though Rev. Ligon might say something. But after a moment, he simply sat down.

The speaker began by reading from Ephesians—"And be not drunk with wine, wherein is excess; but be filled with the Spirit." And on he went reading progressively stronger scripture about drunkenness and sin. Then he proceeded to relate all present-day crime to alcohol, everything from robbery to adultery to murder.

I glanced at the congregation. Most sat stone-faced. Some looked down like Mama, who was wearing her specs and reading scripture of her own choosing. I tried to will the sermon to end, but all I could do was straighten the music sheet for the closing hymn, "Shall We Gather at the River."

The speaker reached a maddening singsong delivery as he condemned South Carolina's dispensary system, saying it ultimately made citizens of our state "immoral." Suddenly, one of the McGee brothers stood up, bumped his way from the pew to the center aisle, and departed the sanctuary. Willis was close behind him. More members followed them.

Rev. Ligon pushed the speaker aside, said a prayer, and nodded at me for the closing hymn. I charged into "Shall We Gather at the River" and played two sped-up verses. He said a fast benediction and dismissed what was left of the congregation.

I hurried out to the churchyard in hopes of seeing Willis, but he was gone.

The Allens arrived shortly afterward to fetch Mama and me. Feaster was driving. Preston jumped down. "Where are all the fine Baptists?" he asked as he helped us into the carriage.

"Gone home to hide their liquor," Mama said, leaving Bessie and Preston speechless for the moment. Feaster concentrated on the horses.

"We had a 'visiting temperate brother,'" I explained. "I guess you'd better hide your brandy."

"I hope it won't come to that," Preston said.

Mama sniffed. "It won't in Varennes. Too many Irish!"

"Mrs. Emily, if you mean the McGees, they're Scotch Irish."

"Close enough," she said.

Feaster clucked to the horses, and back to the Allens we went. At the Sunday dinner table, the conversation turned from prohibition to a power plant to be built at nearby Gregg Shoals and what it would mean for Varennes.

Bessie had already sent Janey home shortly after dinner was served, telling her that we would do the dishes ourselves. So after dinner, Mama went to her room to read, Preston and Feaster went outside, and Bessie and I fell back into a familiar routine from childhood. Bessie washed, and I dried. Once we finished the tumblers, we started on the cups and saucers. And as in our youth, we chatted to make the task go faster.

"I'll admit I was reluctant to move in with you and Preston and Feaster," I said, "but I've really enjoyed my stay."

Bessie handed me a cup. "You're not thinking of leaving, are you?"

"Oh, no," I said, turning the cup over and swiping inside

with a dish cloth. "Anyway, where would I go? Preston rented out our house."

"Mama asked him to find renters," she said. She snagged another cup from the sudsy water and dipped it into the clean. "What I meant was maybe you and Willis might make a decision eventually."

I took the dripping cup. "What kind of decision?"

She looked at me sideways. "You know I mean marriage. For the life of me, I don't understand what kind of dance you two are doing."

I dried the last cup. "He hasn't asked me lately."

She started on the saucers. "He's a fine man—smart, hardworking. I've heard he's got a temper, but I wouldn't think he'd show it to you."

I didn't respond, so she handed me a saucer and continued, "If it's the marriage bed you're dreading . . ."

"Stop," I said, waving the dripping saucer. "My experience is brief and tarnished, but I would welcome such affection from Willis."

"Then what'n High Heavens is it?" She fished out another saucer and dunked it into the rinse water.

"I'm just not suited for having babies," I said.

There, the truth was out. At least part of it. I went on, "It was the sickest, scariest, loneliest, most miserable nine months of my life. And the actual birthing was worse. I thought I was dying."

Bessie stared into the dishwater. "I can't imagine how you felt or any other woman who bears a child feels. The Lord in all His goodness hasn't blessed me with such joy."

My face flushed hot. I felt awful for being so insensitive. "Oh, Bessie, it's more than that," I confessed. "I could endure the pregnancy and the birth. But what I can't endure again is my utter failure at motherhood."

I dropped the dish towel and turned her shoulders to face me. "You are a wonderful mother, regardless of who bore Feaster. I am not!"

She stood silent. I continued, "I couldn't feed him, hold him, comfort him, stop his crying. For months afterward, I wished I actually had died giving birth." Terrible walled-in feelings of failure came flying out. "He would've died if it hadn't been for you and Mama."

I picked up the dish towel. "I can't do that to Willis, no matter how much I love him."

She wiped her hands on her apron. "I just hate for you to miss out on a good man. You know our days are numbered."

"You sound like Mama," I said.

"So I do. Mama would also say, 'Make hay while the sun shines.'" We laughed a little. She added, "You never know how long you have. None of us do."

By then, the rinse water was cool. Bessie emptied the pan, added water from the hot kettle, and we started on the plates.

She didn't ask about Willis again. But when the whole marriage subject came up less than a year later, it had little to do with childbearing.

'His rod and his staff gon-na comfort you best' ↩

By the summer of 1900, all signs pointed to a record year of wheat, corn, and most importantly, cotton. The stars had aligned to produce the perfect balance of sun and rain.

What was good for crops had been equally good for flowers. Mama's and my flower garden at the Allens' was rich with color, from red hibiscus and bee balm to Indian pink, purple irises, and blue false indigo. Sweet scents of roses and jasmine permeated the grounds.

We were in our own little world of peace, security, and love. And at the center, making it all possible, was Preston Brooks Allen. We eased into 1901 without much fanfare. Whether the new century had begun the year before or was just starting didn't matter to us nor most people in Varennes.

We celebrated Feaster's fifteenth birthday in January. He was becoming a handsome young man, almost pretty, with clear blue eyes and straight, light hair. He was as tall as Bessie. He'd grown past Mama and me the previous year.

February went by quickly letting in the lion of March with its usual gray days. We went about our business assuming that spring would come soon enough.

But there's something about the ending of a season that's unpredictable, like a worn wheel, one that might break a spoke or slip off the axle. Those times you just can't prepare for. You can go through your morning ritual of reading scripture, giving thanks, and asking for guidance. But unless you ask for and receive the strength of a saint, some days will crush you.

Such was the case on a Friday in early March. It had begun as a typical winter morning, cold but not yet windy. Rain had let up the night before although the skies were dark and thick. Preston had business in Anderson. He'd gone a day earlier, but a stomach ailment had brought him home early. So he and Red left home Friday morning to finish affairs in town and get back before the rain returned.

Feaster was in school. Bessie was making a list of the sharecroppers' needs. I was crocheting a tablecloth, one that I hoped to have finished in time for Easter. Mama and Janey were in the kitchen baking bread.

All of a sudden, we heard a commotion at the kitchen door. Then Red rushed in to find Bessie. "Mr. Preston! he done took sick!" he shouted. "He's at the stable. A doc come for him."

He caught his breath, but seemed no calmer. "Mizz Bessie, you gotta come right now!"

Bessie grabbed a hooded coat, and they ran to the buggy. Mama, Janey, and I didn't know what to do. So we kept at our tasks at hand with little talking as though we were afraid to give words to what might be happening.

When Feaster came home from school, Mama told him Preston had taken sick in Anderson, Bessie had gone to see about him, and that's all we knew.

The wait was tortuous.

By early evening, Bessie and Red returned. Both looked frozen, like the life had drained out of them. Neither of them met our stares. We all asked questions at once. But they didn't answer.

Finally, Bessie spoke. "Preston is dead."

The walls collapsed around us and the house turned as cold as I can remember. No one moved at first. Then Feaster went to Bessie. He put his arms around her, hesitantly at first, then tighter.

Mama and I began to hug each other. Janey held onto Red.

Red and Feaster tried to choke back sobs. But we women wailed in one painful, climbing voice, reaching the most forlorn pitch I'd ever heard. And there we stayed until there was no wailing left in us.

Then Bessie looked at no one in particular and hoarsely said, "People will be coming."

This is the account we heard from Red and others: Preston had almost finished his business in Anderson when he began feeling sick again. His last stop was to be Fowler's Livery Stable. When he and Red arrived, his condition worsened to the point that he had to be helped out of the buggy and into a room at the stable. By the time a doctor arrived, Preston had quit breathing. Red had come for Bessie in hopes that somehow she could revive him. But it was not to be.

In an instant, Preston Brooks Allen, perhaps the best man I would ever know, was gone. Ripped from us without warning—incomprehensibly, inconsolably, irretrievably gone. And all the big words in Mr. Webster's Dictionary couldn't bring him back.

The undertaker brought Preston's body home the next day in a mahogany casket with brass hardware. He said it was the best he had. It was placed near my piano in the front room. And so began a thick, steady stream of folks coming to the Allen house. Rain threatened throughout the day, but held off.

Visitors came from morning to early night. They ranged from officials to sharecroppers, colored to white. And family. So much family. Preston's aunts and uncles, brothers and sisters, nieces and nephews—all heartbroken.

Our half-sisters and brothers from the first family were there, too. It would be the last time I'd see them all in one place.

Bessie asked Mama and me to greet folks at the front door while she and Feaster welcomed those who came to the back. After a while, she mercifully sent Feaster outside to help Red take care of visitors' buggies and carriages, and made sure the horses and mules were watered.

Janey managed a nearly endless supply of funeral food. And

as the day progressed, people shared stories of Preston's wisdom, kindness, and generosity. Bessie comforted folks as much as they tried to comfort her.

The next day, the day of the funeral, even more people appeared. Because of the threatening weather, Bessie chose to have the funeral at home even though the crowd filled the front hall and living room and spilled out onto the front porch and yard. Three ministers, one from the Baptist church, one from the Methodist, and one from the Presbyterian, conducted the service.

When they finished, Bessie sent relatives and friends home. She said that Preston wouldn't have wanted a single person to catch cold on his behalf and that we would take care of the burial.

As we prepared for the trip to the cemetery, the rain returned and the wind blew hard. Nevertheless, Bessie told the undertaker to proceed. Feaster drove us in the Sunday carriage to the cemetery.

Red had asked Bessie on the day before if he could bring his choir to the cemetery. I don't think any of us, however, expected them to appear, much less sing, in such raw weather. But there they were, already at the gravesite when we arrived, huddled under several dilapidated umbrellas.

Feaster helped Mama and me out of the carriage. Then he helped Bessie out, supporting her every move. He tried to shield us all with one large umbrella. The undertaker arrived. His men brought out Preston's casket and began to lower it into the ground. Red and his choir took that as their cue. They dropped their umbrellas and began to clap their hands and sway and hum. Then their voices opened, rich and mellow. I expected them to sing "Swing Low, Sweet Chariot," or something similar.

But they did not. Instead they sang:

Lay down my brother, lay down and take yo rest.
Lay yo head up-on the Savior's chest.
We sho love you, but Jesus love you best,
Good-night, good-night, good-night, good-night . . .

And there it was. The song that marked my return to my family, that helped ease Papa's final days, was now releasing Preston from this earth. If only for the moment, their soulful sound, the perfect blend of grief and faith, overpowered the dismal weather.

They continued for several more verses:

Go walkin' the valley of the shadow of death, good-night
His rod and staff gon-na comfort you best, good-night. . . .

They sang as though they were warm and dry and in the presence of God. When they finished, Bessie stepped to the grave and dropped something in. She seemed unsteady at the edge, and I was afraid she'd fall in herself. Or jump in. But she straightened her back and returned to us.

As Feaster drove us away from the cemetery, I looked back to see the undertaker's men who'd begun shoveling the wet dirt. I was certain they were well paid. Preston would have insisted.

Papa once said he believed that when you're dying, an angel
in the form of a person who loved you in life comes for you.
That's if you "didn't do nuthin' too bad."

I wonder who came for Preston. Maybe his first wife, who died in childbirth. I never knew her name or anything about the baby, and I never asked. Bessie never mentioned them either. But now I wonder if his dead wife and baby called on him to rise from the grave and follow them.

I wonder who will come for me. What if it's someone I don't want to come? Do I still have to go? Papa never told me that.

PART VIII

Seeing to the living

Obelisk ᕫ ᔓ ᐀

Bessie didn't have time to sit down and mourn. With more than 2,000 acres and no telling how many tenants and sharecropper families to think about, she had to carry her mourning with her.

First, however, she said was determined to find the right headstone for Preston's grave. She could've bought one already carved out and ready for Preston's name and dates to be chiseled into it, but she wanted one made especially for him from start to finish. She and Feaster huddled in the dining room over Preston's Freemasonry and architecture books looking for the proper way to memorialize a Master Mason. They did so almost every evening for a week. With Bessie's guidance, Feaster made notebook sketches of the designs they were considering.

I tried not to intrude, but I was curious. After several evenings thus spent, I peered over Feaster's shoulder at the latest drawing. It looked to be a tall, tapering stone. It rose out of a larger rectangle of stone, which rested on another larger stone, which rested on yet a larger stone. It peaked into something that looked like a tower. It made me think of a giant wedding cake except the top layer was much taller and ended in a peak.

"What kind of monument is that?" I asked.

"It's an obelisk," Feaster said without looking up.

"What's an ob-blisk?" I asked.

"It's ob-EH-lisk," he said. "It's an Egyptian memorial."

"Egyptian?"

Bessie intervened. "It has to do with the Masons."

"What's that draped over the top?" I asked.

"It's a Mason's apron," she said.

I wondered why you'd drape cloth over a gravestone. I'd heard of covering mirrors during a wake so the departing spirit wouldn't catch his earthly image and slow his heavenly ascent. But not on the gravestone itself.

"It's carved into the stone," Feaster said, as though he read my mind. "It signifies that Uncle Preston's work on earth is done."

After Bessie and Feaster settled on the design, Bessie began looking at headstone facilities. She started in the upcountry and proceeded southward. Mama and I did our best to take over the household duties so she could settle the headstone business and get back to managing the farm.

Feaster would've quit school in a minute and joined her if she'd let him. And truth is he already knew more than he could learn in regular school. But he hadn't graduated, and Bessie had plans for him to go to Furman College in Greenville as soon as he did. Red continued to care for the livestock and to manage the day-to-day work with the help of tenants and sharecroppers.

At the time, which was late winter, the land didn't need too much attention. But we all knew that the first planting season was only a month away. It was an unsettling time for everyone who lived on Allen land.

In the aftermath of Preston's death, Willis McGee became increasingly important to us. And I got a glimpse of his temper as well as his passionate heart.

The McGee brothers were using a combination of day workers and their own farm hands to clear some land before the planting season. The mix was volatile. And soon a fight broke out between Willis and one of the day workers. Rather than try to break it up, the others evidently let it go on until Willis nearly killed the man.

The Sunday after the fight, I heard whispers about it at church, but no one would tell me the specifics. Normally I would have asked Bessie, but she was too busy to bother with gossip. So I waited until I could corner Red. His sister, Anah, and her husband, Henry, worked for the McGees. I knew Red would've heard details from his brother-in-law if not from Anah.

My opportunity arose when Red came to the back door to take Janey home. I opened the door. "Good evening, Red," I said. "Come in out of the cold."

He stepped inside the kitchen and closed the door behind him. Janey went to the pantry to fetch her wrap.

"Tell me," I continued, trying to sound vaguely interested, "did you happen to hear anything about a fight involving Willis McGee and a field hand?" Red didn't answer. He looked toward the pantry.

I repeated the question as though he hadn't heard me.

He gave in. "Yes'm."

I pressed on. "I heard he almost beat a man to death. Is that true?"

He didn't look at me directly but said, "They had to get'm a doc." Janey came out of the pantry, shawl in hand. Red looked relieved.

"What was it about?" I asked. Red stared at Janey as she threw the shawl around her shoulders.

"The fight," I said, "what was it about?"

Janey looked up at Red, then quickly down. I thought I saw the hint of a smile. She began studying a slipped stitch near the edge of her shawl.

"Cain't say, Mizz Icie," he answered, reaching for Janey's elbow.

"Please tell me," I said, no longer trying to sound casual. "No one else will."

He hesitated, looked at Janey again, then said, "That boy, he done said what he oughta not. Not to Mr. Willis."

"Boy?" I asked.

"Full growd," he said, "but he be actin' like a boy. Sassy mouth."

"A share cropper?" I asked.

He shook his head. "One of 'em what goes from field to field, gets fed and some shoes or sumpin, dudn't do much work."

"Go on."

"Some of the others put 'm up to mouthin' off at Mr. Willis."

"What about?" I asked.

"Cain't say. I wadn't there."

"It couldn't have been so bad as to deserve a beating," I said, digging for details.

"Yes'm," he said. He had Janey by the arm, pulling her toward the door.

I tried to keep him talking. "Red, would you beat somebody half to death just for saying something?" I asked.

"No, Mizz Icie, I don't reckon I would." He put his hand on the doorknob. "But I cain't say for Mr. Willis."

"What about his eye?" I asked quickly. "You know he has a glass eye."

Red gave the tiniest of smiles. He let go of the doorknob. "Henry say 'fore Mr. Willis took to fightin', he popped out his 'evil eye' and . . ."

I gasped. Janey shot Red a hard look.

"Just field talk, Mizz Icie."

I nodded.

"He put dat eye in his coat pocket and laid it in his wagon. Then Mr. Willis he let loose his fists like a swarm of hot bees," Red said, his voice surprisingly animated. "Henry say all amount of folks come runnin' to watch. There was cussin' and spittin' and bleedin' the likes they never seen! Least not in the field." And on Red went, giving blow-by-blow details as told by his brother-in-law, Henry, this time with Janey pulling at his elbow.

Somewhere between the popping out of the evil eye and the summoning of the doctor to the field, I came to realize two things. One, I really didn't want to know the details of the fight. And, two, I may very well have been the subject of the insult that nearly cost a man his life.

I was almost sure I'd been at the center of the ugly fight a week later when Willis came calling. I ran out to his buggy before he'd had time to tie Sugar to the post. His hat and coat were specked with mud. The buggy itself was as dirty as I'd seen it.

"Are you all right?" I shouted, catching him by surprise. He turned his bruised face to me. He looked tired. Before he could answer, I exclaimed, "What on earth caused you to beat a man nearly to death?"

His expression went from weary to stone-faced. He finished tying up Sugar. Then he looked at me again, his beautiful eyes smoldering. He took me by the shoulders and said, "Icie Jones—I—have—never—once—judged—you." He pronounced each word as though it weighed a ton. He caught a breath and continued in the same cadence, "I expect likewise from you."

I took a half-step back and blinked. I tried to regain a morsel of composure. "What if that man had pulled out a knife?"

"Then Doc Dixon would've stitched me up."

"What if the man had died?" I asked, trying not to blink again.

"I'd have to live with it." He let go of my shoulders. And with that, he clearly closed the book on the hapless, sassy-mouthed day worker.

My heart was still racing but I tried to start over. "What brings you out this day?" I asked awkwardly.

"I've come to see Bessie."

My face must have looked stricken because his expression softened and he quickly added, "Oh Icie, you know I want to see you. But I need to talk to Bessie. Is she here?"

When I didn't answer, he put his hands on my shoulders again. But this time, he gently pulled me to his chest and wrapped his arms around me.

He felt warm and strong. My emotions erupted. The loss of Preston had shaken the very ground I stood on. Maybe that's what the earthquake in Charleston had felt like, where life had been calm and secure one minute and broken into jagged little pieces the next.

I fought back tears as best as I could, and I held onto Willis as though he was the only solid thing in my life. "You'll have to be satisfied with just me today," I said, sniffing and still clinging to him. "Bessie has gone to Columbia to find an ob-EH-lisk."

---- ℮ ----

Before Bessie left on her gravestone quest, she'd asked Mama to order several mourning dresses from the seamstress in Anderson, the same one who'd made my concert dress.

Mama objected, saying, "I can still sew with my spectacles on. I'll make your widow's weeds."

To which Bessie replied, "I've already got an account with

the seamstress. She probably could use the business. But I do want you to pick out the cloth and style for me," she continued. "Just make sure they're loose enough to work in."

My duty was to see to the pantry and household supplies. I sat down with Janey and made a list. Then Red drove Mama and me into town, and while Mama gave instructions to the seamstress, I took my list to the general store.

As for Feaster, Bessie had insisted that he go back to school. When he objected, she told him that's what Preston would have wanted. Given how grief-stricken he was, it was a wise choice. Having lost the head of the household so unexpectedly was devastating to us all, but it must have been the hardest on Feaster.

At the age of fifteen, he'd seen so little of death. When I mentioned it to Mama, she agreed. But then she pointed out that my half-brother Dock had turned fifteen beside a Confederate campfire. It was difficult to reconcile the two—Feaster, a schoolboy, and Dock, a soldier, both at the same age.

I was reminded again of the differences between Papa's first family and us. I'd lived a blessed life, except for my own foolishness, free of the war and hardships that the first family had endured. Even with Preston gone, we still had much to be thankful for.

Feaster spent his days in school and his evenings doing what he loved best—caring for his menagerie and helping Red with the livestock. Mama and I did what we could to take care of day-to-day needs. But, in the meantime, mail was piling up. And according to Red, the sharecroppers' "hearts be sot with worrin'."

We were understandably relieved when Bessie returned from State Marble Works in Columbia and declared, "The headstone is settled."

Preston's obelisk would take at least three months, maybe

more, to complete. Then the chief stonemason and several of his men would accompany it by rail to Varennes and install it in Cross Roads Cemetery. We didn't expect it before fall.

Mama and I'd seen to the household and grounds fairly well. But the farmland, creditors, and sharecroppers were another matter. Once back at home, Bessie used the mornings to visit families living on the place and to reassure them of their shelter and livelihood.

As for the mail, she divided it into two piles—personal and business. She began work on the business mail during the afternoons, and the personal mail in the evenings.

A week after she'd returned from Columbia, Willis came calling again. It was early afternoon so Bessie was at her desk in the front hall. I'd decided to sit on the front porch for a bit of fresh air. I'd wrapped myself in the old gunboat quilt and settled into a rocking chair.

I hadn't been rocking for more than a few minutes when I caught sight of Willis's buggy. Actually, I'd been looking for him for several days although I hadn't told Bessie about his earlier visit. Nor had I told her about his fight with a field hand.

I dropped the quilt in the chair and went out to meet him. I noticed that he was dressed in his Sunday clothes, which I found a bit odd. He wore a starched white shirt under a black knee-length coat. His trousers looked brand new, and his boots shone with polish. He had on a deep blue necktie I hadn't seen before. Even with his hat on, I could tell that his hair was neatly trimmed. So was his moustache. In fact, as I got closer, I caught a whiff of the barbershop.

Evil eye or no evil eye, the man was heart-pounding handsome. Even Sugar gleamed. His silvery mane and tail had been currycombed smooth. And the buggy was so clean that it looked new. In fact, the whole scene seemed to be straight out of one of the romantic stories Aunt Eliza had told me. This visit appeared to be totally opposite of the last one.

"You look dapper this afternoon, Mr. McGee," I said.

He tipped his hat. "You look quite lovely yourself, Miss Jones."

Lovely was an exaggeration. I was wearing suitable mourning clothes, not black like Bessie's, but a faded purple. I'd added the gold watch that Willis had given me after he'd recovered from the mule incident. I'm not sure Papa would have approved of jewelry during mourning, but one should keep up with the hour, I'd told myself. I'd dabbed on a bit of lavender water for good measure.

When Willis and I entered the front hall, Bessie looked up from her desk. She sniffed the air several times. She looked from Willis to me and back to Willis. I thought I saw a slight smile between sniffs. I wondered which one of us she smelled.

"Hello, Willis," she said. "What brings you out on this way?"

He took off his hat and held it against his chest. "Why, I've come to talk with you, Mrs. Bessie."

Bessie stood up from her desk. She was wearing a new mourning dress. Despite her instructions, Mama had told the seamstress to make it fitted in the bodice because, she said, a mourning dress shouldn't look too comfortable.

But as Bessie stood there, greeting Willis, I realized how much weight she'd lost in the past few weeks. Despite Mama's best intentions, the dress hung on Bessie like bedclothes.

She asked Willis to take off his coat and sit on a loveseat nearby. She turned the small desk chair around to face him and sat back down. I took his coat and hat, hung them on the front hall tree, and then started to leave the room.

But he said, "Icie, please stay." He patted the empty space beside him on the loveseat. I sat down and waited.

"Mrs. Bessie," he began, "you know how very sorry I am for your loss."

She nodded.

"For the whole upcountry's loss," he added. "Preston Allen was one of the best men I've ever had the good fortune to know."

She nodded again.

He hesitated.

She glanced at me, then back to Willis.

"Everybody I know admires this fine plantation that he— that both of you—established here." He leaned forward. "Mrs. Bessie, most . . ."

"Just Bessie," she interrupted.

"Bessie, most growers out there don't realize how much your hand is in the day-to-day operation."

She frowned. "'Out there'?"

"I should say 'around here.'" He paused, then added, "I do, because I've been close to the family for some time now."

He glanced at me. My face grew warm.

"What I'm trying to say is this—there are those who don't think you can manage the land without Preston." He hurried on, "Some of them will try to take advantage of you."

Bessie rubbed her palms down the front of her skirt. "Go on."

He took a long breath then said, "I would be honored to look after your interests. As you know, my land adjoins yours across your southern boundary. So what's good for you is good for me."

She didn't reply.

He continued, "I'd never try to take anything away from you or Feaster. I realize he'll be a man soon enough and will help

shoulder the responsibility of what you and Preston have built."
He sounded as eloquent as I'd ever heard him. I wondered if he'd
practiced.

He straightened his tie and glanced at me. "I'd also have
your best interest at heart if I'm fortunate enough to become
your brother-in-law."

It was my turn to catch a breath. And I did, louder than I'd
have liked. Willis looked at me. His face seemed younger than it
had in years. His eyes were shining and hopeful.

Bessie looked at me too.

Time stood still on the outside while it rushed through years
and years inside my head. I remembered Mama saying, "Time
and tide wait for no man," and Bessie saying, "Our days are
numbered." But I also heard myself declaring I could never get
married because I couldn't be a good mother. Then I wondered
what Feaster would think, what Sallie would think, what the
whole first family would think.

Bessie cleared her throat. "Well?"

The past dropped away.

"Yes!" My voice seemed to come from somewhere deep
inside. "Yes," I repeated, with more eagerness than good man-
ners allow.

Bessie smiled. Willis and I hugged. He seemed almost as
surprised as I was.

She waited for us to regain some self-control. Then she said,
"Yes, for me too. I'm already getting demands for payment of
services that weren't provided."

At that point, Bessie and Willis began to talk about the
business at hand—reassuring sharecroppers, planting the most
profitable crops while cutting back on others, contesting claims

against Preston's estate, and on and on. But truth be told, I heard little else. Papa would have said that I was "giddy as a schoolgirl in pink pantaloons."

After they finished talking, I walked Willis to his buggy. We hugged again as though we were newly in love. And when we stopped, I smelled more like barbershop than lavender.

I picked up the gunboat quilt from the rocking chair and wrapped it around my shoulders. I had to stop myself from dancing around the porch. Such joy in the midst of mourning was as a slippery as crossing a creek on wet stones. I would have to remind myself often throughout the spring and summer to slow down and watch my step.

I wonder even now how quickly the saddest of times can give birth to the happiest. Reliving that Jesus-God moment of Willis's unusual proposal still gives me great joy.

Sometimes I wish I could have ceased to exist at that moment, at the height of happiness and expectation. But, I suppose, if life ended at the happiest of times, none of us would appreciate it. We wouldn't want to let go.

Perhaps I'm holding on too long, hoping for one more flash of grace. Or at least some understanding.

Court

Spring 1901 arrived on time regardless of our mourning for Preston. Bessie approached life with a new surge of energy. When

Mama questioned her busy comings and goings while she was supposed to be in mourning, she replied, "I see to the living in daylight. I do my weeping in the dark."

As soon as the winter wheat had been cut and stored, it was time to plant cotton. Bessie and Willis talked at length about whether to plant the usual Egyptian and Sea Island varieties or to try one of the new hybrids. They discussed the price of fertilizer and worried about cotton wilt, boll weevils, and insufficient rain. But well into June, we'd already had more rain than usual, which made local farmers, large and small alike, confident in crop estimates.

The rain continued straight through July. Peaches grew larger than I'd ever seen. Yet the extra rain diluted their sweetness, leaving them watery and bland. Green tomatoes broke open and rotted on the vine. String beans were more tender than usual, and lima beans were larger, but constant rain and muddy fields made bean-picking nearly impossible.

Then August, usually our driest month, turned into the wettest. It rained the entire month almost without ceasing. Folks who kept records said that Varennes got nearly a foot of rain during August 1901.

Fortunately, the rain didn't seem to hurt most of the cotton other than pushing the usual harvest time of late August and early September well into October. It did, however, destroy much of the corn grown to feed livestock, especially corn that'd been planted in bottoms. And there arose a problem for Bessie. She lost more than half her corn crop. She'd have to buy it elsewhere.

In years past, the Allens had hired extra tenant labor from other farms when needed, with the farm owner's permission, to make fast work of harvesting the corn. But this year, Bessie wouldn't need to hire extra labor. In fact, she noted, "There's a silver lining after all. I don't have to put any money in ole Whatley's pockets."

"Ole Whatley" referred to one Mr. J. S. Whatley, who made a living by renting out his tenants to larger growers for short-term labor. Preston had used his laborers in the past to help harvest corn.

Bessie never liked the idea. She'd say that Whatley was making money on the backs of his tenants and not giving them fair wages in return. Preston would say, "It's Whatley's men or convicts." And Bessie would give in.

But, lo and behold, Mr. Whatley demanded payment in 1901 anyway for labor never rendered, saying he had a contract with Preston for corn-picking whether or not there was corn. Bessie ignored him. She and Willis went about seeing to other farming matters. Late-summer, Whatley sent word demanding $100 or else he'd sue.

Willis got angry, but Bessie said, "Let him sue. He's got no contract."

She concentrated on the cotton crop, which, despite the rain, or perhaps because of it, had turned out to be spectacular. By early October, just as Preston had done many times, she had the first bale of cotton to go on sale in Anderson. Willis was as proud of that first bale as though it had been his own.

By mid-October, most of Bessie's cotton had been picked, baled, and sent off to market. Her crop was declared to be among the finest in the upcountry. By the end of the month, she could sit down, rest, and thank God for His infinite blessings.

But she couldn't rest for long. Whatley made good on his threat. In early November, she received a summons to appear in court. Willis insisted on going with her, and he wanted me to go too as his bride-to-be. He said, "It'll look more fitting."

Mama agreed although she made it clear that she didn't like the idea of either of her daughters in court. "It's no place for ladies," she said more than once.

County court was in session from time to time, but not on a regular basis. A traveling judge would hear up to a dozen cases in the duration of a day. Bessie's was scheduled for late morning, so we got an early start.

Willis wore Sunday clothes. So did I. Bessie wore a high-necked black dress with a somewhat fitted bodice and loose skirt. It would have been almost pretty with a colorful scarf or bright shawl, but, obviously, it was a mourning dress.

As we were about to leave, Mama hurried into the front room with something in her palm. "Here, Bessie, I want you to wear this brooch."

Bessie looked surprised. "Mama, I don't think it's proper for a widow in mourning to wear jewelry."

"It's not proper for a lady to go to court," Mama chided. "But it's fitting to wear a mourning brooch." She pinned it to Bessie's dress just under the neckline. It was oval with a black and bone inlay. Delicate gold scrollwork decorated the front. The back was smooth gold.

Bessie felt the brooch. "I'd look in the mirror," she said, "but that wouldn't be proper either."

I couldn't tell whether or not she was sincere. "It looks lovely," I said.

"It's been passed down through the women in my family," Mama said. "It'll bring you luck."

Once we were in the buggy and some distance from home, Bessie and I began to giggle.

"What on earth tickles you ladies?" Willis asked as we headed toward Anderson. Bessie and I said in unison, "a lucky mourning brooch!" We laughed like little girls for at least another mile. It felt good.

I'd never been inside the Anderson County Courthouse, so I was surprised to see that it looked like a church with rows of pews separated with an aisle up the center. The pews faced an elevated pulpit-like desk where the judge presided. Some folks stood before the judge, others sat in various clusters, and still others came and went.

We sat in the back. I recalled what Mama had told me about my half-brothers and sisters suing Papa over some property. I wondered if he'd sat in one pew while his children had sat in another. It was a sad thought.

Soon Bessie was called to the front along with Whatley. The simplest way to describe him was ordinary. Nothing about him stood out. He wouldn't have caught my eye any other time, and if I'd ever met him, I didn't remember. He and Bessie moved to the front pews, she on the left one and he on the right. Willis and I took the pew behind her.

The judge read the suit. It said something to the effect that Mrs. Bessie Allen, the defendant, had failed to honor a contract between the late Preston B. Allen and Mr. J. S. Whatley, the plaintiff. And that the defendant's failure had cost the plaintiff in excess of $100 in missed wages.

The judge looked at Bessie and asked for her response.

She stood, straightened her skirt, and began, "Your Honor, I know of no such contract. I keep the records for our operation and have done so for some twenty years. I would know."

The judge looked at Whatley, who stood and said, "I had a verbal contract with Preston Allen, your Honor."

"Go on," the judge said.

"We had an agreement that two of my laborers would aid

Mr. Allen's laborers in harvesting corn in August of 1901. It's been my practice for several years to lend him labor for such needs."

The judge looked at Bessie. "Is this true, Mrs. Allen?"

"They have done business in the past. I have no record of any such agreement for the latest crop."

The judge turned to Whatley, who said, "Your Honor, everyone in the county knows what an honorable man Preston Allen was. His word was his contract. We didn't have a paper contract because I knew none would be needed with such an honest man."

The judge seemed to digest Whatley's testimony. He turned back to Bessie. "Mrs. Allen, is it possible that you might not be privy to all such verbal agreements having to do with business and given man to man?"

Bessie's head snapped back. She made a snorting sound something like Mama's.

"Given man to man," the judge repeated.

Willis clinched his jaw. He squeezed my hand so hard I nearly yelled. I elbowed him.

Bessie twisted her wedding ring while she regained her composure. "But, your Honor, I had no corn to be picked. Mr. Whatley is asking for payment for a service never rendered."

The judge looked to Whatley. "Your Honor, my laborers still need a livelihood whether or not the good Lord decides to obliterate the corn crop. I don't have the acreage or the resources of the large growers. So my tenants depend on extra work from outside farms to help them get by."

The judge appeared to be considering Whatley's argument. Whatley quickly continued, "Everyone in the county knows how generous Preston Allen has been to his tenants and sharecroppers.

Surely he would not have wanted to shortchange those on a lesser farm who sought work but were deprived of the opportunity."

The judge turned to Bessie. "Would Mr. Allen have honored such an agreement even if there was no corn to be picked?"

"As I stated before, your Honor, I know of no such agreement." She touched the mourning brooch at her throat. "But I do know Preston Allen never would have wanted his widow to be taken advantage of, especially by someone who already takes advantage of his own tenants."

Whatley's head snapped back. I glanced at Willis. He looked straight ahead, but he was smiling.

No one spoke for what seemed an eternity. Then the judge declared, "This court finds the defendant in debt to the plaintiff and rules that Mrs. Allen shall pay Mr. Whatley $124.50."

He looked at us. "Good day, Mrs. Allen."

Then he looked back to Whatley. "Mr. Whatley, I believe you have another case on the docket today."

"I do," he replied.

The judge sorted through some papers. "And in it, I believe you're the defendant."

And there it was. J. S. Whatley was a litigious fella. Aunt Eliza's word. She'd once described the Joneses as being a "litigious bunch." I hated to think the same word might apply to both.

On the ride home, I tried to lighten Bessie's mood. "I've never heard you speak quite so eloquently," I said. I wondered if she'd practiced too.

"I can when I need to," she replied. "But it did no good. What I really wanted to say was Whatley and the judge could both go straight to the depths of hell."

"Bessie!" I exclaimed in my best Mama tone.

"Straight to hell!" she repeated louder and several notes

higher. "Preston Brooks Allen would never have lost such a suit, nor any man in his position!"

We rode home the rest of the way in silence, but she'd given me something to consider, something I doubt Papa or Willis or Preston or any other man had ever given much thought. As for the mourning brooch, it apparently brought Bessie no more luck than all the other grieving women who'd worn it.

Spirit level ↶↷

This morning I'm back in Papa's woodshop. Dreaming or remembering, it's getting difficult to know the difference.

Papa is humming a hymn—"How Firm a Foundation." Mama and Bessie have gone to town leaving Papa to look after me. The dizzying smells of pine and cedar hang in the air. As he hums, he works on a small, skinny table atop his workbench. The table is wider than Mama's desk but only half as deep. I hope it's for me even though it looks too tall.

"Is that a desk, Papa?" I ask.

"Nope," he says without looking down at me. "It's a sewin' table for your mama."

He goes back to humming so I begin to sing, "How-ow firm a foun-DAY-shun, you SAINTS of the Lord, is-uz laid for your FAITH in his ex-SEE-lent word."

Papa stops and smiles. "That's real pretty, Icie," he says. "Didja know that was Gen. Lee's favorite hymn?"

"No, sir," I say.

"Yep, they sang it at his buryin'."

He turns his attention back to the work at hand. He hunches down until his eyes are even with the table. Then he picks up one of his tools and lays it on the top. It's a smooth, flat piece of wood the width of a chair leg and about a foot long. It has a small, clear tube attached to it. The tube appears to have water inside.

"What's that?" I ask.

"Spirit level," Papa says as he moves it around the table. "It shows what's level and what ain't." He holds it low for me. "See the bubble? When things are nice and even, the bubble floats to the middle, right there on the line. See?"

I watch the magical bubble slide from side to side, then float to the center in Papa's hands. He sets it on the workbench, flips the table upside down, and begins scraping a blade across the end of one of the legs.

I pick up the spirit level to examine it for myself. I seesaw it in my hands, watching the bubble race back and forth. Then I try to coax the bubble to the center. I begin to understand the level part, but not the spirit.

"Papa, does it have a spirit?" I ask.

"Yep," he says. He flips the table right side up and lays the level on top again. "Yep," he repeats. He seems pleased with the adjustment.

"Is the spirit inside the little bubble?" I ask.

"Uh huh," he says. He places a yardstick on top of the table and begins marking inches along its front edge.

"What if the spirit gets out?" I ask.

"Then the level don't work no more," he says.

I spend a long time watching Papa carve a yard's worth of inches into the smooth tabletop and trace each line in ink. And all the while, I secretly hope the spirit bubble will escape.

I want to stay right there in Papa's workshop forever. But I hear Anah's voice. "Time to wake up, Mizz Icie," she says, "time to eat some grits and butter."

Papa, his magical spirit level, and my childhood— disappear in the morning light.

Bessie had scarcely returned from the Anderson Courthouse when she received word that Preston's headstone was on the way. The stonemason and four of his men were to bring it by railroad into Varennes the next day.

She asked Red to choose another three men to work with the stone crew. Although it was a weekday, she let Feaster stay home from school, saying she'd needed him to drive the buggy for her to and from the cemetery throughout the day.

So, the morning after Bessie's court appearance, the monument arrived at the depot in pieces. The stonemason needed four wagons to haul it to the cemetery. The base and the second layer required one wagon. The third layer, which was skinnier but much taller, took another wagon, and the obelisk took a third. The fourth wagon held a large pulley device and tools.

Because the installation was a daylong affair, just about every man in town who had an hour or two to spare stopped by Cross Roads Cemetery to watch.

Mama stayed away, saying it wasn't fitting to spend the day in a graveyard around a bunch of men out of just plain curiosity. But I tagged along with Feaster and Bessie in the buggy to watch. The stonemason and his men spent much of the morning scraping and pounding the ground at the head of Preston's grave.

The mason kept sliding a long, flat tool across the packed earth. It was something like Papa's spirit level without the mystery. I'd learned long ago that the only spirit in Papa's level was liquor in the little glass tube. He'd let me think otherwise much too long although I'd found the truth disappointing.

The stonemason's level was larger than Papa's and made of metal. He swiped it back and forth across the cleared dirt, pointed at a spot, and waited for a worker to scrape it with the edge of a shovel or slam it with the back.

I flinched with each scrape and bang, fearing the commotion would tear open Bessie's heart. Yet she stood motionless.

Feaster glanced at me, then back at the workmen. After several more flinches on my part, he said, "They're preparing the ground for the foundation stone. It needs to be level and compacted."

Once the stonemason was satisfied with the plot of ground at the head of Preston's grave, he turned his attention to removing the foundation stone from the wagon. The driver steered the wagon bed as close as he could. Then the mason and his men assembled the pulley contraption almost directly over the bare ground.

Beneath the stone were several metal rods. A worker slipped the end of a chain attached to the pulley over each end of the center rod. Then several other men tugged on the rods while another operated the pulley. Soon, men surrounded the stone and somehow eased it down at the head of Preston's grave.

Bessie, Feaster, and I exhaled simultaneously. The stonemason ran the level over it and seemed satisfied.

I noticed four small, evenly spaced holes in the stone. Soon workmen began hammering metal stakes into the holes, leaving about half of each stake exposed. The crash of hammers on metal seemed sacrilegious. When we were children, Mama had often warned us to be quiet in the cemetery. "You don't want to be waking the dead."

I began to understand her way of thinking. I felt as though I'd surely get a case of the nerves if the hammering didn't stop. It didn't, so I excused myself and walked the mile back to the Allen house in the coolness of the November morning.

Bessie and Feaster stayed long enough to see the second stone lifted and threaded onto the bottom stone. Then Feaster brought Bessie home. She said she had work to do and would return in the afternoon. But she didn't go back until the end of the day.

Shortly before sunset, Red came to the back door and told Bessie that the work was done and the crew was ready to leave. She got her purse and settled up with Red including pay for the local men who'd helped.

Then she pulled on her coat and called Feaster to drive her back to the cemetery. Since the workmen were finished, Mama and I decided to ride along to see the completed headstone. He hitched up Preston's spirited sorrel pair and helped us women folk into the carriage. Blaze and Star seemed excited to be out.

Although the sun had nearly set, we could make out the

top of the obelisk some distance from the cemetery. Once there, Feaster, Mama, and I admired the stonework close up while Bessie settled with the mason. The monument was an imposing blend of architecture and art. The obelisk was draped in a stone apron, as Feaster had drawn out earlier. Along the edge of the apron was engraved "AT REST."

On the stone beneath the obelisk was the Masonic vector. It was a combination of an architect's square and compass with a "G" in the center that stood for God or Great Architect. I knew what it was because Preston had explained it to me in great detail more than once. For him, it was second only to the cross.

Centered below the vector was "Preston B. Allen, born Jan. 16, 1856, died Mar. 8, 1901." Beneath that was a smaller inscription in stylized lettering—"It was hard indeed to part with thee, but Christ's strong arm supporteth me." Tears welled up as I read it over and over in my mind. "ALLEN" was engraved in large letters on the bottom stone. The rest of Preston's grave was outlined in strips of marble like a picture frame.

As the stone crew drove away, Bessie joined us.

Mama said, "It's the tallest headstone I've ever seen."

"Twelve feet," Feaster said.

"It's certainly appropriate for the good deeds he did on the earth," I added. Everyone agreed.

Then Mama said, "Let's go back to the carriage and let Bessie be with Preston."

Bessie didn't object. She stood at the headstone while we waited in the carriage. All was quiet except for the swish of Blaze's tail and a bit of neighing. I thought I heard Bessie whispering, but I couldn't be sure. She ran her fingers across Preston's name. Then she slowly and carefully traced the smaller inscription.

Night had fallen by the time she made her way back to the

carriage. "Janey will have supper waiting," she said without looking at any of us. We rode the short distance home in silence with
the chill of the evening creeping in. Feaster helped each of us
out at the front door, then drove around back to take care of the
horses and the carriage.

Inside, the air was noticeably warmer. The wonderful smell
of supper wrapped around us. It felt good to be back among the
living.

Mama stopped at the front hall tree and hung her coat. Then
she hurried into the kitchen to help Janey. I quickly removed
my coat and hung it next to Mama's. I noticed that Bessie was
staring at Preston's empty hook on the hall tree. Then she slowly
hung her coat on her usual hook next to his. I tried to think
of something to comfort her. But nothing came. She seemed
unsteady so I positioned myself at her back as though I could
catch her if she fell.

But she did not. Instead, she took a deep breath and
smoothed her ball of hair pinned at the nape of her neck. She
took another breath, straightened the bodice of her latest black
dress, and turned around.

She was almost smiling. She put her hands on my shoulders.
"Isamar Woods Jones," she said, looking me straight in the face,
"it's high time we plan a wedding!"

Cognac ⌒

The evening that Preston's marble monument was installed,
Janey had a chicken pie waiting for us. It was just out of the oven
so Bessie propped open the swinging door between the kitchen
and dining room to let the heat even out.

Although the crusty pie looked and smelled wonderful, I expected a somber meal after such an emotional day. Feaster must have, too. He asked to take his supper in his room to which Bessie agreed. He spooned steaming pie onto his plate along with two cornbread sticks and left the dining room.

After we'd served ourselves, Bessie repeated what she'd told me in the hall, only this time to Mama. "It's high time we plan Icie's wedding," she said. Mama looked up, her fork balanced in her hand, but she said nothing. Bessie continued, "I was thinking we could host a modest ceremony right here in the front room next month. We'll make it a week or so before Christmas."

Mama's fork clanged against the china plate and flipped onto the floor.

"Next month!" she shouted in disbelief.

"Yep," Bessie continued, "just a few guests, and the minister."

I watched Mama. She seemed frozen in mid-breath. I was afraid she'd sucked a chunk of chicken down her windpipe.

"Are you all right, Mama?" I asked, about to stand and come to her aid.

"No!" she cried. "I don't know how we can plan a wedding in just a month!" She lowered her voice a bit. "And in a household that's in mourning."

Bessie took a sip of tea. "As you've told us often enough—'There's no time like the present.'" She glanced at me.

"'Gather ye rosebuds while ye may,'" I said, remembering something Aunt Eliza had quoted to me long ago. Bessie raised an eyebrow. Perhaps it wasn't as fitting as I thought, so I tried again. "'Make hay while the sun shines.'"

Bessie agreed. Mama stared. Bessie took another turn. "'Lost time is never found.'"

Mama still didn't respond so I waded in again with " 'Time and tide . . .' "

But she cut me off. "I know 'time and tide wait for no man'!"

"Nor woman," Bessie added. She and I laughed. I thought I heard a giggle from the kitchen.

Then Bessie turned serious. "You never know what tomorrow brings." An obvious reference to Preston's death.

"You girls outnumber me," Mama said, her face softening.

"You taught us well," I said.

This time she laughed with us. She seemed to relax and even enjoy herself as we ate chicken pie and made plans for my December wedding.

Just as we were finishing the meal, Red came for Janey. Bessie went into the kitchen and bid them goodnight. Then she disappeared into the parlor. When she reappeared, she was carrying a bottle of Preston's cognac. She set it on the sideboard and retrieved three brandy glasses.

She poured us each a moderate amount. Then she raised her glass and said, "To Preston Brooks Allen. May his goodness live on in all of us."

Mama and I raised our cognac in response. We Jones women softly clinked our glasses, said, "Here, here," and took a sip. We discussed Preston's greatness as we slowly drank our brandy.

When we'd emptied our glasses, Bessie poured us another portion, a little more generous than the first. She raised her glass again. "To Icie and Willis, may their marriage be long and happy."

"Here, here," Mama and I responded, lifting our glasses in unison. And there began another round of clinking and sipping in which we discussed Willis's many merits.

By the time we finished the second glass, we'd all had quite enough, especially after such an emotional day. But Mama shocked Bessie and me.

"We're not finished," she said. Bessie and I looked at each other. I'm sure my eyes were as wide as hers. "Quit looking at each other like that," she said, "like you girls have done all your lives." She turned back to Bessie. "Pour us another round. And be generous."

Bessie poured like an obedient daughter.

This time Mama raised her glass first. "To William Jones and the life we had with him!"

Bessie and I raised our brandy too and said, "Here, here," not exactly in unison. Then we Jones women clanked our glasses and recounted every pleasant memory of Papa we could recall.

After the third round, little brandy remained. But I wanted to make a toast. So Bessie distributed the final bit of cognac evenly, then held the bottle upside down over her own glass until it dripped no more.

She and Mama looked at me expectantly. I raised my glass. "Here's to the Second Family of Joneses, the best of the lot!"

Bessie and Mama raised their glasses, shouted "Here, here!" louder than before. We banged our glasses and drank. We finished off the night washing dishes and reliving as many childhood memories as we dared. One cup was dropped and two plates chipped. I don't recall the guilty party.

The next morning Janey knocked on my bedroom door, awakening me from a deep sleep. "Miz Icie, wake up!" she said. "It's Mr. Willis." She knocked some more. "He's got his courtin' buggy and his big ole buttermilk stud."

I thanked Janey and pushed out of bed. I'd somehow overslept so I quickly dressed and hurried downstairs. I found Willis at the kitchen table having a cup of coffee with Feaster. A plate of warm biscuits sat between them. I wondered if Mama and Bessie were up. Feaster excused himself and left for school.

"Morning," Willis said. "You're looking a little blurry-eyed."

"And good morning to you, too," I replied, making myself a cup of tea. I added two teaspoons of sugar. "Yesterday was draining. Preston's headstone and such."

"Feaster was just telling me."

"It's the finest headstone I've ever seen," I declared, giving my tea a stir.

He split open a biscuit. "I plan to see it for myself this morning. Wanna join me?"

"I'd love to," I said. I sipped on the hot sweet liquid while he finished his biscuit and ate another one.

Then we boarded his buggy and took the short ride to Cross Roads Cemetery. Willis stopped Sugar at a respectful distance and walked around the buggy to help me down. He reached up, caught me by my waist, and pulled me into his arms. By the time my feet touched the ground, the rest of me was in a full embrace.

"I'm not sure such affection is appropriate in the cemetery," I teased, clinging to him all the while.

He laughed. "I'm restraining myself from much more inappropriate affection. Anyway, we're among kin." He was right. Cross Roads Cemetery held more McGees and Joneses that any other families.

We walked toward Preston's obelisk, careful not to step on other graves as we went.

"There's wide speculation on just how much such a fine marble marker costs," he said.

"I haven't asked. Neither has Mama, although she's wondered out loud more than once."

"I won't be asking either. But it must be a lot."

"Feaster would know," I said. "But he wouldn't tell me. Perhaps, he'd tell you. He seems quite fond of you."

"He's a fine young man," Willis replied. "Smart, polite, eager to learn. He already knows alot about managing the Allen land. Bessie's lucky to have him."

"Yes, she is," I said, somehow feeling pride in a matter that had long been out of my hands.

Willis circled Preston's monument several times. Then he reached as high as he could and touched the obelisk. "This tower of marble must be eleven or twelve feet tall."

"Twelve," I said. "It certainly bears witness to Bessie's love for Preston and to what a powerful man he was."

"And to just how powerful his widow still is," Willis said.

It was an odd thought, something I hadn't considered.

"Bessie Jones Allen is a woman to be reckoned with," he added. "This'll be here long after we're gone."

"If you go first, I'll make sure you have one equally grand," I promised.

"And if I outlive you, which is highly unlikely," he countered, "I'll make yours even grander."

We both laughed. Being in love made dying seem so distant even as we stood in the midst of death's domain.

PART IX

Down the river

Trousseau ⌒

Although Mama had hoped our wedding would wait until after Bessie's first year of mourning, she'd been quietly amassing my trousseau. In fact, she'd started in late March, the day after Willis made his odd proposal.

I say "amassing" because my trousseau had twice as much clothing as I needed, a matter that Mama and I didn't completely agree on.

"Who needs a dozen drawers?" I asked as she went over the list. She was sitting at Bessie's desk in the front parlor, and I was a captive audience of one on the loveseat.

"A lady," she said, without looking up. "Keep your voice down. You don't want to be announcing to the whole household."

"Did Bessie have a dozen drawers when she married Preston?" I whispered.

"No," she said, still working on the list.

"Wasn't she a lady?"

Mama put down her pen, looked over her shoulder, and gave me a stare that could still wither the child in me. "Of course she was! Her trousseau was as complete as I could make it, given our means."

I blinked first.

"Besides," she added, a bit more kindly, "I didn't have time to put together a fine trousseau. Preston was on fire to marry her, and I couldn't make them wait any longer."

Mama went back to her list, "Six everyday cotton petticoats and two silk ones for special occasions."

"What about when you married Papa," I asked. "What was in your trousseau?"

She set her pen down again.

"You were a lady of considerable means, weren't you?" I continued, recalling that Aunt Eliza had said Mama came from old money.

She drew in a long breath and let it out slowly. She turned her chair to face me. "My mother's family had been. And my father's family was comfortable enough. But all that was before the war. Both families lost most of what they had."

"But you married Papa before the war, didn't you?"

"Yes," she said. "But I think we all knew it was coming. Times were too uncertain to be frivolous."

"A trousseau was frivolous?" I asked, realizing the irony of her working so hard on mine now.

"Times were different. Anyway, I had no intention of marrying and having babies. I'd grown up raising babies!"

"But there stood Papa," I said.

Mama smiled and looked past me. A softness came over her. Her cheeks seemed a bit rounder, even pinkish. "You girls asked for that story enough to make a preacher cuss."

"And there stood Papa," I repeated.

"Yes. There stood Mr. William Jones, the handsomest man I'd ever seen."

"And he talked you into marriage despite your best intentions."

She nodded in agreement but seemed to be somewhere else.

"Did you have a trousseau at all?" I asked.

"I hadn't thought I'd need one," she admitted. "While my

sisters were embroidering handkerchiefs and wishing for husbands, I was cooking or gardening or taking care of them. Besides, your papa didn't give me time to put together much." She smiled again and continued, "Despite my mother's loud objections, I went into marriage with just the clothes I already had."

"What!" I nearly shouted.

She returned to the present. "That was a different time and no excuse for you not having one of your own. You're a lady of means."

Mama was right about having means. Since Papa had died and we'd moved in with the Allens, we'd received income from the rental of our house. Preston had continued to farm our land and give us the profits from that too. And I still earned a wage as church organist.

I also knew that I'd inherit the homeplace upon Mama's death. So, without much labor on my part, I'd become a lady of comfortable means. On the other hand, I tried to follow Bessie's example of being charitable. Whether I succeeded or not would be in the final reckoning, which seemed at a great distance in late 1901.

Because Mama had her hands full with my trousseau, she left the wedding dress to me and the dressmaker. A traditional white wedding gown was out of the question. I didn't intend to start another scandal.

Even though we hadn't set a date at the time, I knew it would be in cold weather, well after harvest and winter planting. So I planned accordingly. I'd decided on a fashionable walking suit made out of a wool-and-silk blend in a soft blue-gray color. The skirt was gored, which meant it was made of three triangular pieces, giving it the appearance of an A. I wondered what Papa would have thought about a "gored" skirt.

The short double-breasted jacket was military style, trimmed in black buttons the size of nickels. The blouse had long sleeves gathered at the shoulders, a lacy front panel with pearl buttons, and a stand-up collar. Thank heavens it was silk so that my snug jacket could slide on fairly easily.

For jewelry, I planned to wear the gold watch that Willis had given me a few years earlier. At the time, we'd both known it was meant as an engagement gift though neither of us had said so aloud.

Bessie set the wedding date for December 17 at the Allen house. My guest list was small, but Bessie insisted on inviting the first family. I didn't object, but I doubted any of them would show up unless it was for Willis. Dock and his wife, Sarah, who was Willis's cousin, sent their regrets along with a fine set of leather-working tools. But their eldest son, Dolph, said he'd come and bring his guitar if I wanted.

Mattie, whose deceased husband was also Willis's cousin, surprised me by sending word that she'd come. Johnny would've come to please Mama, but he'd developed bursitis in his afflicted leg and found travel difficult. As for Sammy, we'd practically lost contact with him and his family. We didn't hear back and weren't even sure if we had his latest address.

I knew Sallie and J. E. wouldn't come although I was sure they'd be pleased that I was, at last, being made an honest woman.

I asked Bessie to include Aunt Lou, who'd become postmistress at Dean Station, and Aunt Eliza, who was still teaching in Tennessee. We heard immediately from Aunt Lou. She said she'd close the post office and come. That was Aunt Lou. Aunt Eliza wrote that she so wished she could see "little Icie marry her Romeo," but she had some sort of crisis with her daughter, Willie. Ah, the mysterious Willie.

Other than Aunt Eliza, I didn't care who else sent their regrets. I was too giddy in love to need more than Willis and the Allen household to make me happy.

Several days before the wedding, Feaster caught me alone. I'd just sat down in the front room to make a list of last-minute tasks. He stood in the doorway and looked around, perhaps checking to see if Mama or Bessie was with me. Seeing no one else, he pulled up a chair near my own.

He was very polite at first. "I'm happy for you and Willis," he said looking down at his hands.

"Thank you, Feaster," I said. "That means so much to me." For a moment I thought about reaching out and touching him on the shoulder.

Then he added, "Since you may soon be having children with Willis, the proper way . . ." He paused. I stiffened. My heart sped up. "Maybe," he continued, picking up speed, "you'd be so kind as to tell me who my own father is."

This time he looked me in the eye. My face felt on fire.

"Your father was and still is Preston Brooks Allen!" I declared.

His face flushed crimson and he stared so hard I could see the white all around his blue eyes.

I realized what he must be thinking. "Not that way!" I shouted, "but he was your father in every way that mattered!"

I looked away as he rose to leave. Then he turned and spoke again, "Not telling a child who fathered him is the most selfish, cruel act a mother can do."

That was the last real conversation we had. I was as angry with him as he with me. How dare he call me cruel, I thought.

He'd lived a charmed life with Bessie and Preston! I was afraid looking for a long-lost father would only cause him pain. Bessie too. How was that cruel?

All my fears about being a dreadful mother rushed back. But I was determined not to let them smother me. Love and happiness were within my grasp. I had no intention of letting them slip away. I began avoiding Feaster as much as he had me. And at last I was glad to be leaving the Allen household.

At this moment and in this sorry state, I must admit that Feaster was right. At least about my being selfish. Truth is I didn't want anything interfering with Willis's and my life together. No stirring of the waters. No dredging up the past.

Now, if I could tell him about Alexander from the Lowcountry, I would. I would tell him and let him make his own decisions. He could judge me no more harshly than he already has.

Ah, the irony. Aunt Eliza's sad stories of human frailty are all too true.

For the second time

The morning before the wedding, just as I was trying to persuade Willis to tell me where we were going on our honeymoon, Mama rushed in.

"Willis McGee!" she shouted.

She startled us both. Willis jumped up from the loveseat. She wagged her finger at him. "Don't you know the groom's not supposed to see the bride for a full day before the wedding?"

He didn't answer.

"You'll bring bad luck to the marriage," she said with all the authority Papa had used when dictating "The Rules for Mourning."

Willis looked relieved. He replied, "You're right, Mrs. Emily. If I leave now, I should be in good standing as a groom." He winked at me and pulled on his coat.

"But Willis," I called after him, "where are we going?"

He closed the door. Then opened it partway, stuck his head in, and said, "Pack for ten days." He quickly closed the door again. I ran after him, but he cleared the porch and leaped into his buggy before I could stop him.

I came back in. Mama was still in the parlor, and I was annoyed. "Mama," I said, "he was about to tell me where we're going for the honeymoon!"

She spun on her heels to leave. "Sounds like a long trip," she said over her shoulder. "Guess you'll need all those drawers after all."

Before I could react, it dawned on me—ten days! A ten-day honeymoon would include Christmas. That meant I'd be missing Christmas in Varennes. I'd always spent holidays with Mama and Bessie.

This Christmas of all holidays would be the saddest at the Allen household. Although Feaster would be hostile, Bessie would surely need me. And Mama. I began to regret leaving. I rushed to find Bessie in the pantry. She was hugging the cut-glass punchbowl Preston had given her for their 20th anniversary.

She carried it into the dining room. "I know we're not having a wedding dinner," she said, "but I think we can surely have fruit punch and Janey's angel food cake."

"But Bessie," I said, my voice cracking. "I won't be here for Christmas."

"I should think not," she said, setting the bowl on the table. "You'll be with Willis!"

"I thought we'd be back."

"Even so," she said, "you have another family now. You'll need to be with them." She turned the bowl until it caught the morning sun. Little blades of light shot out and reflected on the wall like a kaleidoscope.

"But not this first Christmas without Preston," I whined. Tears sprung up. I dabbed them back. "It'll be so sad. I should be here."

Bessie left the bowl. She walked across the dining room and wrapped her arms around me. My head barely reached her chin. Full grown, I was still the little sister.

"We'll miss you, Icie. But we'll have a fine holiday." She pulled out a chair for me. Then she sat beside me. "We'll spend Christmas Eve delivering gifts to the families here, the same as Preston and I've done since we had enough land to need sharecroppers."

My throat was too tight to say anything. She put her hand on top of mine and continued, "We've put aside hams for every family. And Mama will bake pies."

"And shawls?" I asked, my voice cracking.

"And the fine shawls you made for each of the ladies," she added. "And the quilt you made for Janey and Red."

I sniffed.

She smiled and continued, "Feaster's been gathering toys for the little ones. He's making some himself out of sticks and string and whatnot, like Papa used to do."

I remembered the stick horses Papa'd made for us one Christmas. I began to feel a little better.

"Besides, if we get to feeling too blue, Mama and I just might get into another bottle of Preston's cognac."

I managed a weak giggle, then another and another, until she said, "I believe you've got a case of the nerves." She patted my hand, stood up, and went back to planning punch and cake.

Our wedding was set for early afternoon in case the weather turned bad and folks needed to get home in a hurry. But the day was as lovely as December has to offer—sunny and mild. Janey and Mama had filled the front parlor mantelpiece with glossy magnolia leaves and heavenly scented winter honeysuckle. They'd added more of the same to the dining room table where punch and angel food cake awaited our guests.

On my side of the family were Bessie, Feaster, Mama, my half-sister Mattie, my nephew Dolph, and Aunt Lou, who did, in fact, close Dean Station Post Office for the ceremony.

On Willis's side were his two brothers and their wives, one of his sisters, and his mother, Mrs. Mary, whom he called "Mam." As far as I knew, she approved of me. She was always kind and gracious and seemed genuinely pleased that her eldest born was at last getting married.

As I came down the staircase in my wedding suit, I fixed my eyes on Willis to settle my nerves. He was dressed in the same black suit he'd worn for the proposal along with a vest and a starched white shirt that must have felt like armor. A tight-looking black bowtie hid the tips of his collar.

Rev. Ligon conducted the ceremony, and Dolph played parlor music on his guitar. Willis seemed eager to get the vows over and done. I barely remember what was said until the "I do" part.

It was another Jesus-God moment. In an instant I'd become part of a world beyond my own little second family. With just a few words spoken before a preacher, I'd graduated into a first family. It was a heady realization, one I'd need to tuck away and think about later.

Bessie surprised us with a photographer. She'd hired him for the entire day so he could take pictures not only of Willis and me but of the guests too. Almost as soon Rev. Ligon declared us "man and wife," we were ushered into a spare bedroom where the photographer had set up shop. He was so lively that I wondered if he'd found Preston's brandy. He had me stand and Willis sit on a stool draped in dark cloth.

I'd never seen such a wedding portrait with the bride standing, looking at the groom, and the groom sitting, looking up at the bride. The photographer kept saying, "This pose is unheard of around here, but it's the latest in the cities."

He fussed with my skirt and jacket until Willis loudly cleared his throat. Then the photographer turned to Willis and commented on how handsome he was and what a beautiful couple we made. Something he probably said to every couple, but it seemed to calm whatever temper might be smoldering in Willis. If only for a moment.

The photographer noticed my gold watch. He said "what an exquisite necklace" it made, and how he wanted it to show in the portrait. With his back to Willis, he leaned toward me reaching for the watch, which hung against my silk blouse and between my breasts.

Willis's jaw tightened and he came off the stool. Perhaps the photographer saw my eyes widen or heard the scraping of the stool legs. He quickly stepped back and asked if I might want to slip off the watch and hold it out in my hand for the portrait. Then he retreated to his camera.

Willis settled back onto the stool. I took off the watch, held it out in my hand as instructed, and tried to relax. Then flash-poof! We had a wedding portrait. Actually, there were a number of flash-poofs until Willis stood up and said, "That's enough."

While the photographer tended his camera, Willis took the watch and chain from my hand and gently slipped it over my head. He adjusted the watch over my blouse. Then he spread his fingers across my breasts and winked. Yes, indeed, I was married.

It was late afternoon by the time we were ready to leave. I should say, "by the time I was ready to leave." Willis had been ready to go as soon as Rev. Ligon declared us one in a state of holy matrimony.

His brother drove us to the Hotel Chiquola in Anderson. The ride was cool and quiet except for the rhythm of the horses' hooves against the road. The air was refreshing. As happy as I'd been with the wedding guests, I was relieved to be leaving the noise behind. By the time we reached the hotel, it was dinner-time. We sent our bags to our rooms, cleaned up a bit, and went into the dining room.

There we ordered roasted chicken, some vegetables, including a kind of squash I'd never heard of, and little puffy rolls. Willis selected a bottle of wine. He said it was a mite sweeter than he liked, but it was pink like my cheeks.

The wine and rolls came first.

Willis poured us each a glass. "To Mr. and Mrs. McGee,"

he said, lifting his glass toward me. I raised mine and repeated, "To Mr. and Mrs. McGee." We clinked glasses, and I took a sip. It tasted just the right amount of sweetness.

"The Chiquola is delightful," I said, after several more sips. "Are we staying here for ten days?"

"No, my beautiful bride, just for the night. Tomorrow we'll take the train to Augusta." He passed me the basket of rolls and then took one himself.

My cheeks did feel rosy. "Augusta," I repeated. I broke open a roll and peered inside. It was hollow. "I've always wanted to go there. The only thing I know about Augusta is that you and Bessie sell cotton there. Oh, and that Sherman didn't burn it for some unknown reason. I suppose you've been there lots of times." I took another sip of wine.

"That I have. For business, always for business." He took a larger sip, swallowed, and continued, "Augusta has a river walk. It's a long stretch along the Savannah River, paved in bricks and lit with street lamps." He reached across the table and took my hand. "Fine fellas take their lovely ladies there."

"To do what?" I asked. "Promenade?"

"If 'promenade' means to walk around and look pretty, then, yep, that's what they do."

I tried the roll. It nearly melted in my mouth. I drank more wine.

By the time our roasted chicken and vegetables arrived, we'd drunk half the bottle of wine. I'd not eaten all day, and if Willis had, it wasn't evident. Perhaps the wine improved our appetites. Or the other way around. The chicken, most of the vegetables, and the rest of the bottle went quickly. We agreed the squash was suspect.

After dinner, we'd scarcely gotten into our room before Willis began kissing me and dispensing with my clothing. First came my jacket, which slid off easily because of the silk blouse. He dropped his own jacket and commenced to kissing my neck.

He got past the little standup collar. But the tiny pearl buttons down my blouse proved difficult. So I took over the buttons while he continued to kiss me and tug on the waist of my skirt.

I thought he'd have trouble unfastening it, too, but my fine gored skirt fell to the floor and turned in on itself. His pants were close behind. He disposed of his tie with one hand and his shirt with the other. By then, I'd unfastened the buttons to my blouse. He quickly peeled it back and off my arms, kissing me up and down all the while.

And so continued a whirlwind of kisses and dwindling clothing until I grew dizzy in his arms. And for the second time in my life, I fell headlong into pounding waves of passion. I felt like I was dying and being reborn in his love. But this time, and every time to follow, I knew the man. I knew his last name. And I knew the difference.

I come back to my wedding day as often as I dare. Remembering now is bittersweet. Yet I am grateful. Then I pack it away in my mind like my wedding suit in the cedar chest.

My beautiful gold watch is packed away, too. Feaster may eventually find it of value. Perhaps, if he has a daughter or granddaughter, he'll give it to her. I wonder what he'll tell her about the name engraved inside.

Augusta

The morning after our wedding, we took the Savannah Valley Railroad for a four-hour ride to Augusta. Until then, the farthest I'd ridden a train was to Greenville on a shopping trip with Bessie. The ride, however, was old hat to Willis who'd taken it many times to market his cotton. He dozed off after the first hour and left me to my thoughts, which turned to Papa.

My first image of riding on a train had come from his account of going to Richmond to get his brother's body in the dead of winter. I imagined Papa on his jarring, dreary, cold ride home with only Uncle James's coffin to keep him company. I felt a deep sadness for him. I wondered what he'd done to pass the time. Most likely he'd tried to keep his mind on Mama and Bessie, only a year old then, his children from the first family, and the struggling farm.

What a difference less than four decades had made. Aunt Eliza would say "fewer than four decades." Either way, I felt amazed at the progress. In 1901, people rode the train to do business or shop or visit relatives or go on honeymoons, while in the 1860s, soldiers had traveled to fight and die or to bring home the dead. I thanked God yet again that I'd been born after the war, if only by a month.

I was glad when Willis woke up and kept me company again. My thoughts returned to our trip. Then it occurred to me that we'd eventually need to cross the Savannah River to get to Augusta.

"How do we get across the river?" I asked.

"By bridge," he said, shaking off sleep.

I shuddered.

"That train trestle is a heckuva lot safer than the track that runs through Anderson," he offered as though that would comfort me. I suppose he was right because we made it across. Of course, I did keep my eyes closed.

When we reached the Augusta Railroad Station, all fear of crossing the river had dissolved. I'd never seen such a busy platform. Once on solid ground, I turned in a complete circle trying to take in all the sights. Willis seemed amused.

He claimed our baggage and sent it ahead to our hotel. Then we walked to a corner where people were boarding a streetcar. He spoke to the conductor and ushered me onto the car. We sat facing out toward the sidewalks.

With so many streetcars coming and going, I wondered how he knew which one to take. But I didn't ask. I just followed along pretending I wasn't such a novice traveler. We rode the car a few miles north to a part of Augusta called Summerville and stopped at the Bon Air Hotel. The hotel was larger and the grounds grander than anything I'd ever seen.

It was five stories tall with carriage stalls at ground level. I didn't know as much about architecture as Feaster and Bessie, but from the giant turret and ornate woodwork, I took it to be Victorian.

"Whadda you think?" Willis asked, as the streetcar stopped and people began to get off.

"I'm speechless," I replied, which I realized was ironic.

He was clearly pleased. "I've watched them build this fine hotel over the last few years with this moment in mind."

He helped me down from the streetcar and into a gleaming carriage, which carried us to the grand entrance. From there we climbed stairs onto an enormous veranda. A butler in a black uniform and shiny black shoes stood at the entrance. He held the door open for us as we strode.

Then I waited as Willis ambled up to the front desk. "Reservations for Mr. and Mrs. Willis McGee," he announced.

"Ah yes, Mr. McGee," the silver-haired lady at the desk replied. She picked up a brass key and a basket of fruit and led us through what seemed to be a mile of twists and turns to our room. She balanced the basket on her hip and opened the door into what would've been plenty of space for a family. She set the basket on a massive sideboard and handed the key to Willis. She recited something about enjoying our stay at the Bon Air Hotel and quickly exited the room.

No sooner had the door closed behind her than Willis and I burst out laughing like children left alone to play.

"How many rooms are in this city of a hotel?" I asked, pulling off my gloves.

"Three hundred, I'm told," he said, tugging at my coat.

I slipped out of my jacket. "I'd surely get lost here quicker than in a forest."

"I'd find you, Mrs. McGee," he replied, now busy with the rest of my clothes.

"And so you would," I said, falling back against the four-poster's feather mattress.

Once we'd broken in the bedding to Willis's satisfaction and caught our breath, we redressed, left the hotel, and took another streetcar back to the river. The streetlights were already starting to come on outlining the brick walkway along the Savannah. Restaurants and shops lined the shore and reflected in the water's shiny black surface. There we had a meal of catfish and squab, which I thought was delightful until Willis told me it was pigeon.

After dinner, he declared, "We've got just enough time to stroll along the river walk. Will you be so kind as to join me, Mrs. McGee?" He bowed.

"I'd be delighted, Mr. McGee," I responded. I followed with a curtsey.

And so we began the much-anticipated river walk, arm-in-arm, with all the self-absorbed joy of two people freshly in love. Our separate strides adjusted—longer steps for me, shorter for him—as though we were dancing side-by-side on the fanciful promenade.

The next morning, Willis took me to what he called the heart and soul of August. The heart, as he and probably most cotton growers saw it, was the Augusta Cotton Exchange, a large structure of brick, stone, and iron. It was four stories tall and sat at the intersection of two busy streets with the main entrance on the corner. It looked to be open so I thought we were going inside, but he stopped at the front steps.

"Shall you give me the grand tour?" I asked. For the first time in my life I actually wanted to explore the business of cotton.

"I would, my dear," he said in a tone I almost didn't recognize, "but women aren't allowed."

I felt a stinging rejection, almost a slap. I blushed.

"Oh, Icie, it's just a tradition," he said in a softer tone. "You wouldn't be comfortable anyhow."

"Why not?"

"'Cause buying and selling's the business of men. No place for a lady."

I was sure Mama would agree. But I wondered about Bessie. So I asked, "What about Bessie now that Preston's gone?"

"This season she trusted me to do her bidding," he said, leading me away from the entrance. "I dealt with her crop same as my own."

"I'm sure you did. I just wonder how she feels about not being able to go inside to sell her own crop."

"Don't know," he replied, as though it had never occurred to him. "She probably knows it's just the way of the world."

Maybe so, I thought as we turned our backs to the no longer appealing Augusta Cotton Exchange, but I planned to ask her just the same.

The soul of Augusta was its wealth of churches—Presbyterian, Baptist, Methodist, even Roman Catholic. The grandest, at least from the outside, was the Church of the Most Sacred Heart. It was quite tall with two spires, all sorts of brickwork patterns, and too many stained-glass windows to count.

"I've never been in a Catholic church," I said. "Have you?"

Willis shook his head.

"Didn't your folks come from Ireland?" I asked, thinking of what Mama said about Irish Catholics.

"Yep. My great-grandfather was born there. Ulster, I think. But his folks before him came from Scotland."

"And none of them were Catholic?"

"Nope. They were Presbyterian. All the McGees. Pap was Presbyterian at heart 'til the day he died, but Mam dragged him to Cross Roads Baptist with her from time to time."

"I suppose they admit women as well as men," I said, "the Catholic church I mean."

"Long as you bring your purse, just like any church."

"Unlike the cotton exchange where evidently a purse isn't enough," I countered.

He didn't reply. He simply ushered me past the beautiful church and on to the next Augusta sight.

After the churches, we saw a series of cotton mills along the river. One looked like a medieval castle in reddish-brown brick. The name "Sibley" stood out in white bricks. In front was a tall, slim freestanding tower made of the same reddish-brown brick. I wondered if it could withstand the kind of storm that had torn through Varennes a decade earlier.

"What's that?" I asked as I stared up. I began to think it might be an obelisk.

"Smokestack," Willis said, shielding his eyes, "all that's left of the Confederate Powder Works."

"Powder what?"

"Gunpowder factory built during the war to supply the Confederacy."

I'd never even thought about where gunpowder came from. "Did Sherman burn down the factory?"

"Nope. The town tore it down to widen the canal. See how water comes up to the bank here?" He pointed to the dark water. "Investors bought the land and built a cotton mill out of the brick. They kept the chimney. I'm not sure why. It's 150 feet tall, so I'm told."

Again I was struck by the difference thirty-five years had made. A place that'd been used for weapons was now used to make cloth. I remembered the Bible verse—"They shall beat their swords into plowshares."

We ended our second evening in Augusta with one more promenade along the river walk. The December air was cool and clear. The stars shimmered across the water. I looked up and found Orion, back in his place, reigning over the night sky.

All was right. All was perfect. I even made peace, at least for the moment, with the great Savannah River.

Savannah ᴄ ꜰ ꜱ

Early the next morning, we gathered our bags, departed the Bon Air Hotel, and took a streetcar toward the Augusta train station.

"Where are we going next?" I asked, not entirely awake.

"The grand old city of Savannah."

"How long does it take to get there?"

"Ten to twelve hours depending on the current," he said as we passed the train station and stopped at the waterfront.

"Current?" I repeated, suddenly wide awake.

He pointed to the riverboat in front of us. "Your ship awaits, my lady!" he said with a flourish.

"I thought we were going by train," I said, not feeling playful at all. I looked around for a way to get back to the station.

"Nope, we're going by water." He stood to escort me off the streetcar.

My heart began to race. I held on to the seat. "Willis McGee!" I shouted. "Crossing that river was one thing, but spending an entire day on it is another!"

He smiled. "And night," he added. He pried my fingers loose and ushered me onto the landing. The streetcar conductor stood and quickly removed our luggage.

"We're a little early for boarding," he said, coaxing me to a bench. He retrieved our bags and sat beside me. "We'll wait here 'til you calm down."

I felt faint. I pulled my coat tight around me. "Think of all

the people who've died in that river!" I said louder than I meant
to. A few other waiting passengers looked our way.

Willis put his arm around me. "Why're you so dang afraid
of the river?" he whispered.

"Because it's so unpredictable," I whispered back.

"It's very predictable," he said, "depending on the weather
and the section of river."

I didn't respond.

"It's also a source of livelihood. My grandfather never
would've come to Varennes if not for the Great Savannah River."
He sounded a bit like a preacher, and I could tell he was trying to contain his impatience. He continued, "Your grandfather
wouldn't have started a store and moved your father and the
rest of the family to Varennes if people hadn't been living here
already." He caught his breath, then added, "Be-cauz-ah of the
river."

I took several deep breaths of my own. His face softened.

"Just think—we wouldn't be together." He nudged my chin
and smiled.

"Jackson Seigler," I sputtered, "Sallie's boy. The way the river
took him. And stories Mama and Papa told us about Yankees
being shot and thrown into the river never to surface again." I
was building up steam. "And it's so dark! You can't see what's
beneath the surface. Or tell how deep it is. Or what lies on the
bottom. Or what's around the bend."

"Oh Icie, you fear the things you shouldn't. The train's a lot
more dangerous."

I stiffened.

"Where there's life, there's gonna be death, too," he added.
"You know that."

I nodded slightly.

"Anyway, I won't let anything happen to you."

As we boarded the boat, I tried not to look down. I reminded myself that it was Willis's honeymoon, too, and he'd evidently been looking forward to floating down this River of Livelihood.

Still, I chose to stay close to the center for the first hour or so. The morning was cold. So was I. But the people at the side railings had blankets. Willis waved a plaid one at me and lured me to the railing. He quickly swept the blanket around my shoulders and pulled me in close. I didn't look down at the water at first but focused on the banks of the river instead.

Before I knew it, I was marveling at how this part of the Savannah was so much calmer than the one at home. As though it had two personalities, the churning one with danger and tragedy, and the calm one with peace and beauty.

Soon the sun warmed us, and we laid the blanket aside. We passed old plantations, some thriving, others in ruins. I could barely make out charred foundations beneath withered vines.

On we floated down the river into the evening with the soft sound of water sliding over the paddles and the occasional startled movement of wildlife along the shore. The air became chilly again, and darkness hung over the river with only the lights of the riverboat. That is until we neared the grand old city of Savannah. Then the riverfront lit up like sunrise.

I was ready to step onto its streets, but Willis said we'd be spending the night in the cabin room on the boat. And so we did, swaying softly throughout the night, sometimes because of the river, sometimes because of my husband.

The next morning, we headed for the Marshall House where Willis had already reserved our room. It was obviously much older than the Bon Air Hotel in Augusta and only a few blocks from the river. The Marshall House was made of dark brick and stood five stories tall. Its wrought-iron veranda ran across the entire front.

"Impressive," I said as we stood outside waiting for our luggage to arrive from the boat. "It looks both old and new."

"It's fifty or sixty years old, but it's been repaired and fancied up several times," he explained. "In fact, a year or two ago, the owners added electricity and running water for warm baths." He hesitated, then said, "I thought we might share one."

"Share one what?" I asked, but I thought I knew.

"A bath as husband and wife." He squeezed my arm.

My face flushed warm. "Is that why you chose this place to lure me into a bathtub with you?"

"Partly," he said, "and because of its reputation."

"As a prime place to honeymoon?" My face still tingled.

"That and the fact that it's haunted."

I looked him in the eye to see if he was teasing. I couldn't tell. "Why would such a fine place be haunted?" I asked, trying not to seem too concerned.

"'Cause Sherman made it into a hospital. Lots of Yanks died inside those walls." He paused for what I took to be dramatic effect, then continued, "The story goes that one winter during the war there was a terrible freeze in Savannah. A 100 years' freeze. The ground was so hard you couldn't break it with a pickax."

The air where we stood seemed colder. He continued, "Doctors had to cut off a lotta gangrene legs to try and save lives. Arms too. But they couldn't bury them because of the frozen ground."

"The severed limbs?" I asked, just to be sure.

He nodded.

"Seems they'd have thrown them into the river," I said, thinking it somehow appropriate.

"The river would've been frozen, too. So they pulled up some boards in a few of the rooms and stored the arms and legs under the floors."

"What happened to them?"

"They meant to go back and get 'em in the spring when the ground thawed so they could bury 'em. But the hospital folks were so busy they plum forgot. Years later, during one of the repairs, workmen found arms and legs under floorboards. What was left," he added, "just bones by then."

I thought of Uncle James, how he'd survived the battle but lost a leg to infection. And how he'd still died a few days later. I wondered what happened to the leg. Papa had brought home the rest of his body to bury. But not the leg.

Willis continued, "Lodgers here have reported seeing a restless spirit clunking around on crutches, looking for his lost leg."

"That's awful," I said. "Just awful! Why are you telling me this?"

He looked somewhat contrite. "I read *A Traveler's Guide to Savannah* when I was planning our honeymoon. I found the ghost story interesting. Anyway, I can protect you."

"No one can protect me from angry spirits," I protested.

"I can," he said, pulling me close. I hoped he was right. I quietly prayed that all such restless souls would find their way home with or without their missing limbs.

Our luggage arrived, and we followed it into the beautiful, frightful Marshall House. A young scarlet-haired lady led us to our room on the second floor. I couldn't stop myself from staring at her. I'd never seen such hair, the color of ripe strawberries.

Little ringlets formed a canopy around her face. She must be Irish, I thought, realizing I sounded like Mama.

Our room faced the street toward the river. "Notice that the French doors open onto the veranda," she said in a joyful tone. "Although it's December, I think you'll find the daytime warm enough to visit some of Savannah's lovely gardens and other sights. Many within walking distance of here."

She floated past us to a bureau, pulled open the top drawer, and produced a sheet of paper. She smelled of magnolia and something else I didn't recognize. I wondered if Willis smelled her too.

"Here's a map of our recommendations," she said, handing the paper to Willis. He took it and nodded. "And we have delightful dining here in the Marshall House," she continued. "In fact, breakfast is being set out now on the main floor."

Willis was still looking at the paper. He nodded again. She turned to me. I nodded. She nodded back. Her ringlets bounced around her face like soft springs. Then she stood aside as an older colored man appeared in the doorway with our luggage. He was dressed in a deep green uniform, and he was dark as she was light.

Willis took the bags and asked, "Any truth to the stories of this fine establishment being haunted?"

"Oh, no," the young lady said, shaking her head. The strawberry ringlets followed suit. Then she laughed softly and floated out the door.

Willis handed several coins to the colored man. "Thank-ya-sir," he said without looking up. He appeared to hesitate as though he'd forgotten something. Then he turned on his heels and disappeared.

Willis began to examine the bathtub, the largest I'd ever seen. He measured it in hands as he would a horse. A folded screen leaned against the wall nearby.

While he scrutinized the tub, I inspected the floor, listening for squeaks and checking for uneven planks. Then we left the tub and floor inspecting for later and headed downstairs to start the day.

Resurrection fern

While we ate breakfast, Willis studied the map from the scarlet-haired lady. He turned his head slightly to the left to see better with his good eye. He'd adjusted so well to his glass eye that I seldom thought about it. He never mentioned it. Nor I.

After several biscuits, strips of bacon, and a pot of coffee, he decided our morning destination would be Forsyth Park, a formal garden about a mile or two away. We would return by a different route and explore the Savannah City Market.

"Eat well," he said. "We have some walking to do."

"Then my walking boots it tiz," I replied, thinking how right Bessie had been. While Mama had made sure I had a dozen drawers, Bessie had insisted I include a sturdy pair of soft leather walking boots. She'd picked them out herself.

"How large is the park?" I asked. I folded my napkin and blotted my lips.

"Twenty-five to thirty acres. Large enough for a family with a good mule to make a living."

"That was the size of Preston's farm when he married Bessie," I said, remembering how proud she'd been.

"And look at her now," he said, "owner of one of the largest farms in the upcountry. And a woman at that."

We soon left the Marshall House to see the sights of Savannah. We found grand old houses surrounded by rich green gardens, despite the chill of winter. Most had shiny magnolia-leaf wreaths with red velvet bows on front doors and garden gates to welcome Christmas.

We passed several lovely churches as well, all more elaborate than the churches in Varennes. Then we came upon the immense Cathedral of Saint John the Baptist. It had towering twin spires and a huge round stained glass window just above the entrance. The window made me think of the kaleidoscope Preston had given Feaster years earlier. Intricately cut pieces of colored glass somehow swirled together in perfect symmetry.

I thought out loud, "That's the grandest Baptist church I've ever seen."

"It's Catholic," he said. "I read about it. It's the mother church of Catholics all over Georgia."

"Catholics are all over Georgia?"

"Around the cities at least," he explained, still looking up. "The Irish pretty much built the railroads before the war. I've heard tell they took on jobs nobody else wanted."

"Irish or Scotch Irish?"

He appeared to think about it. "Maybe both."

We were still discussing the Irish and the Scotch Irish when we came upon our destination, Forsyth Park. What had been a green rectangle on the map opened in front of us like an enchanted forest. Its spectacular fountain reached above the trees and shot out arcs of water in every direction. The sparkling droplets fell back into an immense pool.

In the center of the pool arose what looked like a giant cake stand. On top of it was another, slightly smaller cake stand. And at the very top was a beautiful, half-naked woman, I guessed to be a Greek goddess. She held an ornate staff, perhaps like the one Moses waved around in the Bible. It was taller than she was.

Instead of serpents or flames, water sprang from the staff and slid down the lady into the first stand, where it joined more waterspouts. It tumbled over into the next stand, which had still more spouts. Carved into the base of the fountain were long-legged birds I took to be storks although I'd never seen any real ones.

About midway between the edge of the pool and the fountain were four sculptured creatures, part man, part fish, each blowing water from a horn. And just beyond them were swans, their wings lifted as though they were taking off. Or landing. They too spit out sparkling streams of water.

Willis and I were awestruck. We circled the fountain several times and probably would've stayed there the rest of the day if not for the cold mist against our faces.

Past the fountain, we proceeded deeper into the park. We followed the walkway flanked by live oaks, their branches touching overhead into a canopy. Sheets of wooly gray Spanish moss hung from the limbs.

The magical trees of Alexander from the Lowcountry, I thought but dared not say aloud. In that moment, I was back on Mouchet Hill, hypnotized by the silken stories of Feaster's father, not knowing how much my life would alter in an instant.

I shook my head, trying to erase the image. Willis looked at me. "Just a chill," I said. "Maybe I'm still feeling the mist of the fountain."

Then I noticed the fern that grew in irregular spirals around the trunks and limbs of the plush oaks. The memory rushed back. "Resurrection fern," I said aloud.

"What?" he asked.

"Resurrection fern," I repeated. "Nothing can kill it, not even drought. It comes back like Easter morning." He looked at me but said nothing.

I continued, "A conniving Spanish soldier chased a beautiful Indian maiden up a tree like this one. She jumped into the river to escape him, and everywhere she'd touched the oak, the charmed fern grew."

"What happened to the soldier?"

"He got tangled up in the limbs and died," I said, proud to know something that Willis did not. "The birds left nothing but his beard, which they spread from tree to tree and used for nests."

"Ahh," he said, "Spanish moss."

We continued our walk, another honeymoon promenade, but instead of the Augusta riverfront, it was a Savannah avenue of oaks. I fell in step with Willis, trying not to think anymore about Mouchet Hill.

Then, as quickly as we'd come upon the fountain, we came upon the tallest monument I'd ever seen, as tall as a church steeple. Willis pointed to the top. "That's what I was looking for. The Confederate Memorial."

It was a towering column with at least nine graduated levels of stone. Atop the column was the sculpture of a soldier in full uniform. It appeared to be bronze. His rifle was at his side, the stock at his feet, his arm around the barrel. He looked toward the river.

"I wish Pap'd lived long enough to see this," Willis whispered as though we were in church.

"Papa, too," I added.

The base of the monument sat on a large leveled-off square of grassy earth. Carved into a wider space on the column was a woman sitting underneath a weeping willow. A grieving mother or wife. Angels surrounded her, their wings lifted like the swans in the fountain. But she appeared not to see them.

I thought of Aunt Arabella waiting for the return of her husband, only to find out he'd died and been buried who knows where. I thought of all the McGee and Jones women who'd lost sons or husbands or both.

"I wish Mama and Mrs. Mary were here to see it, too," I said, "although it would make them sad. Mama said not many women in Varennes had wanted the men to go off to war and leave them alone to scratch out a living."

"That may be true for the women, but Pap always said he'd fight before he'd let someone tell him what to do on his own land."

I knew Papa would've agreed. "At least it ended slavery," I said.

"Yep," he added, staring up at the bronze figure, "one form or another."

Then he turned to me, smiled, and said, "Good thing Pap and Capt. Jones came home to wives eager to see them. Elseways, we wouldn't be here!"

That seemed a fitting way to leave the memorial. We completed our stroll through Forsyth Park. Then off we went to find the city market.

The entrance to the market looked like a train depot. Inside was the largest open-air market I'd ever seen, at least four city blocks of booths and simple shelters. Willis and I began our shopping under one of the covered areas. He was immediately drawn to a gun dealer. He picked up pistol after pistol, checking for everything conceivable from the straightness of the barrel to the balance in his hand.

"Look, Icie, look how nice this is. Here. Hold it."

I obliged.

"What do you think?"

I held it carefully in my palms and inspected the scrollwork in the white handle.

"What's the handle made of?"

"Grip," he said, taking it back. "The grip's made of ivory."

"Is that rare?" I asked, happy to be done with it.

"Not on a fine pistol like this." He switched it from hand to hand. "And see, it's a double-action revolver, so you don't have to cock it." He clicked the trigger several times.

I nodded, not sure what to say that would sound intelligent. "It will be a fine weapon for you," I offered, hoping he'd make a decision so I could get to the cloth and yarn.

"Then I'll get it," he declared as though I'd helped him. "But it's not for me. It's for Feaster."

"For Feaster?" He had my attention.

"Yep, for Christmas. I haven't gotten his present yet."

"He will surely love it," I said, remembering my last conversation with him. "I dare not get him anything for fear he'll refuse it," I blurted out. "He's so angry at me."

"Why?" Willis asked, looking from the gun to me.

"For not being who he wants me to be." My heart beat in my throat. Willis and I'd never talked about the matter before. Other than when he'd pointed out in anger that he'd never judged me and expected the same in return.

"And who does he want you to be?" he asked, staring into my face.

"His aunt instead of his mother." My cheeks burned. I looked away.

"Then the pistol will be from both of us," he said, matter-of-factly. "I doubt he'll refuse it."

He settled up with the merchant, and off we went to see the fabric and yarn merchant. I bought several yards of dark-blue silk brocade for Mama and enough lavender cashmere yarn to knit Bessie a shawl on the way home. It would give her some softness and color over her widow's weeds.

Before we left the market, Willis led me to the milliner's booth. "You need a lady's hat," he said, looking through several until he found one for me to try on.

"Why?" I asked, as he set it on my head. I seldom wore a hat, not even to church. None of the Joneses did.

"Because," he said, removing it and replacing it with another, "a proper lady has a proper hat."

"So I'm improper without one?" I asked as he removed the second hat and came at me with a third. I took it from him and put it on myself.

"Just for travel," he said.

The milliner held up hat after hat for our approval. Eventually, Willis saw one he liked for me. It was made of black straw. It looked something like a soup bowl turned upside down on a dinner plate. A band of royal blue grosgrain ribbon circled the hat where the crown met the brim.

Willis placed it on my head. Then the milliner carefully adjusted the brim until it was horizontal to the rest of me. "You look lovely, madam," he whispered as he handed me a mirror. He smiled faintly.

"And what of a perfect gentleman?" I asked, adjusting the hat more to my liking. "Should he not have a proper hat, too?"

The milliner smiled a bit more. He began holding up men's hats. Willis quickly snagged a black felt derby, set it on his head, then tilted it to the left.

"Very handsome," I said. "Now we're both proper." And so we continued through the market with more packages than a Christmas tree.

We returned to the Marshall House in time for dinner—an assortment of wonderful breads, broiled fish, and rice. Willis ordered a bottle of champagne. By the time we finished dinner and made our way back to our room, our bed had been freshly made and a coal fire laid for us.

Willis lit it and began to inspect the bathtub and plumbing all over again.

"That tub's so big it'll take a fire wagon to fill it," I said.

He laughed and turned on the water. While it ran, he lit several candles around the room and turned off the electric lights. He laid three large towels on a chair beside the tub and commenced to shedding his clothes. Soon he was in the water splashing around like a blue jay in a birdbath.

"Come on in, Mrs. McGee," he coaxed.

I knew there was no denying him a shared bath, so I went behind the screen and began to undress, folding each piece of clothing more than I needed to—until I had nothing left to take off. I took a deep breath, wrapped myself in a blanket, and approached the tub.

"Let me help you," he said. He stood up, reached for my hand, and pulled away the blanket. Then he helped me over the edge and into the giant tub of warm wetness.

I slid down as far as I could, then leaned back against the edge of the tub to keep my face and hair dry. I could see the light of the candles reflecting in his eyes, even the glass one. Or maybe I imagined it. Either way it was a Jesus-God moment of the physical kind.

He rolled up one of the towels and slid it behind my head to soften the rim of the tub. Then like a wave, he was on me. And again I was pulled into his passion. But somewhere in the heat of the moment, his hands slipped from the edge of the tub, the towel behind my head rolled out and, whoosh, I went completely under water in a tub full of knees and elbows. Water rushed into my eyes and ears. I was trapped beneath him. In just that instant, underneath the water, I saw the goddess of the fountain covered in an infinite stream. The maiden in the river swimming for an eternity.

Willis scrambled over the edge and pulled me sputtering and gasping with him. My hair dripped over my breasts and down my back. I could feel my heart pulsing in my waterlogged ears

"Answer me, Icie! Are you all right?" he shouted. His voice seemed to come from somewhere else. I opened my eyes. He looked as pale as a ghost, a naked dripping ghost.

I started to giggle, a case of nerves, no doubt. He seemed to relax. He said something about being baptized in his love, and I broke into a full fit of laughter. We spread a blanket in front of the fire and stayed there half the night until my hair dried. Then we crawled onto the thick mattress and pulled up the covers.

And true to his word, he kept the ghosts away—at least for the rest of the night.

Oh my fiery Willis, how I wish you would keep them away now. You'd beat them bloody if you could. But ghosts are like water—heedless to threats or fists.

PART X

The Ivory City

The Battery ⌒⌒

The next morning Willis and I had a quick breakfast and made our way to the Savannah train station. Christmas was still three days away, so I thought we could be going home to be with family after all.

After we boarded, I asked, "Where might we be bound for, Mr. McGee?"

"We might be bound for a lotta places, Mrs. McGee," he said mysteriously. "But today, we're headed to the Ivory City." He reached into his coat pocket and handed me a booklet with a palmetto tree on the cover.

I read aloud, "The South Carolina Inter-State and West Indian Exposition." Then I shouted, "Charleston! We're going to the Charleston Exposition!"

"Yes'm," he said, smoothing his moustache. I thought you mighta figured it out."

I probably should've. The grand exposition had been the talk of the town earlier in the year. But with Preston's sudden death, Whatley's nasty lawsuit, and our speedy wedding, I hadn't thought of it. Charleston had seemed a world away. A lifetime away. A place I still connected to Alexander from the Lowcountry. The last place I wanted to go.

Yet the exposition sounded exciting. To hide my mixed emotions, I began reading from the booklet aloud:

The resources of South Carolina are wonderfully exhibited at this Charleston Exposition, and the people of the world are invited to come and inspect.

I looked at Willis who'd picked up a newspaper. " 'The people of the world,' " I repeated. He nodded.

I continued:

The exposition is beautifully situated on the outskirts of Charleston on the east bank of the Ashley River and covers an area of about three hundred acres of historic ground that formerly comprised the Washington Race Course (I caught my breath) where gentlemen raced their homegrown thoroughbreds.

I let the last line sink in. I turned to Willis. "I wonder if they let women into the race track."

"No place for ladies," he said.

"Even if a lady owned the 'homegrown thoroughbred'?" I asked. I wanted to add, "Like Bessie and her homegrown cotton?" But I didn't.

"Nope. Wouldn't need to. She'd have able men at her disposal." He returned to his newspaper.

"What if she were the jockey?"

"Icie!" he said, looking at me in what was surprise or disapproval. Or both. I looked away first. He lifted his paper again and said, "Read about the palaces."

I skipped down a ways:

As the visitor enters the Exposition Grounds, the eye is immediately attracted to the Court of Palaces, with its

Sunken Gardens, and half surrounded by three palatial
buildings which are severally joined by long classic
colonnades.

"Lots of fancy words," he muttered without looking up.
I went on:

The central building is the Cotton Palace. In its impressive
magnificence it is emblematic of the powerful influence
cotton has long held in the commercial life of the city and
state.

I turned to Willis and asked, "Can women . . . ?"
"Yep," he interrupted me, "women can go in the palaces.
There's no buying and selling."
I read on about the Palace of Agriculture and the Palace
of Commerce. It seemed odd that no buying and selling took
place in the Palace of Commerce. But I didn't point that out to
Willis.
Back to the booklet, I read:

The general building design is typical of Southern character
and motif. And the entire exposed surfaces are covered with a
gysum façade giving an ivory appearance, thus the Ivory City.

Willis didn't comment so on I read:

The making of a lake some thirty acres in extent constitutes
an important feature of the work. In this lake is Electrical
Island, on which stands an Electrical Fountain of unique and
symbolic design.

"I wonder how . . ."

"Don't know," he said, cutting me off again. "Read about the Women's Building."

I skimmed several pages until I found it:

The ladies of Charleston have ably furnished the Women's Building with the finest needlework imaginable from finely crocheted tablecloths to handsomely stitched quilts. It is situated in the grand old colonial home once inhabited by the famous statesman William J. Lowndes, now owned by F. W. Wagener, President of the Exposition.

"I know who William Lowndes was," I said, "but who's F. W. Wagener?"

"German grocer," Willis said.

"How'd a German grocer get rich enough to own a colonial estate and host a great exposition?" I asked in disbelief.

He didn't answer.

"I mean Dock has had a store in one site or another for as long as I can remember. But he's not rich."

He still didn't respond so I returned to my reading aloud:

Near the Women's Building is the Negro Building, designed in the Spanish Renaissance order and resembling a Mexican mission.

"That's odd," I said. "Wonder why it's in a Mexican style." I nudged Willis to make sure he'd heard me.

"Don't know," he said, shaking his newspaper.

I continued:

The exhibit made in this building is designed to show the development of the Negro race in the last twenty-five years.

I held the book open but stopped reading. "Why in the last twenty-five years? Mama told us some of the colored families where she grew up had been there a hundred years or more. She said they had their own language. And you know how rich their music is."

"Since the war and all," he offered.

He folded his paper and took the booklet from me. He flipped through several pages and pointed at a new section. "Look here. Read about the midway. There's a real Eskimo village with honest-to-God Eskimos. See?"

He handed it back to me. "And you don't have to read aloud."

So I read in silence about the Eskimo Indian Village that featured Inuit families from Labrador, Canada, and the Great Bostock's Wild Animal Show with all sorts of exotic creatures including lions.

I squeezed Willis's hand. "There's so much I want to see!"

He seemed less annoyed. "Did you get to the educated horse?" He took the booklet again and scanned several more pages. Here, "The Beautiful Jim Keys, the Educated Horse." He returned the booklet to me, and I continued to read until we reached Charleston.

We checked into the Argyle Hotel on the corner of Meeting and Haskell streets. By the time we settled in and had a light meal, it was late afternoon. The December sun would soon be setting on the grand old city. "Let's get to White Point Garden before dark," he said, ushering me toward a streetcar bound south.

As we stepped down from the streetcar, I was struck with the beauty of the garden—colossal live oaks all around the upper part of the grounds and more of the odd palmetto trees with their lanky trunks and prickly bark. Willis led me past several monuments, a bandstand, and an old cannon to the southernmost point of the garden. He put his arm around me.

"To our left is the Cooper River, and to our right is the Ashley. But straight in front of us . . ."

"Is God's great ocean!" I interrupted. "Water, water everywhere," I said, remembering something from Aunt Eliza as I marveled at the sea's blue streaked infinity.

If not for the oaks behind me, I would've sworn we were on an island. The water smelled of life. I thought of the New Testament where Jesus turned fishers of fish into fishers of men. How he tamed the sea and walked across its back to calm his frightened disciples.

"Look, Icie! Look there!" Willis pointed toward a structure on top of the water. "That's Fort Sumter. That's where it all started."

I stared in the distance until what looked like a floating fortress came into focus.

"Are you sure? I thought Fort Sumter was blown to bits."

"I'm sure. Funny thing is they built it after the fight with the British in Louisiana. But nobody much used it 'til right before the war when the Yankees moved in. They thought they could control the harbor. Then the Confederates wanted it."

We stood silent in the dimming light. Fort Sumter had seemed so distant when we learned about it in school. It still seemed distant even though it was clearly in sight. I wondered how many Confederate soldiers had actually seen it. Still they'd fought. The same for the Yankees. So many on both sides had died. An attack on a fabled fort evidently had been reason enough.

Before I could give Fort Sumter more thought, Willis took my arm and led me westward around the end of the garden. It was then that I realized we were on the famous Charleston Battery, the very place Alexander the Horrible had enchanted me with as we'd sat on Mouchet Hill. That honey-tongued, hissing serpent! I shook my head to clear the image.

Willis guided me farther along the battery until we had a perfect view of the Ashley River. And there we stood, watching the most amazing sunset I'd ever seen. As the sun neared the water, it ignited a flame that ran both up the river and out into the ocean. Such frightening beauty. I looked over my shoulder at the live oaks near the banks. Their trunks glowed golden.

Even the awkward palmetto trees appeared beautiful. And just as it seemed the river and sea could survive no more fire, the sun dropped below the horizon, taking its glorious inferno with it.

Gas lamps flickered on along the battery and into the garden. Drooping Spanish moss took on extra dimension. High above the glow of White Point Garden, Orion looked down on the newlyweds and smiled.

Holy Moses

Willis woke me up early so we could start our first day at the exposition. As we quickly dressed, he told me, "Wear your hat."

I'd forgotten about the dratted hat.

"Wear your hat," he repeated, as though I hadn't heard him. He slipped on his derby and watched as I plopped the black straw dinner plate on my head and stabbed a hatpin through the crown and the topknot of my hair. He nodded his approval, and out the door we went.

We caught a streetcar in front of the hotel. Other folks scrambled aboard until it was full. I looked around. All the women wore hats. Willis looked at me and smiled. Some of our fellow passengers appeared to be as sleepy as I was. Yet the ride was short, and when we stopped at the gates of the Charleston Inter-State and West Indian Exposition, the entire streetcar erupted with excitement.

The grounds were spectacular like a kingdom rising up before our eyes. We began at the central plaza and proceeded to a busy walkway around the beautiful Sunken Gardens. Then we started across a bridge above the largest lily pond I'd ever seen, surely the grandest in the world. The bridge was so crowded I thought it might break. I held onto Willis and looked down at my feet.

As soon as we were across, I looked up to see three gleaming palaces—the Cotton Palace straight ahead, the Palace of Agriculture to the left, and the Palace of Commerce to the right. They were connected with walkways bordered by more flowers, shrubs, and young palmetto trees.

I studied the exterior of the Cotton Palace as we waited our turn to enter. It was even grander than I'd imagined. Tiny lights outlined its domes, rooflines, arches, and doorways. Colonnades fanned out on both sides.

"It makes me think of King Solomon's Temple or the palace of some other great king," I said, still holding on to Willis's arm.

"It is," he said. "King Cotton. The monarch of the South."

Inside we found equally grand furnishings. Displays of cotton's history in America filled the first floor—from when it was first cultivated in colonial times to the newest variety of cottonseed. On the second floor were all sorts of planting and harvesting tools, from the early days to the present. And in the center, elevated above the other displays, was the early cotton gin.

"I wonder how history will view the cotton gin a hundred years from now," I said to Willis.

"As a machine, plain and simple."

"A machine that fueled slavery and caused a war," I replied, realizing I sounded like Mama.

"Nope," he said. "Greed caused the war, not the cotton gin."

"Greed on which side?"

"Both."

I stared at the harmless looking little gin. "I don't think Col. Jesse and Papa were greedy. Do you?"

"I meant it was a rich man's war fought by poor men for all kinds of reasons. I can't speak for Capt. Jones, but Pap was always ready for a fight."

"Why?"

"Something to do with being Scotch Irish. Pap used to say, 'Me and my kin was born fightin'.'"

After the Cotton Palace, we toured the Palace of Agriculture. It displayed all sorts of South Carolina crops other than King Cotton. Next we went into the Palace of Commerce, which showed manufactured products from all over the country. Everything from feedbags to saddles, tin ware to china, furniture to caskets.

I noticed several small caskets. One was decorated with a lamb. Another had angel wings carved into the lid. I traced the outline of the wings with my fingers. "How sad it is to look at these little ones," I said, as I thought of Sallie and all the babies she'd had to bury.

"We're not here to be sad, Mrs. McGee," he replied, leading me away from the morbid exhibit.

We left the last palace and started our stroll around the grounds. We were no sooner inside the midway than we happened upon a bizarre parade. Leading the procession was a man dressed in gold silk, beating on both sides of a large metal drum. He strode about ten feet in front of a dark-haired woman riding a camel and waving to the crowd. How she kept her balance on the enormous, swaying creature was hidden beneath scarlet and gold layers of her skirt.

The camel was decorated with tassels along its halter, reins, across its chest, and around its saddle. The tassels shook with each giant stride. On each side of the camel, young women held their arms high and whirled in unison. Their colorful skirts flew out like spinning tops.

"What on earth is that?" I asked.

"I do believe it's a harem of belly dancers," Willis replied, his eyes fixed on the woman riding the camel.

As if on cue, the dancers began shoving their stomachs and shaking their hips. It was shocking but hypnotic. Following the dancers were musicians in silks as vivid as the young women's skirts, blowing flute-like instruments, creating a melody unlike any I'd ever heard.

The dark-haired woman on the camel beckoned onlookers to follow her through a village façade with giant red and gold lettering that read "The Streets of Cairo—The Beautiful Orient." The only thing I knew about the Orient was "We Three Kings of Orient Are," a song about the wisemen who came to see Baby Jesus. This didn't seem like the same Orient.

Willis and I and most of the other onlookers fell in behind the parade and through the entrance. The musicians and dancers

gathered on a stage to the left. The woman on the camel rode up
to it. The camel slowly bowed on its front knees, then lowered
its backend. The woman hopped off. I realized that she'd been
riding sidesaddle.

Willis seemed entranced. I wondered if she reminded him of
someone he'd known in his bachelor days. I considered a sharp
elbow to his ribcage.

She joined the other dancers on stage, and they began to
shove and shake and twirl in unison. But Willis turned to watch
the camel being led away. The Cairo man took the animal to an
open-sided shelter where other camels stood.

Willis turned back around and pulled me from the crowd.
"Let's ride a camel!"

At first I was relieved he'd been staring at the camel instead
of the Cairo woman. But when he said it again, I realized he
meant it.

"Oh, I couldn't!" I said, my heart racing. "It's as big as a
train car!"

"I won't let you fall," he said, pulling me toward the camel
shelter.

I shook my head emphatically.

"Alright," he said, giving up easier than I expected. Then he
added, "I bet Bessie woulda climbed on a camel with Preston."

I looked him in his good eye. He smiled innocently.

"You scoundrel!" I poked him in the ribs as hard as I'd
wanted to before. Then we headed for the camel ride.

The saddle looked like a large cloth-covered box atop the
camel's hump. "I'll never be able to get on," I whispered, "and
sidesaddle at that!"

"It'll kneel down for us," he whispered back. "I'll get on first
in the back. Then you can just sit down, like the saddle's a chair."

He must have liked his comparison because he added, "Just like sittin' in a chair."

He talked with the man tending the camels, then handed him some coins. The man led a camel out from the shelter. He pressed the beast on the side. It slowly lowered its front half and then its rear half. The man pulled a small platform to the camel's left side.

Willis quickly leaped onto the back of the saddle. Then beckoned me on. Even though the camel had its legs folded beneath its body and I was standing on the platform, the saddle contraption was still higher than any chair I'd ever sat in.

But somehow I sprang backward with Willis lifting me at the same time, and I landed on the saddle. I eased around as far as I could to face forward. I hooked my right leg around the front of the saddle and let it dangle on the left side, all the while adjusting my skirt as best I could. It was no easy task.

Just as I found my balance, the back half of the camel stood up. I fell forward. I would've rolled over its neck if Willis hadn't caught me and pulled me back so far we were lying against the animal's rump.

Then before I could catch my breath, the camel's front half came up. Willis shoved me forward. I felt for my hat. Somehow the pin had held. I was torn between laughing and crying. I tried not to look down.

Willis reached around me for the reins.

The Cairo man shook his head and said, "No sir, I must lead," in a very British accent. It seemed odd for an India-looking fella to sound so cultured. I wondered if they all spoke that way. It was a silly thought. I was nervous.

Willis held me with one arm while he dug into his vest pocket. He pulled out another coin and leaned toward the man who met him halfway. He handed Willis the reins and said, "But I must walk along."

Willis started to object. "What's its name?" I interrupted.

"Holy Moses," the Cairo man said.

"Holy Moses?" I repeated. "How'd he get that name?"

The Cairo man smiled and said, "It's what people say when they see him run!"

Off we went on a slow plodding trip around the Streets of Cairo and the Beautiful Orient like a king and his queen reigning over our temporary kingdom. The fact that I would have to go through an awkward, frightening process of dismounting seemed far away.

And for a Jesus-God moment, I felt exotic, brave, powerful.

Decidin' and doin' ◌ ʃ ↄ

From The Streets of Cairo we made our way to The Eskimo Village. Its façade looked like a bank of fresh-fallen snow, whiter than the ivory palaces. Chilly air blew in our faces as we entered.

Someone behind us loudly proclaimed, "It's cold enough to freeze uh Eskimo's ass off!" Then he repeated it and laughed heartily at his own attempt at humor. Willis turned around and glared. The laughing stopped.

We looked at Eskimo tools and art until several people filed onto a stage about three feet high. They were dressed in skins and fur from head to toe. Most had dark reddish skin and straight black hair.

A pretty young woman and a girl stepped forward holding hands. They waited for the crowd to settle down. The girl, who appeared to be seven or eight, was beautiful. She had long shiny braids and thick eyelashes. Her skin was a shade lighter and her face less square than the others on stage. She looked like a miniature version of the lady beside her, but a bit less Eskimo.

The crowd grew quiet. The girl began to speak in perfect English. "Welcome to the Eskimo Village and our traveling community of Inuit," she said in her clear, young voice. "We are from Canada and Labrador." She turned and gestured to her fellow Inuit.

"But I'm actually from Chicago. I was born there during the Chicago World's Fair eight years ago." She looked at the lady beside her and smiled.

There were a few "ahs" and nodding heads.

"My name is Nancy Helena Columbia Palmer," she continued. "We Inuit have long names." Laughter erupted, and from then on she had the audience in the palm of her small hand.

She briefly described winters in Canada and Labrador, the Inuit people's livelihood, items of clothing, customs, food, and such. She concluded by asking visitors to tour the grounds to see reindeer, sled dogs, and replicas of everyday life in the Inuit world.

As we explored the village, night began to fall. Midway lights blinked out the darkness. Although the exposition was still filled with fair-goers, we decided to return to the hotel and rest up for the next day.

After we boarded a streetcar to take us to our hotel, I looked back at the Palaces, adorned with more lights than stars in the sky. In fact, I couldn't make out any constellations for the brightness of the exposition. I wondered if Orion hunted high above us in the dark.

For the moment, the manmade kingdom appeared brighter than the God-made heavens. The thought seemed like sacrilege.

"I hope I don't turn into a pillar of salt," I said as I continued to look over my shoulder.

"Then turn around!" Willis said in mock horror.

On the ride back, I thought about the Eskimo girl and her mother. Her lighter complexion, possibly the blending of two cultures. She hadn't mentioned a father. But a fatherless child, at least in her case, seemed not so bad. She'd acted confident, happy, loving. Her mother was obviously raising her well.

I thought of Feaster and felt a stab of pain. Perhaps I should have kept him, tried to raise him myself. I might not have done such a terrible job. Maybe he wouldn't hate me so. But that's not why he hated me, I admitted to myself. He probably realized, even at a young age, how lucky he'd been to have Bessie and Preston as his loving guardians. He hated me because I wouldn't tell him about his father.

I thought of the Eskimo girl again. Surely she'd asked about her father. Maybe Feaster was long overdue for the truth. Willis didn't seem to hold my foolish past against me. Feaster might not either. At least his feelings wouldn't be any harsher than they already were.

I decided, right then as we rode through the streets of Charleston, I'd find the courage to tell Feaster when the right time came along. I laid my head on Willis's shoulder and closed my eyes. It felt good to make the decision.

Papa used to say, "Decidin' and doin' are two diff'rent mules. They might pull together in harness, but kick and bite the fire outta each other once they get loose.

He could have been talking about me.

Touché ❧

The next morning, I felt more comfortable in my hoity toity hat as we started our second day at the Charleston Exposition. We decided to tour as many educational and cultural displays as we could before noon. Then we'd have the rest of the day to explore the midway.

We began with the state buildings—New York, Ohio, Maryland, and Pennsylvania—all would have been my family's enemies forty years earlier. Yet to me their displays seemed modern and exciting. Willis called them "citified," but he agreed.

After the row of state buildings, we found the Women's Building. Fine needlework decorated the parlor and hallway. Sweet aromas filled the kitchen. And in the dining room was a massive mahogany table set with several beautiful tea services of fine bone china and sterling silver. A sign announced: "Proper teatime etiquette demonstrated on the hour."

I looked at Willis. He shook his head. So we headed to the final exhibit, the Negroes' Building. In the front room was a lively display of art—paintings in bright, thick strokes and large pottery vessels with glazes that dribbled into otherworldly landscapes. In the hallway we found intricately woven baskets, some as small as biscuits and others the size of cotton bales.

In another room we found the most unusual instruments I'd ever seen. Boards with tightly tuned strings. Gourds made into shakers, drums, and even banjos. Tumblers with varying levels of water. While across the room, musicians played classical pieces on violins, a grand piano, and parlor guitars. From yet another room came the thumping rhythm of an accappella choir.

And in a final room were portraits and biographies of

many colored people. Most I'd never heard of. Some were soldiers who'd fought in the Revolution, the Civil War, and the Cuban War. Others were scientists, engineers, and inventors. I was astounded—both at their accomplishments and my own ignorance.

In the center of one wall was a large portrait of Booker T. Washington, surrounded by other folks in different professions. I spotted the portrait of a thin, distinguished-looking man with a magnificent horse at his side. It reminded me of the beautiful thoroughbred that the Anderson County folks had given Wade Hampton when I was just a girl.

The horse in the portrait seemed even taller. It looked to be a bay. I couldn't tell its exact color but the shine of its coat was obvious.

"Look, Willis. See this picture? It's Dr. William Key and the Beautiful Jim Key. That horse must be at least 16 hands tall, maybe 17!"

He shook his head. "That's a handsome stallion, but I doubt he's that big. The man's probably just short."

I read aloud:

Dr. Key is an extraordinary horse trainer renowned for using kindness, patience, and an occasional apple. He rose from slavery to become a leading businessman and a self-educated veterinarian. He also founded a blacksmith shop, harness and wagon-wheel business, and a restaurant in his Tennessee hometown.

Willis waved his hand to cut me off. "I bet half that's made up."

At noon we stopped at a nearby restaurant, which was an "authentic French café" according to its sign. I asked for something light. The lady serving our table suggested a dish that sounded like, "key-shh." She handed me a menu and ran her finger under the word "quiche." She repeated "key-shh."

I said, "Yes, please."

She looked at Willis. "I'll have the same, but I'll take two."

As we waited, he pulled out the booklet from his coat pocket and asked, "Where do you wanna go on the midway today?

"I know you're skeptical," I said, "but I'd love to see Beautiful Jim Key, the Educated Horse."

Our quiche arrived. It was cut into wedges with strawberries to one side. Where the strawberries came from in December was a mystery. I studied my plate.

"It looks like some sort of pie. Maybe a custard."

Willis loaded his fork, chewed a few times, and swallowed. "Tastes like eggs." He reloaded his fork.

I tried a small bite. "Eggs," I agreed, "in a crust."

Willis continued eating. I took the booklet. "It says the Beautiful Jim Key can spell and do arithmetic. Can you imagine Sugar spelling your name?"

"Nope," he said, halfway into one wedge of quiche. "Sugar's just fine acting like a horse and pulling my carriage. Anyhow, I'll bet that trainer leads his horse to the right letters."

"More than a trainer. He's a veterinarian like Feaster wants to be."

"Feaster'll go to school and learn to how to doctor animals," Willis said. "This fella is self-taught." He tried a strawberry. He made a sour face and swallowed hard. "Kinda green."

I decided to pass up the strawberries.

Willis wiped his mouth. "I'd like to see Bostock's Wild Animal Show myself."

I'd eaten enough so I found the part about the Great Frank Bostock, King of Wild Animals.

"Listen to this," I said. I read aloud while Willis finished his second piece of quiche:

It was he who only a few weeks ago, alone and unarmed save with a riding-whip, faced the man-eating tiger Apollo at the Indianapolis Zoo. This same tiger had killed and partly devoured a luckless fellow only a few weeks before. It was he who at the Atlantic City Zoo rushed into the arena when seven lions and five jaguars were fighting and drove them apart with nothing but a walking stick!

I took a long drink of water for dramatic effect. "Lordy! He's one courageous fella. I suppose he's self-taught too."

Willis smiled and said, "Touché."

"Two what?" I asked.

"It's a word," he said. "T-o-u-c-h-e. There's a little mark over the 'e' that makes it sound like 'a.'" It was his time to take a long drink of water for dramatic effect. Then he continued, "It means 'you made your point.' Do I actually know a word my lovely wife doesn't know?"

"I suppose you do," I admitted. "When did you get so smart?"

He laughed. "My dear Mrs. McGee, I haven't spent all my days farming and courting you."

I thought if he was going to tell me about grass widows, I didn't want to hear any of it. I suppose I looked flustered. He reached across the table and touched my hand. "Icie, when that damn mule left me half-blind, I spent a lotta time healing. I did some thinking about my life. What I'd lost and what I still had. Soon as I could, I started reading.

"I read the Bible, first—as much as I could—then some stuff I was supposed to read in school. And I read books on new ideas for farming and cattle raising. I read history books, one about Ireland in particular. Hell, I even read some of Mam's lady magazines. All that reading was hard with just one eye. But I figured I'd better keep at it should something go wrong with my good one."

I didn't know what to say, so I said nothing.

He patted my hand, laid several coins on the table, and said, "Let's go see this King of the Wild Animals!"

Into the lions' den ⌒ ɾ ⌒

The entrance to the Great Bostock's Wild Animal Show was flanked by two Roman columns and two great lions that looked to be made of wood and plaster.

Inside, spectators sat in rows of raised seating in a semicircle facing the ring. We found seats several rows back with the advantage of height. The ring itself was the front half of a circle with the back half hidden from view by curtains.

And in the middle was a heavily barred cage. In the center of the cage was a platform with a chunky wooden chair. It made me think of a throne. On each side of the throne were stools of various heights.

In the back of the cage was something like a cattle chute with a gate. Curtains wrapped around it keeping its contents from view. Between the cage and spectators was a semi-circular pathway about the width of two wagons side by side.

Once the crowd settled into seats, a tall man appeared from behind a curtain on the far right side. He wore a shiny black, long-tailed coat and matching pants with a ribbon running down the outside of each leg. A black top hat with a red band balanced on his head. People began to notice and point his way excitedly.

"LAY-DEES and Gen-TELL-men!" he boomed in a voice that seemed too deep to be real, "WEL-L-L-COM-MUH to Bostock's Great Animal Show!"

The crowded hushed.

And for the next hour or so we were treated first to a balancing act featuring a huge elephant named Little Karma and her childsize trainer Big Raju that left me exhausted and unsettled. Then came Madame Cleo, a belly dancer, who writhed around with the two largest snakes I'd ever seen. A nightmare come to pass.

As far as I was concerned, the entire show could have ended then and there. My heart and stomach had been tested. But that was not to be. The Great Frank Bostock and his man-eating beasts had yet to appear. And neither hell nor high water could extract Willis McGee from this lions' den until they did.

So there we sat on Christmas Eve beneath a towering brown canvas tent, staring at a cage of iron bars, waiting for the next performance of the odd and the unnatural. It seemed like sacrilege.

Suddenly metal began clanging behind the curtain. Then scraping sounds. Then nothing. Anticipation grew. The audience turned restless. Someone shouted, "Bring on the lions!" Another shouted, "Where's the Great Bostock!" Still we waited.

Then a Jesus-God roar shook the tent like a crack of lightning with rolls of thunder so loud I could feel them in my chest. Cold chills shot up my back. I held onto Willis. Neither of us moved.

The gate to the chute in the back of the cage lifted and out ran an enormous male lion. Dust flew up around him. His thick mane stood out from his face forming a great sable halo against his golden body. His eyes were fiery amber lined in black, and his nose was a wide triangle with the pointed side down.

The only animal I could compare him to was Papa's Angus bull. The lion's body wasn't as big as a bull's, but his head was bigger. And he radiated that same thundercloud of danger. The lion shook his mane from side to side. Then he seemed to notice spectators directly in front of him in the first row. He stood still and stared. I held my breath. He let out another piercing roar and launched himself at the audience.

His claws shot out as he grabbed the bars with all four paws. People in his would-be path scattered, screaming and swearing in a babel of languages. The rest of us sat frozen in our seats. The lion fell back. The bars had held.

The announcer reappeared to the right of the cage. "Sorry, folks!" he shouted. "I should have introduced you to CIM-BAAA! He's a little cranky because he's hung-GREE!"

The door in the back of the cage lifted again and out came another male. He ran to the left side and began pacing back and forth, unnerving spectators as he went. Cimba took to pacing on the right side.

The announcer shouted, "Meet ZEUS! He's not quite as big as CIM-BAAA, but he's still growing!"

Again the chute door lifted and out came another male lion. Lion after lion, mostly males, until there were twelve. All looked as though they'd like nothing better than to rip through the audience. They swiped at each other and threw themselves against the bars.

I began to understand how awful the lions' den in the Old Testament would have been. How Daniel must have felt utterly helpless to save himself. I gritted my teeth and fought back the urge to scream. Tears filled my eyes. Willis didn't notice.

Just when the chaos reached a new high, the announcer started his shouting again. "Ladies and Gentlemen! From the plains of Africa! From the mountains of India! From the jungles of Asia! From the Royal Court of England! The fiercest, smartest, most courageous animal trainer in the world! KING of the WILD ANIMALS! THE ONE AND ONLY! THE GREAT! FRANK! BOSTOCK!"

The curtain flew back and out strolled the One and Only himself to deafening applause. He seemed totally at ease. His coat looked like that of a high-ranking officer. It was detailed with red and gold braid and brass buttons. He wore riding pants, and the tallest boots I'd ever seen. They reached halfway up his thighs.

His light brown hair hung in curls from beneath his cap, the kind a riverboat captain wears. His moustache was in the fashion of the day, but it kicked up a bit more on the ends. He held a long stick and a wagon driver's whip. Neither seemed that well suited to the task at hand.

He lifted the latch on the door and slipped into the cage. The announcer quickly latched it behind him. The lions turned their attention from the audience and each other to the dazzling Bostock. He plunged into the center of what had been growling mayhem and went to work prodding with the long stick in his left hand and cracking the whip in his right.

Tension saturated the air.

Bostock kept moving in a tight circle with his back to the

center. The lions fanned out but seemed to be looking for an opportunity to charge. In an instant, a male to Bostock's far left rushed in and swiped at him just above the knee. His claws glanced off the boot. Bostock somehow kept his balance and landed the whip hard across the lion's face.

The lion fell back. A female dashed in from the other side. Bostock sidestepped her teeth and landed his whip across her face, too. It drew blood.

He yelled at the lions by name and continued to crack rawhide. My heart pounded. My temples throbbed. The lions began to blur. Their roars sounded under water. I felt as though my senses were shutting down.

I hid behind Willis's shoulder. I wondered if that's how a nervous breakdown felt. I thought about Mama's grandmother Isabella who suffered a case of the nerves during Reconstruction. Mama said it was as though her soul had left her body.

Then I felt petty. This was no war, no Reconstruction. But it was more than I could bear at the moment. I remembered the tornado that had struck Varennes and how I'd crouched with Mama and Papa behind their mattress while the storm roared past our house.

As Bostock and the lions went after each other, I willed myself behind my mind's mattress. And there I stayed for what seemed an eternity through roars, cracks, gasps, and all manner of shouting while King Bostock displayed his greatness.

Eventually, the whip quit snapping, and applause grew so loud that I realized the performance must be over. I opened my eyes. There in the center of the cage sat Bostock atop his throne with twelve golden lions calmly seated around him.

Daniel had survived. And so had I.

I've come to realize that the mind extracts itself from what it must. Even from the heart's frantic pumping while its blood slows to a trickle. Oh Mama, here I lie, Daniel of a lesser faith.

Christmas 1901 ⚘

By the time we left the Great Bostock's Wild Animal Show, the sky had clouded over. The ride back to the Argyle Hotel was cold. The stars didn't show themselves and the exposition lights quickly dimmed. Christmas Eve had taken a dreary turn.

I was as tired as if I'd been on my feet all day trying to keep up with Mama. Even Willis seemed tired. I just wanted to go to bed and wait for Christmas. And that's pretty much what we did after a light supper and our usual honeymoon benediction.

I'd fallen asleep somewhat dreading my first holiday away from family and home. But when I awoke in Willis's arms, I felt the unexplainable joy of Christmas morning. We got up quickly and pulled out gifts for each other. Willis started a fire, and we settled into chairs close to the hearth.

He handed me a small, finely carved box wrapped in deep pink velvet ribbon. I slowly untied the ribbon and wound it around my hand, careful to smooth out tiny wrinkles where it'd been tied. My mind wandered as to how I might reuse such lovely ribbon.

"For God's sake, Icie," he said, "quit playing with the dang ribbon and open the box!"

I slipped the ribbon off my hand and lifted the box's thin brass latch to discover a shiny writing set. I balanced the box on my lap and pulled out the pen. It was sterling silver and embossed in a delicate wheat pattern.

"It's beautiful!" I said, rolling the pen between my palms until I saw the inscription—"Icie McGee"—followed by the outline of a heart.

I squealed in surprise. It was a pitch poor sound but Willis just smiled. "It's the finest pen I've ever seen!"

"Look at the pencil, too," he said, leaning forward. "I got it so you can write even when you can't dip ink. Like when we're on a train, you can still write. There's extra lead, too."

I examined the pencil. It reminded me of the one I'd given Feaster several Christmases ago. I wondered what Feaster and Bessie and Mama were doing this Christmas morning.

"This goes with the writing set." Willis handed me a large book.

The cover was coffee-colored leather, embossed with golden ferns. I opened it to find pages of thick white paper, something like Mama's ledger only much finer and without columns.

I looked at Willis. "It's blank."

"It's a journal. You write in it."

The thought of filling blank pages had never occurred to me. Except for an occasional letter to Aunt Eliza in my head and a few birthday messages, I seldom wrote anything.

I glided my hand down the snowy pages. "What should I write?"

"Some of those stories you've told me about." He looked at me expectantly. "Or write about places like Varennes. Or the Charleston Exposition."

I thought a bit, "Or Savannah?"

"Yes!" he replied. "Or you can write about people like Capt. Jones and Mrs. Emily or Bessie and Preston."

I hesitated. My family seemed riskier. I thought again of Mama's saying—"You don't have to tell everything you know."

"What about the McGees?" I asked. "I bet you know some good stories!"

"Hmmm," he said, less enthusiastically, "I'll have to think on that one."

Still he'd lit a fire. I decided I could write about Papa and Mama, after all, maybe how they'd met.

I turned a page. Then there was the bushwhacker story, how Aunt Lou's husband ran barefoot in the snow to escape capture. Surely no one would object to that. And I could write about the first family—Dock, Mattie, Sammy, Sallie, and Johnny.

I turned another page. Then there was Aunt Eliza. I could retell some of her wonderful stories.

I looked up to find Willis staring at me with a smile that made my heart flutter. Light from the fire flickered in his eyes, both eyes. It was a Jesus-God moment of pure love. I leaned forward and kissed him.

Then I handed him one of his gifts. It too was a book, though much smaller, wrapped in white paper and tied with a blue-green velvet ribbon as close to the color of his eyes as I could find.

He quickly tore the paper and let the ribbon fall to the floor. He read the cover aloud, "*The Old Farmer's Almanac, 1902.*"

He opened it and continued reading:

1902, being the 126th year of American Independence. Containing, beside the large number of astronomical calculations and farmer's calendar for every month, a variety of new, useful, and entertaining matter.

He turned the page. "There will be five eclipses this year." And on and on he read "astrological highlights" and "predicted weather events" until I stopped him so I could give him his other gift. It was in a small walnut box about half the size of my writing set. I'd tied it with the same blue-green ribbon, which he quickly dropped beside the first ribbon.

He opened the box to find a dark-finished brass compass straight from London. The cover popped open when the crown was pushed in. The upper half of the face was black with white lettering for directions. The lower half was white with black lettering. On the inside of the crystal was a red vertical line intersected by a red horizontal line in the center. The dial was bright blue.

Willis carefully slipped it from the box and popped open the cover. "It's a hunter's compass!" he said, laying it flat in his right hand. He held it out and rotated his palm from side to side. The blue arrow pointed true and steady. "A fine hunter's compass!" he added.

He continued to move his hand around until I cleared my throat and pointed at a note that I'd tucked in the box beneath the compass. He unfolded it and read aloud, "May your compass always bring you home to me. With all my heart, Icie."

He leaned in close and whispered, "My arrow always points home to you. As long as we both have breath, nothing could turn it away."

Ah, my passionate Willis. I wonder where your arrow points now. I shouldn't fault you if it be away from home. And yet I still breathe. I breathe and remember.

Beautiful Jim Key ❧

We'd agreed to spend our last afternoon in Charleston at the exposition. But as to how was subject to debate. I had my heart set on seeing Beautiful Jim Key, the Educated Horse. Yet Willis thought we'd be better entertained at the track watching a camel race, evidently a popular event at such expositions.

Truth be told, I felt I'd been lucky not running into Alexander the Dreadful at the exposition. Not that I was sure I'd even recognize him. But my luck had held and I wasn't about to chance it at a race track.

"You know, this may be your only chance, as a lady, to get into a race track," Willis said. "And just imagine seeing Holy Moses run!" He held out his elbows and pretended to be riding a loping camel.

"Going to the race track on Christmas is sacrilegious!" I said. "A-n-d, you promised we'd see Beautiful Jim Key. That's what got me through that lion tamer's stomach-wrenching act."

"That may be true, my lovely wife," he replied. "But I bet Bessie Jones Allen wouldn't miss a chance to watch a camel race."

"That won't work again, Willis McGee!"

He exhaled in exaggerated disappointment. "Then we'll go early and sit on the front row so's I can see how this wonder horse does his tricks."

We arrived at one o'clock for the two o'clock performance. A short line of people stood at the entrance. The arched façade featured the painting of a beautiful bay horse with white markings. It was attached to a large blue-and-white striped tent, much more cheerful than the drab brown canvas of Bostock's tent.

At the top of the entrance, in giant block letters was "JIM KEY." In smaller letters beneath it was "Arabian-Hamiltonian hundred-thousand dollar" and beneath that was "EQUINE WONDER." And last, in cursive letters was "the most wonderful horse in the world." I read it all aloud.

Willis looked around. "Not many people here for the 'equine wonder.' Guess they're all at the race track."

As if on cue, a crowd of people began joining the line in front of Jim Key. I silently thanked God for His attention to detail.

Out came an attendant who began admission. Willis chose our seats dead center in the front row just a few feet from the ring. As with Bostock's tent, the seats rose from front to back. It seemed somehow unmannerly to sit so close to the ring, but that's where Mr. McGee planted himself.

He made himself comfortable, slipped *Old Farmer's Almanac* from his coat pocket, and began reading as the seats filled in behind us. From time to time, he'd make a "hmm" sound.

The space inside the ring was divided into two areas. One was a classroom of sorts with numbers and letters displayed on several racks. The other looked like an office with a cash register and mailboxes. In the back was a large banner with red block letters that read: "BE KIND TO ANIMALS."

As more and more people filled the tent, chatter grew louder until my ears began to ring. I looked at Willis. He appeared to be deep in the almanac.

Then the noise ceased. A lone, thin colored man appeared from seemingly nowhere. His face was a rich chestnut with high cheek bones. His hair and beard were white. He wore a tailored riding suit with soft looking boots the color of his skin.

Altogether he seemed ethereal—Aunt Eliza's word. He stood quietly surveying the audience. Then he spoke in a rich, deep voice, "Welcome, fellow human beings. I'm William Key from Tennessee, where I'm an entrepreneur and a self-taught veterinarian. I'm often a teacher and always a student. But you didn't come to see me." Soft laughter rippled through the crowd.

"You've come to see my friend, family member, and business partner, Mr. Jim Key." Just as he said "Jim Key," the curtain at the back opened and into the ring trotted the wonder horse himself. I looked at Willis. He still held the almanac, but he was staring at the stallion.

Jim's coat was a deep shiny brown that glowed as though he'd been polished. His black silky mane covered one side of his neck and hung to his shoulders. His tail barely cleared the ground. It was as finely combed as a young lady's hair.

At first he stood still. Then he surveyed the crowd the same as Dr. Key had done. His ears perked forward. After he'd taken in the audience, he looked at Dr. Key and bobbed his head up and down.

And there began a conversation of sorts between the two.

Dr. Key asked Jim if he felt like trotting around the ring. Jim nodded yes and showed the fine stepping of his Hamiltonian bloodlines. The audience applauded. Jim took a bow and returned to his place beside Dr. Key.

Then Dr. Key said, "Jim, I've just been offered $100,000 for you. What do you think of that?"

Jim looked at Dr. Key and rolled his ears back. Then he looked at the audience with his ears perked forward. He repeated several times, rotating his ears forward to the audience and backward to Dr. Key until people started laughing and clapping.

"But Jim," Dr. Key continued, "imagine how rich I'd be." Jim lowered his head and slowly began to limp off as though he were lame.

When he'd almost reached the curtain, Dr. Key called after him, "Jim, come back! You know I'd never sell you! You're family!"

Jim spun around, trotted back to Dr. Key, and nuzzled him under the chin. The audience laughed and clapped again.

"Tell me, Jim," Dr. Key said. "Do you like pretty ladies?" Jim nodded.

"Do you see any here today?" he asked. Jim looked around, then nodded again, this time in exaggerated fashion. "Then why don't you introduce yourself to one of the pretty ladies?"

Jim began to walk around the edge of the ring closest to the audience. He went back and forth several times and then stopped dead center of the front row. He was so close I could have stood, taken one step and touched him. He was even more beautiful close up.

"So you found a pretty lady?" Dr. Key asked. Jim nodded. Then he leaned toward me and puckered his lips into what looked like a kiss.

The audience erupted. I blushed hot and giggled awkwardly.

Dr. Key spoke up. "Jim! She might be married! You'd better ask." Jim quit puckering. He looked at me with his ears perked forward.

Before I could answer, Willis shouted, "Yes! Yes, she is!" He put his almanac back in his pocket.

Jim looked at Willis. He rolled his ears back, lifted his upper lip like he'd bitten into a green apple, and backed away until he reached Dr. Key. The audience laughed harder and applauded.

Dr. Key moved to a large bin of envelopes next to mail slots like in a post office. "Let's leave the pretty ladies alone and sort some mail. Jim, fetch me a letter."

Jim trotted to the bin and pulled out an envelope. "Why, Jim, it's for Mr. Medlin. Please place it in the right box." Jim took the letter and pushed into a mail box marked with "M." The audience clapped.

"Bet they're all for 'Mr. Medlin,'" Willis whispered.

As if he'd heard, Dr. Key said, "Actually, the envelopes are all blank."

Then he invited members of the audience to call out different names for Jim to sort. "Johnson, Lawton, Brown," and on the names went. Just being able to pick up an envelope with his lips and teeth and place it in a box was impressive enough for me. But Jim filed each piece of mail into the right box according to the alphabet and the name he was given.

Willis whispered, "They're in on the act."

I ignored him and applauded with the rest of the folks.

"Jim," Dr. Key said, "while we're dealing with the alphabet, let's go to the classroom and see how many names you can spell."

Jim trotted to a long rack that held cards printed with letters of the alphabet. Each had the same letter on front and back. The rack held at least two complete sets of the alphabet with a few extra letters. Dr. Key stood next to a second rack, much shorter and currently empty.

He asked for volunteers to give their names so that Jim could spell them. And the wonder horse did, name after name. He would lift a letter card from the long rack in his teeth, trot over to where Dr. Key stood, and slide it into a slot on the empty rack until he'd completed the name.

Sometimes he'd hesitate over a letter and lift it to get Dr. Key's reaction. Occasionally Dr. Key would shake his head and sound out the name in question. After each name, Dr. Key would return the cards to the alphabet rack.

Jim had just finished his fourth name when Dr. Key asked for one more volunteer. To my surprise and embarrassment, Willis stood and loudly proclaimed, "Willis McGee!"

"Oh, the gentleman married to the pretty lady," Dr. Key said as he exchanged a look with Jim. Maybe I just imagined it but Jim seemed to grin.

"A name with double letters," Dr. Key said, "Scotch Irish, I believe."

Willis nodded. Jim hovered over the letters.

"Wil-lis," Dr. Key pronounced. Jim went to work. He quickly selected and placed W, I, and L into the empty rack. Then he looked at Dr. Key, who slowly pronounced "l-i-s." Jim returned to the alphabet rack for L, then I, then S.

The crowd applauded. Willis sat down. Dr. Key rewarded Jim with a small lump of sugar. "Now let's finish," he said, "with 'Mc-Gee.'"

Jim trotted back to the alphabet rack. He quickly selected and put in place the M and C. Then he returned to the letters and chose a K. He held it up for Dr. Key.

"No," Dr. Key said. "It's 'Gee' not 'Key.'" Jim dropped the K, chose the G, and added it to the rack.

Next he chose an E and put it in place without even looking at Dr. Key. He returned for the last letter and hesitantly lifted a Y. Dr. Key shook his head. "It's not like our name," he said. "It's a double letter."

Jim dropped the Y from his teeth, picked up an E and completed the spelling of "WILLIS MCGEE."

I looked at Willis. He looked at me. The flecks in his blue-green eyes danced.

Dr. Key and Jim continued with unexplainable feats—adding and subtracting numbers called out by the audience, making change from a cash register, and plucking a silver dollar from the bottom of a glass barrel filled with water.

Jim even wrote his name on a chalkboard, making large cursive strokes with his neck and head.

And when the performance of Beautiful Jim Key came to an end, we all jumped to our feet and applauded long and loud. None more enthusiastically than the newly converted Mr. Willis McGee.

Sea of secrets ⌒ ♪ ⌒

After the amazing Jim Key, we decided to return to White Point Garden to watch the sunset and take one last promenade along the Battery. We reached the park just in time to see the sun explode like orange fireworks across the sky and sink into the sea. Soon street lamps flickered on along the Battery.

The night was clear and cool. Constellations took their places high above us. Waves lapped beneath them. As we strolled, we talked about our honeymoon travels and our first Christmas as man and wife. I felt almost worldly. A bit sophisticated. Certainly wiser.

Aunt Eliza once said, "A woman's heart is a sea of secrets." But as I looked over the darkening waters, I thought my heart to be about as open as it'd ever been. I was with the man I loved. I'd put my fears of the river to rest. Alexander the Miserable was clearly in my past. I even felt strong enough to face Feaster.

In the distance, another couple walked toward us. Perhaps

newlyweds too. They appeared underneath one street lamp and then seemed to disappear, only to reappear under the next lamp.

I felt a Christmas kinship with them. Another couple like us on this sacred holiday fading in and out along the edge of the ocean.

Something about our walk this night felt ethereal, a touching of heaven and earth, land and sea, dream and reality, life and eternity. I let my mind drift in the experience.

Then as we came closer to the couple, something about the gentleman seemed vaguely familiar. The way he held his head. His casual stride. Something.

Still closer, I caught the sound of their voices—a melody of conversation between male and female timbres. Their laughter.

His laughter. Laughter I suddenly recognized. Or thought I did. Dear God in Heaven! Could it be Alexander from the Lowcountry?

No, I told myself. It couldn't be. I'd thought I'd seen him many times over the years only to realize it was my foolish emotions wishing for something my mind had given up on long ago. Still I just needed to make sure.

As we approached, time slowed to a crawl. The very thing Papa had talked about happening on the battlefield. At the point of greatest danger, he said, everything slowed down so much that he could see the squint of the Yankee soldier aiming at him, hear the click of the trigger, smell the charge, see the ball flying toward him, feel the slow agony as it sank into his thigh.

But instead of a minie ball hurling at me, it was just a man. A man who looked at a distance like Alexander the Terrible. I held my breath.

Then we converged.

We crossed paths at the point where the street lamp shone brightest. The young lady pushed back auburn curls and smiled through dainty lips and even teeth. I wondered if she was the man's wife. Or soon-to-be conquest.

He tipped his hat to Willis and then to me. And that's when I knew for certain. His cursed hair, the color of corn shucks, shone in that moment of light. I could even make out little lines scattered around his eyes and across his forehead. His eyes locked with mine. We were so close I could see the pupils of his eyes expand almost past the blue.

My legs felt paralyzed. My heart pounded in my throat. Love, hate, anger, grief—all churned inside my veins.

Just as I thought I would faint, a voice whispered, "Keep walkin.' Keep walkin.' Don't go lookin' back now. Just keep walkin'." The voice was Papa's.

Willis said something.

I struggled for my own voice. "What?"

"That fella looks familiar. Wonder where I know him from."

I shivered.

"You cold?" he asked, putting his arm around my shoulders. "We can turn around."

"No," I said too quickly. Then added what I hoped sounded calmer, "A rabbit ran across my grave."

Willis stopped walking. "What?"

"Just a cold chill," I said, pulling him forward. "That's what Aunt Eliza used to say when she had a cold chill. She'd say a rabbit ran across her grave."

He laughed. "Never heard that one." As we fell back into step, he said, "If we see that couple on the way back, I'm gonna ask the gent where we've met."

We walked on a little farther until Willis wouldn't take no for an answer. He turned me around. I held my breath and looked along the Battery between us and the park.

Nothing. No one. Not another soul appearing underneath the street lamps. The couple had disappeared like phantoms in a dream.

Still, my senses were on alert. I heard barking dogs, a crying baby, a singing child—all in the distance but separate and distinct.

Papa used to say sound traveled farther at night and clearer in the cold. He said the night he'd brought Uncle James's body home, he could hear "wolves howlin' like banchees above the racket of the rails."

I felt Papa close by walking with us.

By the time we reached the park, only a few people remained. None, thank God, who looked familiar.

On the ride back to the hotel, Willis declared, "I know where I met that fella!"

I swallowed hard and muttered, "What fella?"

"That couple we saw on the Battery."

"Which couple?" I said, trying to delay whatever revelation he was about to make.

"For God's sake, Icie! The only couple we saw."

He looked at me for a response but didn't get one.

He went on, "At the Cotton Exchange—not in Augusta, the one here in Charleston. Somebody introduced us a few years back. Seemed like a nice enough fella. A little cocky. Had land here and all the way up to Pendleton."

"Oh," I replied as though it made sense.

"Funny thing is," he added, "I remembered his face, but I'll be dang if I can remember his name."

I stared at the street lamps out the window of the streetcar, willing my heart to slow down. And suddenly a laugh rose up from my soul and ripped loose.

"Oh dear Lord!" I wanted to shout, "the irony of memory!"

PART XI

Going Home

Columbia ⌐ɾↄ

Aunt Eliza used to say "Ignorance is bliss." I'm sure she
meant it to be ironic. Mama would counter with "Ignorance
is no excuse." I'm sure she meant it to be literal.

   Lying here now, I recall their words as I think back on
the magical Ivory City. How it broadened my little life's
experiences. How much I learned about my husband and
myself. How I thought of it as eternal.

   I didn't know the grand exposition would close down
within a few months. The gleaming gypsum façade would
soon crumble in the salty air. Weeds would overtake the
fairytale grounds. And the whole undertaking would be
considered a financial failure. Ah, ignorance.

The morning after Christmas, we began our trip home. I hadn't
taken in Charleston on the arm of Alexander as I'd dreamed of
years earlier. I'd gone as a grown woman on the arm of the man
who truly loved me, whose last name I not only knew but shared.
I'd faced my fear and stayed on my feet. I felt vindicated, if still
a little shaken.

   We decided to go home by way of Columbia, our state capital, on to Greenville and then Anderson. As the trained pulled

out, Willis checked his compass. "Northwest," he announced. Then he opened *The Old Farmer's Almanac*.

As we rode, I began to see much of the grand old city I'd missed in our brief stay. The northern part seemed rundown, sad, like it was a separate city. I saw boarding houses and old hotels in disrepair. I wondered who lived in them, certainly not the people we'd been among at the exposition.

An old woman appeared on the edge of the street carrying a bucket. Two children followed her, sloshing another bucket between them. I saw broken windows, boarded up doors, more of the city's poor.

Then I noticed a dilapidated building with a raised platform attached to the front. "Look, Willis," I said, pointing. "It must've been an outdoor theater in better days."

"Nope, I do believe it's the old auction house." He returned to his reading.

"For what?" I asked, remembering the busy Charleston City Market.

"Slaves," he mumbled without looking up.

The blood drained from my face. I felt ignorant. Repulsed. I suddenly envisioned men, women, children standing atop the auction block to be bought and sold. I'd never understood slavery. Since it'd ended before I was born, I'd never had to face it. But the sight of the rundown auction house made my stomach churn.

I wished I hadn't seen it. It would've been easier not to face history even though it was all around me. We rode on in silence.

Once we were clearly out of the city, I let myself think about Alexander again. I suppose I did see the beauty he'd spoken about—the live oaks, magnificent sunsets, grand houses, lush gardens. But I also saw the uglier side of the city that he didn't mention—the place where the city's lesser citizens lived. The

godawful auction block attitude that those born into good fortune were entitled to all the beauty and power it held, regardless
of consequences to others.

To some degree, I saw it in myself. A sobering realization.
Varennes had its share of poor, too. Tenants. Sharecroppers. Day
laborers. But property owners like Mama and Papa, Bessie, the
McGees took care of them to a certain extent. Yet, there was no
denying.

Willis looked up from the almanac. "When we get back," he
said, "I plan to get you some help."

"Help for what?" I asked.

"For the house."

"I can run a household," I said, somewhat put off. "I did
while Papa was bedridden. Mama saw to him, and I took care
of the house."

"What about cooking?"

"I can cook!"

He looked surprised.

"Not as well as Mama but better than Bessie." I felt a touch
of guilt.

"Bessie'd rather run her business, turn a profit, and hire a
cook," he said flatly. "There's something to be said for providing
other folks' livelihood. Don't you think?"

I hadn't.

"You'll need some help, whether it's cooking or cleaning.
And there's plenty of willing hands that need the work."

"I see your point," I conceded.

"So what about Anah?"

"What about her?" I asked, looking out the window at a cow
pasture, glad for a change of scenery.

"I think I'll hire her to help with our house. I know you

like her. And she and her brother have some sorta connection to your family."

"She works for your mother," I pointed out. "Mrs. Mary won't let her go."

"I do the hiring for Mam," he said, returning to the almanac.

"Which happens to be the Big House," I said, not ready to give in. "What if Anah doesn't want to leave the Big House?"

He looked at me like I was speaking in tongues. "What?"

"She might rather stay with Mrs. Mary," I repeated.

"I suppose I could ask 'em," he mumbled. I felt I'd made a point.

"But they won't refuse," he added. So much for my point.

Then he whispered innocently, "I just want you to have time for me." He slid closer and put an end to our conversation about Anah, at least for the time being.

I took out some knitting and settled in for the ride. Willis alternated between reading and dozing off. Each time we stopped, he took out his compass and checked the direction.

As we neared Columbia, it began to rain. The outskirts of town seemed sadly piecemeal. Some structures of wood, but few of brick. I expected Columbia to be like Augusta. It was not. All the visible streets, at least from the train, were dirt. Not a stone or brick paver in sight.

The rain had made the streets muddy. Blobs of straw lay strewn around the train station. The ground reminded me of a barnyard.

"Not how I expected our state capital to look," I said, as we waited to get off the train.

"It looks pretty dang good for being burnt to the ground." He glanced around. "I doubt Atlanta looks much better. Hard to come back from ashes."

We stepped off the train and onto the wooden sidewalk. Willis paid a train attendant to load our bags onto a cart and follow us to the hotel.

After an early trip to the dining room for warm chicken pie almost as good as Janey's and sweet baked apples almost as good as Mama's, we returned to our room and settled in for the evening. Willis pulled out a ledger and borrowed my new pencil to begin plans for his winter planting.

"Hope we're getting this at home," he said, referring to the rain. I thought of Papa and the way farmers were always hoping for rain.

I'd intended to spend the evening writing in my new journal about the Ivory City. But Columbia's condition made me think of the war. How the South was still hurting despite the monuments and busy markets in the cities we'd just visited.

I began to think of Papa again and his account of bringing home Uncles James. He'd told it many a time when I was young, but it suddenly seemed more real. Not that something can be more real, Aunt Eliza would say. More personal, I guess. He'd been in his thirties—like Willis and me now. I began to see Papa not as a parent but as a younger man with hopes and fears for the living as he brought home the dead.

At the top of the page, I wrote "Lay down my brother."

Fresh paint ❧

The next morning, we loaded our things back onto the cart and wheeled it to the Columbia train station. Then on toward home we rode from Columbia to Greenville to Anderson with many short stops along the way.

The sun was sinking by the time we reached Dean Station. Willis's brothers had left Sugar and the buggy in the station's small barn. With help from the attendant, we unloaded our belongings once more.

Willis brought around the buggy, and we filled it to almost overflowing. Then we squeezed ourselves in, and he pointed Sugar toward home.

By the time we neared Bessie's farm, the moon and stars had taken over the night. The glow of lights in her house made my heart swell with homesickness. But as we passed, I reminded myself it was my home no more.

We rode on to Willis's house. It was about halfway between the Allen farm and the McGee Big House, a large colonial-style home of brown brick, where Mrs. Mary lived.

When Willis had turned twenty, he'd built his own home, similar to a farm manager's cottage. Quite modest compared to his birthplace and even to my childhood home but just the right size for the two of us.

The house was basically a square wooden box with a metal roof. On the left side were two bedrooms, and on the right, a parlor and kitchen. A hall ran down the middle and a shallow porch across the front. Most of the back porch had been converted into a water closet.

The outside, including the roof, had been in need of a fresh coat of paint. So while we were honeymooning, Willis had left instructions to paint the outside white and the roof a grass green.

I'd asked to have the beadboard walls and ceilings painted white to brighten the inside. To be honest, I intended to block out the aura of any other woman who may have cast a shadow on those walls. Superstitious, I know, but I wasn't taking any chances.

We soon turned up the narrow road that led to our freshly painted house. It shone softly in the moonlight. Sugar bobbed his head and picked up speed.

As soon as we reached the front porch, Willis jumped down, quickly tied up Sugar, and forbade me to go inside until he'd lit several lanterns. Room by room, light reflected off the white walls and poured out the windows.

I made myself busy unloading lighter things from the buggy onto the porch until Willis rushed through the door, lifted me off my feet, and carried me inside. He smooched me hard, swung me around until I was dizzy, and proclaimed, "Welcome home, Mrs. Icie McGee!"

Then he promptly led me back outside so we could haul in our belongings. Once that was done, Willis made a fire while I tried to close windows. They'd been left open, probably to let out the fumes. But the chill of the night seemed more daunting than the smell of paint.

Since I couldn't get the windows to budge, Willis banged on the jams and sills with the palms of his hands until he could force them down. I thought surely the panes would break, but evidently there was a method to his attack.

Most of the furniture had been left in the center of the rooms, so when Willis finished muscling the windows, we pushed a few things back into place. Most notably his bed.

While he put away Sugar and the buggy, I added clean linens and a quilt. We were both tired from travel, but no sooner had he returned from the barn than he launched himself onto the freshly made bed. He patted the space beside himself, smiled charmingly, and said, "Welcome to your wedding bed!"

I tumbled in beside him, and we began our married life in his little white house under a little green roof in our little hometown. Afterward, I quickly fell asleep with the smell of paint in my nostrils.

The next morning, we picked through our shopping spoils, selected the ones to go to Bessie's house, and loaded them back into the buggy.

"In hindsight," I said, "we should've left the buggy loaded last night."

"Probably better to do our sorting in the daylight lest we take Bessie and Mrs. Emily our dirty drawers!"

"How rude!" I replied. "Speaking of which, don't you think we should wait until after breakfast to show up unexpected?"

"They'll be expecting us," he said as he pointed Sugar toward the Allen farm. He was right. Bessie and Mama met us at the front door.

Willis brought in bags of rice, tea, and other staples from the lowcountry. I'd packed gifts into a large basket covered with silk cloth. So I carried it with me and set it next to my chair at the table where Janey was putting out breakfast. Feaster joined us.

Then we sat down to the hardiest meal we'd had in nearly two weeks—a platter of scrambled eggs, thick sliced bacon, steaming grits, tender biscuits, and Mama's wonderful peach jam.

After breakfast, we gave out our late Christmas presents. First, I took off the silk cloth I had covering the basket. It was dark blue brocade with gold leaves.

"Mama, this is for you," I said, as I handed it to her. "It's silk from the West Indies. It's enough to make a scarf and wrap and probably something else."

Mama wiped her hands on her napkin several times and then on the front of her dress. She gingerly took the cloth. "It's beautiful," she whispered. "I've never seen cloth quite like this."

"It'll bring out the blue in your eyes," Bessie said.

"Oh, it's too pretty to wear," Mama said. "Much too pretty."

"Then drape it across the back of a chair or on the foot of your bed," I suggested. Bessie agreed.

I reached into the basket again and pulled out the lavender shawl I'd knitted for Bessie. It was made of alpaca yarn imported from Peru according to the merchant at the Savannah Market. Its heavenly softness reminded me of the shawl I'd made for Mama before the Faith Alliance concert.

Bessie held it to her cheek. "It's a lovely color, and so-o soft."

"And it won't overpower black," I added. Mama nodded. Bessie wrapped herself in it, and for a moment, she looked almost girlish. Everyone at the table seemed to notice.

Then I pulled out Feaster's gift and handed it to Willis.

He cleared his throat. "Feaster, here's something Icie and I thought you might like." He held out the gun he'd bought in Savannah.

It was wrapped in a square of thick, black fabric. Feaster laid it on the table and carefully peeled back the cloth, a corner at a time, until the gleaming barrel and ivory grip lay framed in black like a portrait. He slowly picked it up, pointing the barrel down and away from the rest of us.

He handled it much the same way Willis had. I studied Feaster as he examined the pistol. He looked older, more mature, as though he'd aged several years in the past two weeks.

I realized I hadn't really looked at him closely in recent times. I'd dodged him as much as he had me. But I remembered my decision to tell him about his father and let him think what he must. Now that I was home, the thought made my heart race.

Mama and Bessie watched Feaster, too. "What a beautiful piece," Bessie commented.

"Yes," Feaster said. "Yes," he repeated. Then he looked from Willis to me and back to Willis. "Thank you."

Lastly I took the basket, now empty, and gave it to Mama. "We brought this for you, too. It's made of Charleston sweetgrass."

She ran her fingers over the intricate weave. "It's too pretty for bean picking," she said.

"Then use if it for flower fetching," I said as I hugged her.

We stayed at the table discussing what had happened the past two weeks at home and away until Feaster asked to be excused, and Willis and Bessie adjourned to the parlor to talk farm business.

That left Mama and me. I began to tell her about the beautiful sights we'd seen—Augusta's river walk, the boat ride down the Savannah, Forsyth Park and its wonderful fountain, the amazing sunset from the Battery, and the Ivory City.

"Oh Mama!" I said, "I wish you could see those places!"

She looked past me for a moment. "I expect your joy is joy enough for me. Anyway," she said, focusing on me again, "I haven't given you your Christmas present yet."

"Yes, you did! My trousseau! And, yes, I needed all those drawers."

She smiled and slowly pushed herself up from the table with both hands. She seemed smaller. Evidently, I hadn't really looked at Mama in recent days either.

"I have something else for you," she said. She led me to the sideboard and a familiar set of china, though I hadn't seen it in years. China that I'd grown up with but that we'd never actually used. It had been my great-grandmother Isabella's bone china from better days.

The story was that Isabella had given the set to her daughter, who probably never used it either other than to instruct her daughters on the difference between bone china and plain ole china. Mama inherited the dishes upon her marriage to Papa.

The sight of the set took me back to childhood. When Bessie and I were young, Mama would occasionally take out a plate decorated with little bouquets of yellow, pink, and blue flowers and a gold border. She'd hold it up to the window like a fan and put her other hand behind it.

"Can you see how many fingers I'm holding up?" she'd ask. Bessie would guess first. Then I'd quickly guess a different number thinking it was some sort of trick like Sallie's. Bessie would be right.

"The point is," Mama would say, "this is bone china from England. It's so thin you can see through it with a little help from the sun. You can't see through other china."

Sometimes she'd let us each hold a cup. I would feel the raised flowers on the delicate handle. Often I'd find a tiny dead thing in the bottom, almost too small to be seen.

Mama would take the cup, dump out the powdery remains, and repeat the history. Then she'd carefully wipe off the freshly handled pieces and put them away in the maple china cabinet Papa had made for her.

One time during our bone china lesson, Bessie asked, "Why don't we ever use it?"

Mama quickly replied, "Because it's too fine."

"Too fine for us?" Bessie asked.

Mama looked surprised. "Oh, no, honey. Too fine for everyday."

That seemed to satisfy Bessie who was probably in a hurry to dispense with the dish lesson. But not me.

"What makes it so fine?" I asked.

"Bone china is thinner but stronger than regular china,"

Mama said, as she put the pieces back. "It won't chip or crack so easily."

"Why's it 'bone'?" I asked.

"Because it's made of bone," she said.

Bessie and I'd looked at each other with alarm.

"What kind of bone?" I dared to ask.

"Ground-up cow bones," she said, closing the cabinet door and the discussion on bone china. That settled it for us. Neither of us wanted to eat off ground-up cow bones.

"Icie," Mama said, bringing me back to the present, "I want you to have Isabella's bone china."

"Oh, but what about Bessie?" I replied.

"She's got more dishes than she knows what to do with. Anyway, you know she doesn't give a hoot about such."

"Then I'll take good care of the set," I said, not entirely sure I wanted it. "And I promise not to use it except for very special occasions."

"No!" she shrieked, catching me off guard.

"Then I promise not to use it at all," I said bewildered.

"No!" she shrieked again. "You must use it often."

I looked at her for signs of dementia. I wondered if she'd had a mild stroke while we were away.

"You don't understand. Those dishes have passed through three generations without touching so much as a slice of ham or a hot roll or a drop of coffee."

"Then you must use them yourself." I felt her forehead to be sure she wasn't feverish. "And what about your Christmas gifts?" I added. "You said the silk's too pretty to wear and the basket might get dirty from beans!"

She laughed and admitted, "Old habits die hard." Since that sounded more like Mama, I relaxed a little.

"I'm not losing my mind. I'm just too set in my ways to change now."

I wanted to agree but thought better of it.

"I can imagine the mismatched dishes at Willis's house," she continued. "Chipped plates and cracked bowls from his mama's table. Tin cups for coffee. Need I go on?"

So while Bessie and Willis talked about livestock and fertilizer and early planting, Mama and I carefully wrapped up Isabella's bone china, piece by piece, and packed it into several wooden boxes.

As we worked, Mama told stories about some of her happier days as a daughter and granddaughter. Stories I'd never heard before. I began to think the value of objects such as china passed down through generations lay not in their fineness but in the stories they held.

And perhaps the real value of those stories, of all stories, was in the telling and retelling. A way of reliving joy or coming to terms with something not yet settled in the teller's mind.

It was something to write down and think about.

Catch-as-catch-can ⟨ ⟩ ⟩

While frosty cedar boughs gave way to delicate dogwood blossoms, I stayed busy inside our little house.

I made curtains of unbleached muslin. But once I'd finished the curtains, I realized the unbleached muslin was plain against the white walls. Too plain. Then I remembered something I'd seen in one of Mrs. Mary's magazines—*Ladies' Home Journal.*

The instructions showed how paint a border of leaves on fabric. So I used magnolia leaves in dark shiny green, oak leaves in rusty red, golden yellow maple leaves, and fern fronds in the same dark green paint as the magnolia leaves. The border made me think of resurrection fern.

On the day that Willis put up rods and we hung the curtains, he fetched Mrs. Mary from the Big House to see our handiwork. She seemed impressed and brought more magazines for me.

In early spring, I turned my attention outside, planting Lenten roses, small camellia bushes, and iris and lily bulbs that Mama shared. She visited often and helped with the flowers. She kept saying I was getting too thin, so she usually brought baked goods and other dishes she and Janey had cooked up.

Mrs. Mary must have thought the same about Willis because she often sent beef stew, ham, or fried chicken. Whatever she had at her table, she evidently had extra made for us.

I hardly cooked a lick, as Mama would say, other than biscuits for breakfast or a pan of cornbread once the vegetables started coming in. Not that I had my own garden. We got beans and corn and tomatoes from the Big House garden.

Willis's mother also sent Anah to help with laundry once a week. But if Mrs. Mary thought I was helpless, she didn't let on. In fact, she complimented me often on how lovely the house and yard had become. When I returned her dishes, I filled them with whatever was blooming in our yard. She seemed genuinely happy with her firstborn's choice of wife.

Mrs. Mary reminded me of Mama in her independence. But she was considerably younger. Actually she was closer in age to my half-sister Mattie than she was to Mama. She'd been nearly twenty years younger than Col. Jesse when they'd married, which made me think there must have been an interesting story about their courting days. Story or no story, she was still mighty spry. She often drove herself when she came to visit.

Another way she was different from Mama, other than age, was her fondness for magazines. She said they were her window to the world. And the world of fashion, she could have added. Not that she dressed beyond the confines of Varennes, but she sometimes included a bit of flair such as a bright scarf held just so by a brooch.

Willis didn't object to my playing for Cross Roads Baptist services. And I continued to have my own purse though he gave me plenty to manage the household.

As for the sharecropper families on McGee property, I wrote down the birthdays of babies born there and gave them crocheted blankets and caps and booties. I kept small presents on hand for their brothers and sisters too. Something I'd learned from Bessie.

She'd arranged for Feaster to go to a college in Greenville beginning in the fall. Even though he was young, he was ready for something more. Until college started, he worked on the Allen farm. So far I hadn't been able to catch him alone. At least, that's what I told myself.

Willis continued to help manage Bessie's land in addition to McGee property. He kept saying he'd build us a larger house closer to the Allen home whenever I wanted. But I was in no hurry.

And so passed the happiest seasons of my life.

Early one morning, as I walked around the yard to see what was blooming and what needed a trim, I found a single butterfly wing glittering on top of the grass near the well. At first I thought it was just an odd clump of dew until I crouched down and began to study it.

I picked it up and held it carefully in my palm. It was so light I could hardly feel it. The wing's top side was sparkly black with yellow dots around the edge like a decorative border. I turned it over.

Underneath was the same black with yellow dots around the outer edge. But on its lower half, the black dissolved into every shade of blue under the heavens. And across the shimmering blues was an explosion of large orange spots.

With its wings folded back, the butterfly must've looked like a tropical flower. It was a Jesus-God masterpiece on a tiny canvas. Such a minute, fragile, essential part of the whole. And oh so beautiful. I continued to stare at the single wing until my legs ached.

I stood and looked around for the rest of the butterfly—the other wing, a mirror image for the one I held, and the slender body that joined the two. I found neither. Perhaps they'd fallen into the well. I returned the wing to its resting place as though the wounded butterfly might somehow reclaim it and fly away.

At the end of the day, just as the light was beginning to fade, I returned to the well to look for the wing. But it was gone.

That evening after supper as I wrote in my journal and Willis read from his almanac, I thought about it again.

"Does your almanac say anything about butterflies as an omen?" I asked.

"You mean the one about the first yellow butterfly in spring?" he said without looking up.

"No, not that one. Anything about butterfly wings?"

He flipped through several pages. "Matter of fact it does." Then he read aloud, or pretended to read, "'If a lady finds a butterfly and bites off its head," he paused for dramatic effect, "she'll get a new dress the same color as the wings.'"

I gasped. "That's awful! Just awful!" I was sorry I'd asked.

"Yep, awful for the butterfly." Then he added, "Hope it wasn't black" and returned to his reading.

I didn't say. And I didn't think about the wing again until summer gave way to fall. Before I knew it, September rolled in with its devotion to King Cotton. Picking, hauling to the gin, baling, weighing, hauling to market. In a normal year, September was the busiest month for farmers in Varennes.

Yet I hadn't been married to it before. A stress, a kind of competition permeated just about every step. Hiring the best pickers, getting at the head of the line at the gin, getting to market first. It needed as much managing as it did labor and luck.

I saw little of Willis during daylight hours throughout the month of September. The stress of managing the McGee crop with his brothers and helping Bessie get her crop to market took its toll. Some nights we hardly had a conversation.

But at the end of the month, as summer dissolved into fall, all things cotton seemed to slow down. Sensing as much, in early October, I planned a special meal to be waiting on Willis. Rolls and baked sweet potatoes, ham his mother had sent, and my own apple pie. I'd bought a new blue dress, one Willis hadn't seen, that I planned to wear.

I set the table with a wedding present tablecloth, Mama's bone china, and a large shallow bowl I'd filled with pink autumn camellia blossoms.

By late afternoon I had the house in order and as much of the meal prepared as I could until time to heat up the last bit. So I took my rest on the front porch. As I sat enjoying the coolness of early fall and wishing Willis would come on home, I saw a ball of dust rolling up the road to our house. But it wasn't Willis, it was Mrs. Mary.

When she reached the porch, she leaped out of her buggy and slung the lead rein around the post.

"Willis home yet?" she asked, clearly agitated.

I quickly stood. "No," I said, my heart picking up speed. "What's wrong?"

"Fighting!" she shrieked, "just like his father!"

"What fight?" By then my heart was about to explode.

"He got into it with Harve Higgins," she said, still at the bottom of the steps. She reached for the rein. I was afraid she was about to drive off.

"Whatever for? Harve Higgins is his friend! He's Bessie's neighbor!"

"Goes back a ways, I expect." She left the rein and came up the steps. "Seems there was always some rooster strutting between Preston Allen and ole Harve."

"Roosters?" I asked. "A cock fight?"

"No!" she said. "Well maybe," she added. "It was more a cotton fight. Guess Harve thought he'd have a leg up this harvest since Preston passed away. God rest his soul."

"But not so," I said for her. "Not with Willis helping manage Bessie's farm."

Mrs. Mary nodded. "Hard words passed between them, and they went at it in one of the barns near the gin." She straightened her dress and attempted to knock off some dust.

"I don't know much else," she said. "I just hope he doesn't die. Or isn't left crippled."

My heart stopped beating. Mrs. Mary started to fade.

"God in Heaven!" she shouted, grabbing me under my arms and pushing me back into the chair. "I've scared you to death!"

I regained some of my senses, then burst into tears. "How bad is Willis hurt?" I asked between sobs.

"Oh not too much I don't think," she said, fanning my face with her bare hands.

"But you said, 'die' and 'crippled'!" I sobbed louder.

"Oh, honey! I meant Harve! I'm hoping Willis didn't kill him or break him up too bad."

I felt some relief, enough at least to slow my tears.

She stopped fanning me. "My boys can take care of themselves as long as it's a fair fight. And there's not a mule involved."

She sat beside me and looked toward the road. The dust was beginning to settle. "I suppose Harve has his side, too," she said.

We sat in silence for a while. Then she stood.

"Mainly, I worry one of my boys might end up in jail or get sued." She hugged me, went down the steps, grabbed the lead rein, and bounced up into the buggy.

I watched her drive away. I wanted to be a strong woman like Mrs. Mary. Like Mama. Like Bessie. But I had a long way to go.

I sat back down and considered the possibility of becoming a widow. I'd seen Mama in widow's weeds. And the same for Bessie, but I hadn't thought about that fate for myself, not so soon after getting married. Yet there it was—if not from this fight, from one down the road.

I thought about the butterfly wing until the sun set and the stars began to show. I went back inside, washed my face, and put on my new dress. I didn't feel pretty like I had when I'd first tried it on. But I told myself I didn't have to feel pretty. I just had to be strong.

I remembered how angry Willis had gotten when I questioned why he'd nearly kill a hired hand for insulting him, or more likely, insulting me. I knew he'd be angry again. I kept repeating the word "strong" in my head. I put out supper and I waited.

When Willis finally came home, he was an exhausted mess. He shirt was torn and dirty. His cheeks, puffy. His hands were covered in cuts and scratches. And his left eye was swollen shut.

"What on earth happened?" I shouted, already knowing but shocked at how bad he looked.

He mumbled something.

"What?" I repeated.

"I'm alright," he said.

"But what happened?" I asked again.

"Fight," he mumbled.

"A fight! Willis McGee, you could have gotten killed!" He didn't respond, so I added, "Or killed somebody!"

His face turned hard. "Goddammit, Icie!" he said in a voice as hard as his expression. "We already had this conversation!"

I didn't flinch. "Yes," I said. "Yes we did."

He turned away.

I continued, "That was before you had the responsibility of a wife you could leave without a husband." My voice shook. I took a deep breath. "And, a child you could leave without a father."

He turned back around so fast he nearly lost his balance. He stared but said nothing. I nodded. He continued to stare. I nodded again although I wasn't really sure. I'd meant to wait at least another month until I was positive. But it just came out.

His expression softened so quickly I thought his face would melt and run off his head.

"When?" he asked.

"One of so many nights. How should I know which one?"

He laughed and wrapped me in his arms. He smelled of sweat and blood. "You've made me the happiest man in the world," he whispered.

"Even in your bruised and battered state?" I whispered back.
"Even in this state."

Then I remembered the glass eye, or lack thereof. "What about your eye?" I asked, worried it may have been crushed and driven into his brain. I tried to look.

He held me tight. "It's safe in my coat pocket. I knew there'd be a scuffle."

As for the "scuffle," it made the Anderson newspaper after Harve Higgins swore out a warrant on Willis.

The article read:

Last Friday afternoon, two local gentlemen in Varennes, Willis McGee and Harve Higgins, had a difficulty, which from present indications, will have to be settled in the Courts. McGee, a prominent farmer, related by marriage to the late Preston B. Allen, has the supervision of Mrs. Allen's farms in connection with his own. Harve Higgins owns an adjacent farm. Hot words passed between them a week ago last Saturday but no blows. Afterwards, McGee was told that Higgins was saying some pretty hard things about him. They met Friday afternoon in a cotton barn. McGee demanded that Higgins retract; Higgins refused to do so, and a catch-as-catch-can fight followed. A seed shovel, fists, fingernails and everything available was used, and when the dust cleared away, Higgins was pretty badly "done up." The next day, Higgins came to the city and swore out a warrant for McGee, charging him with "assault and battery with intent to kill." McGee appeared Monday and gave bond in the sum of $500. They were good friends, and it is hoped they will adjust their troubles before the case is called to court.

I didn't know whether to laugh or cry. But I didn't bring it up. Instead I waited for Willis to read it himself. And when he did, he let go a string of swear words, balled up the paper, and threw it into the fireplace.

"I oughta go back and finish the job!" Then he looked at me and softened. "But I won't. I have more important business to take care of."

I just hoped he was right.

Second chance ❧

The worst of the fight blew over in a few weeks. Willis's face had healed enough by early November to return his evil eye to its rightful place. I didn't see Harve so I don't know how long it took for him heal. They settled out of court. Willis didn't say how much and I didn't ask.

As for the other matter, I'd been right. Funny how you can hope against something one day and hope for it the next. Regardless of what I wanted or didn't want, Willis had taken seed. And he was about as happy as I'd ever seen him. Which was a good thing because I was about as sick as I'd ever been.

I kept thinking about the first time I'd seen birth up close. It was during Reconstruction when times were unsettled and the Red Shirt movement had just begun. I was barely ten. By then, I knew where babies came from, more or less, at least how they got out. But I hadn't actually witnessed birth's long, loud, messy ordeal.

One of Papa's two beef cows was set to calve. She didn't have a name. Molly, our milk cow, had a name because we kept her until she died on her own. But the beef cattle didn't stay that long—except for the bull, Samson. Papa called him "Samp-son." He was huge and black and built like a freight train. He bellowed like one, too.

Papa traded out the females after a few seasons. He said changing up the cows for Samson kept the calves strong. Which also meant big.

Those days, when Papa needed help, he'd call on one of the neighbors or a sharecropper on the property. But middle-of-the-night emergencies fell heavy on Mama.

One of the nameless beef cows had been trying to give birth to Samson's big calf most of the day and into the night. Papa kept going out to check. Then he'd come back in, wait a while, then go back out. After the rest of us had gone to bed, he rushed in, woke up Mama, and out the door they went.

Bessie and I followed. Normally, Mama kept us away from the barn at such delicate times, but she was too intent on helping Papa and not losing a perfectly good beef cow. She held onto the cow's halter as best she could while Papa fumbled around at the dark end. The cow bellowed in pain and lifted Mama off the straw. When Papa saw us, he yelled for Bessie to bring around the lantern so he could see what he was doing.

I watched as Bessie held the light, Papa pulled, and Mama hung onto the cow's head. I had to do something, so I grabbed onto Mama's waist and started singing, "Hush little BAY-BEE, don't say a word, Ma-ma gon-na buy you a MOCK-in-bird . . ." I reached up and stroked the cow's neck as I sang. I don't know how many times I sang it, but every time I got to the end, Papa yelled, "Keep singin'!"

So I did until the cow gave a blood-curdling, freight train of a bellow every bit as loud as Samson's. Bessie gasped, and Papa fell back with a bloody, drowned calf in his arms. I looked away in horror. But Mama seemed absolutely ecstatic. As soon as she let go of the cow's halter, the cow wheeled around and began licking and nudging the apparently dead calf. Then, miracle of miracles, the calf began to move. Papa wiped off its bloody face with his shirt while the cow inspected every inch of the shiny thing that had come from inside her.

We watched as the calf tried to stand. Wobbly, wobbly, wobbly, down—again and again until what I'd given up for dead was not only standing but obviously hungry.

Mama and Papa smiled at each other, and even in the dark of the barn, I could see the light between them. I looked at Bessie. She was staring at Papa's bloody shirt. Then Papa fetched a pitchfork and lifted up the mass of blood that had come out with the calf—the darkest, thickest I'd ever seen, held together by shiny strands of something I didn't have a word for. It dripped down from the pitchfork prongs like horrible, lumpy, runny grape jelly mixed with straw. Papa took it somewhere. Where I never knew nor did I want to know.

Mama brought Bessie and me back inside while Papa cleaned up. We talked about the sweet little calf and how happy the mother looked. But we never talked about the ugly part. Mama soaked Papa's shirt in a tub on the back porch over the next few days, changing the water from time to time until the muslin took on a uniform pink.

More than twenty years later, I wished I could just remember the calf and not the other part. But every time I tried, I thought of that pitchfork's gory load and I threw up.

The alternative was to think about giving birth to Feaster. How I'd ridden that lurching train of pain on a godawful track with my eyes closed. How absolutely alone I'd felt even surrounded by Jones women.

To make myself feel better this time around, I sang the Mockingbird Song. I sang it a lot. Occasionally, I heard Willis whistling the same tune. He was a happy, happy man. Part of me was also happy. I wanted so to be a good mother, and I was getting a second chance.

I didn't plan on telling Mama and Bessie for a while, but Mama knew almost as soon as I did. From time to time, she'd say something about Willis chirping around like a song bird, bruised face and all. So I knew she knew. And if she knew, Bessie knew.

Still, we thought we'd wait until Thanksgiving to tell our families officially. We planned to eat dinner at the Allen house. Feaster would be home from college for the first time since he'd started in September. I worried what he'd think.

We wore our Sunday best, but the dress that otherwise hung on me was uncomfortably tight in the waist. The rest of my good dresses were snug in the middle too. So I left three buttons at the waist undone and tied on a pinafore. I realized I'd need more pinafores.

We went to the Allen home early so I could help with the table and Willis could talk farm business with Feaster.

When we arrived, Feaster greeted us at the door, probably at Bessie's prompting. He was dressed in his school uniform, a tailored jacket and pants in dark gray wool. The jacket had a standup collar and shiny black trim. It looked uncomfortable but he wore it well. My heart swelled much like when he was a toddler.

I was sure he looked like his father, at least his eyes and hair. I stared at Feaster until Willis helped me down from the buggy and up the steps. Then Feaster rode with him to the carriage house.

Inside, Mama and Janey bustled about in the kitchen, and Bessie wrestled with the tablecloth in the dining room.

"I can never get this fancy knitted thing to lay straight on the table," she said, trying to stretch it one way and then the other.

"It's crocheted. Aunt Eliza made it," I said, remembering how she'd worked on it while she was in mourning. "Put a bed sheet underneath it."

Bessie went to the linen closet and returned. "The is the best I can do." She billowed out the sheet. I helped straighten it from the opposite side of the table. Then we added Aunt Eliza's handiwork.

"Much better," she declared. She lifted a stack of dinner plates from the sideboard. I recognized them as Preston's last anniversary gift to her.

They were snowy white with blue and yellow flowers around the edges. The blue flowers had tiny yellow dots for centers and the yellow had blue centers. Silver filigree bordered the flowers.

"So glad you're using these today," I said as I helped set them out.

"High time, don't you think," she said.

"Wonder if Mama has held them up to the window," I joked.

"Not in front of me," Bessie said, "but I'm sure she has."

Then almost in unison, we both said, "Remember how she taught us to thump crystal to see how good it was!" We burst out laughing.

We set out the goblets. "I bet these beauties have a fine musical ring. Preston had excellent taste." I resisted the urge to thump one.

Bessie agreed, then asked, "Is that a new pinafore or a new

dress?" She handed me several bread plates for my side of the table.

"It's a new combination," I said, "worn out of necessity."

That's all it took for her to rush around and hug me.

"I'm so happy for you and Willis! Mama told me not to say anything about it 'til you actually told me. That was close enough." She let go of me and fetched the silverware chest. We began putting out the flatware.

"Both of you know me so well. I'm just worried about Feaster. I wonder how he'll take it."

"He'll be happy to have a brother or sister," she said working her way through the sterling forks, then knives and spoons.

"Half," I said.

She waved her hand as if to erase the half. "Anyway, he loves and admires Willis."

"But not me," I said without self-pity, finishing the flatware on my side.

"He'll work it out," she said. We added linen napkins and completed the table.

Bessie propped open the door to the kitchen, and we helped Mama and Janey set out platters and bowls and baskets of Thanksgiving. Then she called Feaster and Willis to the dining room.

She motioned Willis to one end of the table where the golden turkey waited for the knife. She sat at the other end. Mama took her usual place on Bessie's left and Feaster on her right. I sat between Mama and Willis.

As we settled in, Bessie said, "Feaster, you do the blessing, and Willis, you do the carving."

Feaster bowed his head. We did likewise. He prayed, "O

God, we praise thy gracious care, which does our daily bread prepare. O bless the earthly food we take, and feed our souls for thine own sake. So mote it be."

I recognized it as one of Preston's masonic blessings complete with "So mote it be." We followed with "amen."

Willis positioned the platter to his liking. "Feaster, what have you learned in school so far?" He steadied the turkey with the carving fork.

"A lot," he said as he spread the napkin across his lap.

Mama started the dressing around. "What's your favorite class?" she asked.

"I pretty much like them all. Then he looked thoughtful and added, "My language class, I guess."

Willis sliced down across the breast.

Bessie served herself some dressing and passed it to Feaster. "How so?" she asked.

"When my French professor found out I'm from Varennes, he told me the history and etymology of the word." He served himself a generous mound of dressing.

"What's that?" Bessie asked. She took the gravy from Mama.

"It's the origin of the word," he said, his face animated. "And my professor doesn't pronounce Varennes like we do, he calls it 'VAAH-ren'" He said it again, "VAAH-ren!" not quite as nasal as Aunt Eliza but just as loud.

Bessie, Mama, and Willis were suddenly struck deaf and dumb like Paul on the road to Damascus. Willis stopped mid-slice. Bessie nearly dropped the gravy. Mama's hand was frozen on the breadbasket.

"Did he tell you about King Louis XVI and his wife Marie Antoinette and their flight from Paris to VAAH-ren?" I asked nonchalantly, remembering Aunt Eliza's fine lesson. I helped myself to some sweet potatoes and slid the bowl toward Mama.

Bessie, Mama, and Willis turned their Damascus faces toward me, and Feaster joined them.

I smiled and took a sip of tea.

Feaster recovered first. "Yes, and he said it means 'Cemetery of the Gods.' Makes us sound like something out of a Greek tragedy."

Willis regained his voice. "Too bad it isn't 'Farmland of the Gods.'" He resumed his carving duties. Mama and Bessie agreed.

And so progressed dinner as the sliced turkey at last made the rounds, followed by cranberry sauce, green beans, and Janey's peach pickles.

Between polite chews, Feaster talked about quantitative philosophy, the humanities, and social sciences. I don't guess I'd ever heard him talk so much. He was clearly in his element, but Bessie looked bewildered.

Luckily, Feaster seemed to notice. "The goal of my studies is to prepare me to think critically and independently," he said, looking at Bessie, "just like Uncle Preston."

If we'd had brandy at the table, we'd have raised our glasses and shouted, "Just like Preston! Here! Here!"

Bessie glowed, and Mama and Willis relaxed. All was right with the Allen household again and in our little town regardless of what we called it. After-dinner coffee was rich and smooth, and Mama's pecan pie never tasted so good.

At dinner's end, I realized I'd eaten an entire meal for the first time in months.

While Mama, Bessie, and I busied ourselves in the kitchen,

Willis and Feaster adjourned to the parlor. I knew he planned to tell Feaster about the baby away from the women folk. Bessie sent Janey and Red home with their own feast. As we washed and dried Bessie's fine china, we relived past Thanksgivings including the last ones with Papa and Preston.

And when it was time to leave, Feaster shook Willis's hand and said, "I'm happy for you." He looked at me and added, "for both of you."

Miracle of miracles, I thought, so mote it be.

Anniversary ⌒

When we told Mrs. Mary our news, she was no more surprised than Mama. She'd had five of her own and gracious plenty grandchildren. But she seemed as happy as if it were her first. Her firstborn's firstborn. Biblical, no doubt.

And before I knew it, we were marking our one-year anniversary. I was more grateful than I thought possible. Our honeymoon had taken us down the Savannah, which no longer seemed so scary, and across to the Ivory City, a world away from our little VAAH-ren. I'd even seen the ocean with its watery vastness.

From time to time, I read in the Anderson newspaper about Beautiful Jim Key dazzling skeptics somewhere far off. And I saw that Nancy Columbia and her Inuit family had taken their Eskimo Village to Coney Island in New York.

The Charleston Exposition had closed only six months after it'd opened, according to the paper, "following a stretch of extraordinarily wet weather, a plague of pigeons, and a serious shortage of capital." I would've mourned the demise of the palaces and magical grounds if I hadn't become enchanted with my own little castle, my own little yard, my own little kingdom.

In the meantime, Feaster was thriving in college. Bessie missed him terribly. She didn't say so, but I could tell. Since Mama and Janey ran the house quite well on their own, Bessie threw herself into making her farming operation even bigger and better than the year before.

Willis continued to help her when needed, but he kept a closer eye on me. Which was nice to a point. He didn't want me lifting anything heavier than a pan of cornbread. And he tried to make sure I ate well, meaning twice as much as my stomach could hold.

Actually, I did regain my appetite, for the most part. And, except for nearly constant tiredness and leg cramps, I felt better. I tried to do honest-to-goodness housekeeping in the mornings—sweeping, dusting, washing dishes—when I had a little giddy-up. Papa's word. I didn't have to do much else because Mama kept bringing food, and, praise the Lord and Mrs. Mary, Anah still came once a week to help with laundry.

Needlework didn't take much energy, just reasonable concentration, so I continued to make caps and booties and blankets for sharecroppers' babies and our own soon-to-be little McGee. I sewed more pinafores for my growing middle. And I wrote in my journal.

Odd how writing down a family story causes you to look at it more closely. To go beyond the familiar telling and look deeper at the teller. What he's giving away and what he's holding back. What the telling means to him. Or her.

There's the story on the surface, like Papa's account of going after Uncle James's body during the war. Then the details. The bad weather. The long, cold walk from his camp in Petersburg to catch a train to Richmond. The makeshift cemetery there. The digging. The unrecognizable face. The jarring, frigid train ride home with what was left of Uncle James.

I imagined Papa had a long conversation with his young brother, almost twenty years his junior. Probably longer than any conversations they'd had in life. Uncle James couldn't answer in the conventional sense, but maybe he heard just the same.

Writing down the story made me think more about kinship. It pulled me below the surface to the place where life and death mingle. Where the living take care of the dead or the other way around. I went back and rewrote it several times, thinking of more questions with each new version.

I remembered and wrote down the happier stories, too. Some made me feel like a little girl again as though the adventure had just happened. Sometimes I'd have a laughing fit. Other times I'd burst into tears.

Mama, who found me one way or the other from time to time, said, "Oh, Icie, it's just your condition. It wears on the body and frays the nerves. You'll get better."

Maybe I had too much time to think. But that's pretty much the way I spent my afternoons. Writing and needlework. Aunt Eliza would have approved. If not Mama.

That Christmas, Mrs. Mary gave us a family Bible. She said, "You'll get the McGee Bible when I go over the hill. Until then, you need your own." She'd already filled in the McGee side. Mama helped me with the Jones side.

The family Bible brought home the need to decide on names. I thought for sure if we had a boy, Willis would want to use Jesse, his father's name, or Willis, his and his grandfather's name.

I brought it up one night at supper. Red had brought us several servings of Janey's chicken pie and Mama's baked apples.

As soon as Willis finished asking the blessing, I said, "I think we need to settle on names. How about Jesse or Willis Jr.?" I spooned myself a moderate serving of chicken pie before he could serve me. Then I pushed the pan toward him.

"Nope," he said, helping himself more generously and looking at my plate as though he might try to add some more. I propped my arm between my plate and the pie. He laid down the spoon.

"Nope," he repeated. "My folks used 'em up already."

I hadn't thought about that, but I should have. His nephews were populated with Willis, Jesse, Elias, and Thomas in various combinations. I helped myself to a baked apple and slid the dish to Willis.

"How 'bout William or James from your side?" He scooped out two apples.

"The Joneses have worn them out, too." I started on my chicken pie. The crust was crisp. The meat and vegetables were oh so tender. For the moment, I forgot about names and enjoyed Janey's creation.

Then I thought about Mama's side. "I don't think there's but one Euphronius," I offered.

Willis looked like he'd bitten into a bone. He shook his head. "No offense, it's just a lot to saddle on a young'un."

We ate on. I finished most of my chicken pie and started on the sweet, soft apple. Suddenly, I had an idea. Willis must have read my mind or had the same exact thought.

"How 'bout we name him Preston Allen?" he said. "Assuming it's a boy." He cut into the peel of his second apple.

"Preston Allen McGee," I said slowly, "a fine name after a fine man. That'd surely make Bessie happy. And Feaster."

"Then it's decided," he said. A sizeable portion of apple disappeared into his mouth.

"But if it's a girl?" I asked.

He looked thoughtful but continued to chew.

"What about Mary Bethia?" I asked. "In honor of your mother and my sister?"

He swallowed. "McGees are full up on Marys. How 'bout Emily Bethia?"

"Emily Bethia McGee," I said slowly, giving equal time to each syllable. "It's almost like singing."

"Then we got 'em covered." He reached across the table, squeezed my hand, and served himself another apple.

Our baby was no longer anonymous. He or she had a first name, a middle name, and a last name. "Preston Allen McGee" or "Emily Bethia McGee"—fine names. Now I could call the child growing inside me by name.

⟜

The new year bought a mild winter. Daffodils bloomed in early February, followed by little snowball blossoms on the Lenten roses. And by early March, the hyacinths were up and showing color. All seemed right in our little corner of the county.

Then, in late March, one of the McGee barns caught fire during the night. It belonged to Willis's brother. Willis raced out to help fight the flames but forbade me to leave our house lest the smoke upset something.

He returned hours later soaked in ashes and exhaustion. Once he'd cleaned up and consumed almost a pitcher of tea, he reported on the damage. No one was hurt, and thanks to

quick work by neighbors and sharecroppers, most of the livestock was saved. But two mules and a horse perished along with
the contents of the barn and obviously the barn itself. The fire
was considered arson.

The thought made my heart race. It reminded me of the
night Bessie and Preston's new carriage house had burned down
in the middle of the night and nearly taken their house with it.

"Who would do such a thing?" I asked.

"Lowest of the low! It takes a goddam evil bastard to unleash
fire on sleeping souls."

I flinched at the word.

He softened, "Somebody musta been mad at my brother
about something."

He fell into bed and I crawled in beside him. I held him close
while my belly stirred with tiny arms and legs. I prayed to God
to keep us safe from evil.

April progressed as usual with farmers fretting about the
likelihood of a late freeze. But Willis didn't worry because his
almanac predicted an early spring. It was right.

As soon as the weather was warm enough, I spent time outside tending to my flowers. I deadheaded the ones I could reach
without stooping, and I kicked at the weeds. Neither was especially tiring or effective, but it was enough to feed my gardening soul.

Each evening after supper, Willis and I went for a stroll
around the property. We called it our country promenade.
Sometimes we walked down to the branch where ferns rolled
out new fronds and spring rains created small waterfalls. The
woods smelled of evergreens and wild plum blossoms.

Occasionally we'd take a buggy ride along the edge of the
fields where the McGees had planted feed corn. Other times,

we'd ride by the Allen house, through town, past the cemetery, and back home while the sun descended and the horizon turned every shade of pink under the heavens.

By Easter, I was bigger than I'd been with Feaster, which again presented the problem of reaching the organ pedals. I remembered how, years earlier, church members had stared at my belly, then turned their heads in disgust. The second time around, they looked, smiled, and nodded approval. I had, after all, become an honest woman. But honest or not, I still had trouble reaching the pedals.

I was determined to play through April, then take my leave. Truth was I enjoyed having my own little money and using it as I wanted. So I played on as long as I could.

Willis and I'd settled on names but not on who should deliver the baby. My family used Dr. Dean, who lived north of Varennes in Dean Station, and Willis's family used Dr. Dixon, who lived south of town along the Savannah.

My half-sister Sallie Seigler had delivered Feaster much to Mama's and my chagrin. But she'd done a fine job even with me at my worst. So, wonder of wonders, I wanted her to deliver my baby again. Mama did, too. We'd softened toward Sallie as she had toward us. Besides, she'd brought more babies into the light than both doctors put together.

So I asked her the last Sunday I played at Cross Roads Baptist, and she agreed without hesitation. She even smiled and patted my hand.

Willis had gone to the Presbyterian church, which he did from time to time, to see some of his father's kin. It always let out before the Baptist. Willis said the Presbyterians already knew what the Baptists evidently forgot during the week.

He and Sugar were waiting for me when I got out of church.

As soon as he'd helped me into the buggy, I told him I'd asked Sallie to do the delivering.

"But I just asked Dr. Dixon," he said turning Sugar toward home.

I was dumb-founded. My heart sank.

"I can't un-ask Sallie," I cried. "She'll never forgive me, nor will the entire first family." I wiped away tears.

We rode on in silence until he spoke up, "Then we'll be well covered. One or the other might already be delivering when it's your time."

I hadn't thought about that. Sallie was in demand, especially with the sharecroppers who seemed to be having a record number of babies.

"Anyhow," he added, "Dr. Dixon isn't known for showing up early."

He could have added, "or entirely sober" as I would later learn.

Birthday

By the time May settled in, I gave up on being comfortable ever again. I couldn't sit and do needlework for long without my back aching. Everything felt sore and stretched beyond what it was intended for. My ankles hurt and swelled if I walked much. My legs cramped if I didn't. And I still wasn't even sure when the baby was due.

With Feaster, I knew the exact date, time, dastardly moment of conception. But with this baby, I couldn't narrow it down other than for womanly matters I thought to be signs.

I took to fretting. What if it was about to come? What if it wasn't? Could I stand another day? Could I take care of it once I had it? Would I have enough milk this time? I'd gone back to thinking of the baby as "it." Shameful, I know. A living, kicking, rolling thing that needed more room than I had to offer.

I tried reading Mrs. Mary's latest *Ladies' Home Journal* to take my mind off the present. It was full of interesting stories.

One was about a lady photographer who went around the country taking pictures of children "in poverty." On the one hand, I thought it was wonderful that there were female photographers. On the other hand, something seemed sort of underhanded about taking pictures of poor children just because they were poor. On the third hand, those photographs might bring attention to their plight and produce something positive. In other words, I thought about it for a while with no clear conclusions.

So I read "Making Good Candy at Home" and "Ten Pretty Designs in Modern Lace" for something lighter.

Then I made the mistake of reading "Dressing Well on Small Means." Actually it was more a matter of looking at illustrations of beautiful dresses with tiny waists. I burst into tears. What I did at such times was to lecture myself as though I were Mama, take a walk around the yard, and count my blessings. Some I counted twice. Then I'd come back inside and try to do something useful.

With Feaster, I'd been a mental and emotional wreck. But my body hadn't taken such a beating. This time I was considerably older. Maybe age made the difference. That and the fact that the McGees had big babies.

At least that's what Willis told me more times than I wanted to hear. Things like—"Grandpap Willis came out looking to be a year old. Pap himself weighed as much as a calf. My brothers were bigger than that. What, Icie? You alright?"

I don't know how he stood me when I couldn't stand myself. But he managed to be exceedingly patient. For him. He even planned a little birthday dinner for me with Bessie and Mama.

By late May, the feed corn was up, and the cotton was in the ground so there was a lull in spring planting. My birthday fell on a Saturday, which was usually a workday for growers. But on that particular Saturday, Willis took the afternoon off. Bessie did likewise.

At dinnertime she and Mama rode up in Preston's Sunday carriage. Bessie had been driving it herself since Feaster was away at college. She looked at ease holding the reins. Willis brought in Mama's sweetgrass basket "slap full," he said, of birthday dinner. Bessie followed with a cake, and Mama brought up the rear with a jug of tea.

The basket held potato salad, pickled peaches, yeast rolls, and baked ham cut in thin slices. Aunt Lou had sent the cake, a beautiful strawberry pound cake drizzled in a pink glaze. She knew it was my favorite from my younger days. Her kindness touched my heart.

I covered our small dinner table with a cloth I'd sewn the same time as the curtains. It was bordered in dark green fern fronds. I set the table with Mama's bone china and the silverware Mrs. Mary had given me and filled a vase with lavender mop-head hydrangeas. None of the colors went together, but Mama said how pretty the table looked. Bessie agreed.

They put out dinner, and Willis asked a blessing, short as usual, but with more emotion. I made sure Mama sat between Willis and me so he couldn't help my plate.

As we passed around the food, Bessie talked about Feaster. How he'd soon be home from college for the summer. "I think Doc Harris might let Feaster help out with his vet practice a month or so," she said.

"Good experience," Willis commented. Then he mentioned that he was looking to buy a cross between a quarter horse and a mountain pony. "It oughta be fast and surefooted for a small rider."

Mama talked about her youngest brother, Euphronius, and his wife, who'd recently come from Hartwell for a visit. "His wife writes for a newspaper," she said. I couldn't tell if she thought it a good idea or not.

"She's editor and chief," Bessie added, clearly impressed. "Why, Icie, you know lots of big words. You could write for the Anderson paper."

I knew they were all trying to give me a happy birthday, these people I loved. I didn't say anything. I just listened. It was so nice to hear female voices other than my own. And to hear Willis talk about something other than cotton and cattle. To be fair, he'd learned not to ask me how I felt.

So I enjoyed the conversation and did the best I could with the potato salad. And I ate an entire pickled peach except for the pit. I didn't want to push my luck, so I skipped the ham although the others commented on how good it was. No one saved room for cake, so we decided to have some later.

Willis fetched a small box tied in pink ribbon. He stood over me while I untied and opened it to find a beautiful gold ring, set with a fiery opal. The intense layers of pink and blue made me think of the brilliant sunset across the ocean at White Point Garden. A Jesus-God moment as large as the universe captured in a delicate stone.

"It's beautiful!" I gushed. I showed the ring to Mama and Bessie.

"Beautiful!" they agreed in unison.

Willis took my hand in his and attempted to slide on the ring. But it was too small for my fat finger. He went to another finger. Too fat. He switched hands and kept trying fingers until he reached my little finger on my left hand.

Bessie watched in apparent shock, her mouth open, while Mama eyed me like a hawk as I fought back tears.

"No," she said in her stern mama voice, "No, Icie. You will not get upset."

I looked at her, feeling like I was ten years old again.

She softened. She patted my fat hand and said, "All that puffiness will go away. It's just baby water."

I had no idea what "baby water" was. I'd heard not to throw out the baby with the bathwater, but I didn't think that was it. I looked at Bessie. She didn't seem to know either. She rolled her eyes and made a face. I started to laugh. So did Bessie. Then Mama. Then Willis. And in that moment, I felt it was surely a happy birthday after all.

When we stopped laughing, we agreed maybe we would have a taste of Aunt Lou's pound cake. As Bessie began cutting the cake, I pushed back from the table and stood up to get dessert plates.

At that very moment, the baby water broke loose and spilled down between my knees like a waterfall.

Mama looked at the puddle surrounding my feet and said, "It's time!"

As if on cue, a cramp struck me in the middle and bent me double. Bessie dropped the cake knife, yelled, "I'm going for Sallie," and took off in the carriage.

Willis turned white as cotton. Once the contraction lessened and I could straighten up, he ushered me to the bedroom with Mama at his elbow. Mama ran him out and helped me take off my wide pinafore and already unbuttoned dress. She put extra sheets for me to lie on and helped me under the covers.

"I'm going for the doctor!" Willis yelled. The door banged and he was gone.

Then I was seized with another contraction that twisted me to the core. I knew I was on the labor train again and there was no getting off. I lay there balled up in a zigzag of pain with Mama at my side. My mind rode from Varennes to Augusta to Savannah to Charleston. I tried not to groan or cry.

Soon I heard the front door open and women's voices. Sallie began washing up in the kitchen where a pan of hot water stayed on the stove. "Just delivered a baby over at the Pruitt farm this morning," she said to Bessie loud enough for Mama and me to hear. "It was breech. Like pulling a calf. Now that was a mess!"

All I could think of was our poor beef cow and Papa's bloody shirt. I began to rethink my choice of midwife. Then another contraction ended all thought.

The Jones women took their positions, Mama on my right, Bessie on my left, and Sallie at the business end. She set down her basket of birthing wares, pushed the covers aside, and began poking around.

"I feel a little head," she said. "Thank the good Lord! I couldn't handle two breeches in one day."

"Amen!" Mama said.

The pain train seemed faster than with Feaster. I could tell the contractions were inching the baby along. I bore down with each new pang.

"I see the top of a head!" Sallie announced. "You're doing good, Icie, real good."

At that moment I heard the front door swing open followed by a rush of footsteps. In swept Willis and Dr. Dixon. Mama cut Willis off at the bedroom door, shooed him into the parlor, and quickly returned. I could hear the parlor floor creak beneath his feet.

Dr. Dixon stepped in and announced, "I'll take over from here, little lady." If he had a black bag, I couldn't see it.

Sallie didn't budge. "You didn't even wash your hands," she said.

"I cleaned 'em up in alcohol on the way," he replied.

"I can smell it," she said in disgust.

Evidently Mama could too by the way she sniffed. I was more intent on pushing than smelling.

Since Sallie wasn't giving up her space, Dr. Dixon tried to tell her and me what to do. I'm not sure he ever looked at my top half. I ignored him and kept pushing, pushing, pushing until I felt a tremendous swish.

"It's a boy," Sallie shouted, "and he's breathing just fine!" I heard the same little meow sounds that Feaster had made.

She tied off and cut the cord before Dr. Dixon could finish explaining the proper procedure of something that sounded like "om-fuh-lotta-MEE." He said it several times as though it felt good to his mouth.

Sallie quickly wiped the baby off, wrapped him in a blanket, and handed him to Mama. I wanted to hold him but I was still seized with contractions.

Bessie hurried to the doorway and shouted into the parlor, "It's a boy!"

The creaking stopped. Willis yelled back, "Can I see?"

"Not yet!" Mama shouted as she cradled the beautiful little pink, puffy-faced creation. The creaking in the parlor resumed.

Then Dr. Dixon whispered to Sallie loud enough for me to hear, "Wonder why it's no bigger, given the size of her belly."

I'd had it with him. "Shut your mouth!" I yelled, between waves of pain.

Sallie ignored us both and declared, "There's another loaf in the oven!"

"Little lady, that's just pla-cen-ta," Dr. Dixon said slowly. "You know it as af-ter-birth." He slurred his words so that it sounded like "af-ter Berth-a."

I raised up on my forearms and looked between my knees at what appeared to be a standoff.

Then Sallie elbowed him out of her way. "You're not finished, Icie," she said. "Keep pushing."

And so I did, though I really didn't have a choice. A contraction strong enough to turn me inside out delivered the second baby in short order.

"Another stem-winder!" Sallie announced. She repeated the process and handed the second baby boy to Bessie.

"Now, Icie, we gotta get rid of the afterbirth," she instructed. So I finished with my last bit of strength.

When she was satisfied that the delivery was complete, she cleaned me up, tugged the birth-stained sheets from beneath me, replaced the top covers, and propped me up on both pillows.

Then she told Mama and Bessie to lay the two little bundles on my chest where I could hold them both safely at the same time. They quickly complied, probably the only time either had taken orders from Sallie or ever would again.

At last I could see my babies up close, touch them, smell them, cradle them in my arms. I felt a rush of gratitude as big as the deep blue sea.

Sallie called Willis. When he saw the two babies I thought he might faint, but I guess he'd heard enough to know. He knelt beside the bed, kissed me softly on the forehead, and enfolded all three of us in a wide, soft hug.

And that's the way he remained until we realized Dr. Dixon had disappeared.

"I expect he's in the buggy, celebrating," Willis said. "S'pose I should drive him home."

After he left, Sallie showed me how to nurse twins. "Two mouths and two spigots, but if it was me, I'd feed 'em one at a time. Least 'til everybody knows what to do."

We began with the baby that was making the most noise. He latched on without much coaxing and set about getting supper. I could feel the milk rush down. It felt like it was coming from high underneath my arms. My free breast started dripping, too.

"Looks like you got aplenty this time," she said. "Let 'em nurse when they want. It'll be hard on you but good for them."

So that's how it should have been with Feaster! Poor baby, I thought. He never had the mother's milk every baby deserves. But before I started down that old painful path, I reminded myself he did have Bessie, the best mother any baby could ever want. And now he'd have two brothers. Half-brothers but by a man he truly admired.

As soon as we heard Willis's buggy returning, Sallie kissed me on the forehead and gathered her basket of midwifery. She glanced at Mama. And for just a moment, an unsettling look passed between them. Then Sallie and Bessie were gone.

"What, Mama?" I asked. "Is something wrong with them?

Something missing?" I tried inspecting each without disturbing the other.

"No," she said. "No. They're perfect."

"Then what?" I asked again.

"They're just mighty small, Icie. And twins are hard. They'll need lots of care."

"Then I'm not worried," I declared, feeling a surge of power. Maybe it was from having given birth to twins. Maybe it euphoria brought on by the end of intense pain. Whatever it was, it made me confident. More confident than I'd ever been before. "We'll give them all the care they need," I added, looking from one to the other.

Willis soon returned, and so did Bessie. Mama offered to stay the night, but Willis thanked her and sent her home with Bessie.

That night we put the tiny babies in the big crib that Willis bought for the big baby he'd anticipated. Of course they didn't stay there long, and we got little sleep. Willis held one while I fed the other. Then we switched babies. After several such feedings I forgot which was which.

"I can't tell these little fellas apart," I said, some of my new-found confidence waning.

"We'll figure it out tomorrow," he said, returning the fed baby to the crib and handing me the other one.

Then another problem occurred to me. "We don't have enough names. We can name one Preston Allen, but we can't call the other Emily Bethia!"

"We'll figure it out tomorrow," he repeated. He lay beside me and waited for the baby on my breast to let go.

I was sore, exhausted, and confused. Yet it was my happiest birthday of my life.

God's in His Heaven ❧

I have the Alexander from the Lowcountry dream again. I've had it enough times that it fails to upset me at first. It begins as always. He rides the magnificent stallion beneath my window in the black of night. He pushes open the window that always sticks. I expect Willis to rush in any second and beat him bloody. And I expect Alexander to escape to ride another night. It's as though I'm awake and dreaming at the same time.

But this night, as the dream unfolds, something is different. A storm brews in the distance, the kind that lights the black air with soundless sheets of lightning. I hear Alexander outside my window, hear his stallion stomp the soft ground, feel more than hear him slip into my bedroom.

Then he's on me! I try to pull away but I am powerless to move. He whispers, "Isamar, lovely Isamar, I've come back for you."

My throat is frozen. I can barely breathe. Still I manage to mutter, "My babies!"

"You can leave them," he says. "They'll be taken care of."

The night lights up, I see the curtain of blond hair across his forehead. His eyes glow like fiery blue opals.

"No!" I shout, my voice bypassing my throat and coming straight from my chest. "I won't leave my babies!"

"Then we'll take them with us," he says in the same even voice. "I'll be their father."

In a panic, I remember that Willis has gone west to buy cattle. He's left Feaster to look after us. Suddenly, the bedroom door flies open and in rushes Feaster. He's carrying the pistol Willis gave him. He lifts it and takes aim.

Alexander stands. "No, Feaster!" I scream, pushing up from the bed. "He's your father!"

Another sheet of lightning illuminates the bedroom, and the two stare in mirror image. They seem frozen in an eternal instant. Until Feaster says, "Prepare to meet your Maker," and pulls the trigger.

Alexander falls back through the open window. His body thuds across the saddle, the stallion snorts, leaps forward, and disappears. I turn to Feaster, but he is gone. I collapse onto the floor. There I lie until the sun lifts the night and Anah finds me.

On Sunday, the day after the twins pushed their way into our hearts, we solved the name problem. We decided to name one baby Preston and the other, Allen. In fact, we skipped middle names altogether.

Our babies looked even smaller in the morning light. I inspected each one closely and discovered that Preston had a tiny birth mark on his left shoulder. It looked like a fairy slipper. Allen did not. Otherwise there were identical.

As much as I wanted Willis to stay with me and the babies,

he had to get back to the business of farming. But bright and early Monday morning, Anah showed up at the back door. I don't think Mrs. Mary would've let her go, despite what Willis had said, for just one baby. But with two, I suppose she couldn't refuse.

Anah seemed to come willingly. After Willis had gone for the morning, I asked her if she minded leaving the Big House.

"Oh, no, Mizz Icie," she said. "Sometime a big house is too big. Anyhow, a little change don't hurt nothin.'"

"But you don't feel like you have to, do you?" I asked. I don't know why I was questioning good fortune.

"Lawdy, no. I 'spect I could work at a whole lotta places. We not sharecroppers, you know."

I didn't know. And I felt foolish not knowing.

"We got our own house and plot of land," she continued. "We don't be sharin' nothin' we don't want to. But Mr. Willis, he do pay good."

I hugged her like I did when she was a young girl and I was just a few years older.

"Your mama, Mizz Em'ly, she mighty good to us when we was little," she said, her voice breaking. "People was crazy back then. Some still is."

One of the babies started to cry. Then the other. I picked up the louder one, which turned out to be Allen, and started him on his meal. Anah picked up Preston.

"Twins is somethin' alright," she said, swaying back and forth. "God's makin' up for lost time."

Anah and I fell into the same feeding routine as I had with Willis. But she managed to burp them faster and get bits of housework done in between switching babies. It was comforting to have her with me, especially as the twins' frailty began to sink in. Neither was bigger than a loaf of bread. A skinny loaf at that.

But then Feaster had been small, I reminded myself, and he'd been deprived of mother's milk. Preston and Allen got all their little bellies could hold.

I longed for more than an hour or two of sleep at a time and an honest-to-goodness bath when I could soak until my bottom felt better and the water turned tepid. But I was determined to do whatever I could to start the twins off right. I thought if I could just get them through a month without any problems, they'd be safely on their way.

Anah went home in the evenings, and Willis took over helping me at night. But after the first week, he realized he couldn't run a farming operation without sleep. So he hired Anah's oldest daughter, Bernice, to help with the night feedings. She was sixteen and already knew more about babies than the both of us.

Bernice was pretty, the image of Anah, although she wasn't as tall and her skin was a shade deeper. Willis put a small cot for Bernice in the front bedroom with me and the babies, and he moved into the back bedroom.

The babies regained the softness they'd lost shortly after being born, and their little umbilical cords soon dried up and disappeared. I wasn't sure where they went, so I asked Anah. We were sorting clean laundry at the time.

"Them belly curls?" she said, folding and stacking diapers in one fast motion. "They come off and I buried 'em."

"Why?" I asked as I tried folding like she did.

"So Death don't want no more." She started another stack.

"Of what?" I asked, still not clear.

"Of them babies, Mizz Icie. So Death don't try to take 'em 'fore their time."

ℒ

The next few weeks were a blur of crying babies, sore dripping breasts, and lots of diapers. The bed became my throne for much of the day and night. I could lean against the headboard without putting undo pressure on my bottom, which was still quite sore. Willis had bought a beautiful mahogany rocking chair, shipped all the way from England, that I planned to use once I'd healed.

Most days Willis came home for the midday meal. Since I'd be nursing the babies, he'd usually come into the bedroom with a plate for me and sit on the bed while I ate and nursed at the same time. I learned to eat with one hand. For a while I lived on ham biscuits. Then it was sliced roast in a yeast roll. And tea. Always lots of tea. I'd never been so thirsty.

Mama came to visit every other day. She could burp a baby as well as anybody. Certainly better than I could although I was improving. She talked about when I was born. She said I'd been small, too, and that the twins looked like me "except more Irish."

Mrs. Mary came every other day, too, but not the same times as Mama came. I suspected they'd coordinated visits, though neither said so. Mrs. Mary liked to help bathe the babies. She always checked the bath temperature with her elbow before she put them in. She said the twins looked so much like Willis when he was born. She didn't add "only lots smaller" for which I was grateful.

She did say more than once, "Why, Icie, you're glowing. You make a beautiful mother." She sometimes read aloud a feature from her latest magazine while I nursed the babies. One was about a lady who'd traveled to Paris, France, to study art.

"I'd love to go to Paris," she said. "Wouldn't you?"

"I'd love to be in Paris, but not to ride a boat to get there," I said, handing her Allen to burp while I fetched Preston. "Floating down the Savannah was plenty water travel for me. But if

I did go to France, I'd want to see the original Varennes. Or as they say 'VAAH-ren.'"

She softly patted Allen against her shoulder. "Oh, Icie, you're braver than you think."

Bessie came on Sundays. She said the babies looked a lot like Feaster when he was an infant. She told me that he was home from college and making rounds with Doc Harris.

"He's happy about the babies. But he's waiting to see them until they have time, as he said, 'to build up a little immunity.'" She smiled, clearly proud.

I thought about Mrs. Mary's "glowing" comment, how that was exactly what I'd seen in Bessie when I'd given Feaster to her. How she'd radiated a halo of love. How she still did when she talked about him. But I'd never really looked beyond the fact that she'd made a wonderful mother while I had not. At least not back then. Now I understood.

Two weeks after the twins were born, Sallie and J. E. stopped by after church. While Willis and J. E. talked about crops and cattle, Sallie inspected the babies. I proudly pointed out which was which.

"Their color's good," she said, eyeing their bottoms as well as their faces. "Not chapped or red, and their limbs are filling out a little." She seemed impressed, as much as she could be.

Then she looked at me. "Icie, you're doing real good. You look worse for wear, but the babies look better. You can recover later."

So much for the glow of motherhood. "Thank you, mostly," I said.

She patted my hand and added, "You're doing what needs to be done. That's all you can do. Course, you can always pray." Then she hugged me, gathered J. E., and left.

And so we managed. Anah during the day. Bernice at night. Willis inbetween. Mama had been right about my fatness going away with the baby water. After a few weeks, I was smaller than before I'd gotten married.

When the babies reached four weeks, I felt like marching into the church vestibule, yanking on the bell rope until I deafened myself, and shouting to the good people of Varennes, "ALL'S RIGHT WITH THE WORLD!"

Not that Preston and Allen were normal size yet. They still looked lost in that barge of a crib. Yet they were thriving, their color was rosy, and their little arms and legs were almost pudgy. God was in His Heaven. I was certain.

Today Mama read to me from the Book of Isaiah: "When thou passest through the waters, I will be with thee; and through the rivers, they shall not overflow thee: when thou walkest through the fire, thou shalt not be burned."

'All my pretty ones' ❧

Papa used to say, "They's a heap of slips 'tween the cup and the lips." He was usually talking about farming. Mama used to say, "Don't count your chicks before they hatch." She was usually talking about life in general.

But I wasn't farming and my chicks had already hatched. So I continued to celebrate the twins' first month as a milestone. I was convinced they were out of the big bad scary woods.

Then one morning, nearly a month later, I noticed that little Preston was taking less milk. I thought maybe he'd gotten more than I realized and was just going longer between feedings. But by afternoon he felt hot and he coughed at my breast more than he nursed. I held him against my cheek and felt the fluttering of his small heart.

I sent Anah to find Willis. By the time they returned, the baby was burning with fever. Willis took one look. "I'll go for the doctor," he shouted, rushing back out the door.

"Dr. Dean!" I called after him. "I want Dr. Dean!"

Just at sunset, Willis hurried back in with Dr. Dean behind him. Dr. Dean felt Preston's forehead. He looked into his mouth. He listened to his chest. Then he studied the baby's tiny fingernails.

"Looks like winter fever," he said.

Willis yelled, "How'n the hell can it be winter fever in the middle of the summer!"

Dr. Dean glanced at Willis, then back at little Preston. "Pneumonia doesn't care what season it is with babies. At this stage their lungs are still forming. Once fluid gets in, it's hard to recover."

"Fluid? Like milk?" I asked, thinking that was the only liquid going into his body.

"No," he said, looking at me for the first time since he'd arrived, "from inflammation."

"What can we do?" Willis asked, panic in his voice.

"Try to keep him cool with wet cloths. Otherwise, give him love, and hope for the best."

He patted my shoulder. "Icie, it's nothing you did or didn't do." He sounded tired. "Some things just happen. I've often wondered how any of us made it through childhood." His voice trailed off.

As if on cue, Allen started to cry. Dr. Dean looked in on him and said, "He seems alright. Maybe he's stronger." Then he left.

Throughout the evening, Allen was his hungry little self. But Preston stopped nursing at all. Willis sent Bernice home and stayed up with me, alternating between Allen's feedings, burping, diapers, and Preston's cool cloths and rocking.

Eventually, Willis fell asleep on the bed beside me, and Allen went to sleep alone in his vast crib.

I remained with my back to the headboard, holding my sweet little Preston. By the time the sun began to rise, I knew all the cool cloths and love in the world weren't going to save him. I swayed to the rhythm of his jagged little breaths until he gave up air altogether.

Then I let myself cry with as much anguish as I dare release.

Willis woke up. He encircled me and Preston's small body in his wide arms and wept, too.

An hour later, Anah arrived along with Bernice. Willis had just left to make burial arrangements. I was feeding Allen. They took one look at the little body wrapped in a baby blanket at the foot of the bed and began to cry.

There was nothing to say, so I kept nursing Allen. Anah soon composed herself. But Bernice sobbed louder.

Inside my head, I heard Sallie's words after her first son had died. They tumbled out of my mouth. "Don't cry, Bernice. Little Preston is in Heaven. God has a special place for babies."

Being July hot, there was no time to think through a regular funeral. One of Willis's brothers came up with a small coffin, not much more than a wooden box you might store apples in. His other brother dug the grave in Cross Roads Cemetery.

With Mama, Bessie, and Feaster from my side, and Mrs.

Mary, the brothers and their wives on Willis's side, we laid little Preston to rest on what would have been his two-months birthday. The minister read something from the Book of Job. I'm sure there was more, but all I remember was "The Lord giveth, and the Lord taketh away."

Bessie offered to get a granite marker where she'd gotten Preston's obelisk. We didn't refuse. We still had Allen to care for.

He remained well for more than week. Then symptoms started creeping in. His nursing slowed and his temperature rose. He began to cough, and soon his little fingernails went from pink to lavender blue.

I wiped him with damp cloths and prayed to God over and over, "Take my breath and give it to this baby."

Dr. Dean had been right. Allen was stronger. He fought pneumonia for four days before it took him. And like some godawful déjà vu, twelve days after our first baby died, we made arrangements to bury our second baby.

Someone must have said something to the minister about the twins not being baptized because at Allen's funeral he made a point of saying, "Baby Allen and his brother Baby Preston have been christened in their parents' tears, baptized by the blood of our Savior, and welcomed into the kingdom of Heaven through the grace of God."

Those words were much more comforting than the dreadful Book of Job. I remembered what Papa'd said about dying babies—"They're too young to sin, so their little spirits get new bodies and come on back down." If that was true, I hoped the twins would fare better in their next mother's womb.

When we got home from the funeral, I folded up the baby things, put them in a cloth bag, and stored them in the chest at the foot of the bed while Willis took the crib to the shed.

I was sticky wet from August heat and leaking breasts, so I undressed and washed off as best I could. Then I slipped on a light, loose dress.

My heart was numb, but I tried to get my mind in order. I thought about Mama after she'd lost her first baby and Sallie after she'd lost more children than most. I thought about Bessie and how she'd carried on without Preston. They'd been as heart-sick as I was, but they'd managed to go on. Somehow I would be as strong as the other Jones women, I told myself.

But first I needed to lie down for a while. I stretched out on my back for the first time in better than two months. The last thing I remember before I drifted off was the sound of a wasp bumping against the ceiling, then the window, then back to the ceiling trying to get out. Bumping, bumping, infernal bumping. I wondered how an insect's wisp of a body could create so much racket. Then I fell asleep.

I don't know how long I slept. Hours or days. I'd start to wake, then fall back. However long, it was plenty of time to have a nightmare.

The dream started out deceptively pleasant. Willis and I were on a ferryboat about to cross the Savannah River into Georgia. It was a beautiful day, and we were going to visit my half-brother Johnny and his family in Elberton.

Several other travelers boarded with us. They chatted about the weather and what they planned to do on the other side. The ferry had railings and a covered seating area where I chose to stay. But most passengers, including Willis, stood at the railings.

As we reached the middle of the river, the wind began to whip. All at once, the river rose into a dark wall above us. Then it crashed down and ripped away the boat's cover and railings and most of the people who'd been standing!

I held onto the seat, bolted down in the center. I looked for Willis. I could hear him calling but I couldn't see him for waves and tree branches flying around in the air. Then the water crashed down again and washed away everyone else on board except me. I tried to scream, but the hurricane wind blew my voice back in my face like wet leaves.

I awoke to hear Willis still calling my name. He seemed at a great distance. But when I opened my eyes, I saw him beside the bed. Dr. Dixon was on the other side peering down at me. He kept poking around my neck, pressing his fingers just below my ears.

I opened my mouth to tell him to stop, but nothing came out. I breathed as deep as I could and tried again. Nothing. Just like in the nightmare. Maybe I was still dreaming.

"She shows signs of de-crep-ti-tude," he said, carefully enunciating each syllable. Then he added, "aphasia, debility . . ."

"What the hell does all that mean?" Willis interrupted.

"I believe your wife has suffered a stroke, possibly a postpartum stroke."

I listened for a slurring of his words, hints of a drunken mistake. But he sounded stone cold sober.

"From what?" Willis asked. His voice shook.

"From childbirth," the doctor answered.

"How can that be?" Willis asked. "She had the babies ten weeks ago!"

Dr. Dixon lifted my arm by my wrist. Then let it go. To my horror, it fell back beside me. I began to realize I not only had no voice, I had no control over my limbs. I tried to push up on my elbows, but nothing worked.

"I've seen it as late as twelve weeks after giving birth," he continued. "Of course, it could be other causes. She's been under a great deal of stress," he said in a maddeningly even voice, "physical and mental. I bet she's lost half her body weight since I last saw her."

If I could've, I'd have sat straight up and slapped his face. Coming and going. I hoped Willis would punch him in the mouth.

But my fiery Willis seemed broken. "Will she get better?"

"She might," Dr. Dixon said. "But I doubt it."

Neither quick nor dead

'Tween the stirrup and the ground, much is sought, some is found"—another one of Papa's sayings that came to me just now.

At first I was determined to get better. I remembered that Mama had gotten up on the third day after taking to her bed to mourn little Frances. That Sallie had kept delivering babies and having more of her own. That Aunt Lou's aphasia had lasted nearly a year, but she kept going and eventually regained her voice. I promised myself I would go on, too.

I perceived time by degrees of darkness and light. Days of the week by footsteps in the house. Seasons by the maple tree outside my window and the fruit inside my bowl.

Anah took care of me during the day. She was careful to feed me soft foods. She'd say things like "Mizz Em'ly done made her sweet baked apples." Or "That Janey, she sho can cook. Now eat up this boilt custard she sent." Or, "Look at these juicy peaches! They goin' melt in your mouth. You won't even hafta swallow much."

She cleaned me up in the mornings and in the evenings as gentle and pleasant as she could. "You light as a feather, Mizz Icie," she'd say. "I'm goin' roll you to the side to change this sheet. Keep them bedsores away."

At first Willis spent time sitting beside my bed in the evenings talking about the weather and crops. Sometimes he read from *Old Farmer's Almanac*, usually a poem about the particular month.

I remember the September one:

O moon of golden fruit and ripened grain
Of skies and peaks that melt and mist together
And streams that sing in murmurs soft and low
A tender requiem for the summer weather.

He continued to sleep in the back bedroom where fern-bordered curtains framed the windows. Perhaps he needed resurrection ferns more than I did. He was mourning the loss of his precious twins and our almost happy little family. I was numb, and all the resurrection ferns in Charleston and Savannah weren't going to change it.

After the first autumn came and went, it became obvious I wasn't getting better. Willis grew more and more distraught, and I was powerless to comfort him. His sad visits became unbearable. I began to close my eyes when I heard him coming. I thought if he believed I was asleep, he wouldn't feel the need to sit with me.

The first few evenings when I pretended to sleep, he held my hand and wept. After a while, though, he changed his nightly ritual to stepping into my room, kissing me on the forehead, and saying, "Good night, my love." That was enough.

Mama kept up her every-other-day visits. She usually read from the Bible. But occasionally she chose something from the newspaper. Once she read a feature about Bessie from an Augusta, Georgia, newspaper. The title was "Make Way for the Ladies."

Mama read:

The male planters and farmers of the South will have to hustle in the presence of some of the female agriculturists of this section. No doubt many of our Southern women are performing great deeds as in the case of Mrs. P. B. Allen of Anderson County in the neighboring state of South Carolina, a decided executive genius for managing successfully a large cotton plantation. Many men find it hard to match her record. No one without experience can adequately imagine what brains, skill, and vim are required to accomplish successful planting these days. She is a noble captain of industry. She is a conspicuous example of what a brave, strong, brainy woman can accomplish.

There was more, but I held on to what my own little brain could manage. Odd how a numb body can warm with words. I was filled with pride for my sister's astounding accomplishments. I imagined Bessie's expression as she read "a noble captain of industry." I laughed inside.

When Mrs. Mary visited, she usually read from her latest *Ladies' Home Journal* inspiring stories of other women like Bessie. Occasionally, she held up illustrations for me to see. She would say, "Icie, those models are pretty, but not as pretty as you." A barefaced lie told in kindness.

Bessie came, too, usually on Sunday afternoons. Sometimes she talked about when we were little, like the time we hid in the loft and watched Johnny talk the warts off our milk cow. When she did, she'd break out laughing, then end by saying, "I haven't thought about that in years."

Other times, she talked about the Bethesda Methodist Church. She told me about putting in a ten-foot stained-glass window in memory of Preston. It sounded beautiful. She said in the center was Jesus Christ in a glowing robe with His hand reaching out. I tried to imagine the rays of jeweled glass surrounding Jesus, their intensity heightened by the setting sun.

Bessie would always tell me what Feaster was doing. At times, I thought he might be lingering in the doorway. At other times, I felt sure Preston was standing behind Bessie. Obviously, my perception was suspect.

Others folks stopped to see me from time to time. My half-brother Johnny came once that I remember. He said a long prayer over me in words I didn't recognize.

Aunt Lou came several times. She talked about when she had aphasia and how she'd miraculously gotten her voice back. Then she leaned close and whispered, "Icie, I've never told another soul, but I think I got a new voice altogether."

One afternoon my nephew Dolph brought his parlor guitar and strummed songs from the Faith Alliance concert, nearly a dozen years earlier. He played beautifully and seemed to enjoy each note. He said he was surprised he remembered the songs at all.

Anah brought Red to sing for me twice. He stood in the

hall outside my room and sang a capella. The first time he sang "Amazing Grace," and the next, he sang the Goodnight Song.

I sang along in my head—"Lay down, my sister, lay down and take yo rest; Lay yo head upon the Savior's breast. I do love you, but Jesus loves you best." His smooth, rich baritone filled the house and my heart.

But when I was alone, I tried to understand my fate. Why I'd been cast into the lions' den. Was I to have the humble faith of Daniel? The arrogant courage of the Great Frank Bostock? The patience of Job? I lay in my bed suspended between ending and unending. And wondered.

I remembered what Papa had said when he was making coffins—"I think the fella what lingers got somethin' unfinished, maybe in his head. He gets extra time to look over his life, tidy up, let go."

I wondered what I was supposed to tidy up.

My journal just might be the answer. If I could read through it, maybe I could see what's in order and what's not. Perhaps I could review my life, page by page, give thanks for what I received, and ask forgiveness for what I did wrong or failed to do.

Obviously, I couldn't get up and retrieve it from the chest at the foot of the bed. The same chest where my concert dress and wedding suit lay folded, where I'd packed away the twins' things. My journal lay among them. At the heart of my hope chest. A bit of irony, I recognized, even in this state.

So I began going through it in my head, trying to remember each page as though it might hold some hint of what I'm supposed to understand, to let go. A way to endure this slow unwinding. Neither quick nor dead.

As I tried to remember each entry and relive each moment, I

made imaginary notes in imaginary margins. That's how I filled my solitary waking hours. A slow process, often interrupted by the ramblings of a stricken mind, unsure of what was real and what was not.

I began with Papa and a war I never understood. There'd be no tidying it up although it weighed heavy on my family and cast a shadow throughout my life. From the war, I wound and lurched forward through my childhood, to Bessie and Preston, and then to Alexander.

Then on to the arrival of Feaster. I'd given out of chances to make things right with him, so I tried to let go of the guilt. I reviewed my life with Willis, the happiest of days. And the birth of the twins. But I didn't relive their deaths. That was not the ending I wanted regardless of what was real or unreal.

If I thought I'd mastered my waking hours, nighttime was a different matter altogether. Dreams came uninvited. The return of Alexander was the most disturbing. And I had it over and over in various forms until God had mercy on me, Feaster shot him, and Alexander rode beneath my window no more.

As those nightmares ebbed, the ones about the Savannah River flowed, both in frequency and detail. Sometimes I'd see dead, bloated soldiers floating on its surface. Sometimes drowned babies. Always crashing waves and helpless solitude. And when I awoke, I actually felt relief in my current godawful state. "Gallows irony," Aunt Eliza would have said.

Dreams or no dreams, I do believe my tale is nearly told. A second summer has come and gone. I hear whispers of pneumonia. My lungs are weary. Anah no longer coaxes me to eat. Mama reads only from the Book of John. I hear Willis's footsteps in the hall coming and going, but if anyone else comes, I am oblivious.

I'm still left wondering what's the value of a story like mine with no remarkable accomplishments, no great charitable causes, no vast sacrifices. Yet I loved and was loved. I felt more joy than pain. I planted flowers. I knitted shawls. I made music. I had babies. I wrote in my journal. And I remembered stories about my family.

Maybe the value lay not in the story itself but in the telling, if not by me, then by someone else. Perhaps the teller learns more than I have. I hold tight to that conclusion until sleep overtakes me and brings a familiar dream.

Willis and I are crossing the Savannah again. Scarlet leaves float atop the water. We board the same ferry. People chat about the beautiful autumn day.

And, as always, a storm blows up. But this time, instead of seats to hold onto, a single iron ring, the size of a wagon wheel, lies bolted to the center of the deck.

The river rises into a dark wall above us, higher than the trees along its banks. Willis pushes me toward the iron ring. "Hold on!" he shouts as the water crashes upon us.

I hold on with every bit of strength I can summon. The waves seem to subside. Heads bob in the dark waters. Everyone has been washed overboard except Willis and me.

Then I lose my grip and slip toward the edge. Willis lets go of the ring to pull me in closer. Just as I regain my grasp on the curve of wet iron, another wave crashes over us. I see Willis fly past me and into the dark waters.

I scream his name over and over as he fades into the distance. I pray he can reach the crumbling bank and pull himself out.

I grip the iron ring and brace for the next wave. But it doesn't come. The ferry boat has become a raft. It continues to rush down the river. Someone will see me, I tell myself. Someone will stop this wreck. Maybe in Augusta where landings and shops cover the banks. But when I reach the charmed city, the river walk is empty.

Even dreaming, I know it's time to wake up. I try to escape the nightmare, but the river continues flowing with me its sole passenger. Surely I'll be rescued in Savannah where lights line the nearly endless docks and ships are always coming and going. I set my hopes on Savannah and watch for the glow of the city.

But the lights wax and wane without interruption. As I reach the salty solitude of the great Atlantic in the dark of night, despair washes over me. I wish I'd let go of the ring miles ago. I try to summon the same strength that I used to hold on, now, to release my death grip, to pull my arms away from the ring, to roll my body over the edge.

As I struggle, I see a face push up from beneath the black water. A beautiful face illuminated by moonlight. A circle of gleaming black hair floats around her neck and shoulders.

She says nothing but beckons me to come closer. My

fingers release from the ring. I ease to the edge. She swims to the raft, holds on with one hand, and reaches out to me with the other. I take her hand to help her out of the water. But she gently pulls against me until I slide in myself.

At first I float comfortably on my back buoyed by the warm, salty water. I've never seen quite so many stars. I try to name autumn constellations above me. They seem close enough to touch. I think I could stay here for an eternity. But soon I realize my raft has drifted away.

I look back at the lady in the ocean. Her face is as bright as the moon, and stars hang in her hair. Suddenly I realize she's the maiden of the resurrection fern.

She takes my hand again and pulls me beneath the shimmering surface. I breathe in the beautiful water as she leads me down, down to where the sun rests and Orion plans his return.

Acknowledgments

Much gratitude goes to Gail Woodard, publisher and CEO of Dudley Court Press, whose skilled, multifaceted, and innovative approach to publishing made this book possible. I also appreciate the constant support and attention to detail from Winsome Lewis, publishing assistant, and Lora Arnold, project coordinator.

As for the content, I'm greatly indebted to Rebecca Akins, my cousin whom I met on the Internet, for her research and generosity in sharing some of the stories and characters in these pages. Also I'm indebted to two excellent writers and skilled editors—Aïda Rogers, who spent an entire summer going over every word in the manuscript, making it better with each suggestion, and Bob Lamb, who gave story-by-story advice on what to keep in and what to leave out.

A special thank-you goes to my sister, Dee, who reviewed the roughest of drafts as they rolled off the printer, and to my husband, Billy, who constantly encouraged me and asked, "How's it coming?" often enough to keep me on track.

About the Author

LIZ NEWALL grew up in Starr, South Carolina, a town rich in history and stories, characters and contradictions, much like her fictional Varennes.

She earned degrees from Anderson and Clemson universities. Her greatest education, though, came from teaching high school and raising children.

After an early career in teaching, she worked as a freelance writer along with picking peaches in the family orchard—a sweet, itchy, iffy enterprise.

During this time, she wrote her first novel, *Why Sarah Ran Away with the Veterinarian*. She soon discovered that freelance is a little too free. She found a writing position at Clemson University and became managing editor of *Clemson World* magazine. There she stayed until retirement.

She then began searching for the stories of characters who'd lived in her mind for much too long. She found them in old newspapers, a diary, Bible entries, antique jewelry, and family stories. The result is *You Don't Have to Tell Everything You Know*.

Liz lives on a farm in Pendleton with her husband, Billy, where she no longer picks peaches.

Connect with Liz on Facebook at Liz Newall Author

Made in the USA
Middletown, DE
10 December 2021